LIFE IS A BALANCE

It isn't only about you

PHILIP NORK

ALL THINGS
THAT MATTER
PRESS

ISBN 13: 9780985778965

Library of Congress Control Number: 2012946000

Cover design by All Things That Matter Press
Published in 2012 by All Things That Matter Press

PREFACE

The journey of self-discovery is a lifetime trip; and just like the fingerprints you possess, yours will be uniquely different than anyone else's. There *are* things that are common in each—such as good and bad times, emotional highs and lows, and choices that will need to be made.

These choices that are presented to you can greatly define how you live your life. They may be influenced by the people you meet, symbols that are strategically placed along your journey, and especially by your religious or spiritual choices. Being that no choice ever comes without consequence, there really is no right or wrong answer; the road taken will eventually get you to where you're supposed to be. Although, some roads take longer than others in order for you to reach your ultimate goal.

The stories in this book tell of choices made and roads taken by one man. While all of them are based in truth, some characters or scenarios have been slightly embellished. Like Mark Twain once remarked, "Never let the truth get in the way of a good story."

The sweetest thing about the life we live is that we all get to lead it differently. What's right for one may be totally wrong for another; and while perception truly is your own reality, don't forget there is always something more than meets the eye. You will be well served if you learn to see the whole picture before passing judgment on others, if at all.

INTRODUCTION

This is the second leg of one man's journey into self-discovery. The first was full of joy and pain, love and hate, and his realizing that everything experienced in life doesn't have to be perfect in order for that life to be considered good. It was a unique time of discovery, remembrance, and lessons to learn. It ultimately became seventeen years of practice, which in turn led to many unusual and special experiences which helped shape the thinking and actions of that one man.

* * *

My name is Phil and I'll be guiding you through the utter confusion that once was my life. Growing up a product of divorce really added some adverse complications to how I was living, and how I thought other people saw me. I was small and quiet, but a smart child, one who relied much more on the support of others than on my own choices. After my dad left us when I was eight, I fell into the thinking I wasn't good enough. And the more men I met, the deeper the wound went. Not only did I believe my dad left the family out to dry, but in eighth grade a mean old basketball coach told me I was better suited to be a cheerleader.

As soon as I was able to recognize the brilliance and the intelligence of the "fairer sex", I began to trust females much more than their male counterparts. In fact, these *special ladies* of my past introduced me to several life lessons which I attempted to put to good use. The woman who first influenced me was my great grandmother. I called her Nana. She taught me that in order for girls to notice me I needed to be a little different, sincere, and learn how to treat them extra special. She died when I was ten, but I never forgot her talks. I believe she is still with me at all times guiding me through this thing we call life.

While these "secret insights" for understanding and impressing women helped me regain the confidence I had lost when my parents divorced, I soon found out the way I chose to use them sometimes clouded my judgment. While I was a teenager, I let the girls influence my major decisions about sex. I felt I was helping them by being a concerned listener to their problems; but, it could be argued that what they saw as "sensitive and caring" was a fine line between that and using them.

Although most of the time the girls initiated the sex, I followed through without a question. For most teenage boys, this would be a dream come true; lots of sex with lots of partners. But I began to wonder if this so-called "gift" of mine was in fact a curse. I know the question that comes to most people's minds: "How can tons of sex be considered a problem?" Perhaps until you've been there yourself, it's difficult to understand. I'll answer the question with the one word I was feeling most often: *emptiness*. At first it was fun, being wanted by so many, but there comes a point when you begin to feel empty. Not empty of energy, or excitement, or adventure. What you feel is empty spiritually. And trust me, that is the worst kind of empty. When you finally can admit to yourself you've reached that lowest level, there's hardly anything that can make you feel good or fulfilled.

So there I was, in high demand, but in way low spirits, without a clue of how to reclaim my sense of self or my sense of purpose. The logical solution, you'd think, would just be to abstain from sex all together. But when I tried that, another girl did a good job of convincing me I had made the wrong choice again.

I was now close to becoming a grown man and needed to know if the ladies of my future would continue to influence my decisions or if by some miracle, I could take control of my own destiny. Although I didn't have a clue as to who I truly was, or how others *really* perceived me, I did know I had already lived more than a lifetime of experiences.

I was aware there are many reasons we are put through this life phase—on this planet—but that the most important one is to *learn*. The teachings come from the people you know, strangers you meet on your way, and strangely enough, from symbols which are strategically placed throughout your life. You just have to know how to first recognize and then interpret them.

* * *

The first part of my journey had been an emotional roller coaster ride, trying to find the real person lost so deep down in my soul. I wanted to please every woman I met, and I sure tried. But in the meantime, I completely lost the one thing I really needed to please the most … me. I had gotten too absorbed in meaningless sexual encounters, which I rationalized as "helping" these young girls have a highly pleasurable, guilt-free experience. I began thinking I had been handpicked as the one who was supposed to make these ladies happy again at a time when they needed something to go right in their lives. Family and boyfriend problems were the main reason the girls came my way.

I'd listen intently to their problems, be very understanding, and then do their bidding in bed. I was always sincere and, unlike the other boys who only cared about themselves, I was much more in tune with what the girl wanted and enjoyed. Because females talk about these things to other females, this became the circle of my life. I never had to be "on the make." The women were in total control, and for a while, I was just fine with that.

Whether you were the jock everyone else looked up to in school, or the girl who "did" every guy around just for the attention it brought, or even if you were the person no one else knew, you can't deny that the people around you made you do things you never thought you would for acceptance.

But I figured there had to be something more to life, though I had no idea what it could be. I was almost eighteen, and I knew that acceptance and happiness were my ultimate goals. This became my new mission: *To figure out what was missing and make it happen.*

CHAPTER 1
THE BEGINNING

It was early spring of 1979 and what I needed was a fresh start—a do-over, if you will.

So I called Lisa to get a few suggestions. She had been my sounding board and best friend since age seven; she also was my very first date, and later on I was there for her during her parents' divorce. To say we had experienced a lot together was putting it lightly.

She said, "Ya know what I'd do if I were you? I'd try to reconnect with your father."

Lisa knew my dad had left the family when I was eight and that I hadn't heard from him since. Although I thought about him often, looking him up never occurred to me. "Besides not knowin' if he actually wants to see me, I don't even know where he is," I said. "But it does sound like an interesting adventure, and you, better than anyone, know how I like new experiences."

After a little bit of interrogation of my paternal grandmother, I was able to find out where he lived. I decided I would go, unannounced, to Florida, and visit this mysterious man.

I now knew where I was going, and what my reasons for the trip were. I still didn't know what I was expecting to happen, but I had taken a big step. I had finally made a decision on my own. Even though this one had absolutely nothing to do with sex, it still counted in my book. That being said, I asked my fifteen-year-old brother, Tim, to come along for moral support.

Although we were from the same family and experienced the same divorce, my brother and I were totally different. He had many close friends, being that he easily trusted people, and had the luxury of having the same girlfriend for a long time. I, on the other hand, didn't allow people into my life for very long. My life was much more complicated than his easygoing, down-to-earth approach.

I was still intent on maintaining my recent commitment to abstain from sex until I met someone who was clearly relationship material. But the urges I had been suppressing for the last few months were coming more and more to the forefront. I found myself once again yearning to "help" any female in whatever way they needed me.

Another big difference between my brother and me was that I was thoroughly interested in just about anything abnormal, such as UFO's, ESP, and especially the afterlife. Although Nana had passed on, I was sure that she was still communicating with me through signs and sensations that I felt.

I truly believed we were here, in this human life form, for just a short period of time and then "developed" into another phase of life. The way I saw it, we are eternally alive, just in different forms.

My brother just thought I was crazy.

* * *

The two of us jumped into my car to leave our small town in Missouri for this adventure. We immediately began to discuss why I wanted to go.

"You know, Tim, the last few years have been tough on me ..." I rambled on about how I thought that I'd put a lot of pressure on myself. I was always trying to figure out what was morally right and wrong, and which way I wanted my life to go. I sometimes felt like a rock star, what with all the girls who wanted to spend time with me. "It's not easy being in such demand, ya know."

"You're so high on yourself." Tim shook his head as he stared out the side window. But he didn't have a clue what my life had turned into, and now wasn't the time to try and explain it.

* * *

We stopped at a local gas station to fill up before leaving town. I noticed two girls using the pump next to us. While Tim filled the tank, the prettier of the two girls waved at me and said, "Hi."

Here we go again, I thought to myself.

"Right back at ya!" I said, glancing at her license plate. "I see you're from out of state ... so, where you ladies headed?"

She looked me over and said, "On our way to Georgia to check out a college we may go to. How about you?"

"Well, we were on our way to Florida, but it seems like we may be going to Georgia now to see about a college." I raised a sly eyebrow.

She smiled, getting my joke. "I have an idea ... if you're game."

I hadn't a clue where this was going, but was open to her suggestion. "Let's hear it."

"My name's Mandy. Why don't you guys follow us and we can stop later for some dinner and some small talk? It'll make the long drive more fun."

I nodded, and then upped the ante. "Why don't *you* come with me, and my brother will ride with your friend, so we can talk on the way? That will make the long drive even more fun."

So that's how I started on my journey to change—by not really changing at all.

CHAPTER 2
MANDY

Mandy was short, skinny, and big chested; very easy to look at. I noticed a gold four leaf clover earring in her left ear. I assumed she was about my age. She had the look of a cheerleader; long blonde hair pulled up in a ponytail, a great big smile showing off perfect white teeth, and a perky bounce in her step. I also noticed something emanating from her eyes. It was the "secret" gleam that Carmen, a lesbian friend of mine, had clued me in on. It indicated Mandy was open to sexual banter ... and possibly more.

Mandy introduced Tim to her friend. Right away I could sense Sue was a little on the shy side. She was a tad overweight, had short brown hair, and came across as the "girl next door" type. I wondered why they were friends, they seemed so different. That's when I noticed the same gleam radiating from Sue's eyes, and understood what they had in common. I believed these two traveling companions were ready for whatever sexual desires they had to come to fruition.

* * *

I drove out of the gas station and Mandy immediately started talking about herself—which I didn't mind. Over the years I had learned to be a caring listener.

"I'm a cheerleader from a small town in Iowa ... Harlan," Mandy said. "Everyone in school knows each other, so I wanna get away from all that and meet some new people. I feel like I'm not like the other kids. I'm really into the occult. I love bowling, and my favorite thing is disco dancing. Right now I just wanna relax and not worry about the future all that much. What about you?"

Wow, she sounded just like me. Those were my exact favorite things.

"I'm a little different, too," I said. "Back when I was eight I overheard my mom, who was recently divorced, talking with some of her female friends about how *all* men are untrustworthy, selfish, and only care about themselves."

Mandy's expression indicated she couldn't disagree.

"I set out on a mission to be a guy *all* women respected. And for a while I had it down. But now some do and some don't, so I'm tryin' to find the 'real me' after leadin' a life that's veered so far away from what I had expected."

Mandy was clearly interested in what I was saying, and wanted to hear more.

"Starting when I was fifteen," I said, "I tried to make every girl I met 'feel good' by being there for whatever they needed from me. I was able to see the girls differently than the other boys did. I made a point to remember everything they said to me, and to see things about them that others missed."

Mandy looked at me strange. "So, whatcha *seen* about me so far?"

"That's easy," I said, "two things right off the bat. First, you wear a gold four leaf clover earring in only one ear. I'm guessin' that it means somethin' special to you."

I smiled as she grabbed at her ear.

"Second, a certain gleam radiates from your eyes; it tells me that you're very comfortable with your sexuality, with few or possibly no hang-ups at all," I said, rather proud of myself. "I bet none of the boys back home can tell ya that much and I've known you for a lot less time."

Mandy was impressed. "You're right about that, no boy has ever commented on my earring before. It was given to me by my grandma when I was eleven. She's dead now and I never take it off cuz it's the only connection I have to her."

A lone tear ran down her face. She wiped it away and said, "As for the other thing, I'm not so sure I agree. But tell me more."

"A lesbian friend of mine once pointed out that you can tell how good a person will be in bed by how well they dance. And later—just by lookin' into my eyes—she knew when I'd had my first sexual encounter the very next day after I had it. She was the only one who sensed it. She then taught me how to read what people are sayin' with their eyes. They can't lie, you know? Think about it. Have you ever noticed how sometimes a person's mouth is saying one thing, and their eyes are sayin' something totally different?"

I stopped, turned to Mandy and awaited her reaction. When she shot me back a smile I realized she now understood what I meant.

I went on about my past. How I felt as though I was "forced" into my first sexual encounter by a demanding girl. How I "helped" many others when they wanted to "escape" from their life for a short amount of time by first listening with heartfelt concern to their problems, and then by having sex with them on *their* terms. And later how I became what would be considered a hired "gigolo" after I met an older lady—a madam, in fact—who thought my "gift" should be shared with her middle-aged female clients.

I told Mandy, "I had it worked out in my head that I was just puttin' a talent for selflessly pleasing lonely women to good use. And the pay wasn't bad either."

"So …" Mandy hesitated as if unsure she really wanted to know, "all told, girls and older women combined, how many would ya say you've had sex with?"

I never kept a scorecard, if you will, so I didn't really know the exact number. "Rough estimate," I rolled my eyes skyward while doing the mental math, "probably in the neighborhood of twenty or thirty."

I knew the number was much higher, seeing that for just about three years almost every Friday and Saturday night I was out 'sharing myself' with those who asked. And that wasn't even counting my time with Nancy and her 'friends.' But I didn't want Mandy to get the wrong idea about me, and I didn't want to look like I was bragging. I always told the girls: *What friends do together should stay between them.* Besides, I was hoping that part of my life was over now.

Mandy sat quietly in the seat and took in what I had just said. She didn't make a weird face, and she didn't make any crude comments. After some contemplation, she turned to me and said, "I don't recall I've ever met someone like you before."

I felt a sense of relief that she didn't pass judgment on me.

Mandy rolled the window down to let a cool breeze flow in, and said above it, "Man, it's kinda weird, you're so easy to talk to, and you have this calming effect on me. I like listenin' to your stories, but I'm not sure if I believe everything you say. Anyway, my grandmother told me when I was a kid to 'Always keep an open mind', so that's what I'll do.

"My grandmother said that, too," I nodded. "They both sound like ladies who knew what they were talkin' about."

A big smile appeared on Mandy's face. "Do you believe in fate, like me?"

I shot her a sideways glance as if to say, *What do you think?*

* * *

About 400 miles and five hours later, Mandy and I got out of the car to refuel. She walked up to me and gave me a long hug. "After thinkin' about all the things you've told me, I've formed an opinion—I like you … and your stories … and I want more."

More? More of what?

I started to think about the possibilities, but was jolted back into reality as Tim and Sue pulled into the gas station just behind us. We all decided to get something to eat at the restaurant next door.

We filled up on greasy hamburgers while Mandy told Sue some of the things she had learned about me. I just sat there watching Tim. He didn't seem to be interested at all. When Mandy announced she needed to use the restroom, Sue tagged along, as girls have a tendency to do.

I knew right away they were going to talk about me.

Tim and I discussed the slight change in itinerary as a result of hooking up with the girls. Finally, I asked him, "So, whaddaya think of Sue? She's pretty, huh?"

"If you like that kind of girl," he said. "I'm happy with Denise, back home, thank you."

"You're 500 miles away, and all you can think about is your girlfriend?" I shook my head. "Well, I like Mandy. And who knows, maybe she's the one I've been lookin' ...," I had to stop my thought because the girls were coming back.

* * *

We finished off our meals with hot fudge sundaes, and then headed for our cars to drive about two hours into the future—to find a place to spend the night.

Mandy jumped in the passenger side door, only this time she quickly slid down the bench seat to sit right next to me. She placed her hands along the sides of my face so she could look directly into my eyes. When she smiled brightly, I was able to see a new sparkle in her eyes—one that meant she trusted me. This was a totally different look than the sex gleam, and actually meant more to me.

We drove down the road and Mandy happily started telling me more about herself, concluding with, "Ya know, I've had some experiences of my own. Some were good and some not so good. I'm not too sure I learned from mine like you did, though."

Her upbeat mood was suddenly replaced with a frown. "My last two boyfriends just used me cuz-a my looks and cuz I was a cheerleader. I was just another notch in their belts and nothin' more. You'd think I'd learn, but I never do."

I reached over to hold her hand.

Mandy began to cry softly. "Football jocks are only interested in the thrill of the chase. And then once they've had ya, they're through with you, and onto the next conquest they go. That's the real reason I wanna get way."

My heart went out to Mandy. I'd known too many girls who'd fallen for the "sports jock" type and had made the same mistake.

She looked up at me and noticed my eyes had teared up, too.

"I've never seen a boy cry listenin' to my story before." She shook her head in disbelief. "You're so sweet to listen to me complain about my life. I think I'm beginnin' to understand why those girls said you always make 'em feel better."

"Thanks," I blushed. "I've found you can learn a lot about a person just by listening, by *really* listening, ya know?"

"So … what have you learned listenin' to all my blubbering?"

"Mandy," I let out a long exhale, "you're a girl who cares way too much what others think about you, and you're oversensitive about being judged by 'em." I thought about my next words very carefully, not wanting to overstep my bounds. "If you ask me, I think you're lookin' for the wrong type of guy. Your whole life seems to be about outward appearances and status. I've found that those types of relationships never pan out cuz they don't let you connect emotionally with the other person."

Since Mandy wasn't protesting, I continued. "My opinion? I'd say you oughta start lookin' at what a person has going on *inside* of 'em, instead of what they look like on the outside. Everyone has somethin' special they want you to know about—you just need to find it. You need to learn to trust in your feelings more and what they have to tell you."

Mandy placed her head on my shoulder and kissed me gently on the neck. I felt as though I may have helped her a little. In fact, for the first time in a long time I felt a warm sensation radiate through my heart.

I smiled to myself and put a favorite cassette of mine by Bread into the player, and turned the volume low so we could listen to their songs in the background as we traveled down the road in reflective silence.

* * *

It was about ten at night when our cars arrived at the hotel parking lot. We registered for our rooms, then stood in the small lobby and discussed a swim before turning in. We made plans to meet at the pool in half an hour, then Tim and I went to our room to change into swim suits.

Tim nonchalantly asked, "How was the rest of your ride?"

"It was pretty interesting. I learned a lot about Mandy, but I think she needs to 'talk' some more. I'll find out later."

He looked at me quizzically. "What the hell does that mean?"

"Just that she needs more *help* and I think I've been chosen once again to be the one," I shrugged. "This is just my lot in life."

My brother shook his head. "You are so full of yourself."

* * *

I went down to the pool alone; Tim was on the phone with Denise, and wanted no part of what was likely to happen next. The small pool was empty except for Sue. I watched as the water glistened off her tanned body when she exited the pool. She looked nice in her bikini, although as

I said earlier, she was a little overweight. She walked closer, and I was taken aback when I saw the sex gleam staring back at me. Guess she wasn't as shy as I first thought.

"Mandy told me more about you when we got back to our room. She thinks you guys have some kind of connection. She believes in fate and stuff like that, ya know."

I didn't see it coming when she said, "The more Mandy talked about you, the more I began to feel somethin', too. Your brother's a nice kid, but way too young for me."

I really wondered where Sue was going with this as she continued to walk toward me, stopping only inches away. What happened next floored me.

Sue winked and said, "Mandy and I wanna know if you'll show us this 'gift' you told her about, and if you'll share it with *both* of us at the same time."

I was dumbfounded, and although I had taken that vow a few months earlier not to have sex until I'd worked things out in my head, I followed Sue to their room.

When I called Tim to tell him not to wait up for me, I could just picture him rolling his eyes. "You stupid boy," he said, "you're goin' down the exact same path you're tryin' to get off of."

* * *

Sue, Mandy, and I did spend the night together. It was my first threesome—another new experience.

Using some of the things I'd perfected in my previous sexual adventures, like intimate and prolonged touching of body parts, including both of their G-spots, I began to share myself with Mandy and Sue. All of the feelings I had been suppressing for the last few months quickly came rushing back to me. Although I never expected this, and wasn't sure I wanted it to happen; I was happy that it did. But at one point a question sprung into my mind: *Am I being just like Mandy's football studs?*

I remembered how I used to "teach" the inexperienced girls I went out with how to lose themselves in the pleasure of sex. I realized I missed sharing this great feeling. Luckily, or unluckily—it was yet to be seen—I had just gotten it back.

When the three of us finished and Sue left to take a shower, Mandy and I stayed in her bed. She kissed me lightly on the lips, and as we cuddled under the sheet I asked, "Well, how'd that make you feel?"

"The sex was real good and different than normal for me," Mandy smiled. "And I have to say, I've never felt so comfortable afterwards. You were so much more caring than any of my old flames."

I felt a smile appear on my face as she said that. Perhaps staying away from sex was the wrong thing for me to do?

"You made this a terrific experience for both of us," Mandy continued, "you were also very considerate and sensitive to both our needs. It felt like you were more concerned with what Sue and I were feelin' than what you were. Like I said it was different."

She reached under the covers. "And I was hopin' you could make me feel that way one more time."

* * *

Before I fell asleep with Mandy next to me, I debated whether or not I should pursue a relationship with her—we had shared so much in such a short time. This was partly what I was going to Florida to discover about myself. Maybe I didn't have to go there after all. Was it possible I'd lucked out and found just what I needed in Mandy?

I awoke in the morning alone; Sue and Mandy were gone. Near my pants Mandy had left a handwritten note:

Phil, I had a great time. I hope you enjoy Florida, and find the happiness you're looking for. The person I met last night is just fine with me. You treat people with kindness and the respect that they deserve. I hope you're not mad I didn't say good-bye. I just needed someone like you to help me find a new perspective, and I'm a happier person today than I was yesterday. While we have a lot in common, our destinies are different. I think we both know that FATE has other plans for us.
Thanks, Mandy!

I didn't know what to think. I know, most guys couldn't have cared less that they'd bailed—maybe even seen it as having done him a favor, living out a fantasy and never having to see the girls again.

Maybe I was insane. Here I was doing the same thing as I always had and expecting a different outcome. I guess I'm just better at this "meaningless sex thing" than finding the emotional connection I really want.

My memory of that experience may be fading, but Mandy always comes to mind whenever I hear the particular lyrics from Bread's *Today's the First Day.*

These two ladies reawakened some buried feelings in me—ones of conceit and conquest. These traits were always present in me, but not as obvious as in other boys. Mine was a "decent" type of conceit, at least in my mind. But now, instead of thinking more about sensitivity and caring, the thoughts going through my head were maybe I am something special and maybe my life needs to be all about me.

CHAPTER 3
LORETTA

After arriving in sunny, warm Florida a day later than we anticipated, Tim and I finally got to meet Dad. We followed the directions Grandma gave us and arrived in front of a very large house situated on a cul-de-sac with only a few other houses. Neither of us could believe how big it was and the golden colored iron fence around it made us even more skeptical.

"Are you sure we're at the right place?" Tim asked.

"The number on the mailbox is the same," I said, looking at the note with directions on it.

"If this is his," Tim said, starting to get a little mad, "I can't wait to tell Mom."

Mom was always telling us even though Dad was sending money to help raise us, it was never enough. I had to say I agreed with Tim this time.

I pulled the car into the driveway and when we hit a certain spot the front gate opened up on its own. I followed the stone pavement until we were in front of about ten other cars. They ranged from a beat-up old Datsun B-210 all the way to a nice brand new BMW convertible.

Tim and I walked to the front door. When I rang the doorbell, I became aware of the sweat pouring down from my face. I wasn't sure if it was nerves or the Florida weather.

Shortly after the bell sounded, we heard the echoes of footsteps coming nearer to us through the door. The nerves hit me hard, but when the door opened they almost knocked me down. There stood a magic mirror; I was looking at an older version of me—a man in his mid-thirties who was thin, tanned, and very well dressed. The only thing that bothered me was his receding hairline. *Will that be me in about fifteen years?*

"Ha, it's about time you guys got here," he said. "I was expectin' you yesterday."

Expecting us? We came without any announcement.

He saw our confusion. "Mom called to let me know that my two sons were coming to spy on me," he laughed. "I'm really glad you did."

He invited us in and introduced us to a big crowd of his friends. "Hey guys, these are my kids, just down from Missouri."

I quickly noticed everyone in the room was a man. I wasn't totally comfortable being around groups of boys or men. They often made me nervous and feeling down about myself. *Wonder how this is going to affect our visit?* But when everyone smiled and waved it helped me to relax a little.

I had a real hard time calling him "Dad" since he had been absent from my life for so long. I hadn't seen or talked to him since he left nine years ago. I couldn't remember very much about him. He knew very little about me as well; I had grown up a lot since his leaving, in more ways than one.

And I thought, Other than looks, and our names, we have absolutely nothing in common.

After a few minutes of small talk, he said, "Look, we were just going to dinner. Wanna come?"

Tim and I said yes. Since there were so many of us we took four separate cars.

I was once told, "Your deepest inner feelings never lie to you, learn to trust them." Although no words were exchanged between us, there was an immediate connection with a friend of his named Lawrence, so I chose to ride with him, and let Tim have some time alone with our dad.

* * *

Lawrence was a big man—six-foot-five, weighed about two hundred and seventy-five pounds; had jet black hair, and bushy eyebrows to match. He also sprouted a thick, black mustache. I detected an attitude— a Brooklyn, New York way about him. I then saw, hanging from his right pierced ear, an earring in the shape of small golden handcuffs.

After we climbed into his BMW convertible I had to contain myself from laughing when he said, "So, what brings you here to Florida?"

Here was this gigantic man with a New York twang, but his voice was really more of a feminine tone—I was expecting a deep sounding baritone, but got a Marilyn Monroe squeak instead.

I usually didn't like talking. I was always more of a listener. But I came to Florida to change my habits, so I volunteered, "I'm here to get away from my 'normal' life for a while. It's gettin' pretty confusing back home, so I thought a change of pace might help."

He nodded as if he understood my dilemma. "Well, *this* will be a change all right." He added without any hesitation, "You do know that your dad and all of us are gay, don't you?"

I sat there in silence thinking this over. Now I understood why my parents couldn't remain together. Mom must've known about dad's sexual proclivity, but I wondered why she didn't tell us? Did she feel the need to protect me from the knowledge my dad was gay? Or was she trying to protect herself so us kids wouldn't ask, "How'd you not know he was gay when you married him?"

"Hello, are you there?" Larry said, snapping me out of my reverie.

"Sorry, just thinkin'." I looked over at Larry. "No, I didn't know that fact about Dad. But seeing all guys in the house, and your earring, I get it. I may be young, but I do know that when a person wears an earring in their right ear only, it signals they're either gay or lesbian. I have a few friends back home who fit that description."

I saw Larry relax some.

"It's really no big deal to me," I said. "It just means that you like the same sex, nothing more. I think all of God's people are exactly alike inside and all want the same two things from life—to be accepted for who we are, and to be as happy as we can be."

"You really are your dad's son," Larry said as he smiled at me. "I know you don't know him very well, but believe me, he has the same exact thoughts. I sense that you're much more mature than your seventeen years let on."

I sighed and thought, If I really am I wouldn't feel so lost.

* * *

The restaurant was called Area Code 305. That was an interesting name and I wondered what it meant—until we walked in. Every table had a telephone on it and a corresponding number hanging over it. The phones were a unique way to pick someone up who you saw sitting across the room. Hence the name; the area code for Florida was 305.

When the waiter came around and started asking everyone for their drink orders, two things came to mind. One, was this a gay restaurant? And two, could I drink here? I sure could use one.

"You want somethin' to drink?" Dad asked both Tim and I. "A beer maybe?"

"I'm not old enough to drink alcohol," I said, although I was already partaking at home when no one knew about it. My preference there was white wine.

"Here in Florida the drinking age is eighteen," he said, "and you're with me, so it's okay if you want something."

Not wanting to be a party pooper, I ordered a Miller Lite like most of the others. *I'm not really a beer man, but what the hell!*

Tim went with a cola.

Our phone rang shortly after we had finished eating and Larry put it on speaker for all of us to hear. The voice on the other end was young and female. *At least I know it isn't a gay spot now.*

She asked, "So what's a group of good looking men like you doin' without a lady? Lemme talk to someone who wants to meet a pretty girl."

Larry took it off speaker and laughed as he handed me the phone. Lesson number one; *be different*, entered my mind. I said with an edge in my voice, "Hey there Florida babe, are ya sure you want to talk to me? I may be bad for you."

"What a coincidence, I only like guys who are bad for me," the voice snickered. "My name's Loretta, why don't you come over here so we can talk face to face? I'm at table 444."

I approached her table with a beer in my hand and met not only Loretta, but also her parents. *Not too awkward!*

The four of us discussed many things, none that were too life changing. Things like how old I was, how old Loretta was; and I thought the most interesting thing they found out about me was that I was from Missouri.

Well, that's not entirely true.

Her mom asked me, "So, what's the 'H' for?"

She was referring to the solid gold letter "H" earring I had in my *left* pierced ear.

"It was given to me by a friend back home. It stands for 'healer.' I helped her and some of her friends through many tough times." I smiled as I reminisced. "It brings back some fond memories, and besides it's a great ice-breaker. It always gets noticed."

She laughed, and as she did I saw one of the signs I always wanted to see emerge from a female; the sparkle of trust emitting from her eyes.

* * *

We spent an enjoyable hour together and then Larry came over to tell me it was time to leave. I wanted to spend some more time *alone* with Loretta, and I said to her dad, "I know it may seem odd that I'm asking this, but I'd like to get to know more about your daughter. Is there any way she can stay here with me, and you can pick her up later?"

He and Larry had a little conference and when they were done, he said, "Your dad and I agreed that since you haven't had too much to drink you can use his car. Just be safe and don't be too late."

I shook his hand and said, "Larry's not my dad, he's just a friend of my dad's … over there." I pointed to him and he waved back. "I promise to take good care of your daughter and bring her home safe and sound."

He smiled, reached for his wife's hand, and they started to leave. When she passed by Loretta, her mom said jokingly, "Watch out for these out of town boys, they all have just one thing on their mind."

Little did she know that Florida girls had the same thought!

* * *

Loretta decided to show me the Fort Lauderdale strip. We parked the car and strolled hand in hand past the big hotels. I noticed the sidewalk area was extremely well lit, allowing a close-up look of Loretta. She was about five-foot-two and had beautiful red hair flowing down to her shoulders. I could see her green eyes already had the sparkle of trust in them.

"Is this area always so busy and bright?" I winked. "Isn't there somewhere else we could go to be more alone?"

She smiled back, getting the real question I was asking and I saw the sparkle of trust magically turn into the sex gleam. She eagerly volunteered, "We could go down and walk along the beach."

We started toward the ocean, and I slipped my arm around her slim waist. Loretta asked, "So how long are you stayin' in Florida?"

"I'm leavin' later this week, but I've been seriously thinkin' about moving here."

"If I make it worth your while, will you move here for me?"

I laughed—then got serious. "Right now, I wouldn't even know what 'worth my while' is. But how about we sit and I tell ya more about me before you decide if you really want me to?"

We stopped at a beachside stand to buy a cold drink and the place had lemonade, which was my favorite drink as it brought back fond memories of my Nana, so I bought us each one.

We found a bench overlooking the ocean in a remotely quiet and somewhat hidden section of the beach. We started talking and I looked into the dark night sky above the ocean. I was amazed at how much brighter the stars looked here in Florida. Immediately, memories of my times in Wisconsin at Nana's special cottage, which I had loved so much, came to me. Loretta saw me gazing upwards and asked, "So, whatcha thinkin'?"

I smiled and told her about Nana, our times together, and how even though she had been dead for a long time, I still felt like I could talk to her. I shared with Loretta the last "talk" Nana and I had—the one where I was trying to figure out if what I was doing was right or wrong. That's when Nana told me in a dream, "I can't tell you why you do the things you do—only you can. I can tell you though, in your own special way, you are there for those who need you and that's what living this life is all about: helping others, respecting them, and building relationships. In return, you get love and respect back. God is helping you understand all this. As one of many signs, every time you feel warmth in your heart, God is letting you know the Spirit is around. The Lord believes in you and is a fair and good God who works in miraculous ways. And although you may not always understand what God does, you need to know and trust that everything happens for a reason. Sometimes the Lord sends real people, as human angels, to assist those who need help. It looks as if God picked you by giving you the gift that you possess. Your way of helping may not be the preferred way, but as long as you use it for the right reasons, the Lord continues to understand. You have made a great difference in your young life to many people already."

Loretta exclaimed, "No wonder you wanted to get away."

I took a sip of my lemonade and again smiled.

Loretta asked, "Now what?"

I explained the way Nana would put a sprig of mint in her lemonade and I, not liking the taste of mint, would pluck mine out and put it in my pocket in order to smell it later. Whenever I smelled the aroma of mint, I knew Nana was near.

"You sure have a lotta strange memories, but I have a few questions," Loretta said. "The first one is what is this way of helping that isn't His way that you talk about? And more importantly, just what is this 'gift' that makes others feel good?"

"They're actually one in the same," I explained. "After my parent's divorce I escaped by lockin' myself in my room and listenin' to records. When that didn't help me break through, I began experimentin' with somethin' else. It seems as though I have helped many ladies find respite from their troubles by sharin' intimate conversation and sometimes physical intimacy. If I felt a warm surge in my heart I knew that I had helped them somehow. I've stopped havin' that feeling lately, which is why I'm here in Florida—to see if I can get it back in some other way."

"I'm no expert, but why change a good thing?" Loretta smiled.

I just shrugged my shoulders.

Loretta surprised me by kissing me and whispering in my ear, "Do you think this girl from Florida can help you find it?"

When I kissed her back I felt a much different feeling come over me— wonderment—could I really make it in this old world not believing that everything revolved around me? That sensitivity and sex weren't the same thing? And, finally, by truly feeling good about who I was? I wondered if Loretta could be the one to help me with this and if it was really what I wanted anyway.

When I asked her to stop kissing me and she did without shooting me a strange look, I realized that she had no preconceived expectations of me, like the girls back home did. I took it as sign from above.

* * *

My main mission with this trip was to help me figure out whether I could handle only one girl in my life, or if I truly needed the chase to stay interested. I had already experienced the feelings of satisfaction and conceit begin to enter my body again after Mandy and I had sex and I knew I liked how it made me feel. And although I still had no idea which way to turn, I did know that I had a friend, and probably a life in Florida, if I wanted it. I told Loretta I was leaning toward moving.

* * *

I walked Loretta up to the front door of her house, got her phone number and promised to call her if I decided to move. I started to kiss her good-bye when the door suddenly opened and there stood her mom.

She said jokingly, "I warned you that those out of town boys only wanted one thing."

Loretta gazed up at her with a faraway look in her eyes, and quietly said, "You're right, and I hope he moves here to Florida just to prove it."

* * *

I drove back to Larry's house to drop off his car. When I arrived, he was sitting in his hot tub which overlooked the lit-up strip. He invited me to join him, and then said, "So, how'd it go?"

I declined the offer to jump in the water, but sat nearby on a recliner.

"It went fine. I think I may be movin' here. By the look on her face when I left, she's infatuated with me," I said. "But I'm not too sure that's what I want right now—"

Larry interrupted, "That's because of the strong aura of sexuality radiating around you. Your colors are red, which obviously is the color of love and sexual energy, yellow, which means joy and freedom and green, which means healing. With those colors surrounding you, whatever you experienced tonight is only the beginning."

Once again I had to contain my laughter—me getting sexual advice from a gay guy. But seriously, here was another person who saw primarily the sexual side of me coming through. I wondered why and if I should be worried about it.

* * *

The next morning at breakfast I casually asked my dad about living with him if I decided to move. To my surprise, he was excited about the idea. As I debated internally over the decision which lay ahead of me, some tough questions came to mind. Was this the right choice? Would this be good for me, or blow up in my face? Was Florida what I needed, or was there something I was trying to avoid? Would I get a sign to let me know what would be best for me?

Silently, I prayed for help, but didn't feel I'd gotten any response.

With all the questions running through my head, I felt more confused than before my trip. Back home I would have retreated to my room and turned on some Rod Stewart records. I really related to his songs, and for some reason they helped me to think clearer. Instead I walked out to the backyard for a swim, and turned on the radio by the pool. It was a shock when Rod's song, *Hard Lesson to Learn,* came on. This sure sounded like a sign to me.

I could only think of one thing. Whatever was going to happen next on this incredible journey of mine was going to happen. It was in that instant I chose to move to Florida. But first I had to say good-bye to my life back home … and I hoped I could actually do it.

CHAPTER 4
BACK HOME

On Sunday night, after I got back to Missouri from my Florida trip, I was talking to my best friend. Billy was one of the few guy friends that I had. He was there on my first date—we doubled. He was there as the two of us roller skated every Friday night for three years, and he was there lending me support whenever I needed it. When I told him I was moving, the first thing he said was, "Can I have some of the girls you know from skating?"

All Billy ever wanted was pure unadulterated sex ... and the more variety the better.

Billy had no idea of why I was so popular. He did know that a lot of the girls at the rink liked to talk to me, and I think he was envious of that fact. Even though we spent a lot of time together here at the rink, Billy never figured out my technique for attracting so many girls. Not that I could teach him about it anyway, there was a certain discipline required which I thought most teenage boys, especially a horny one like Billy, didn't have the patience for, nor the understanding.

The skating rink we frequented, The Roller Wheel, was what really made me who I was. It had become my second home, and I felt the most comfortable there, more than anywhere else except for Wisconsin where Nana had that summer cottage. Every Friday night Billy and I arrived in separate cars, because on most of these nights I knew I'd end up at a private parking lot which overlooked the Mississippi River. This was where I shared what the girls called my "gift" with them.

I'd spend some quality time with these girls, most times culminating with sex in my back seat, and then would present them with a silk rose. The particular color of each rose had a hidden meaning, which I knew the real reasons for, but wasn't so sure the girls did.

Leaving this rink, the girls associated with it, and the popularity I had experienced here was going to be harder to do than leaving my family.

* * *

I started telling a few of the girls I was moving and the word spread quickly. They all said Friday nights wouldn't be the same without me, both in the rink *and* out of it. Even though I had started out extremely shy three years ago, "Disco Phil" allowed me to become the center of attention rather fast. Because of "him," I was able to drastically change my personality. And that was where I found myself thinking the world, and all the girls in it, revolved around me.

All these young girls knew me only as Disco Phil. This alter-ego was the brainchild of Joyce, a lesbian friend from work. She helped me to feel comfortable around the straight girls, allowing them to see I was friendly and approachable to all types of girls.

Since I liked disco music so much, Joyce reinvented me as this character because I was much better at playing a part than I was at being myself. The image she helped me project was enhanced by the clothes she chose for me to wear: black Angel Flight pants, styled polyester which hugged my body like a second skin, and bright colorful metallic shirts with matching belts and socks. The shirts she chose for me had low cut necklines. I wore a tiger pendent around my neck which my father gave to me when I was younger, and a gold charm with my astrology sign written in Greek. Nancy — the madam I temporarily worked for — gave it to me.

I even had my own song which I skated solo to each Friday night. Week after week, the DJ would announce me over the PA system as he plunged the old place into complete darkness and then started playing my song. Joyce had me buy clear wheels for my black skates which had lights in them. So as soon as my wheels were seen rolling through the darkness, the girls would line up around the rink and as I whizzed past them, they'd try to slap me on the ass.

Joyce started this routine and Steve, the owner, approved. He told me, "Phil, you helped save my business when you started skating here. You're by far the best known kid here, and I feel like I owe you something."

When he learned I was leaving town, Steve said, "I'm going to throw you a going away party here at the rink. You're my best customer so I want to send you off the right way. Since Mondays here are for special events, that's when we'll hold it. You can invite anyone you want to, and I'll pay for everything … the skating, the food, and I'll even throw in a cake. These Monday night parties normally have about forty people. Do you think you can get that many to show up?"

I started talking to the girls, while Billy talked to some of the guys he knew, and we came up an initial list of sixty names.

Little did I know what would happen next.

* * *

On the night of the party, a surprisingly warm and muggy one, Billy and I once again arrived separately. I *knew* I would be getting lucky, and Billy hoped that he would. When I pulled my red 1978 Monte Carlo into the lot that night, Steve was there waiting outside for me, looking a little nervous.

"Instead of entering the front doors, let's have you come through from the back of the rink so you can make a grand entrance," he suggested.

That night, instead of wearing my usual black outfit, I had on a white disco suit, which included white pants, a purple shirt, a white vest, and even white boots.

John Travolta step aside.

I'd made a necklace from some green glow sticks left over from Halloween for around my neck, just for kicks. After changing into my skates, I heard my song, *Hot Stuff*, by Donna Summer, start up as the DJ announced I had finally arrived. He turned off all the lights and I skated out from the back room glowing from head to toe as I made my way to the center of the rink.

The large room, which normally had loud music resonating off its three carpeted walls, was unnaturally quiet. I silently prayed that someone—anyone—had shown up.

When I finished my first jump, a thunderous applause arose from the darkness. The lights clicked on and as I looked up from the middle of the rink, I saw at least 100 young girls were standing around it clapping. I was stunned. When I looked closer at them all, I noticed more than half of them were wearing different colored silk roses in their hair. These were the same roses I gave to them after spending our special times together.

I felt something inside—not sure if it was a sign from above or the rumblings of self-centeredness growing. Whatever it was, I silently thanked God that people actually showed up. I dropped to my knees and started to cry, but quickly attempted to compose myself so I could finish my routine.

Steve came out after my song ended and said some stuff to the crowd, most of which I don't remember. He then whispered to me, "This is the most people ever to show up for a private party. You sure must have touched these people somehow."

Little did he know just how.

* * *

I sat down to relax for a minute and Billy plopped down beside me. "Man, whatta turnout! There's only ten guys here, not countin' us? But there has to be at least a hundred chicks. I wonder where they all came from."

It was time for me to come clean ... as much as I could.

"Billy, these last three years have been busy ones for me. All you ever knew about was that the girls loved to share their problems with me here at the rink, or while sittin' in my car," I explained. "But many of 'em ended up going to the private lot down by the river with me. Believe it or not, all the girls with roses in their hair tonight have had sex with me."

Man that sounded so bad to me. But on the other hand, it also made me smile. Boy, was I messed up.

Billy laughed. "Stop fuckin' around. You always said it was all talk and no action."

"Do you think any of 'em would have slept with me if I was braggin' about it to you, or to anyone, for that matter?"

Billy maintained his doubtful stare.

"Look, if you don't believe me, go ask 'em," I told him. "Since I'm leavin' for good, I doubt they'll mind telling ya the truth, now."

Billy skated away and talked to a couple of the girls and came back dumbfounded. "Just why the hell are you leavin' again? These girls love you."

"Nah, they don't love me at all. Maybe they love what I do, but I just helped them get through some rough times, that's all."

I then reminded him, "In fact, you're the one who told me never to confuse love and sex."

I finally got to my point. "I gave 'em guilt-free, no pressure sex, and *they* were always in control. Now I don't know if it was right or wrong. So I need to start fresh someplace where there are no expectations on me, and I sure can't do that here."

I don't think Billy totally understood. He just shook his head and asked, "Why do they all have different color roses?"

"Ya know how I believe in symbolism?" I said and waited for him to nod back. "Well, the roses all have hidden meanings. Each color represents my feelings about that girl. Red was for love—not even one of those out there. Yellow was for friendship. Pink was thankin' 'em for somethin'. And finally, the white ones … those can have different meanings, but to me they mean that the girls were much too young to understand love."

Billy looked around and noted all the white ones. "You suppose I can take your place?"

"I doubt it. You've already got a reputation as a player, and that's not what they're lookin' for," I said. "Besides, it's not always as fun as it may seem, and it can really mess up your mind if you're not careful."

Billy surveyed the room a second time and sighed with resignation, "I'd take my chances anyway."

* * *

27

I wanted to be a good host and spent some time with as many of the girls from my past as I could. Star was my first real sexual encounter; the first girl I couldn't say no to. At the time, I thought I believed I didn't want to have sex until I got married. Still, I reluctantly gave in to her persistent pressure. Even though I felt as though she "corrupted" me, I was happy to see her again.

Cece showed up, too. I hadn't seen her since she became my first one-night stand; well, actually I was just one of *her* many one-nighters. Her friends, a cop and his buddies, actually owned the parking lot I frequented and only allowed a precious few to use it in the evenings. She also played a big part in starting me to hand out those silk roses.

Deidre was an older girl who had sex with me in order to get over her ex-boyfriend. She taught me a few special things which I'd never experienced before—like locating a woman's G-spot, and treating women as special as I possibly could. I was then able to incorporate all this into my sexual routine. I gave her a big kiss and thanked her for her expertise.

Sex with both Cece and Deidre led to my first experience of the warm surge I sometimes felt in my heart. Although I didn't understand it at the time, I now believed they both needed someone like me right when I showed up in their lives.

I wished I could be that innocent again.

Diane also showed up, and I was extremely surprised. She was the girl who I just wanted to be the "real me" with, not Disco Phil. I really liked her a lot, but chose not to have sex with her. I felt more for her than any of the others. But since sex was the main thing she wanted from me, and it didn't happen, she left me. Our brief time had ended unhappily for her.

But I had a happy memory of her. It was Diane who helped me to "see" Nana again. That's when Nana let me know that no matter what, God still loved me.

I gave Diane a hug. "I'm so sorry that you didn't get what ya wanted from me. I liked you way too much, and wanted to offer you so much more."

"I'm sorry, too." Diane stared at me with tears in her eyes. "All I really wanted was a rose."

* * *

Seeing these girls again made me reminisce about our times together. I was happy to be remembered by them all, but also felt confused and somewhat ashamed about some of the things I'd experienced with them.

The more these thoughts rambled around in my head, the more I felt an odd need.

Here I was, in the middle of 100 girls and I suddenly wanted to be alone. Why? Was this a new sign I needed to pay attention to? How was I going to enjoy Florida when I was probably going to start missing some of these girls? Or was I going to miss any of them at all? Did they really mean anything to me? Did I actually mean anything to them? Or was it just the uncomplicated sex I provided that made me special? I felt an emptiness develop deep inside.

* * *

The emotional night was coming to what I thought was a close. From a corner of the rink a young girl, probably about thirteen or fourteen, with long black hair skated over to me.

"Hi, I'm Juanita," she said. "I've had a massive crush on you for the last three years. You've said hi to me before, but that was about it. I need to know … is it cuz I'm Mexican?"

I never saw a person as a certain color or persuasion. I always thought I was more interested in what they had to offer on the inside. This question, and the frankness of it, took me by surprise.

"No, that's not it at all."

"Then prove it, take *me* to the parking lot tonight."

It was a first for things: the first time a girl so young played the guilt card; and the first time it worked.

* * *

I waved good-bye to everyone and then Juanita and I left the rink. She was extremely excited and wouldn't let go of my arm. We sat in my car in silence as I said good-bye to The Roller Wheel. Memories flooded my mind and I started crying—not a slow, controlled cry—but a big ol', nothing held back bawl.

Juanita looked at me with an understanding far greater than her years should have allowed. "I'd heard that you were sensitive and emotional." She stopped to consider her next words carefully. "I really hope I can meet someone like you when I get older, and marry him."

With all I had done and who I had become I thought, If you only knew.

"Are you sure you really wanna go to the parking lot?"

"I wouldn't miss this for anything in the world," she said with a sparkle in her eyes.

So I drove over there for the last time, unlocked the gate with my key, and parked along the grassy space between the concrete lot and the river. Once again past memories of the girls I had brought here came rushing back to me. The finality set in and I started to cry again.

Juanita slid over next to me, then slowly kissed my ear and quietly whispered, "Tonight it's just you and me. Can you help me feel the way you've made the others feel?"

That question had often come up in the past, and I had a pat answer, "Yes pretty lady, I can help you feel good." I wasn't so sure this time the answer was appropriate, but there, I'd said it.

I kissed her back, but wasn't fully into it. I think she felt the same thing because she suddenly became very shy. "Maybe I made a mistake. I'm not sure I wanna do this."

"I think you just made the right decision," I said. "Sex is something everyone should experience, but only with the right person and only when they're ready for it. I have a feelin' that you're still too young right now."

She smiled at me and said, "Thanks for understanding. Now I *know* someday I wanna marry someone like you. You've just made me feel so special, and without even havin' sex. Imagine that."

When I dropped her off at the rink, Juanita asked me one last question, "Can I still have a silk rose like the ones you gave to everyone else?"

I opened my glove compartment and handed her the first red rose I had ever given out to a girl from the skating rink. I hoped she would be extremely happy when she walked back in with a one-of-a-kind flower, for a one-of-a-kind girl.

It was hard to believe this truly was the end of an era for me.

* * *

On the way home, I talked out loud to Nana as I had become accustomed to doing. I asked her for some help, for understanding, and I asked her for forgiveness. Nana believed God used rain as a way of rinsing away your sins. Back when I was a boy we used to dance together in it every time a storm came around. I pulled over to the side of the empty road, got out, and looked upward for guidance. I felt a warm mist hit my face and soon it began to rain harder. I started dancing and more than ever, I hoped that Nana was right.

* * *

The memories of the night before still lingered the next morning when I woke up. I began to doubt my choice to move, but knew I didn't dare change my mind. The thoughts of all the girls and all the times that I spent with them kept running through my head. At the same time, I knew I wanted one person to call my own, but wasn't even sure if I could sustain a monogamous relationship.

I remembered what Colette had said to me after a party we attended back in high school, "You'll never have just one girl in your life cuz you'll always be lookin' for the next best thing."

So far she was right. How did I ever veer so far off course?

I felt as though many of the things I truly wanted out of life—happiness, understanding, and being accepted by others—hadn't happened to me yet. And that I couldn't depend on anyone except myself.

The one thing I could depend on was all the time I spent alone. During these times I would think about the *real me*—who I was, what I had become, and what I wanted to be. This was the time I spent in deep thought listening to the soothing words and music of others. I didn't want anyone else around in order to lose myself in certain lyrics trying to understand what they really meant—all songs have hidden meanings, just like roses. Right then, Rod Stewart was singing *Drift Away.*

I would drift away to Florida, a faraway place where I didn't know any of the girls, except Loretta. I wondered if she was the "one and only" I was looking for. But for some reason, my gut was telling me it could be Juanita—who'd said she hoped to find a guy just like me someday and marry him. Normally my gut never let me down, but how would I be able to follow through on this in Florida? Eerily, I had a feeling we would meet again, later in life.

That thought quickly passed out of my head as my heart began racing faster. I was always open to experiences that could help me learn something new. I was hoping this move to Florida would help me find the correct path in life.

I also hoped and prayed Nana and God would be by my side to strategically place some signs along the way for me to follow. In all instances, the die was cast. I was going to Florida, come good or come bad.

CHAPTER 5
HELLO FLORIDA

I celebrated my eighteenth birthday with my immediate family and some other relatives. One of these was my great-grandfather. I spent many of my early years with him and Nana up in Wisconsin at their summer cottage. He gave me a special going away present ... and a story that went with it.

Handing me an old Saint Christopher medal, he said, "This medal was found by Nana in 1911, the first summer we owned the cottage. She was on her knees, tending to the small flower patch which she had started, and found it as she was digging a hole to plant the first rose bush. It was dirty, but she knew right away it was Saint Christopher, and he being the patron saint to gardeners, she took it as sign from God that all would be well there. She polished it up and kept it around her neck the rest of her life. When she got sick, she took it off and handed it to me. She then told me that she believed somewhere in the future someone else in our family would need this medal more than she did. With you leaving soon, and Saint Christopher also being the patron saint of travelers, I realize you're the one she was talking about."

Thanks to my religious upbringing, I knew a Saint Christopher medal helped you remember to turn to God when you needed Divine help. And as I put it in my pocket, I also remembered my Nana, and took this as a sign that both she and God would be with me.

* * *

I was saying good-bye as everyone was leaving when the emotions I tried to keep in check all day finally came flooding out. Two girls back in junior high taught me how to explore these emotions and explained it was just fine for a boy to cry. I had cried before, but this time it seemed to mean much more. I guess leaving my family wasn't as easy as I thought it would be.

* * *

I climbed into my car the next morning, Florida bound, and the first hundred miles were the worst. While I listened to my favorite cassettes, my mind would wander back to previous experiences and people. The tears got so bad at times I had to pull over. Every time I thought I was back in control of myself a different song would start playing, which made me remember someone new, and I'd start all over.

I occasionally reached into my pocket to feel for my medal. I had bought a new air freshener that smelled like mint for my rearview mirror before the trip, hoping it would relax me on the long ride. But nothing seemed to help. I finally turned off the music all together, was able to gain control, and drove straight through to Florida.

* * *

I pulled into my father's driveway late in the afternoon and the empty feeling inside welled up again. I remembered that I knew practically no one, nobody knew me, and I knew nothing about Florida. I felt scared when I realized I was really alone for the first time in my life. Even my father was new to me.

He left when I turned eight and I had lost all contact with him until the day Tim and I showed up on his doorstep a few months ago. I still had the tiger pendant he gave me one Christmas. I felt it meant something special to the both of us.

I composed myself, put on a fake smile, walked up to the front door, and rang the bell.

Dad greeted me with a big hug. "Welcome to your new home. I hope you like it here. I'm sorry, but I don't remember all that much about you, so let's take this time to reconnect."

"That sounds good to me," I said. "The only connection I've had with you all these years is this tiger pendant you gave me. I wear it every day."

I showed him the gold chain and pendant which hung around my neck.

"I gave that to you?" he said, scratching his head. "I sure don't remember that."

So much for it having special meaning to both of us.

I made a mental note to take the pendant off my chain and replace it with the Saint Christopher medal.

* * *

My dad gave me a refresher tour of my new home. It was magnificent. The house was located about three miles from the main Fort Lauderdale strip, sat high on a hill off the beaten path with only a few other houses on the block. It had five bedrooms, four bathrooms, a huge kitchen, a nice-sized living room, a laundry room, and a unique space he called "the Florida room." This was actually an outside area in the middle of the house which separated one half from the other and led to the pool and the Jacuzzi in the backyard.

This mini-mansion was custom built by the previous owner and had all the latest amenities. The coolest thing about the whole place was that it was built with two master bedroom suites, one on each side of the house. The whole property was enclosed with a golden rod-iron fence and gate.

I thought I had died and gone to heaven.

I was given the bedroom suite with French doors which opened up to the pool. Dad's room was located on the other side of the Florida room with the exact kind of doors which led to the Jacuzzi. My new room was furnished with a king size bed, two dressers, a few nature pictures, and a full-length mirror. There were also a large screen television and a full stereo along one wall, with speakers in each corner. Above the bed was a fan, and recessed lighting built directly into the ceiling.

I thought about my mom and her saying that Dad never sent enough money home. I wondered how he could afford a place like this, but figured he would explain it all to me when he was ready to.

I also knew I was in Florida to try and change my habits, but I wondered about the reactions the women I brought home would have.

When we walked through the rest of the house, I noticed something rather strange—each room had a vase full of flowers. Most were lilies or some exotic Florida flower, but my room had roses; pink, yellow, and white ones. I was used to seeing roses at my grandmother's house as symbols of how we felt about each other, but didn't understand why my dad had them in his house.

"What's with the flowers?" I asked. "Especially the roses?"

"I *do* remember your grandmother loved the hidden meanings of roses." He coyly added, "This whole house has a hidden meaning."

"I wanted you to feel comfortable, so I put some in your room." He went on, "The pink ones mean thanks for sharing time with us, the yellow tells you that friendship is what we're all about, and the white are to remind you to never forget where you came from."

I didn't understand the comment about the house, but the roses did mean something special to me. And strangely I felt a little more comfortable.

I also wondered why Dad was going out of his way to make me feel so welcome. Here I was intruding on his lifestyle and he didn't seem to mind. What was going through his mind? Was there some weird plan he had? Or did he really feel bad about leaving us and wanted this to be his way of making it up to me? But those questions would have to wait.

* * *

I had just settled in when two of my dad's friends came by. One was Larry, who I had met on my last visit. With him was another guy—shorter, much more feminine demeanor, and balder than an eagle.

My dad asked us all to sit down at the kitchen table, then looked directly at me. "There's something we need to talk about right away. I probably should have told you this the last time you were here, but I didn't know how to. You know Lawrence, and this is Dewey. I know Lawrence told you we're all gay. What he didn't tell you is ... Dewey and I are life partners. We've been together for about five years. This is my house, but Dewey lives here with me and we share a room. Understand?"

Now I know what he meant when he said the house had a hidden meaning.

"Yeah," I smiled. "Didn't Larry tell you we already discussed this? I have some very close lesbian friends back home. The way I see it, we're all the same inside, they just happen to like women rather than men. So you guys like guys, no problem for me."

"That makes me feel much better," Dad said.

I sensed Dewey relax, too. "Want somethin' to drink?"

I nodded. "Do you have lemonade? It makes me think of special days gone by."

"That's your Nana's influence," my dad said. "I know I don't always remember everything, but I know she was a wonderful lady, and someone you really looked up to. Unfortunately, we don't have any lemonade or any *mint sprigs.*"

I was impressed by this recollection.

Dad asked if I wanted a beer like at the restaurant on my last visit.

"Do you guys have any white wine instead?"

"Ah, you'll fit in here just fine." Dewey smiled at me. "That's all I drink, too."

"I want you to treat Dewey the same way you'd treat me. We do have our own special lifestyle, but I promise that it will never interfere with yours," Dad said. "That's the reason you have the master suite leading to the pool. It allows you your own space. We don't want to be in each other's way, you know?"

"I don't care what ya do. I'm sure there's enough room for all of us to be very comfortable together," I said. "As long we respect each other as adults, I see no problem."

"That's very mature of you." My dad proudly looked at me.

"I think to make this arrangement work out we should have more of a friendship instead of the typical father-son relationship," he said. "I don't know how to be a father anyway, so I'll never try to tell you how to live your life. I'll be there if you ever need me, but I won't get in your way."

"Sounds good to me," I said.

"This house has only one main rule—you must learn to enjoy life," he stressed. "Once again, I promise that our gay lifestyle won't be pushed onto you in any way. If you'd like to experience anything we do, or go anywhere we go, you're more than welcome, but there won't be any pressure."

I think I just understood what Dad wanted; to be part of my life, to see what I was all about, and possibly to help me understand his lifestyle a little better.

Larry added, "I want you to think of me as a 'father figure' type of friend, too."

I was taking a small sip of wine when I noticed something uniquely strange. Now, I was used to seeing the sex gleam radiate from the eyes of the girls I met, but I swear I saw this same reaction in the eyes of Larry as he smiled at me.

* * *

The next few days I played tourist. Dad, Dewey, and Larry showed me the hot spots—both straight and gay. I also noticed about a block away from the house there was a strip mall with a convenience store, a dry cleaner, and a small florist shop. I made a point to remember the flower shop, promising myself to keep fresh, colorful roses in my room at all times.

One day my dad took us to a bar called Behind the Scenes. It was a large building just off the main strip hidden away among warehouses and factories. When we walked in, I could see it was two stories high. The first floor was lined wall to wall with bars—on all four sides. In between them stood a dance floor made of lightly-colored wood with a glittery shine to it. Above it hung disco balls and lighting.

In a soothing way, this place reminded me of the skating rink back home.

Standing at the front looking in, I could easily see a stage situated on an angle near the back corner. Next to this stage was a big wooden door, it looked like a sliding barn door. When it slid open, and disappeared behind the stage, it revealed an outdoor swimming pool, along with some tables and chairs.

Looking up past the disco balls, I could see the second floor was designed to watch the dancers below. There were tables along the railings and even more bars along the walls. There was another door nestled near the far back corner, this one dark black in color—which led to who knows where?

Being that it was the middle of the day, there wasn't much action. As the four of us shared a bottle of white wine, my dad asked, "So, whaddaya think of the place?"

"It seems nice." I looked around again and said, "I wonder what it's like at night."

"You should see it!" Dewey smiled. "I'm glad you like it, cuz it's ours."

"What do you mean yours?"

"Your dad and I own it. And it's *the* hottest locals bar in South Florida," Dewey proudly announced. "Both straights and gays like comin' here to hear the newest disco singers perform. You know you're always welcome, and you and your friends—when you find some—can come here for free, as long as you don't abuse the privilege. If you want, we can also give you a job."

"Great! I promise not to overuse the welcome," I said. "Thanks for the job offer too, but right now I feel the need to try to find somethin' on my own."

* * *

The next day, Larry took me to see some strictly straight clubs. He was a hair stylist and had many straight clients, so he knew most of the happening places.

"I remember that you have a sexual energy aura around you," Larry said. "I can help you get started here in Florida if you want me to. Some of my clients are recently divorced ladies who are always lookin' for company, if you know what I'm talkin' about."

My mind flashed back to Nancy and my gigolo days.

I smiled. "I know whatcha mean, all too well. But before I take you up on your offer, I'd like to explore on my own and see what I can do. I want to get a job fast, and then start creatin' my own circle of friends."

With the sex gleam radiating brilliantly from his eyes Larry said, "I'm always willing to help … in any way that I can."

Once again I let that comment *and* that look pass right by me.

* * *

My first few fun days in Florida were over and I was relieved everything seemed to be going well. I was intrigued by the fact my dad and his friends were gay. I was going to be able to see how they lived and how they related to each other. I did, however, have some questions which popped into my mind. Did these older guys have the same fears Joyce did back home? Were they just as scared straight people would find out the truth about them? Or were gay people more openly accepted in Florida?

Then I remembered I needed to kick start my own life and even more questions came to mind. What kind of job and friends would I find here? Would I meet anyone at all I could relate to? Would I ever be as popular in Florida as I had become back at home? And just what was my place in Florida going to be?

And the last two questions rolling around my head were the most important ones to me at the time. What was the reason that Larry always had the sex gleam beaming from his eyes whenever he looked at me? And what exactly did it mean?

CHAPTER 6
LORETTA, REDUX

Instead of trying to answer any of these questions, I decided to call Loretta. "Hey, it's me, Phil, and I'm back here in Florida. How'd ya like to help me explore the town tonight?"

"I can't believe you actually moved here," Loretta said excitedly. "Of course I would. Do you remember how to get to my house, or do you need some help?"

"Give me the directions, please!"

I grabbed a beautiful pink rose from the full vase in my room and then followed Loretta's directions to a tee. I confidently walked up to her door and rang the bell.

Her mom answered and asked with surprise in her voice, "I see you've made it back. So, now that you're here, what's your next move? Like, where are you staying?"

"I'm staying with my dad in Fort Lauderdale. My initial plans are to have some fun today and tomorrow, and then look for a job," I said. "I need to settle in and get on with my life."

"It sounds like you have put some serious thought into this and that you may be here to stay." She smiled, clearly happy for me. "Well, welcome to Florida. I hope you and Loretta have some fun together."

The three of us spent a few minutes talking as a group and then I decided it was time to go exploring. Loretta and I were getting ready to leave when her mom said, "Bye guys, enjoy your evening, but don't get into any trouble."

"Don't worry," I said, "I'll take good care of her."

Loretta grabbed my hand and whispered, "You bet you will," and led me toward the front door. I didn't know what she meant, but just before she shut the door behind us, she yelled to her mom, "Don't wait up for me, I'll probably be late."

* * *

We hopped into my car and I gave Loretta the pink rose, explaining it was to thank her for helping me choose Florida. Then we went for a drive along the ocean. Florida was so exciting to me—the colors, the sounds, and especially the smells. These were new aromas that were scintillating to me. The saltwater had a unique odor all to itself. The smell of hot sand and the aroma of suntan oil lingered in the humid air.

I couldn't believe you could drive right along the beach for so far. I looked out at the cascading white water coming in and going out and it sort of reminded me of my life in a way. The waves just came and went as the wind beckoned it to do; as if they had no thought in the matter. I felt a parallel with that—back home I used to listen to what the girls told me and obediently followed their lead, also without thinking at all.

* * *

We continued on our way and Loretta asked, "What's in store next?"

"I'd like to get a job, find some good friends, and I need to find *myself* in order to proceed with my master plan."

She winked, "Am I part of this plan?"

"*You* are my plan right now," I said. "I don't know anyone else and besides, I don't need anyone else. Tonight you, and a bottle of wine, are all I need to enjoy my first 'date' here in Florida. Would you like to see where I live?"

Loretta smiled. "Of course I would."

I was feeling good about myself for the first time in a long time. I was surprised that absolutely no thoughts of sex were in my mind … and hoped this would continue.

* * *

When we pulled in front of my new house, Loretta couldn't believe her eyes. The sheer size and the location of the house surprised her. And being so high above the strip allowed us a panoramic view of all the lights down below. Seeing the house was completely surrounded by the gated fence, she wondered out loud how my dad could afford such a place. I ignored her, not wanting to explain my dad's lifestyle just then.

We entered the house and she was again taken aback by what she saw. We stopped in the kitchen where I opened a bottle of white wine and grabbed two glasses. I proceeded to show Loretta the rest of the house and when we got to my room she became very excited about the pool she could see through my French doors.

"Wanna go for a swim?" I nonchalantly asked.

"I'd love to," she replied. "But I don't have a suit with me."

"But you do have underwear on, right?"

Loretta got my drift and removed everything except for her bra and panties in record time and threw it all in a bunch on my floor. She started to walk toward the French doors which led to the pool when she suddenly stopped and asked, "Can I use your phone?"

I was already down to my briefs but walked with her to the kitchen where she quickly dialed a number and said, "Hey mom, it's me … I'm spendin' the night at Phil's … No, nothing like that, we've just had a little too much to drink and his dad offered me one of the guest bedrooms for the night … of course, he's here. Great, I'll see you tomorrow."

Loretta hung up the phone, grabbed me by my right arm, and began to lead me to the pool. It was my turn to be taken aback. Here I was, a guy who always tried to tell the truth and wanted the same from my friends, but she just lied so easily to her mom. I wondered what else she could lie about. I didn't have much time to think it all through because, as we waded into the shallow end of the pool hand in hand, Loretta made some remark about how sex in a pool is so cool.

I didn't have any indecent objectives, but realized Loretta probably did. All I really wanted was to swim, share a little wine, and get to know more about each other better. But it seemed as though she had something completely different in mind. She confidently turned toward me, let loose a great big smile, grabbed at my briefs and quickly yanked them off. "There, isn't that much more comfortable?"

Without letting me answer, the next thing I knew she had her bra and panties off and was flinging them over to a poolside chair. "This is why I love Florida so much … the freedom to do what I want to."

Loretta took control immediately, and I let her. We splashed at each other, then sat next to each other on the inside ledge of the deep end of the pool sipping cold wine, and finally she kissed me. It was a kiss like I'd never experienced before. It was wet, it was long, and it meant much more than she just wanted to be friends.

And I wondered if this was the start of something good … or something bad.

* * *

We were basking in the moonlight when, at about 3:00 in the morning, we heard voices. Coming through the open Florida room were my dad and Dewey. When they got closer to the pool, Loretta suddenly became nervous about being naked and hid behind me.

They reached the side of the pool and my dad said, "Hi. Are you guys enjoying this great Florida night?"

"You bet! Hope ya don't mind us bein' out here at this time of the night," I said. "By the way, you remember Loretta from my last visit, don't you?"

"I do indeed," he smiled. "Come on out and say hi. Neither of us care that you're naked."

"We'd be much more interested in seeing what *he* has to offer anyway," Dewey said jokingly, elbowing my dad.

Loretta slid tighter next to me and had a perplexed look on her face, which my dad saw.

"This is Dewey … we're gay," he explained. "Being a friend of my son makes you welcome here anytime. But while you're here you need to play by our rules. First, you can be whatever you wanna be—gay, straight, drunk, or sober—it doesn't matter to us. Second, you must learn to enjoy the experiences that life brings your way. And third, you must learn to share the pool."

With that, he and Dewey undressed down to their boxers and jumped into the water across from us.

Loretta looked at me, and then said loud enough for them to hear, "Now I see where you get your personality from. I guess the apple doesn't fall all that far from the tree after all."

For the next half hour we all sat in the pool and shared some small talk. We drank some wine and a funny thought went through my mind: *If this is my new family, what a wacky one it was.*

Still, this was the coolest thing I had experienced yet. Here I was skinny-dipping and drinking in my own backyard with a girl and my dad didn't even get mad. Instead he joined us. He treated me as an adult, Loretta liked me as a friend, and I really thought that neither had tried to control my actions … well, sort of.

What a difference a state makes!

* * *

Loretta and I left the pool shortly after this to take separate showers. When she saw the huge vase of flowers on my desk she asked, "What's with all the roses?"

I explained how I meditate on them every morning to remind me of things. Each of them told their own story, but when I put them all together they mean something totally different to me.

"So, what are the meanings?"

"The yellow roses mean I need to make good friends who I can trust. The pink ones remind me to give thanks every day for what I have. The white ones are for remembering where and why I started on my journey, and finally, the single red one stands for always loving myself and God. All together, they mean 'don't forget to live a balanced life' and that's what I try to do."

Loretta smiled and gave me a little kiss. I think she understood.

* * *

Shortly after she climbed out of the shower, Loretta took control again. "I wanna feel you next to me," she said, reaching for my hand. "I can't wait to make love to you."

I wasn't sure I wanted to. I had moved to Florida hoping sex wouldn't matter so much to me anymore, and it had been a long time since I had *made love* to anyone. Sex was always there for the taking, but making love was special to me.

"Are you sure?"

"I've never been surer of anything in my life."

So, I gave in to the moment. I put one of my Air Supply cassettes in the player and their song, *Closer You and I*, came on. While Graham and Russell sang this appropriate song, Loretta and I shared a small memory that night. I hadn't planned it this way, but afterwards felt the room was perfect, the music was perfect, and that the company was perfect. I also found myself thinking, If this is going to be my new life, I made the right choice in moving to Florida.

* * *

We were awakened early the next morning by the sun's warm rays radiating through the French doors of my bedroom. Loretta said, "Last night was great. I had a dream a few weeks back that this would happen. I can't believe it actually has. I'm so glad you moved here."

I didn't say anything out loud, but I was happy, too.

We showered, got dressed, and I proceeded to drive her home. On the way to Loretta's house we passed a large Burger Shack. This was the fast food chain I'd worked at back home. I didn't even know they had them in Florida, but I thought I'd stop by later on to see if they were hiring.

Then I heard something on the radio which made me do a double take. Loretta had put on her favorite Florida radio station, since I didn't know any of them yet. The DJ announced they were giving away free tickets to an upcoming Air Supply concert at various locations throughout the day. One was right down the road from The Burger Shack.

If both of these weren't signs directed right at me, I had no idea what would be. "Hey, if I can get tickets, do ya wanna go with me?"

Loretta laughed. "Of course, I would. After last night, Air Supply is one of my favorite groups."

* * *

I dropped Loretta off and then returned to The Burger Shack to talk with the manager. I decided to use a lesson I'd learned back home; *tell the blunt truth*, to see if I could get hired. When John came to the counter, I told him, "I know I'm not dressed for an interview, but I'm looking for a stable job. I just moved here from Missouri where I worked for your company. I was a very good assistant manager and really could use a job here. Whaddaya think?"

He looked me over very serious like. "I like the fact that you started looking for a job so quickly, most kids come here to party, not to work. I'm impressed that you told me all that up front, it shows me that you're probably trustworthy. So, where are you stayin'? And how long do you plan on being in Florida?"

"I'm living with my father," I replied. "And I hope to stay here forever."

When he heard me mention my father, his eyebrows went up. "Sounds real good to me that you have family here, it'll help keep you grounded. I'll need to call your old job though to get a reference. If that comes back acceptable I'd love to have you on my team. See, I'm looking for a new assistant … had to fire the last one for gettin' too involved with a coworker. I'll call you later to let you know."

I gave him the phone number to my old work and to my new home before I left. I really wanted to work for him; he seemed like a man I could actually trust.

* * *

I left The Burger Shack with a good feeling and I hoped it carried on as I looked for the Air Supply ticket giveaway. I finally saw the radio station van, along with a short queue of people. After parking the car, I took my place in line and waited for my turn. I wanted these tickets badly, so I decided to use a lesson in observation I had learned to insure that I got them.

I listened intently to what the girl and guy giving away the tickets were saying to the people ahead of me when they walked up. They were asking everyone questions such as, "Why do you deserve these tickets?" I also noticed the girl had a bandana tied to her upper leg with the call letters of a familiar radio station from back home.

I figured this was my in.

When my turn finally came, the tall lanky girl sized me up and said, "So why should I give you tickets to the Air Supply concert?"

"Well, I'm new to Florida—this is my first week here. Right now I have no job, no friends, and I'm feelin' a little homesick," I said. "I actually got to meet these guys after one of their concerts in St. Louis, and they've become one of my favorite groups. I think it would help me feel at home if I could see 'em again. I'm sure you understand what I mean, seein' that you're from Missouri, too."

She looked surprised. "How'd you know where I'm from?"

I pointed to her leg. "I noticed that your bandana has the WLUP call letters. I listened to that station back home. So either you were from Missouri or this radio station is affiliated with it. Whatever the reason, I'm sure you know what I mean about sometimes feelin' homesick."

"That's very observant. I'm from St. Louis, and I do know that feeling all too well." She handed me what I wanted. "Here's a pair of tickets to welcome you to Florida. By the way, who're you gonna take with you?"

"I don't know …" I pretended to ponder the question. "I may have an idea though, if your station will go along with it," I said. "Why don't you run a contest with me as the prize? You could offer the tickets, a free limousine ride, dinner, and a date with the newest guy in Florida to the girl who promises to show me the best time?"

Her partner, Bob, eagerly said, "What a great idea. We can talk to you on the radio, ask a few questions, and then let you pick a date from those who call in. Are you sure you're really game?"

"I think so," I said. "But listen, I haven't had lunch yet and I'm starving. Let me grab a quick bite and I'll be right back."

"That's fine," Bob said. "I have to get clearance from the station manager anyway. You go eat and I'll call him on the CB. We'll talk more when you get back."

I left and headed over to the hot dog stand I'd seen around the corner. I placed my order and as I waited for it to come up, I spotted what I was looking for, a pay phone. I called Loretta and explained the whole thing to her. She promised to call in and "make it worth my while."

After returning Bob explained the stations terms, I signed a waiver, and the contest was on.

Bob was excited and announced on the air: "We have a brand new contest going on out here. We need a lady who wants to see Air Supply in concert later this month, *and* also have dinner with the newest, coolest resident of Fort Lauderdale." He then briefly described me. "Let's get to know him. Phil why don't you tell our listeners what kind of lady you like."

It was a foregone conclusion I would pick Loretta, but I still couldn't help wanting to hear some of the other offers.

"Well, age means nothing to me … it's just passage of time," I stated. "What really matters is whether you feel a connection with someone. I don't care what a person looks like. What's more important to me is what they have going on inside. We're all on a life journey. I want mine to be fun and exciting, so I'm open to any and all new experiences."

This answer apparently went over very well with the ladies who were listening. As the calls rapidly came in, Bob told me the station has high school girls, college girls, and even moms and grandmothers call in whenever they have this type of dating contest.

Of course, they also had Loretta. Bob and I narrowed it down to the top five lucky contestants, with her being one of them. I was able to ask their name and only one quick question. My question to all of them was simply, "What, pretty lady, could you do to help me feel good?"

I heard all of their sexy responses and indeed was feeling pretty good about myself, *one could even say conceited.* If Loretta hadn't been one of the five, I could have easily picked any one of them and had a fabulous and exciting time. Wisely though, I picked her.

* * *

After the arrangements were made and telephone numbers were exchanged, I got a little surprised when the girl from the radio station said to me as I was getting in my car to leave, "That contest idea went over very well. Your answers made quite an impact on our female listeners. They all said they liked your voice—some said that it sounded ultra sexy. We've had over a hundred phone calls askin' all about you. It looks like Florida will be very good for you."

She smiled and I saw the sex gleam radiating from her eyes.

Oh no, I thought, Here we go again.

"I have somethin' special for you." She handed me a folded slip of paper. "Don't read it till you get back home though."

Of course, I couldn't wait that long, and pulled over to the side of the road as soon as the radio station van disappeared from my rearview mirror. I opened the note and read the feminine handwriting:

I like your philosophy on life—you seem honest, sincere, and I must say, totally different. I could get to like you. I can make you "feel good" by sharing a night with me. My name is Bunny and my number is (305) 555—1129. Call me for an experience you'll never forget.

There it was, the very thing I was trying to escape—another sexual encounter with someone I didn't really know.

I wasn't sure if I'd ever call, seeing how Loretta and I were just getting started to know each other. Still, it was nice to know that I still had the touch.

I drove home feeling rather satisfied with what had happened to me in Florida so far. I had met a few new people, possibly gotten a job, was given a free night on the town with my girl, and reinforced the notion the *real me* was someone not only others, but also I, could get to like. I just had to tone down the sexual aura thing Larry had referred to.

* * *

I walked into the house and my dad stopped me. "There's a message for you on the refrigerator."

I dialed the phone number on the piece of paper and spoke to John, the manager from The Burger Shack.

"I called that number you gave me and talked to the manager, Joyce. She had nothing but good things to say about you. She said you were great at dealing with the staff. That's good enough for me. When can you start?"

It was the best day so far in my short Florida stay. I opened a bottle of wine, put on a swimsuit, and headed for the pool thinking, This is the simple life I was looking for.

CHAPTER 7
STACY L.

I started work two days later and the first person I met was Stacey. I found that kind of ironic since I knew a Stacey at my old Burger Shack, too. That Stacey was a strange sort with magenta colored hair who turned me on to *The Rocky Horror Picture Show* and then actually got me to dress up like a transvestite (Dr. Frank-N-Furter) before bestowing me the honor of being her *first*.

This new Stacey, Stacey L., was the manager who was assigned to help me review the ropes. She was a rather large girl, two years older than me, and was very open about things. She said exactly what she wanted to, and never outwardly showed that she cared what others had to say about her. She had long stringy black hair and a minor acne problem. But thanks to another lesson I'd learned; *see the small things people want you to notice,* I saw she had the most beautiful fingernails. They were perfectly manicured and covered in a bright red polish.

"I really like your nails; you take excellent care of them," I stated. "That must be a lot of work."

Stacey blushed. "Thanks. It's so nice of you to notice. Most guys don't look past my acne."

"Then they don't know what they're missing, do they?" I said.

Almost immediately I felt a warmth in my heart. And thought to myself, Maybe I am heading down the right path, after all.

* * *

Stacey and I soon became good friends—actual friends—not just acquaintances like I had so many of back home. I remembered friendship leads to other opportunities, and it is so true.

The two of us would go out drinking most nights after work, just to talk. Loretta wasn't always around—she was real tight with her girlfriends and loved spending time with them—plus, I felt it was fine to have more than one friend who was a girl. I was very relaxed around Stacey and told her *everything* about me: Mary, my first actual girlfriend; Star and her friends, Cece and Deidre; Disco Phil—the skating rink, the parking lot, the sex at the drive-ins—the whole kit and caboodle. And finally I told her about the four months I worked for Nancy, the madam, and *took care of* her lonely clients.

Stacey just took it all in without judging or criticizing me. Sometimes there was a look of disbelief in her eyes, but through it all I saw the trust sparkle coming through loud and clear.

I also began to feel something special developing for Stacey. She was nothing out of the ordinary, but we had shared something—a very open, no holds barred honesty—much more than I felt comfortable sharing with Loretta. While I felt Loretta and I had a great sexual connection, I didn't feel as though we had much more going on. Stacey had cemented a special spot in my life by being there and accepting my past for what it was. I really liked this girl and wondered where it may lead.

One night at the bar Stacey said, "Phil, you see things in such a different way. I really respect you for your sensitivity and honesty. Do you have a girlfriend in town yet?"

"Actually, I can't say for sure," I replied. "I met this girl, Loretta, and we've been hanging out. Not sure if she's a girlfriend, but I do have some feelings for her, and I need to explore what they mean."

"Again, there's that honesty," Stacey stated. "Let me share with you my thoughts on life, now that I know yours."

She gently took both my hands into hers and stroked my fingertips. "I believe since we are now friends we can share many special things together. One of these can be sex."

Oh, no. I thought, not again.

"There won't be any emotional involvement, just the physical act of sex whenever we want it. I sense by your red and yellow aura, your attitude on life, and your past, that you'll be interested. Am I right?"

Here I was again in the same predicament I always found myself. I wasn't looking for basic sex here in Florida, but so far that was all I had encountered. Just like back home it was the girl who actually brought up the subject of sex and wanted to be in complete control of the situation.

I wasn't sure what to do. I already had Loretta in my life and we'd had sex, on her terms. Bunny wanted the same thing from me. And now there was Stacey. I found myself thinking, Am I ever going to break this pattern? Or should I just resign myself to it for the rest of my life?

* * *

Stacey and I decided to go dancing while she awaited my decision and we ended up at Behind the Scenes. When I introduced Stacey as *my special friend* my dad slyly smiled at me knowing what I really meant. To bad I didn't.

We danced for about an hour and then retreated back to my house. After a few more drinks and some more prodding by Stacey, I finally gave in to her wishes.

We were cuddling afterward when Stacey proclaimed, "I've been looking for someone honest, fun, and understanding. I know we agreed to only being *friends with benefits,* but I think I may want more."

My head started spinning. What was I thinking? That's the problem, I wasn't thinking. What's that insanity definition again? Doing the same thing and expecting a different result.

I probably shouldn't have had sex with her. I should have taken a stronger stance against it. I was here to settle down, to change from what I was doing back home. I liked Stacey, but I really needed more of a close friend than a lover at the moment.

I kissed Stacey lightly on the lips and said, "Please don't take this the wrong way, but can't we just be friends for right now?'

"I knew I was pushing the envelope." She smiled at me. "Of course we can. This just goes to show me that you really are different than the other guys here in Florida."

* * *

I had been in Florida for only about a month and was suddenly starting to second guess myself. I had moved here to slow down, to find one special person, and to get to a point where I liked myself again. What I found instead was that sex was all around me and, once again, I didn't know what to do about it … when to say yes and when to say no.

I was confused as to whether or not this *one girl* thing was what I really wanted after all. I didn't tell anyone about how I felt, but I think Stacey knew it. Every time she asked me about Loretta, who was only in my life when *she* wanted to be, I quickly changed the subject. I began to spend more time alone listening to music just like I did back home when I needed to think. I had to choose which road I was going to take in life, and fast. At least here in Florida I had a pool, enough wine, and a Saint Christopher medal to help me think it all through.

* * *

I started a new routine. Every Monday I would go buy fresh roses from the local florist. I noticed they would start to fade, dehydrate, then shrivel up and die if I didn't pay close attention to them. I found myself thinking, That could happen to people, too, if they let it.

I became a regular at the shop and got to know the owner pretty well. She was an elderly Asian lady who spoke only in broken English. Since there was no way I could pronounce her name, I called her Rose.

One day she said to me, "Ah, some lady bery, bery lucky, with resh flowers ebery week."

"No, these are for me," I explained. "I keep them around as a reminder to live life to its fullest and to make the correct choices in life."

Rose giggled through yellowed teeth and said, "Hope dey work fo you."

CHAPTER 8
THE CONCERT

The day of the Air Supply concert finally arrived and I wasn't sure how I was feeling about the whole thing. I was excited to see Air Supply again, and I thought I still liked Loretta, but I wasn't overly convinced she was what I needed in my life right now. It seemed the more time we spent together the more pronounced our differences became.

Late in the afternoon, the radio station called to say the concert had been cancelled for some unexplained reason. But they were still giving me a free dinner and the limo for the night. A driver would take Loretta and me to some of the hottest night spots on the strip.

I called Loretta. "The concert's been cancelled, but the rest of the night is still on. The station will be calling you. They'll have the limo pick you up at 7:00 to take you to the restaurant where we will meet 'for the first time.' Then it's on to some of the nicest hot spots down on the strip afterward. Make sure to dress for a night of dancing."

Loretta replied very excitedly, "I can't wait. I have a feeling this'll be a night I'll never forget."

* * *

I arrived at the restaurant first, drank half of a bottle of white wine and received a bouquet of yellow roses from Bob to hand to Loretta as she walked in.

Bunny, the girl I met before, was there, too. She gave me a small hug and with a wink said, "Hey, why haven't you called me yet? Are you too busy for me already?"

"Now's not really the time to discuss this," I said calmly.

Bunny seemed unhappy to hear that.

The limo dropped Loretta off and she played it up big for the sound crew by giving me a sexy "nice to meet you" kiss, and then made some crude comments which the radio station had to bleep. I felt we had a spotlight shining on us.

The station people took a lot of pictures, got us to say what they wanted to hear and then they left. It was nice to finally be alone together without any performance pressure.

Loretta and I drank wine, ate dinner, and then exited hand in hand to the limo. The driver took us to a few clubs on the strip, but after a few minutes in each of them we didn't feel the right vibe. When we climbed back into the limo after the third stop, I politely asked, "Please take us to Behind the Scenes—it's just off the strip."

"I know where that is," the driver replied. "Unfortunately the station has no contacts there, so I can't get you in for free."

"No sweat. This is the son of the owner. We'll get in free, ourselves," Loretta said curtly. "Just drop us off and be gone, we won't need your services anymore."

I thought she was being a little harsh, but I didn't say anything.

On our short trip to the bar we finished off another bottle of wine. When we were getting out of the limo, the driver said, with his hand extended obviously for a tip, "I hope you found my hospitality satisfactory and you enjoy the rest of your night."

I reached into my pocket, but Loretta snapped, "This night was on the radio station—let them give you your a tip."

Again, I thought she was rude, but ignored her. As she started to walk ahead of me I slipped the guy a ten spot and just shook my head. I think he understood my dilemma.

There was a long line, half of which were pairs of young women, waiting to get into the club. As we approached the entrance the bouncer recognized me and waved us to the front. I noticed several girls looking at me as if I must be someone special. And I felt a tingling sensation inside of me.

There were two plain looking girls waiting to get in near the end of the line. I read what their eyes were saying, *Can you please help us?* I surmised they would probably never get in, even if they had made it to the front of the line. I asked the bouncer if they could join us and as the four of us entered the bar together, Loretta turned on me.

"Who are these girls, and why do you want 'em to come with us?"

"Look, I just helped them get in faster. Don't read into it."

I didn't understand why Loretta was always so mean to others.

* * *

We got some more wine, and then Loretta and I got busy dancing. Dad's bar was so different from the drab ones on the strip we had just left. It had a much more happening feeling to it—the people were looser, and they seemed to enjoy life more, without trying to impress anyone. We saw guys with no shirts on and women in tight mini-skirts. Some men were kissing men and some women were kissing women. The whole atmosphere was so hot and exciting to me.

While we were on the dance floor "busting a move" I saw a few of the others sniffing something out of a little black bottle. I had no idea what it was, so when I saw Larry across the room Loretta and I made our way over to him.

"Larry, what's the stuff in the bottles?" I asked. "What's it for?"

A devilish smirk crossed his face. "That, my friend, is a liquid drug called 'poppers.' It induces a short-lived, light-headed euphoric state of mind." Instead of continuing with this scientific explanation Larry shrugged and said, "Basically, you sniff it, it kills some brain cells and makes everything go black, and then you slowly come back to reality. It's good to use when dancing, and especially cool to experiment with during sex. Do you want some?"

I looked at Loretta who said, "We're here to have fun, so let's give it a try."

Larry gave us his bottle but cautioned, "Now be careful. Sometimes you forget what happens when you use this stuff."

We tried the drug as we were dancing and both of us found it enjoyable. Loretta coerced Larry to give her another bottle for later that night. She licked her lips and told him, "To use while we're having sex."

* * *

A couple hours later, we were getting tired of dancing and wanted to get over to my house. Lucky for us, Larry was ready to leave, too, so he gave us a ride home. Loretta started to kiss me passionately and I thought I heard Larry whisper under his breath, "Someday he'll kiss me like that."

I couldn't say for sure if I had heard him correctly, or if it was just the alcohol and drugs playing tricks with me.

Loretta grabbed my hand and led me to my room as soon as we entered my house. Before I could even turn on some music, she had us both undressed and was practically begging for sex. What could I do but to give her what she wanted?

While I kissed and caressed her whole body, Loretta began squirming and getting a little loud. When I went down on her she started screaming for more. I handed her a bottle of poppers hoping to quiet her down. "Sniff this stuff and see what happens."

Loretta took a hit and then got real quiet. But suddenly she screamed, "What a rush! Here try it!"

She jammed the small bottle under my nose and I took a big whiff. At the same time, Loretta grabbed my erect penis with her other hand and put it inside of her. The drug kicked in immediately and I found myself immersed in total blackness and totally out of control of my bodily functions. It slowly began to wear off and I felt my whole body shake and I saw everything in the most fantastic clear colors that I had ever seen.

What a feeling, I felt so alive, so excited.

Unfortunately, when I had fully returned from my brief euphoria, I was still inside Loretta, but I noticed I was totally limp. I always prided myself in the past on how long I could keep an erection, but with the combination of all the drinking, the drug, and the excitement, I knew I had already come. Loretta didn't seem to notice or care. She had already fallen asleep underneath me.

I, on the other hand, couldn't sleep. I was still reeling from the effects of all the alcohol and the drugs and I wondered if I had done something wrong this time. I'd never lost control like this before. My mind immediately had this thought, What is the worst thing that could happen? An unpleasant image—one of a little baby coming into my life—popped into my head, so I got up to take a shower to try and sober up. Before I entered the bathroom, I saw the bouquet of yellow roses I had given to Loretta laying on the floor and instinctively put them in the vase on my dresser.

When I returned to my bed and saw Loretta sleeping there naked, two more thoughts came to me. Did I really want this girl in my life? I felt she ultimately wanted something totally different than I did. I was here to slow down, she was here to party. And I wondered what was going to happen next?

I had no clear answers to these questions and realized that once again whatever was going to happen was going to happen. Instead of worrying about it, I climbed in next to her hoping sleep would dissolve away all of my concerns.

* * *

We awoke early the next morning as the sun came shining through my French doors.

"So how ya feelin'?" I asked Loretta as she stretched some life into her body. "Whaddaya remember about last night?"

She smiled brightly. "I know you're a great lover … and that you made me feel things I never had before. You got me much more excited than anyone else ever has. However, I seem to remember more about the foreplay than the actual sex part. I may have fallen asleep before you were finished. If I did, I'm sorry, and will make it up to you later. I hope you were able to finish without me."

Little did she know!

Loretta kissed me. "I'm so lucky that I met you. I think I may be fallin' in love already. Wouldn't it be something if we got married someday and started a family together?"

"Yeah, that sure would be somethin'," I said under my breath, not believing a word of it.

I had dealt with some demanding ladies in the past, but this time my reaction was different than I expected. I wasn't too happy about the way Loretta was just using me for her sexual pleasure whenever *she* wanted it. But my main concern was the way she treated others. It made me wonder if she could be just as mean to me sometime in the future. I was becoming convinced that I didn't want this girl in my life anymore.

And to underscore these feelings, I noticed the yellow roses, which I put into the vase on my dresser just last night, had already started to wilt.

* * *

In the morning, Loretta asked me to drop her off at one of her girlfriend's house, so her mom wouldn't know she spent the night with me.

I thought it was interesting she had her own key to let herself in. Then I noticed the black Camaro SS in the driveway, and I knew the lowlife that it belonged to. Dad had thrown him out of the club a month ago for trying to deal coke there. My mind went crazy. *Circumstantial evidence? Perhaps. Maybe Loretta's girlfriend lives with, or is dating, Camaro drivin' drug dealer guy? But at the very least, doesn't this mean that Loretta is probably into heavy drugs? Or am I jumping to conclusions and blowing things out of proportion for an excuse to get out of this relationship?*

With all these questions swirling in my head, I decided to call the only other person who I really knew in Florida for some help.

* * *

After I explained everything to her, Stacey L. said, "It sounds to me like what you're really sayin' is you don't want one person in your life right now."

Of course she wanted me to herself, so I wasn't sure I could take this advice at face value.

"I think you used that 'finding the one and only' excuse in order to give yourself the courage to move here in the first place."

Interesting. I found myself thinking, Maybe I did.

"Deep down you know exactly what you want. You want to leave your mark in Florida just like you did back in Missouri."

Ah-ha! A small light bulb went off in my head. Although the thought of the empty feeling I used to have came to mind as well.

"You want that spotlight back—you love the attention and the feeling that being something special brings to you."

Now that I couldn't argue with that.

"You wouldn't have gone to bed with me with Loretta still in the picture if you didn't like the excitement of possibly getting caught."

Again, I couldn't really argue with that either.

Stacey then said the same thing I had heard from Colette back home years earlier. "You're just going through the motions of wanting only one. You're totally afraid that if you did settle down, you'd miss the next best thing to come along. This leads you to relish the uncertainty of where your next 'best friend' will come from. You attract girls who fall for your 'charm' because they know what you can do for them. Loretta already proved that. I betcha she's already told you that she loves you. But she's too mixed up to know what true love really is. Trust me, she's just playing a game. Watch out or she might get herself pregnant in order to win."

I remembered how easily Loretta had lied to her mother and it made me wonder, *Could she be doing the same to me?*

I hung up and was even more confused, but I also felt a little bit of relief. With Stacey's help, I was finally able to see that my mission to change my ways wasn't going to happen exactly like I had planned. I agreed with her that my reason for me moving to Florida was just an excuse I made up to get me here. The challenge of meeting all new people and having many more sexual experiences was what really drove my move. Larry sensed it the first time I met him, my dad knew what I wanted, and Stacey had just confirmed it for me. Whether it was right or wrong I chose to move on in a whole different direction all together.

Later that night, as I sat at my desk looking into my mirror, I wrote this poem describing how I was feeling:

Recollections of times before
Not knowing what's behind every door
Trying hard to find out who I really am
Slipping backwards in time and not giving a damn.

* * *

I called Loretta the next day, but was surprised when she wouldn't let me say anything. I guess I shouldn't have been, she had taken control of most every other situation when it came to us.

She said, "I'm very confused. I think I may love you, but I also know I can't be in love this quickly in a relationship."

I agreed with the "but" part.

"You came here trying to find yourself and now I think I need to do the same thing. I'm gonna move in with my grandmother in Georgia for a while so that I can think some things over. If we meet again, then it was meant to be. If we don't, it wasn't. I'm moving on with my life and hope you can do the same. Please don't come looking for me," she said as she hung up the phone.

I found myself thinking, I guess no matter how many lessons I learn about them, I'll never fully understand women and what makes them tick.

A small sigh of relief came over me. Loretta had just given me my freedom, or did she?

* * *

One weekend day about four months after that one-sided conversation, Loretta strolled into The Burger Shack. Stacey was working the register and when Loretta asked for me, she told her I wasn't there.

"Where the hell is he?" Loretta demanded. "I've tried calling him more than once, but he never answers."

"I think he chose to move on like you told him to," Stacey said. "I thought you'd moved to Georgia, anyway?"

Loretta snickered. "Nah, I just told him that cuz I didn't know how I felt about him and I needed some time to decide."

"Real nice move," Stacey said sarcastically.

Loretta ignored her comment. "You know, we had sex the last night I was with him. I remember tellin' him before we did that I felt as though it would be a night I would never forget. Well, it was. He got me pregnant."

"So, you're pregnant now?" Stacey said warily, not seeing any sign around her belly that could confirm it.

When Loretta nodded her head yes, Stacey said, "You sure this isn't just a ploy to get Phil back into your life?"

"Go fuck yourself. This is none of your goddamned business."

Loretta stomped out and Stacey immediately called to tell me about Loretta's visit and then added, "I don't believe she's pregnant at all. I think she's lying just to get you back cuz now she knows what she's missing. I told you she'd try something stupid like this. I'd just forget about it."

What now? What if Loretta was pregnant? Should I step up and take responsibility? Or should I ignore what I just heard? I had started on this journey of mine wanting to be respected and have all females like me. I didn't want to be looked at in the same way as the "no good men" my mom and her friends talked about when I was young. Everything that experience had taught me said I should meet this challenge head on.

Now knowing Loretta was actually at home, and not really in Georgia, I called her that night. I started the conversation, but once again she interrupted me.

"Stacey must have told you about our 'little visit.' Well, I've changed my mind. I don't want you in my life. In fact, I never want to see you again."

I ignored her outburst and calmly asked, "Loretta, are you pregnant? Cuz if you are, I want to be there for you. Let me help."

"I can take care of myself. Leave me alone, you'll never know if I am or not." She slammed down the receiver and that was the last time I ever talked to Loretta.

* * *

P.S. Stacey was sitting at a stoplight, about five months later, when she saw Loretta walking across the street. She wasn't pregnant and didn't have a kid with her. Did that mean she never was and indeed had tried to use it as a ploy to get me back into her life? Or was she, and she took care of it? Could she have had the baby and given it up for adoption? If she had the baby how would I know it was mine anyway? She lied about practically everything else.

I wondered if I would ever find out the answers to those questions.

CHAPTER 9
LARRY HELPS?

After Loretta hung up on me, I was feeling like I wanted to get away from it all. I decided to go to my dad's bar for a drink. I walked in, got a glass of white wine, and went upstairs to watch the dancers below. I figured this would give me some time to think about and digest what had happened the last few months of my life. I hoped I would be by myself long enough to accomplish this.

But I wasn't alone for more than ten minutes when Larry came up to me. "Why're you so glum? Anything I can help you with?"

I ignored him for a second, took a long sip of wine, and then answered. "Probably not. Loretta and I are through. But what's really bothering me is, looking back, I have no way of knowing what was true or false, so I just wanna forget the whole thing."

"Well, you came to the right place to forget." He smiled. "How about a dance?"

I raised an eyebrow. "Ya know, I'm not quite drunk enough to dance with a guy, but wait a while, I'm sure I'll get there."

* * *

Two glasses of wine later Larry returned with a girl attached to his arm. I knew just by looking at her she was a lesbian, but was sure Larry didn't know that I knew. "How about dancin' with both of us then?" he smiled.

It may have been the alcohol talking when I said, "What the hell. At least it's just a dance … I know no one can get pregnant by doing that."

The three of us went downstairs and I found out the beat of the music was just the medicine I needed to forget my problems. The louder the music got, the more I began to loosen up, and instead of the three of us dancing, it quickly became everyone on the floor dancing with each other.

I sniffed some of the poppers which were arbitrarily stuffed under my nose and felt someone start grabbing my ass and someone else rubbing my penis. I hoped it was some of the women in the circle, but couldn't be sure. After about fifteen minutes of gyrating to the music, it didn't even matter to me who it was. I started grabbing and touching anyone around me back. This made me feel like I did the night I danced with Carmen so long ago in the lesbian bar back in Missouri.

The more I danced, the more drugs I did, and the more I perspired, the better this feeling became. The disco music had grabbed me and I was lost in it. I was now sweating profusely and the next thing I knew my shirt was ripped off of me by someone in the crowd. Even that didn't stop me. Someone poured a wine cooler down my chest and a girl—who could have easily been either straight or gay—started to lick it off. That's when I felt someone move up behind me, start dancing to the exact beat I was keeping, wrap their arms around me, and start rubbing my penis again. I figured it was a girl … until I felt an erect penis move up and down my ass and my legs.

* * *

The disco beat came to a screeching halt as a slow dance song came on. I went back upstairs to cool off and ran into Larry. He ordered each of us another glass of wine and then said, "You're feelin' pretty relaxed here, huh?"

"Yeah, it reminds me of a place back home. I love the smells, the music, the lights, and the amount of freedom that is allowed here. I wish the straight bars had this kind of excitement in them."

Larry saw his opening. "Well, there's another piece of this bar that you haven't seen yet. Remember that big black door up here in the corner you noticed the first day? Inside is a place you'll never see in a totally straight bar."

"Really? Why?"

"I'm not sure if it's for you or not." He hesitated. "Now I did see you touching many bodies down on the dance floor. I even saw you touch some of the guys. I saw, and felt, your reaction when that trans-sexual started licking the wine cooler off your chest. That dick of yours sprang into action real fast—"

"Wait," I stopped him. "That was *you* rubbing me?"

He looked at me with a gleam in his eyes and fessed up, "Yep that was me. Look, I know you're twenty years younger than I am, and I'm a friend of your dad, and most importantly, that you're not gay, but I find you very attractive. I have since we first met. In fact, when I drove you and Loretta home that one night I wished it was me you were going home with."

Now I knew it wasn't the drinking that had affected my hearing that night.

"I know I sound like an innocent school boy, but you make me feel young again. You're everything I'm looking for and will never find," Larry said all melancholy. "Now I'm sure I'm not what you need in your life right now, but you got me very excited."

Larry stuttered a little as he came to the point. "L-L-Look, the area behind the black door is a quiet place for people to pair off and experiment with each other. Mostly the gay guys here use it to feel each other out."

Larry took another deep breath. "I know you've never been with a man, and I'm not askin' you to have sex with me, all I wanna do is give you a blowjob. It feels just like when a girl gives you one. Just close your eyes and pretend I'm a female. Throw an old man a bone. Are you up for it?"

I was flabbergasted. I was also drunk and horny, so I went with him.

* * *

I let Larry have his fun. We entered the darkened room, settled into a corner, and I lay back while he gave me a blowjob. I didn't feel too much as he was doing his thing. I started sniffing more and more from the little black bottle of poppers I held in my hand. Larry was right in one aspect; the feelings I got from him—which were next to nothing—were the exact same way I felt when a girl did this to me.

He went along doing his business when a funny thought entered my head, I guess my lessons also apply to gay men.

I made myself a promise laying there naked from the waist down that night; I was never going to use them this way again—but it was good to know everyone could benefit from them.

Larry finished and then pleaded, "Please don't tell your dad. He warned all of us that you were off limits."

I laughed. "Relax. What I do is my business. I hope I helped you feel better tonight. It seems as though that's what I'm all about right now."

As I finished getting dressed I let Larry in on a little secret. "I gotta tell ya something though. I didn't feel a strong sexual pleasure. You may wanna work on your technique. One of the lessons I learned long ago is that practice makes perfect."

Larry blushed as we both left the room smiling.

* * *

Larry and I became friends after that night. No more talk about sex or being straight or gay. We accepted each other for what we were.

At least I thought we did.

We started going out to dinner together and I felt good being out and about again, but I was still a little confused as to what my place in Florida was going to be, and how I was going to fit in.

Larry took me to only his favorite restaurants. Little did I know they were all gay spots, my awareness sensor had been off since moving to Florida. I didn't see things the way I used to. I should have seen that there were only guys sitting all around us, but I never did. At least the food was always good.

"How about a change in appearance to help change your mood?" Larry asked one night as we sipped white wine at one of his clubs.

"Why? What's wrong with the way I look?"

"Nothin' at all, just thought it was time."

My mind swept me back to times in my past when others had performed a makeover on me. There was the time Lisa helped me pick out new clothes just before junior high. More importantly there was the time when Joyce turned me into Disco Phil. Both had turned out well for me, so I agreed with Larry's suggestion.

The next day *Lars*, as Larry was known at his salon, wet down my long curly brown hair and set upon turning me into a new person. I trusted him and hoped all would be well.

"Just relax. I know what I'm doing. Take a small nap and when you wake up you'll be a new man."

So I did. I was off in another land when a vision of Nana came to me. "Keep a sharp eye out, things may not be as they seem." With that warning, she disappeared.

I awoke as Lars was putting some sort of gook into my now short and stylish hair. "So what's that?"

"I'm adding a little bit of blond to help highlight your natural brown color," he said, almost giggling with excitement. "It's so Florida! Close your eyes. I have another surprise for you."

I did and felt someone take my fingers and start massaging them. Then I heard the small faint sounds of a nail clipper start and realized that I was getting my first manicure. It felt nice, and I liked the pampering, so I just went with the flow.

When Lars washed my hair I felt his strong fingers as they moved the shampoo through. I laughed to myself as I thought, Strong masculine fingers, but still a girlish voice.

Lars used a blow dryer to get all the excess moisture out of my hair and then I was allowed to see "the new me." I actually liked it. After years of long curly hair which I hated to keep up, now I had very short brown hair with streaks of blond in it. Lars also decided my mustache and beard, which had become like a second skin to me, must be trimmed back. He hacked off most of the beard, leaving only a goatee behind, and neatly framed my mustache against my upper lip. I thought I looked handsome, and obviously so did Lars.

"Almost there!" he shrieked.

I had been wearing Red for Men as my cologne of choice since Nancy gave it to me years earlier. Lars changed that without even asking. He took a small green bottle and splashed some new fragrance onto my face and neck. At first it smelled a little fruity to me, but then a few of the older ladies at the salon nodded their approval.

"Tonight, two more changes and you're good to go," Lars said, almost singing.

That night he took me shopping at his favorite place. I had never heard of Nordstrom's before, but soon was very happy I now did. First, Lars took me to the cologne area where he bought me some Paco Rabanne, my new scent. This also came with a moisturizer, liquid soap, and a gel for my hair. Lars told me, "You can never be too careful when it comes to your appearance here in Florida."

Then off to the men's section we went for new pants and shirts. A few hours later, after shopping like a girl and having me try on many new outfits, Lars finally picked out the best look for me. I was now sporting brightly colored flower patterned short sleeve shirts, with khaki colored pants. He wanted me to get a few shorts, but I never liked showing my skinny legs in public, so I declined. After getting a few pairs of different colored boat shoes and a new tuxedo, Lars was very happy with what he saw.

"Now, let's get rid of those glasses. Let's see about ordering you some contacts so I can see your bright shining eyes?" he clapped with glee.

I went home with a bag full of new clothes and accessories that night which Lars had bought me, along with a new feeling. Although I still didn't know my place in Florida at least I was happy again, this time thanks to a gay man.

* * *

The very next night Lars took me to the most expensive restaurant I'd ever been to. He had me dress to the max, putting on my new tux, so we could celebrate. As we sat at the table eating delicious lobster and sipping ice cold champagne, I noticed we were in a place filled with men only.

Maybe my awareness was coming back.

"Is this another gay only joint?" I asked pretty undignified.

"It sure is. I wanted to show you off. I know you're not gay," he softly giggled under his breath, "but these guys don't. I just want you to see how popular you could be if you open up your mind a little."

"So, all this is a ploy to make me *want* to be gay?"

"Not at all," Lars backtracked. "This is so you can see how the girls feel when you court them. Maybe you'll learn something from it."

I was lost as to his logic, but was feeling no pain. After downing two bottles of champagne and even dancing with Lars to some of the faster music the band played, I felt something happen inside of me—sort of an acceptance of myself—and I liked the feeling.

As the night progressed, men of all ages came up to say hi to Lars and then have him introduce me to them. I felt two old friends of mine, conceit and high demand, rush through my body. And surprisingly these feelings, although brought about by men, made me feel real good about myself. I also realized that even if Lars *was* trying to change my lifestyle, I could handle whatever came up.

This same sort of thing happened repeatedly night after night wherever we went. Lars would parade me through bars and restaurants while men of all backgrounds would try their best to make me theirs. And I started to play the game.

One night in The Rainbow Room we saw a guy standing at the bar. Lars told me, "That guy, William, he's a 'real player.'"

"Really?" I asked. "Does that mean the same thing in 'gay lingo' as it does in straight?"

"You bet. He gets everyone he lays his eyes on," Lars swooned. "Those eyes are so dreamy and he knows it. He's a little conceited, but he knows how to handle whoever comes his way, and his 'chosen one' does whatever he says. Most times they aren't disappointed either, if you know what I mean?"

Just about that time, we both saw him glance my way.

"Watch out, he's set his sights on you," Lars whispered. "Can you handle it?"

My mind went into overdrive. I never liked these overly aggressive guys—straight or gay—who so outwardly acted like they were God's gift to women, or men. "Yep, just watch me."

The man, a younger looking forty-something, was indeed very good looking. He was tall and slender, deeply tanned, and had a touch of gray in his hair. And Lars was right about his baby blue eyes, they practically sparkled. In a different world who knows what may have happened. But here's what I actually did.

William walked up to me and said, "Heaven must be missing an angel, cuz you're standing here tonight."

I laughed at his well-practiced pickup line. But I played on.

William then asked if I was there alone. Although Lars was near me, we hadn't been acting like a couple or anything, so I convincingly said yes. When William offered to buy me a drink I gladly took him up on his offer for a free glass of wine. After a few more drinks, and way too many more corny pickup lines which made me smirk, he asked me to dance. I followed his lead. The fast music took me away and I pretended I was dancing with a girl. Obviously William liked what he saw. He attempted to kiss me, but I quickly turned away and he just brushed the tip of my ear.

Not deterred at all, when a slow song came on, William began to put his arms around my waist. But I walked away before he could finish.

"Hey," he asked, surprised. "Where ya goin'?"

"Sorry, I don't dance the slow ones."

"Why?"

"Too much pressure."

William looked at me strange, but followed me to the bar. He bought me another wine, and then started to seemingly pour his heart out to me. He told me about how he had never been in love, but how I could change all that in a second. He laid it on thick, using the same basic techniques a man would use to try and bed a lady. About fifteen more of his sleazy pickup lines later, I'd had enough.

Man, now I knew why I hated those SOB's that Mandy had fallen for so often.

William finally got around to his point. "You are so nice to look at, I would love to spend some time with you alone, if you know what I mean."

"I sure do," I said, winking at him. "But I can't do that."

"Sure you can," he said. "Just walk out the door with me."

"I'm so sorry, but I'm in a threesome right now and I won't do anything to upset the apple cart."

"A threesome?"

Then I let him have it. "Yep, I'm in love with me, myself and I. And I'm as straight as they come. Guess you were barking up the wrong tree there, stud."

I saw the blood drain from his face and he quickly scurried out of the bar. When Lars saw William bolt, he couldn't believe it. "Man, you really put him in his place."

Lars was right, I did learn something from William, in fact, more than one thing. I now knew how it felt to be on the receiving end of bullshit pickup lines. It was a good reminder that honesty and sincerity were to be my watchwords when interacting with females. Also I would start looking at only the prettiest of the bunch, and who had the sex gleam radiating from her eyes. I was feeling as though if a super-handsome man would want me, every stellar looking girl would, too.

I knew that last statement went against all I used to stand for—I knew looks shouldn't be the deciding factor—but I didn't really care about that anymore. For a second I worried what Nana would think of me now. But only for that second.

And not that it was all that useful of a tool, I had honed my gay-dar. I knew how to spot lesbians, thanks to Joyce and Carmen, and now I could tell a gay man from a mile away. I also learned how to let them believe I was fair game. So whenever I wanted a free drink I knew what buttons to push to get one.

* * *

I was already comfortable around lesbians, and now gay men, but I wasn't too sure what to think when Lars showed me there were other kinds of people in this world, too.

We were sitting upstairs at Behind the Scenes one night and I saw a very beautiful lady dancing on the floor below. She was tall, lanky, and had bright red hair—my favorite. Her legs seemed to go from her neck all the way to the floor. She was dressed in a short red mini-skirt with matching five-inch stiletto heels. It was a little weird though that she also had white panty hose on, and I thought it's way too hot to wear those things in Florida.

I wanted to go down and dance with her, but when I pointed her out to Lars he stopped me. "She's beautiful all right. But in a whole different way than you think."

I was lost to his point and kept staring at this vision of loveliness for another few minutes. That's when Lars asked, "So do you really wanna meet her?"

"You know her? And we've been sitting here all this time?" I shook my head in disbelief. "Of course, I do."

"Okay, I'll bring her up, but do me a favor."

"Anything you want," I said, but backtracked. "Well, almost anything."

"Just have an open mind," Lars said as he stood up to go downstairs. "She has a secret to let you in on."

I had no idea what I expected to happen next, but what did was beyond anything I could imagine.

Lars returned and introduced me to *Regina*. I was smitten. She was even more beautiful up close. Her red hair glistened every time the strobe light above us rotated around, and her makeup—although a little heavy—was applied perfectly. I especially liked her bright red lipstick. I found myself wondering how her lips would taste when I kissed her. She gave me a little hug and the scent of her perfume was intoxicating, it was the smell of cinnamon. I could feel myself getting extremely turned on.

The three of us sat down at a corner table away from all the action and the noise. We talked for a few minutes about nothing special, shared a drink, and it was here I found out why Lars wanted me to have an open mind.

"Are you ready for Regina's secret?" Lars asked.

"If her secret is that she loves me, then yep, I'm ready."

Regina laughed. "No, that's not it. Brace yourself, honey, I'm a guy. My name is really Reginald."

I almost fell out of my chair. I was stunned. How could such a good looking girl be a guy? I was suddenly embarrassed about my thoughts on her … him, and found myself blushing.

"Phil," Lars chuckled, "here in Florida there are many kinds of people. With your open attitude, this should come to you as no surprise."

On closer inspection I noticed Regina's hands, although they had beautifully manicured nails, were rather larger than any girls' I'd seen before. Dropping my gaze down to her legs, I also realized the stilettos on her feet looked to be about size twelve.

Regina could see the look of disbelief on my face.

"Don't be so hard on yourself," Regina smiled. "I take it as a compliment that I can turn on a straight guy."

My sexual orientation had never come up, so I asked, "How'd ya know I was straight?"

"I can sense it," she explained. "We all have auras and energies that we let off. Yours tell me that you're straight as an arrow."

"But some of the gay guys think I'm gay."

"That's cuz most men don't actually take the time to really look, they think with their dicks," she said point-blank.

I had to say that statement had more truth in it than I liked to admit.

Regina explained in more detail about her lifestyle and I found everything she said very interesting. She told me she had some gay friends who were female impersonators, and others that were into cross-dressing, and by the time she told me she was a trans-gender, and what that meant, I didn't care why she did what she did, rather I found myself accepting her for what she had become; a new friend.

She said the same to me. In fact, she told me that I was her first and only straight friend. So when she asked if I wanted to dance, I gladly accepted.

"You're very easy to get along with," she said. "Watch it or one of these gay guys will try to take you home."

"Too late, it happens all the time," I said.

"Just be true to yourself and you'll find happiness in life."

I had just learned another lesson from another special person.

* * *

Regina was correct; the attempts to pick me up continued every time Lars and I went out for dinner and drinks. I eventually found it to be flattering and let it go at that. I thought, the games people play to get what they want.

And the more we hung out together, the more I got to know Regina. He became my best lady friend, all caught up in a man's body!

I finally decided it was just fine to wear what Lars bought me, go where he wanted to take me, and to pretend to be what he wanted me to be when I was around him, just as long as I knew who the real me was.

CHAPTER 10
BUNNY

One rainy night I sat on my bed and reviewed what had happened to me since I moved to Florida. As Rod Stewart sang softly in the background, I noticed a crumbled slip of paper on my dresser. I reached for it and saw the note Bunny, the sexy girl from the radio station, had written to me.

She answered my call, and after she remembered who I was, I got right to the point. "Do you mind if I use you as a sounding board? I have some things that are confusing to me and I'd like your insights."

"Whatever you want to talk about I'll gladly give you my honest opinion on." Bunny seemed eager to help. "But *only* if you and I can get together later for what I really want from you."

"That's exactly what I want to talk about. Not you and I specifically, but that subject. I'm trying to understand some things."

I started to tell Bunny about the lessons I had learned, and the people I'd encountered back home. I then talked about why I moved to Florida in the first place, what I had experienced so far, and all the people I had met. I said, "I met a girl named Mandy on the way here and she just used me for what she wanted. I'm not complaining, but once I got here I met someone else who I had some feelings for, but she only wanted me to help her party. Then a girl at work wants me to have sex with her whenever she needs it, and now you. You don't know anything about me, but you still want the same thing from me. Even gay guys are trying to lure me to their side of the street for sex. I'm beginning to feel Florida is all about making big impressions and having lots of sex. So, tell me, what did you see when you first saw me?"

"That's easy." Apparently Bunny didn't even have to think about it. "I saw a young man who was nice, polite, and honest. There was this person who seemed to be in control of his life and, therefore, had an air of confidence about him. Your looks didn't hurt the situation either."

I liked what she was saying to me, but still had to ask, "So, why do all these people feel I'm interested in sex?"

Bunny laughed. "*Everyone* is interested in sex, whether they flaunt it or not. Sex is a way of connecting and feeling important to someone else. The biggest compliment you can get paid is that someone likes you enough, trusts you enough, and is comfortable enough to share this part of them with you."

Probably because sexual encounters always came easily and naturally to me, I never thought about it that way before.

Then she got even more real. "Having grown up there, I know people in Missouri are pretty much how they present themselves. But here in Florida most people play games. The guys tell lies. Ones that make them feel better about who they are. They're more aggressive and toss out all these stupid lines to impress us girls. But most Florida women just look at the guy's appearance, and how much money he has, as their guiding point. We may sometimes get what we want from each other, but more often than not all of these relationships end up very badly with someone getting hurt."

She stopped as if she was recalling some bad memories of her own.

"You're just like all the other guys." She hesitated as if to gauge my response and then giggled. "What I mean by that is—you want sex as much as they do, you just go about it in a way that the girl relates to better. You're honest, up front about your feelings, and you know how to talk *to* us, not *at* us. Girls want someone they can trust. Here's a secret, we don't like all the games guys play—we just want what we want when we want it. Fortunately for you, you know how to give it and make women feel good about it at the same time."

As Bunny was saying this I felt my vanity level growing sky high. I wasn't sure if it was a good thing or bad, but God I loved the attention I was getting from everyone. Now I knew why I liked being around Lars and his merry men of gay guys so much.

I felt for the first time since I arrived in Florida, and maybe in my entire life, that I was beginning to truly understand myself. I had always wanted the girls I met to like me and respect me, most of the time not really thinking about my needs. But how I needed to use the lessons of my past now was to meet new people, *preferable girls,* in order to have sex with them to make *me* feel better about myself. Although I seriously doubted it, I hoped God would also see I was making a difference in both the girls' lives and my own. Maybe this time I'd get a clear sign to let me know if I was doing the right thing.

I agreed to meet Bunny later that week to keep my part of the bargain we'd made. I hung up the phone and retreated to my desk. I noticed the mirror on the wall and saw my image staring back at me. I looked deep into the eyes of the reflection and realized something. In the past I played the part of an innocent young boy who loved to help the girls I met experience a new sensation without all the head trips most guys deliver. Now, thanks to almost everyone who I had met in Florida so far, what I saw instead was a conceited, self-centered guy looking back at me. I had actually started believing I was indeed super hot, and in much more demand. And that I had won some sort of conquest over Bunny, even though she was the one who initiated the whole thing. And I found that feeling was one I enjoyed, maybe too much.

And as *You're So Vain* started to play on the radio in the background, I should have paid closer attention to the yellow roses in my vase. They were wilting and fading fast. But once again, since my arrival in Florida, I missed another sign.

CHAPET 11
THE SKATING RINK

Now that I understood myself better and how the girls of Florida saw me, I decided to put it all into practice. The self-centered person lurking inside of me had now become my reality, so I needed to learn how to use it to the best of my ability. That night I decided there'd be no more wanting to fall in love for me, no more gay experiments, and no more pretending to be someone I wasn't when I was around the ladies. I chose to start using the "secret insights" I knew to help me, *and only me,* feel better.

* * *

I figured the best place to go was where I would feel the most comfortable—a skating rink. I drove to the closest one, The Palms, and the minute I walked in it felt just like back home. Even though I didn't know a soul in the place, I felt in complete control. I knew my confidence level was at its highest and radiating very strong. I was sure it wouldn't take all that long for someone of the opposite sex to notice this. And within a brief few minutes of skating around the rink, I felt a pair of eyes honing in on me.

Imagine my surprise when it turned out to be a boy about eight years old.

"Hi." He rolled up next to me. "You're pretty good. I really like the lights on your wheels." He began to spit out questions one after each other, not even waiting for an answer. "So, what's your name? Do ya live nearby? How old are ya?"

I wasn't really interested in having a pint-size pal, but felt there was a different reason why he was bothering me. I finally found out, right after the DJ announced a couple skate over the PA system, what he actually wanted from me. I was exiting the rink when the kid asked, "Hey, wanna skate wiff my mom?"

I was surprised and started to wave him off when she skated up next to us.

"Well, I see you've met my little Bobby. I'm sure he talked your ear off." She looked at him with a mother's love radiating from her eyes. "I suppose he asked you to skate with me, too. Well, how about it?"

I took her in and saw a twenty-something young girl smiling hopefully at me.

She was about five inches shorter than I was, had long black hair which she wore in pigtails, and actually looked quite nice. I gazed deeper into her eyes and saw that neither the trust sparkle nor the sex gleam was present. However, a quick glance at her left hand revealed no wedding ring so I assumed she was divorced.

I hadn't answered her question yet. She shrugged and said, "If you're not interested, that's fine."

"No, it's not that. I was just thinking about somethin' else," I replied with a wink. "I'd love to skate with you and I hope it makes your little boy very happy."

When we skated around the rink, hand in hand to two songs, I saw Bobby smile big every time we passed by.

I skated with Jane and Bobby the rest of the night. At closing time, Bobby said, "That was fun. Wanna come wiff us to the ice cream store? Mom promised we could go, and she never breaks her promises."

I really wasn't in the mood to spend another hour or so with an eight year old—albeit an eight year old with a hot mom—so said, "I can't tonight, but I'll be back next Wednesday night and skate with you and your mom again. Will that work?"

Bobby sighed and said, "I guess so, but don't break your promise like my daddy does."

I had no idea what he meant and didn't want to know.

I was saying good-bye to my two new friends when the owner of the rink approached me. "Where'd you learn to skate like you do?"

"Missouri," I replied, "in a lesbian skating rink."

"I don't care about the details," he interrupted. "I like your personality and want someone like you as a skate guard. You'll keep an eye on the skaters and help them up when they fall. Occasionally, you might have to tell a hot-dogger to slow it down a bit. And once in a while, you'll do a couples skate with some of the shy girls; make their night a little more enjoyable for them. Are you interested?"

"I already have a full-time job, but maybe I could do somethin' part-time."

"Look, I really like you and will pay you double what I pay my other employees, if you can keep it a secret," Paul said under his breath. "And you can pick your nights to work. The weekends have the best scenery to look at, if you know what I mean."

I knew exactly what he meant, so that's how I started to guard at The Palms every Friday night. The regular skaters started to accept me for who I was. I didn't have to play the role of Disco Phil, my alter ego from back home. I wasn't able use the lessons as I had planned to at first—I was taking my time in order to scope out my options—but I was able to make many new acquaintances.

* * *

I did return on Wednesdays to skate with Jane and Bobby, mainly to keep my promise to him, but also to see how long it would take for Jane to "make me feel better." I still had the initial plan in the back of my mind, you know.

Jane and I skated together and talked about nothing in particular as I bided my time. Just seeing us together seemed to make Bobby happy. He smiled a lot, and I was able to ignite the sparkle of trust in Jane's eyes the more she got to know me.

Soon it would be time to put my real plan into action.

* * *

One warm Wednesday night a couple of months later, Jane showed up at the rink alone.

"Where's Bobby tonight?"

"Bobby's with his father. He actually showed up for once." She shook her head in genuine disbelief.

Jane and I sat down to talk about "adult things" without being interrupted by the inquiring mind of a little boy. "I got married at sixteen because I wanted to get away from my parents," she confessed. "I had sex *once* with my husband and nine months later Bobby came along. By then his deadbeat father was long gone. The two of us have been basically on our own ever since, except on the blue moons when Nick decides to act like a dad to his son."

I could tell Jane wanted to get more off her chest, so I suggested we move our conversation somewhere more private, and asked, "Do ya like to swim?"

Jane said yes and we left the rink in our separate cars for my house in order to share a relaxing nighttime dip in the pool and some drinks. She pulled up next to me at a red light, rolled down her window and said, "Follow me to my apartment. I need to get my swim suit."

We parked in her lot and she went in. Jane returned about ten minutes later with a small travel bag. I was waiting by her car door, and before she got back into the car I asked if she wanted to ride with me.

"No, I'll take my car. This way I can leave whenever I feel like, and not inconvenience you."

I found her to be the nicest girl I had met so far in Florida.

* * *

When we entered my house, Jane was impressed. I grabbed a bottle of white wine and two glasses from the kitchen while she changed into her suit in my room. I changed in the hall bathroom and then we headed to the pool together.

We settled into two deck chairs and Jane asked, "How do you afford this house? It makes my little apartment feel so tiny."

I remembered what Bunny told me about Florida guys playing games to impress the girls and decided to give it to her straight.

"This is my dad's place. I'm just stayin' here, but basically have the run of the house. My dad owns Behind the Scenes, a bar near the strip, and works late most nights. I wish I could afford all this," I gestured around me, "but all I can swing right now is to give someone my time. That's enough about me. Tell me more about you."

Jane eased back in her seat, took a few sips of wine, and said, "Since my husband and I divorced, times have been hard. I have a steady job answering the phones at a local dentist office, but it doesn't pay enough to support both Bobby and me. My ex is totally irresponsible, doesn't pay his alimony on time, and never follows through on his promises to Bobby. I can handle all this, but I worry for Bobby. He's got no stable male influence in his life, and I don't know how that'll affect him later in life."

This conversation hit home with me. Jane sounded a bit like my mom and her friends did when they used to get a little sloshed and trash talk the men of the world. Here she was only twenty-four years old and her life was nowhere near what she thought it would be.

Her honesty made me think of Loretta for a second and instinctively made me wonder once again if she really had ever been pregnant. I promised myself that I would be there for Jane and Bobby whenever I could.

"Don't worry about Bobby. He'll be fine. I'll help him if you want me to," I offered. "My parents got divorced when I was eight, and I didn't have any male influence either. I think I turned out okay."

Jane softened. "You're such a sweet guy. You've known us for only a few months, but I feel so close to you, more than anyone else I know. And I know Bobby really likes you, too. There's this calmness and relaxed feeling that always comes over me whenever you're near. I don't know if you've heard this before, but I really feel good around you. Where have you been all my life?"

I could tell the wine was taking its toll on her so I suggested we move into the pool so she could sober up a bit.

We entered the shallow end hand in hand and I wasn't sure if it was Jane or the wine talking when she said, "I haven't had sex since that one time with my husband. I've never had enough confidence to try it again.

I'm more than a little scared seein' that I've only done it once and I have one kid. I have a pretty good hunch that you've had sex many times."

Little did she know just how much!

"I would also assume that since you have no kids you know how to avoid that situation, too."

Not really sure about that comment.

"Look, I know I've had more than my share of wine tonight, and we've only known each other a short time, but I sure would like it if you could help me learn how to enjoy sex again. I'm ready to experience some things I've only read about, and I want to feel things I've never felt before. I wanna matter to someone other than Bobby, and I wanna feel good again." She leaned into me. "How about it Phil, can you please help me?"

My chest began to swell and the feelings of winning a conquest were arising, not to mention other parts of my body.

I knew I could help Jane with her request. The ladies I had met through the madam, Nancy, and several others from my past all came rushing to mind as I said to her, "Yes, pretty lady, I can."

We exited the pool, dried each other off and then Jane and I retreated to my bedroom. I put on a cassette by Bread; Jane poured herself another glass of wine and then went into my bathroom with her travel bag. She returned a few minutes later wearing a long cotton nightshirt—she looked like a teenager on a sleepover. When she climbed into my bed, she slowly pulled the sheet up to her chin, as if she was hiding from what was to happen.

I thought it was cute and so innocent.

I dimmed the lighting, slipped off my wet trunks, dried myself off even more and then joined her under the covers. I gave her a very soft kiss to break the tension in the room. A few seconds after my tongue entered her mouth, and she returned the favor, I felt Jane relax a bit. I slowly kicked the sheet off the bed and started out deliberately very slow and very careful in order to keep Jane at ease.

But the more involved we got, the more she responded. When my hand slipped under her nightshirt, I was very surprised to find Jane had no underwear on. Guess she wasn't hiding from anything after all.

Her body continued to react favorably to my gentle and calculated movements, but I noticed she had her eyes closed. The longer we stayed together, the tighter her eyes clinched. After about an hour of sexual pleasure, I finally heard a sigh of enjoyment emerge from her mouth.

We cuddled afterwards and I asked her, "So, is this *all* you wanted from me?"

Jane kissed me, her lovely eyes wide open, and now I saw the sex gleam emanating. "If I knew it was gonna be like this, I wouldn't have waited for so long. I'm sure that most guys aren't this careful and considerate though. You've made me feel special."

I smiled knowing we both got exactly what we wanted. I stroked her hair gently and asked, "Why'd ya have your eyes shut the whole time?"

Jane blushed. "Two reasons. One, I didn't want you to see me cryin'. I've never felt so wanted before." Jane kissed me. "And I thought I must be dreamin', so I didn't want it to end."

That comment made me laugh. "I'm flattered you enjoyed our special time together. As you can plainly see, I'm very real, and anytime you want more, all you have to do is ask."

"You're so sweet," she cooed, then fell asleep next to me.

I hoped I had helped Jane rediscover her sexuality. I was extremely happy with myself, and with what I had just accomplished. In the past when I did something good for someone I always felt a warm feeling run through my body. This time I didn't feel it at all. In fact, the only feeling I had was one of conquest. And it didn't even bother me.

Well, just like in my past, I had entered yet another woman's life precisely when she needed me to. Consequently, I was able to make her feel better, and the feelings of being something truly special grew twofold. Bunny was absolutely right—I wanted sex, plain and simple— and I felt as though I helped someone new this time around; me and my conceited self. And for the moment I felt real good about it.

Please don't hate me for feeling this way. Deep down inside I was doing that enough for the both of us. Deeper inside, I could sense emptiness returning.

* * *

The next night I stayed home by myself just listening to music in my room. I opened the French doors across from my bed to let a cool breeze come through. I popped open a chilled bottle of white wine, put a Rod Stewart cassette in, and planned on closing my eyes to relax. Instead, many thoughts bombarded my mind. I started thinking about my days back home in Missouri and how it made me feel when I helped the ladies I met. Now knowing I craved not only sex, but the resulting feelings of conquest, much more than the emotional part, and that there were women out there willing to "feed my need" at any time, I needed a new master plan, one that would catapult me to sexual stardom.

I listened to Rod sing the words from *It's Not the Spotlight* and the plan came to me.

I wanted that spotlight he was singing about shining brightly down on me again. I believed if this happened, I'd gain even more confidence— *as if I really needed more.*

I desperately wanted to feel important and special to others, however I could. I once believed my confidence level was directly linked to having a girl by my side. After seeing what had happened so far in Florida, I realized that statement wasn't entirely true. What I really needed was a constant flow of new women coming and going in my life in order for me to stay interested. I enjoyed this thing they called the chase, but was beginning to crave the meaningless sex part even more.

I fell asleep shortly after coming to terms with my new identity. But could I keep that empty feeling that was gnawing away at me at bay?

CHAPTER 12
CONNIE and JOANN

Connie, a new girl at work, had just moved from Wyoming. Back in grade school I knew a girl from Wyoming. I thought I could impress Connie with my accumulated data about her home state.

Red-headed, freckles on her face, and beautiful green eyes, although they never flashed the sex gleam when I glanced her way, Connie was a little shorter than my five-foot-eleven frame, but was just as thin as I was. She possessed this tremendous smile, which produced the cutest dimples I'd ever seen.

When I casually mentioned this to her, her cheeks flushed as red as her hair was. Connie was a little shy at first, but soon enough her eyes developed the sparkle of trust whenever she looked at me.

I nicknamed her Red, which she said she hated, but let me call her anyway. I really liked Red, but didn't want to get too deeply involved in order to keep my options open. We often hung out at a small restaurant, *Poppy's,* mostly with me listening to her talk about being homesick and feeling uncomfortable in Florida.

Was my old self starting to emerge again?

One night I gave her some advice. "I once felt like you do, couldn't get comfortable wherever I was. Then I discovered that I first needed to be happy with myself before I could be happy about anything else."

I continued talking about my journey and some of the life-changing lessons I had learned. I hoped it didn't sound like a sermon. "You have to figure out what your mission in life is. I know mine is to help women understand what makes them feel better."

My new persona suddenly took control and I bluntly said, "I learned that guilt-free sex makes most women feel better. It works for me, too. Maybe that's what it'll take to get you out of your funk?" I winked at her and was expecting a coy smile in return.

Instead, Red just stared bullets at me. "You're so conceited. I'm sure not looking for what you're offering. You may think you're helping 'em, but I think you're taking advantage of those women, and I'm sure God doesn't appreciate what you're doin' either."

Wow, I was taken aback. I never knew anyone felt that way about me here in Florida, although Joyce once told me something similar back home.

I tried to regain my composure. Another girl from work who had been listening to our conversation from the bar suddenly joined in. Joann said, "If what he's doin' helps someone feel better about themselves, what's wrong with that? Isn't that what we're supposed to do as humans? Isn't that what God wants from us?"

For the time being I felt justified.

Still, I pleaded with Red, "Let me try to explain it a little better. I think you've totally misunderstood what I mean. You came into my life when you moved here, right? You knew no one and had nobody to talk to, right?" She slowly nodded her head. "Maybe it was God who sent you to me?"

She shook her head in disagreement.

"I gave you the opportunity to speak your mind freely, and I listened to you. That's what you needed from me at that particular time of your life, wasn't it?" I asked. "I never pressured you for more, did I?"

Red shook her head again.

"Some of the other women who were sent into my life needed more. They were lookin' for help in finding what they thought they were lacking. In some cases it was confidence that they needed. Many others wanted to feel accepted again. Then there were those who just wanted uncomplicated, guilt-free sex from me. Who am I to argue with them? I did whatever they needed me to do in order to make them feel good again. Does that make it any easier for you to understand what I do and why?"

Was I trying to convince her or me?

Red still didn't get it, but Joann did. "Hey, I have a problem. Do you think you can help me?"

"It depends," I said, turning my attention to her.

"I had plans to go to my senior prom next weekend, but the jerk I was going with just cancelled on me," Joann said. "I've already bought a new dress, made expensive dinner reservations for afterwards, and had this special night totally planned. Now I'm gonna miss the whole thing. This is really important to me, so how'd you like to go to the prom with me?"

I thought about it for a second. Here I was older than her by two years and I didn't know a soul at her school. Hell, I hardly even knew her, but I did know that becoming friends with girls always led me to more exciting opportunities later on. And a plan developed in my mind.

I agreed to go with her and Joann gave me a big smile and a bigger hug in return. She stepped back and I looked into her eyes. They had both the sparkle of trust and the sex gleam shining in them.

I shifted my attention back to Red. "See, this is what I mean. I'll help Joann make this special night for her happen and whatever will be, will be. It really couldn't be that much easier to understand."

Red smiled back and reluctantly replied, "I guess I get it. It really looks as though you're happy that you can help her." Of course she couldn't help adding, "But I still think you're conceited!"

Who was I to disagree?

* * *

After finalizing our date, Joann and I set out getting to know each other. Outwardly, we were very different. Joann was much taller than me—a good six-foot-three in stocking feet. She had long silky hair which hung down to her waist. Her beautiful eyes matched the color of her hair—a deep dark brown. She wore a gold Star of David charm around her tanned neck, and had long well-manicured fingernails, which were always painted either a black or gray.

I found out she wasn't too well liked at school, she kept to herself a lot, and no surprise, that she was Jewish. I had never dated a Jewish girl before, so we discussed a lot about her religion, her beliefs, and her overall feelings about life.

The more we shared, the more I felt as though we were the same on the inside—we just wanted to be accepted and happy. And even though I planned to never let anyone into my heart again for fear of getting hurt, I found myself falling for Joann.

* * *

On the night of the prom I wanted to make sure Joann had a great time so I hired a limo to take us to the dance, bought some flowers for her, and then I bought some wine for me. I thought I may need a little boost of confidence to get through this, and wine always helped.

Uncharacteristically, I was anxious when I first approached her door. I normally was in complete control, but for some reason this time something felt different.

When Joann answered I saw a look of nervousness in her eyes, too. But after having some pictures taken by her mom, I felt her relax, which put me at ease, too.

Her mom told her to have a great night and thankfully, not to worry about coming home at any given time. In the limo, on the way to the dance, Joann and I shared the bottle of wine, which eased both our nerves even more.

We walked into the dance hand in hand, and when everyone looked at us Joann tensed up again. She squeezed my hand a little too tight, but after looking me in the eyes and seeing my proud smile, she seemed to be back in control.

And why wouldn't she?

Joann was wearing a beautiful red dress which went all the way to the floor. There were slits up both sides of it which showed off her white lace pantyhose. Her black hair was braided neatly on top of her head and she was wearing silver eye makeup which highlighted the deep dark color of her eyes. She was wearing silver high heeled shoes which made her even taller than she actually was. And even though this made me look shorter, it was her night so I didn't care. On her left dress strap she wore the silver lily I bought her. I took in this vision of loveliness and thought she looked just like a princess—minus the tiara.

Complimenting her dress, I was wearing my black tux adorned with all red accessories. Hands down, we really looked great as a couple despite our height issues. I was thrilled to be Joann's prom date tonight.

When the band started to play I realized I knew them. I always danced at my dad's place and this band was there just the week before. In fact, I developed a dance one night for their new song; hence, I got to know them pretty well. They'd named themselves Johnny and the Fat Girls. They weren't well-known at this time, but did have a song, *Love the Feelin'*, which had just started to climb the charts.

I went up to request their new song and Johnny remembered me. "You bet we'll play the song, *if* you teach everyone the dance you made up. I'll even dedicate it to your date. What's her name?"

"Joann," I said, thinking this was the perfect way for me to be a little different, to be accepted by this younger group of people, and finally to help make Joann's night even better.

And I was totally right. Johnny announced the dedication and started singing. At first, Joann blushed when she heard her name announced for everyone to hear, and was reluctant to dance. But when I started to dance by myself in front of her, she had little choice except to join in. We turned out to be great dance partners, if I do say so myself. And pretty soon, the rest of the kids, and even some of the older teachers, joined us in doing my dance moves.

By the time the song ended, everyone in the place knew Joann and me. Perhaps selfishly, I thought it was the first time in her life Joann had been the center of attention, and that it was all because of me. Whether that thought was right or wrong, it energized me, and reinforced my belief that the spotlight was exactly what I needed to feed my desire to feel special.

* * *

The hubbub died down; Joann and I danced a couple more songs, had a few pictures taken, met some new people, and then decided to leave on a high note. We exited the hall hand in hand smiling from ear to ear.

Back in the limo, Joann asked, "Do ya really wanna go eat? I'm not hungry, I just wanna dance some more."

A friend from my past once told me that all girls like a guy who is good on the dance floor. It also means he's good *somewhere else*. It was girl code which meant this could lead to something I liked even more than a good dance partner—a great bed partner.

It was looking like my plan had worked.

She slid over next to me and gave me a big kiss. "I now totally understand what you said to Connie about being there for those who need somethin'. I just wanted to get over getting dumped and then you showed up. It's like someone upstairs planned this whole thing out."

Joann looked upward as to emphasize what she just said. That's when her eyes caught sight of the sunroof above us. She opened it and added, "I'm so happy that you came with me tonight, I can't believe how great this night has started. You know, this is the first time I've been accepted by the kids at school. God, it feels so cool and, to show you my thanks, just you wait until later tonight."

I didn't know exactly what she meant, although I had my theories!

* * *

I asked the driver to take us to Behind the Scenes and as we drove off, Joann and I shared some of the leftover wine. It was a bit warm, but it didn't seem to matter. Both of us brought a change of clothes for after the party, so as the cool night breeze came flowing through the open sunroof above Joann started to change. She slid out of her dress and I tried not to look … *yeah, right!*

I found my eyes locked on her chest as she took off her bra to put on a halter top. Joann had the nicest breasts I'd ever seen. They were perfectly shaped, perfectly sized, and thanks to the cool night wind, her nipples were perfectly hard.

Joann caught me. "You really don't have to stare," she winked, "you'll get your chance later on. But I do hope you like what you see just the same."

I certainly did. But I blushed anyway.

Joann took off her pantyhose and replaced them with a pair of blue jeans. I slid on a pair of black Angel Flight pants and a bright blue shirt. I left the top two buttons undone and this was the first time Joann had seen me without a tie—I always wear one at work. That's when she noticed my chest hair. She slid next to me again and started to rub her hand through it, and obviously liked the feel. Joann gave me another big kiss and a wonderful smile.

We pulled into the parking lot of the bar and Joann put on a pair of flat shoes while I slid on my cowboy boots. When we stepped out of the limo, for the first time, I was taller than her.

I waved to the bouncer and we were able to walk past the line, right into the bar. After introducing Joann to my dad and Dewey, we started dancing and drinking. Once again, I was very impressed with how well we moved together, seeing how we had just gotten to know each other. I was hoping this would help out later in the night because she moved just like I did, and we all know what that means.

Back home I liked Latin music and danced to a different beat than most anyone else, but clearly Joann heard the same rhythms, and it quickly became very noticeable, not only to me, but to certain parts of my body as well.

We'd danced to a couple more songs, had a few drinks, and sniffed a popper, when a song by disco diva Anita Ward, *Ring My Bell*, began to play. We both looked at each other at precisely the same time, and decided to leave the bar

We both were amped as we jumped into the back of the limo and headed to my house to celebrate whatever was to come. Joann turned on the radio, and sang along with Alicia Bridges to the words from *I Love the Nightlife*.

Being as smitten as I was, I wanted the same thing. And a funny thought came to mind; Maybe she had a plan, too.

* * *

We walked in the front door of my house and Joann saw through the open Florida room the lights of the pool and the hot tub. She led me to the backyard, got both of us undressed without saying a word, and into the Jacuzzi before I knew what had happened.

We were sitting next to each other looking at the Florida skyline. "Thanks for a great evening," Joann said, "This whole night has been so special—and even though we've only known each other for a week, I feel like I've known you forever. In fact, I wanna do something special for you in return."

Joann grabbed my arm and asked me where my bedroom was. I didn't hesitate to point the way.

We left the French doors open so a small breeze could blow through. The wind made the roses on my desk sway back and forth. Joann noticed and asked me about them. So I told her the same story I had let Loretta in on.

Unfortunately, the yellow roses weren't as pretty as the rest of them. They were always shriveling up faster than the other ones. Joann asked if that meant anything to me. When I couldn't come up with any immediate answer, I turned on my cassette instead and let Rod sing to us.

And as we started having sex I felt all was well. Joann must have felt the same way, because we connected in bed just like we did on the dance floor. She anticipated what my next moves were going to be, and she even surprised me with a few new twists of her own.

I guess she did a have plan all along.

* * *

Although initially, I'd agreed to this prom thing out of arrogance, and really only wanting to have sex with Joann, I was surprised when I felt something I hadn't in a long time. I was wanted by a girl once again, and not only for my sexual expertise. So much so, that right then and there I decided to try and make Joann the only girl in my life.

Wow, what a quick change in perspective that was.

Even though I was feeling good about this decision, *and also about the sex we just finished with,* I still didn't feel the surge of warmth in my body as I expected. This confused me.

Was I doing something wrong? Was I really ready to try this "love thing" again? Could this feeling actually last more than just this one night? And most important, just how did Joann feel about me?

I must have been doing something right though, because I saw that it was a smiling Joann who was fast asleep next to me.

* * *

After the success of the prom night, Joann and I did become a couple. For her it seemed an easy transition, but for me it was the total opposite. Many of the girls who attended the prom started coming to see me at work. I was confused as to why, until I remembered that females converse openly about sex with each other. I figured Joann must have done some girl talk about me at school.

That theory was confirmed by Joann a few nights later. "I was in my own little world before you came along. I was always the different one—tall, quiet, and most of the other students ignored me. But ever since the prom, some of the girls started approachin' me, and I really like the attention. One girl asked if you had kissed me and I let the whole story out. I was so proud of the fact that you like me. I had no idea they'd all start stalkin' you. I'm so sorry."

It was cool to see I still had the knack, but I tried to contain the temptation of several different girls suddenly wanting me. "Don't worry about me," I said. "I love that you're happy, and I love our sex together. Let's concentrate on us, and just let the others feel jealous."

I went into this relationship wanting sex only, but the longer Joann and I were together, the more comfortable I felt in having only her. My feelings of conceit, self-centeredness, and even the emptiness I once had slowly started to dwindle. I finally felt as though I had become the person I actually moved to Florida to be. Joann had done something other women couldn't; she had helped me find the real me.

We shared everything—our dreams, our innermost thoughts, and many nights of passionate sex. Wow! I was actually making love to a girl again. And within two short months, the safety barriers around my heart had completely disappeared, along with the emptiness I had learned to live with.

* * *

Our nights always started at a small local bar, Casey Maxfields. We would go there after work to share some wine and listen to the live music. The drinking age in Florida was eighteen, so I was legal, but not Joann. That didn't seem to matter to anyone once we became regular customers. In fact, even some of the other girls and teachers from Joann's school would occasionally join us.

We all enjoyed the music and were in high spirits, but then some of the other girls started approaching me when Joann wasn't around. They told me that they enjoyed the times we spent at the bar, but wanted to get to know me better … in private. In the past I would have leapt at the chance to bed any of these ladies, but I kept pushing them away. For the first time since dating Kim, I was extremely happy with myself. Kim was a girl who I fell extremely hard for back home. She eventually told me I wasn't man enough for her. Despite that outcome, I prayed that my results with Joann would be different this time around.

* * *

One night about six months later Joann and I were swimming at my house.

"I'm goin' on a small vacation," she announced in a bubbly voice. "There's a week long retreat bein' sponsored by my synagogue and I really wanna go. It's for older teenage Jewish girls to discuss with rabbis what this life has in store for us. I love what we have together and I'm hopin' this will help build our relationship even more." Joann's face morphed from excitement to deep concern. "I know you have all these other girls hittin' on you, so please don't do anything that will ruin what we have, I wouldn't want to lose that."

I smiled and put my arm around her waist in order to bring her closer to me. "There's no way I'd do anything to hurt you. I'm very happy with where we are and—"

Joann stopped me mid sentence by kissing me, and then said, "I really think I love you."

At first I didn't say anything back, knowing how love never seemed to work for me, but I was feeling the exact same thing about her. So I finally let it out. "I love you, too."

Joann and I retreated to my bedroom where we enjoyed the best night of lovemaking we had ever shared. Exhausted, we fell asleep next to each other with us both feeling happy and convinced that absolutely nothing could come between us.

* * *

The week Joann was away passed by faster than I thought it would. But on the Friday night she returned I could tell from the get-go that something was different. The connection we shared just last week seemed to be gone and I didn't know why. I had done nothing wrong, so I wondered if she could say the same.

We went to Casey Maxfields and when I ordered our usual—two white wines—Joann interrupted, "No, please just make it one. I don't want any wine tonight. Make mine a ginger ale, please."

This was a total surprise. In the past, Joann had always shared my enthusiasm for a good white wine and I'd never seen her drink anything else at the bar, especially a soft drink.

I tried to listen to the music, but Joann only wanted to discuss things about our life—like what we had already shared and what was to come in our relationship. After downing my first bottle of wine, the chatter started to bother me and I suggested rather loudly that we just leave.

I stormed out alone, but Joann followed close behind. When we got to the car she gave me a small kiss on the cheek and said, "I'm sorry if I made you mad. I just really need to talk to you."

I smiled back and forgave her.

I drove to my house thinking a swim and some love making would change her mind about talking. Joann didn't say a word the whole ride. I could tell she was in deep thought about something and I didn't want to interrupt her thoughts.

When we arrived at my house I was more than a little drunk and ready for some hot sex so I needed to let her get this serious stuff off her chest quickly. "Okay, what's so important?"

"I learned a lot about myself at the retreat," Joann said reflectively. "Rabbi Simmons asked us to think about what was important to us and why. The question of God came up and how we related to the Lord's message. Rabbi Simmons then asked us to think differently about how we celebrated the feelings we felt." Joann got very serious. "We were then asked who was sexually active and who drank."

No doubt her hand had to have been raised.

"Then he told us to try and understand why we do the things that we do. He asked us to give up these superficial vices and to really concentrate on more important religious feelings. So," Joann started to stammer, "I-I-I wanna try giving up sex and alcohol for a while."

What, did I hear that right?

"I know these are a big part of our life, but can you help me through this?" She put her hands firmly on top of mine. "If you really love me like you say you do, I know that you will."

Now what?

At the same time she spoke those words, Rod sang the song *So Soon We Change.*

It felt as though Rod was singing it to us. I downed another full glass of wine in one slurp, looked Joann squarely in her eyes and saw the sex gleam had completely gone out, although the sparkle of trust was still there, along with a look of anticipation awaiting my answer.

I shook my head in disbelief. "What? I thought we had a good thing goin'. Why would you wanna change anything about it?"

When I didn't get a response, I grumbled, "Ya know, I need some alone time to think about this. I'm too drunk to drive, so why don't you call someone to pick you up?"

Joann kissed me gently on the lips and as she stared blankly into my eyes, I now saw that the trust sparkle had fizzled out, too.

She made her call and headed outside to wait for her ride. I saw tears roll down her cheeks as she passed me. I wanted to stop her, to hold her, and to say that everything would be just fine. I also wanted to know more about why all the changes. I wanted to do all this, but unfortunately I was too numb to do any of it. Joann walked out of my life, but something inside of me returned, only I didn't recognize it yet.

Somehow in my inebriated state, I changed the cassette in the player to Bread, a much mellower music, and then stretched out on my bed trying to comprehend what just happened.

Once again I was devastated by a girl who I thought I loved—Mary, then Kim, and finally Diane all came to mind. I felt a twinge pass through me, but had no idea what it was.

I was finally making love to a girl again, along with the emotional connection I desired, and had everything I wanted from a committed relationship. I had let another girl into my heart and once again it didn't work out the way I hoped it would. I couldn't make sense of it. Joann wanted, and thoroughly enjoyed, the sex we shared and then *poof,* something changed.

Again I felt that strange twinge.

I thought this through over another glass of wine. Then it came to me from out of the blue. *I can't be with someone if sex isn't involved.* Talk about being caught up in myself. I thought I really loved Joann, but I found out the hard way I didn't love her enough to give up sex, even if it was only temporary. I started to cry when I realized I had lost in love again.

I was upset with Joann and my life, again. It was then my past feelings of conceit and self-centeredness, not to mention the dreaded emptiness I used to live with, reappeared. *Those were those strange twinges I had felt.*

I glanced at the mirror above my desk desperately trying to see what my red eyes would reveal. I saw nothing staring back. I glanced at the vase below and saw the pink roses had started to change, just like the yellow ones before. Their color was gone, they were ready to die.

I probably should have recognized the sign, but was too distraught to notice.

I guess Colette was right—I didn't want to miss out on the "next best thing" to enter my life. I decided to formally break up with Joann the next day. The safety barrier went back up around my heart again, this time stronger than ever.

I sat there and tried to visualize Nana—I really needed her help. I hadn't had a "visit" from her in a long time and was getting very frustrated with her—and with God. Neither seemed to be around when I needed them to be. Where were they? And what happened to the signs they used to leave me to help me choose which way to go?

CHAPTER 13
STEPHANIE

The next night I went to Casey Maxfields to drown my sorrows. When I walked in the bar I saw a few familiar faces, but chose to sit at the end of the bar by myself. Louie, the bartender, brought me a bottle of my usual white wine. He opened it and asked me where Joann was, but I never answered. Instead I quietly sat back on my barstool and listened to the live music.

Normally on Saturday nights there would be a younger man belting out loud rock and roll songs, but tonight an older lady, Gloria, sang slow love ballads.

Of course, just my luck.

I knew most of these songs by heart. I closed my eyes and let my mind drift. Soon I was able to forget I was at a bar and just let the music take me where it wanted to. When Gloria sang *Two Less Lonely People in the World* by Air Supply, my mind went to Mary. She was my first real girlfriend and this was her favorite song. Anytime I heard it I was reminded of all the things she had taught me. This time the memory hit me real hard. I lowered my head onto the bar and softly cried.

"Hi, Phil," A woman had come up from behind. "Where's Joann?" At first she didn't notice my tears, but then asked, "Hey, what's wrong? You wanna talk?"

I looked up and saw Stephanie standing there. She was a teacher from the high school who had become a semi-regular at our table here at the bar, ever since the prom. I never really paid that much attention to her in the past.

"She's gone." I tried to regain some composure. "If ya wanna sit here and watch my emotions get the best of me, go ahead. I'm sure I won't be too good of company tonight."

I was beginning to feel the effects of the wine I had consumed. Instead of acting so melancholy, I realized that I liked the songs Gloria was singing and actually found myself singing along. I never could carry a tune, but that didn't matter to me tonight.

Stephanie sat down on the stool next to me. In the middle of a Rod Stewart song I didn't remember, she reached for my left hand. Instinctively I held on to hers. As she stroked my palm, I lost myself in the melodies again. I began to feel better—but then Gloria sang a Lennon and McCarthy song that Rod covered, *In My Life*, and I lost control again.

Tears filled my eyes. I looked over at Stephanie and saw an understanding smile. "Would ya like to get outta here and get some coffee?"

We walked to the coffee shop across the street; sat at a small table near the back out of all the commotion that was being made up front.

"What happened?" Stephanie asked. "You're always in such a good mood."

"Joann and I broke up. Somethin' about these new feelings that she wants to explore," I tearfully explained. "I thought I was in love. Ya know, I've been screwed over so many times by girls I thought had the same feelings for me, that I just don't wanna let anyone else close to me. I don't ever want to be hurt like that again."

Stephanie patiently listened to me complain. "Phil, I'm so sorry, but you can't let a few broken hearts change your perspective. We all go through this roller coaster ride. Right now I suggest you focus on what makes *you* happy, and let the rest take care of itself."

Little did she know I had already come to that same conclusion, although you sure couldn't tell it by my actions right then!

A few more cups of coffee and I was sober enough to actually comprehend what she was saying to me. I knew what would make me happy, but it occurred to me, what about *her*?

For the first time I carefully studied Stephanie's features. She was about twenty-eight years old with short blonde hair and blue eyes, and had a smooth, *easy to listen to* voice which helped me calm down. I thought she was pretty. And I noticed she had the trust sparkle in her eyes.

"Thanks for listening to me whine and complain. Ya know, I'm normally the one doin' the listening, but I needed to let all that out," I said.

I took a long sip of coffee, set the mug down, interlocked my fingers, and put on my wise owl face. "So Stephanie, why don't you tell me about you?"

She put two sugars and a small amount of cream into her coffee and then opened up. "I was born and raised in Michigan. I moved here to go to college, learned to like the weather, and accepted my teaching job."

The more she talked to me with that smooth voice of hers the more I found myself wanting her to continue. A few minutes later the waitress came by with refills. After she left, I added two sugars and a small amount of cream to Stephanie's coffee.

"That was very sweet of you," she said raising her eyebrows. "How'd you know how I take my coffee?"

"I see things most guys don't. It's part of this stupid 'gift' I have," I said as if it was a burden. Then I quickly changed the subject. "Can I ask ya what you like in a guy?"

She considered my question for a moment. "I'd say common sense and manners. I can connect with a guy who can share his emotions without feeling he's being 'unmanly'. In fact, I actually was a little turned on when you were crying at the bar."

Here we go, I had heard several versions of this before and most times it had led right to what I wanted—sex. I was beginning to feel a little more like my old self.

Stephanie continued to describe her dream man and I tried hard to listen, but I couldn't stop my mind from picturing how I thought Stephanie would look naked. When she paused to take a sip of coffee, I said, "I really like your voice. It's so soothing."

Stephanie blushed and reached over the table for my hand. "No one has ever said that to me before. I guess that's another one of your special talents." She stopped, as if weighing her next words very carefully. "I think I'd like to get to know you better."

There it was; the hook was set as Stephanie confirmed she wanted the same thing I did!

And Joann disappeared from my mind.

I was almost there, but I wanted to see the ultimate reward; the sex gleam in her eyes. "I'd like that, too, but you need to know that I can't do anything long-term right now, and I sure don't wanna fall in love." I leaned in closer and asked, "But how about us just spendin' some 'quality' time?"

Stephanie understood what I meant. She didn't say another word. She didn't need to. Her eyes sealed the deal.

* * *

We went back to my place, listened to a few love ballads, and ended up skinny-dipping in the pool. The two of us were relaxing in the Jacuzzi, looking up at the stars, when Stephanie suddenly asked me, "Wanna fool around here?"

I said, "I'm yours," and Stephanie took the reins. She wrapped her arms around my neck and started kissing me.

So I sat back and let her do everything she wanted to. She took complete control, kissing me while moving from body part to body part. It was nice for a change having the girl initiating the moves, but after she finished I felt a little out of sorts, just as I had a few times before, being strictly on the receiving end of sex always felt weird to me.

I believed I needed to be the one leading the way when it came to the sex act, so I took Stephanie by the hand and led her to my bedroom, where I started.

I knew I had achieved complete satisfaction when Stephanie said, "My God, why would anyone throw you away?"

I smiled and kissed her. "Thanks for being there for me tonight."

"Any time, any place." She playfully pinched my rear. "Are you up for doing this more often?"

"Yeah, I'd like to. Just remember, I want nothin' long term and I don't want to fall in love again."

And I truly believed that last statement.

Stephanie left for the night. I went back to the pool and looked aimlessly into the night sky for what seemed like forever. That's when I felt the emptiness overtake me again. Guess it's just one of the side effects of being conceited that I needed to get accustomed to.

* * *

The next morning I went to see Rose at the flower shop. I was surprised when she said, "So sowwy, Little Papa, no pink or yellow roses today, only red and white. You wan 'em?"

Not again! Lately, whenever I came to buy new roses, she didn't have the colors I wanted. I took only the white and red ones and went on my way wondering what the hell was happening.

* * *

With Joann out of my life I chose to start a new chapter: meeting new girls, let them know exactly what I wanted from them, and then quickly moving on. I wasn't going to think about the other person, me, or even the outcomes anymore. I was just going to have some fun. I wasn't getting the help I needed from above anyway, so I had to look for my own signs and symbols. Self-centeredness had taken me completely over.

CHAPTER 14
BEGINNING of a NEW FOCUS

I continued to skate on Wednesdays to see Jane and Bobby even while dating Joann. I had promised I'd be there for him, and I always kept my word. I also gave Jane whatever she wanted from me—sometimes it was money, other times it was time itself, and many times, after Joann left me, it was just good old-fashioned sex. The three of us seemed to get exactly what we needed from each other.

I also continued to guard on Fridays. In the beginning I was the dutiful employee, totally focused on doing my job well. But now, lauded down with my renewed self-centeredness, I decided to take advantage of the opportunity to meet new girls.

One night I said to the owner, "You know, almost everyone likes disco music, and we don't play much of it here and you have us guards wearing these referee uniforms, which does absolutely nothing to show off our individual personalities. Isn't that why you hired me, for my personality? I'd really like to dress a little different and skate to one disco song alone every Friday night. Whaddaya think?"

He pondered my suggestion. "Okay, I don't see why not, at least for one night. Dress however you feel comfortable next week and we'll see what happens."

Come Friday night, I put on an old pair of black Angel Flight pants and a light purple metallic shirt that I pulled out from the rear of my closet, and memories of Disco Phil came flooding back to me. I sprayed on some Red for Men instead of Paco Rabanne, adjusted the Saint Christopher medal around my neck, and then made sure my chest hair was showing through the top of my shirt.

I decided to be a little different and straightforward that night. And I hoped it would get me exactly what I wanted; a sexy bed mate with no strings attached.

* * *

I walked into the rink and many of the regular Friday night skaters came up to me to ask what was going on. "The owner's letting us dress more comfortable. He's also gonna play some of my favorite music with the lyrics I like to dance to."

They didn't seem to understand what I meant about the lyrics, but most agreed it was a nice change of pace.

All night I was much friendlier to the girls than normal, and even though many of them were very receptive, none of them possessed exactly what I was looking for.

Then it happened. A girl who I had never seen skate before walked in with three friends. I watched her while she changed into her skates. She stood about five-feet-five, not counting the three inches of skates she had just put on. Her hair was beautiful—blonde with a hint of red in it. She wore it shoulder length with the ends slightly curved upwards, with a colorful scarf that held it in place. She was on the thin side, but I could see she was definitely a girl where a girl should be. She was dressed all in pink—a light pink top paired with darker pink jeans. All in all, she was put together very nicely, and I knew *this* was the girl I was waiting for.

This vision of loveliness skated around the rink with a confidence—almost a stuck-up attitude—about her. But the thing that gave me a green light was her fantastic smile … well, that and her eyes.

I let her skate past me a few times while I rehearsed in my mind how I was going to approach her. The last time she whizzed by, not only did I notice she had bright pink nail polish, but she also had what looked like a charm attached to one of her fingernails. It was gold in color, but I couldn't see what it actually was. This was to be my opening.

I rolled up to her side, slid my arm around her slim waist, and confidently said, "Hi there, Pinky. I'm Phil, tonight's guard. I haven't seen you here before, so I wanted to welcome you personally."

"Hi, right back at ya," she said as her face turned a cute shade of red. "My real name is Kathy, but I like Pinky, so you can call me that. I just moved here from Indiana and I'm with some friends from my new job."

She continued talking to me, and when I saw the telltale gleam in her eyes, that confirmed she was the right one for me.

"Alright, Pinky," I shot back, "I actually stopped you for another reason though. I saw a flash of gold coming from one of your fingertips as you passed by me. I'm curious, what is it?"

"Oh, you saw my rose charm?" she said very surprised. "Most guys never notice it, never mind mentioning it. So what other minute details have you noticed about me?" She flashed a mischievous smile that almost melted me on the spot.

"You've gone to great lengths to make sure that you look very nice and your smile takes away that haughty attitude you have. And finally, your eyes have a certain glint."

Kathy wasn't all that mad I had somewhat dissed her about her attitude. Instead, Kathy was a good sport. She crossed her eyes at me and said, "What kinda glint? And whaddaya think it means?"

"It's a sensual gleam," I said very serious-like.

"Really?" she said with a hint of sarcasm, "You think I have that?"

"Yep, the eyes are the windows to the soul and they hold all the secrets to what a person really wants," I expertly explained. "Your eyes tell me that you desire a sexual connection with someone. And I think that someone might be me."

"Man, you're direct, but I kinda like that." She blushed and looked away. "No beatings around the bush, no games, just say what's on your mind." She turned her head back my way and looked directly into my eyes. "You know, I think I might bite on that. I'll let you know after skating if I'll take you up on your not so subtle offer."

Pinky began to skate away but called over her shoulder, "I've heard that you can tell a lot about a person by the way they dance, show me what ya got, big boy."

"I know that one, too," I laughed. "Just watch me."

* * *

I rolled over to Mark at the DJ box. He knew about my skating routine back home. I asked him to announce me as "Disco Phil" and to play my special song for my solo skate. Having watched me hitting on "Pinky," he smiled and then told me I was on it.

Two songs later, Mark turned down the music and announced that he had a special treat. "All right ladies, gather round the rink. I wanna introduce you to Disco Phil, he just arrived from parts unknown and I want you to welcome him to Florida. As he skates past you to *Hot Stuff* by Donna Summer, feel free to try and touch him. For some reason he loves to get slapped on the butt. Let's see who can get him the most times. Enjoy what you're about to experience."

When the music started, I whizzed around the rink and almost immediately had girls trying to smack my rear. I was really getting into the music so the gyrations coming from my hips made it all that more difficult, but Pinky was right there center-stage leading the way. Even though all the other girls were delirious, laughing and whooping it up, I still felt that special connection with Pinky.

That ol' special feeling of being the center of attention was back in full force.

* * *

Two things happened when the music stopped. First, the owner asked me to repeat the routine every Friday night. Second, and much more important, was when Pinky skated over to me, smiled, and nodded her head once to indicate *yes*. I knew what she was agreeing to.

We left the rink together and went directly to my house. We had some wine, I put some slow music on, and we had sex by the pool. Afterward, as we were laying side by side looking up at the stars, Kathy giggled and said, "Man, that was fun, I hope we can do this again."

"Absolutely, but I have to tell ya, I'm not interested in a heavy, serious thing. If you feel the need, I'll be there for you, but don't get too used to me. Trust me, I'm no good for you in the long run."

"Again that frankness comes through loud and clear." Kathy shook her head. "But, you're too hard on yourself. Cut yourself some slack. You're good—in more ways than one." She began to run her fingers through the hair on my chest. "You're honest and you don't pull any punches. Believe it or not, most girls like that in a guy. We're tired of playing all the games and we just want what we want. And some of us girls also want 'no strings attached.'"

I can't tell you how comforting it was to hear her say that.

"Girls don't want to get hurt either, ya know." Kathy moved in closer to me. "And I sure don't wanna fall in love right now, myself."

Kathy sat up on one elbow and tapped me absently on the chest with her finger. "This whole night reminds me of a song by James Taylor. *How Sweet It Is To Be Loved By You.* I listen to him when I get depressed and just wanna space out in my room all alone. You were truly a blessing to me tonight."

Kathy kissed me and I watched her attitude perk up. "I'm sure you know that girls like us love to talk about the good ones we meet. Mind if I share what we did with my friends from work?"

I didn't know exactly what she meant by the 'girls like us' comment. I thought *all* girls talked about sex to each other.

I smiled at her. "I do know that girls talk openly about sex. In fact, I count on it. I hope you let all your friends know about me cuz this is the only form of entertainment I like. By the way, where do you work?"

"I just got a job at the Burger Shack over in North Pompano. It's great, I'm always meeting new people, and I feel part of the 'in' crowd."

"You're kidding? I work for them too," I said flabbergasted. "I agree, it is a great place to meet people, especially when you're new in town."

This could get interesting.

* * *

Kathy did tell her friends at work about me and the news quickly got back to my location. My Saturday nights began to look and feel like back home. I no longer went to the drive-in movie theater—I was much too sophisticated for that. Instead, all my dates started at Casey Maxfields for drinks and dancing. Then we would retreat to my house for a late night swim and whatever else followed. I know what you're thinking, but it wasn't *always* sex, and I was fine with that. Stop laughing, I was.

I was doing what my dad always told me to do; enjoying the life I was living and the benefits that my que sera, sera lifestyle brought to me. I didn't even think about where it could lead me or whether it was right or wrong. I found myself addicted to the feeling of being in control and finally making all the important decisions in my life. Oh yeah, and I truly loved the meaningless sex part.

But deep down inside the emptiness grew.

CHAPTER 15
FAYE

About a month after my one-nighter with Pinky, my boss said I was getting promoted. I had been picked by upper management to open a new Burger Shack down the coast in nearby Pompano Beach. While there the PB location afforded me the opportunity to meet a whole new group of people. Two guys who were cooks, and were about the same age as me, became fast friends. Barney, Rick, and I would hang out at the local bars after work and check out the "scenery." In fact, a day would come where the three of us would share an experience that none of us would ever forget. More about that later.

During the grand opening of the restaurant I met many of the workers from the other stores in the mall. One of whom was Faye, the manager of Cozy Bug, a ladies apparel shop across the hall. A few weeks later she came in for lunch, went to pay for her order, and realized she didn't have enough money. She got all nervous and flustered until I stepped in.

"Look we've all been there," I said. "Let's make a deal. I'll take care of your lunch, if you'll go out for drinks with me after work tonight."

"Thank you. Meet me at six by the main exit," she said. "I look forward to it."

Since moving to Florida, I'd heard that accent enough times to recognize it as Cuban.

* * *

Faye requested that we go to her favorite bar, Ray's Place. We sat in a small red leather booth and I couldn't help noticing I was the only white guy in the place. Faye was indeed of Cuban descent and we were obviously in a Cuban bar. I had been to lesbian bars, gay bars, and bars that catered to various other nationalities, so I was just fine here, too.

Faye made it even more relaxing with the look in her eyes—her trust was evident.

She talked about her job and I started to size her up. I saw a twenty-four year old with long dark curly black hair. She had the deepest brown eyes—they almost looked black—that I had seen since Carmen's back home. Her eyebrows were extremely full and groomed. Her face was perfect; no blemishes or early wrinkles, just soft, cocoa-colored skin. Her fingers were long and slender with a ring on each one and her perfectly manicured fingernails were painted a color of red I'd never seen before. She wore gold bracelets on both wrists.

I longed to see the parts that lurked beneath by her clothes.

Faye was tall, about six feet, and extremely slender, with a unique smell, one of spices which made me think of Christmas. I later found out it was a perfume from Cuba that she always wore. I focused back on her face and noticed a key thing that wasn't present—the sex gleam. Sex was always on my mind and I took this to mean she wasn't interested in me that way.

Although a man could dream, can't he?

Faye ordered a Cuban drink I'd never heard of before and I ordered my usual white wine. She asked me point-blank, "Are you gay?"

"No," I gasped. "What makes you think that?"

"It is just that most guys I know who drink white wine are, so I just assumed," Faye shrugged. "There is nothing wrong with it if you are."

"Believe me, I'm quite the opposite of being gay."

I could see Faye had no idea what I was implying.

I changed my drink order to a vodka tonic and that seemed to please her.

"Now that is more like what a real man would drink," she winked at me.

Maybe she did know what I was thinking after all.

I let her do most of the talking as we drank. "I came from Cuba two years ago with my grandmother. My parents are still there. I will not get to see them unless the government changes their rules. So I will probably never see them again." A reflective silence hung over us for a minute as Faye slowly took a sip of her drink.

Her Cuban accent was such a turn on. And I loved that she never used any American abbreviations or contractions when she spoke.

"I have a few good friends here, but mainly I am a loner. My boyfriend was killed trying to come to America. I have not really dated anyone since. I do not want to get too close to anyone else for fear something bad will happen to them, too. I am better off alone."

Now the absentee sex gleam made sense to me.

Faye was crying a little and I felt her pain. When I reached for her hand to comfort her, she flinched. She clearly had a trust issue with people.

This prompted a change in the reason I wanted to be with her. I still had a sensitive side, you know!

"That must've been a terrible time in your life. I can see that you're still affected by the feelings you had for him. I've had the same kind of thing happen to me and I reacted the same way."

Faye was busy fidgeting with her straw, but I knew I had her attention. "I found that once I was able to count on someone my life got better. You're a very beautiful lady, so I'm sure that many guys have tried to pick you up using sleazy lines or hollow promises. I'll never do that. I'd rather be there when you need someone to cry on, to listen to you, or just to be there."

And I really think I mean that.

"That would be great. Right now I do not have anyone I can depend on except myself." Faye composed herself. "You are right. Most of the guys I meet are jerks. They think only about themselves, or how to bed me. But you are different. You have a calm effect on me. I know I can trust you already because you actually listened to me. You shared some emotion, which most men cannot. Now let me ask you a question, can you dance?"

The two of us made our way to the small dance floor. The music was Cuban, which had the same beats as the Latin music I used to move to with Carmen so I was able to keep up with Faye quite well. She winked and asked me again, "Are you *sure* you are not gay?"

And I wondered, Could this night be a turning point in my life?

* * *

Faye and I were hanging out together more often. She became a frequent guest at our house. My dad and Dewey got to know her, and she accepted them for who they were. Faye and I shared many nights of dinners, drinks, and dancing together. The more we got to know and trust each other, the more we shared—things like moonlit skinny-dips in my pool while listening to my Rod Stewart and Bread cassettes.

I found it ironic that although Faye was sexually repressed, at the same time she was very comfortable being totally naked around me. I wondered if it was a cultural thing.

Even though I finally got to see Faye in her "birthday suit," it didn't seem the same as when I saw other girls naked. It was comfortable, it was natural, and it was innocent. Maybe it wasn't a cultural thing after all. Maybe it was just a trust thing.

And just like Mary, my first girlfriend, Faye and I never shared sex. The subject didn't come up and I stopped looking for the sex gleam to suddenly pop into her eyes. We were having plenty of fun just being friends.

It had been a long time since I felt so comfortable being with a girl without sharing sex. Faye made me realize, at least for the time being, that I didn't always need sex with a girl if I had a "real friend" to share some time with.

* * *

One night as we were lounging in the pool we heard Bread sing *Baby I'm-A Want You*. A week later Faye and I made plans to go out dancing, but before I could get off the couch, she stopped me with a question: "Why do you wear the clothes that you do?"

"Beg your pardon?" I immediately went on the defensive. "It's my style and the image I want to project. I feel very comfortable wearing these clothes."

"First of all, you *look* gay, and the scent of Paco Rabanne is not for macho men at all," Faye laughed. "Remember you live in Florida, and that you love women, not men. What you need is a new image—one that reflects our lifestyle and our weather. One that will help you be who you really are."

That did it! Instead of dancing, that night Faye and I went shopping. And just like years earlier when Joyce reinvented me, I allowed Faye the pleasure of updating me with a new image.

"I'll buy anything you pick out, as long as you'll be seen with me wearin' it," I said. "I trust that you won't embarrass me."

I'd forgotten Faye was an apparel professional. She knew exactly what she wanted, and where to get it. Faye set me up in both black and blue Sergio Valente jeans. They had the same cut as my old pants, but were a much more relaxed fit. She then had me buy khaki shorts, as the hot summer days of Florida would prohibit jeans—unless I liked to sweat a lot. I reluctantly agreed to the shorts, still harboring the age-old feeling that my legs were too skinny.

As for shirts, Faye favored bright colors. She had me buying colorful, lightweight t-shirts which I was to wear underneath button-down shirts which were made to remain unbuttoned and un-tucked from my pants. She complemented the shirts with the same color belts. She then showed me how to mix and match colors and styles so that I always looked in fashion. I was instructed to start wearing my Gemini charm and St. Christopher medal on the outside of the t-shirts she'd just picked out for me. She had me buy socks which matched the color of the shirts—but I wasn't allowed to wear them anywhere except roller skating—along with a pair of slip-on leather loafers that she said needed no socks.

When I came out of the dressing room all decked out in my new garbs, I said, "Well, I hope this is what ya like, 'cuz I think it makes me look even gayer than before."

Faye just laughed. "Just you wait. The girls will love the new Phil. Now you have a style all of your own. Besides, you have the necessary confidence to wear anything and make it look good on you."

Wow. It had been a while since Faye had given me a compliment. I wondered what that actually meant. Was the way she felt about me changing?

Much to my surprise my new wardrobe actually did work. The next time the two of us went dancing I was the hit of the bar. So much so that I sensed Faye was getting jealous. I had girls wanting to dance with me and some who wanted even more. When Faye would go to the restroom, certain girls would sidle up to me and drop unmistakable hints about having sex with me.

And even though Faye brought out my dominant sensitive side, I could feel my buried ego fighting to resurface. I wondered, Hmmmm. Which one's going to win?

* * *

Faye and I hung out together for about six more months, but I was getting extremely anxious. I occasionally slept with other girls because Faye and I were still strictly friends, but more and more I found myself wanting to have sex with her, plain and simple.

One night after way too much drinking and even closer dancing, Faye and I ended up back at my house. We were skinny-dipping once again when I drunkenly decided to make my move.

I swam up to her, and planted a booze-breath kiss squarely on her lips. "Why ain't we ever had sex? We do practically everything else but. I say it's 'bout time we do the deed."

Faye pulled back as if I had slapped her. "I thought you were different, Phil. I enjoy our time together because I do not have to think about that. I love the way we dance. We can count on each other for good advice and how we always make each other smile. And now you want to risk ruining all that with sex?"

"Look, other ladies are fallin' over each other to have sex with me," I said all cocky, "but you never even think about it." I tossed my head back, lightly spraying her with my wet hair. "The physical part is what I'm interested in now. Yeah, I enjoy your company, but I need more from you. In fact, if we don't have sex soon," the alcohol and my ego teamed up to say, "I just may have to move on."

"Do not worry about that, Casanova," Faye jumped out of the pool. "I will." She got dressed, and stormed out of my house, and out of my life.

I never saw or heard from her again.

Well, I proved to myself once more I really was a self-centered man. Thanks to my selfish actions, I knew I had lost a friend that night, but I wasn't overly concerned. In fact, nothing except the wonderment of who would be my next conquest was my initial thought. But deep inside, there were a whole lot of rotten feelings rumbling around. I soon hated myself for what I had done to Faye, and to some of the other ladies I had been with. Since when did sex become so damned important to me that I stopped caring for the girls I was with? And I also began to hate myself for what I was becoming, and God for letting me become this person.

I went inside to my room and I immediately noticed the vase of white and red roses on my dresser wasn't in full bloom anymore. The white roses were still bright and alive. But the red ones were shriveling up, ready to die. I had bought them at the same time just the other day when Rose didn't have any yellow or pink ones left. Why is this happening all the time? I wondered.

I knew I had made another stupid mistake in my life. Was that why all my roses were rapidly dying on me? I put my head in my hands and thought I was going to cry. I couldn't imagine what could possibly cheer me up, until I looked back up and my eyes drifted to the calendar on the wall. That's right; *Spring Break* is coming to Florida!

CHAPTER 16
DONNA

I'd been told Spring Break was a huge deal in Florida, especially in Fort Lauderdale and Daytona Beach. I was getting all psyched up to hang out at the bars on the strip with Barney and Rick in order to "work my magic" on some out-of-state girls. That was, until I received a phone call from Missouri—it was Billy.

"Hey, my brother and I are comin' down to Florida for Spring Break with a few friends. I know you live in Lauderdale, but we're going up to Daytona. We'll be there tomorrow," he said. "It's a ride, but can you make it?"

"Make it?" I whooped. "I'll be waitin' for ya."

The next morning I packed, jumped into my car, and set off on the four hour ride to Daytona Beach. Along the way I pondered what kind of trouble Billy and I could get into.

I pulled into the hotel where Billy had booked four rooms, and parked the car. When I walked into the lobby, a tall lanky brunette with her hair in a bun, slightly oversized glasses, and wearing a dark brown vest strutted past me. I swear she winked at me, and I said to myself, This is going to be fun.

* * *

Billy and his group pulled in about two hours later. When we shook hands, he said, "Man, you look great. You're smiling, you seem happy, and the tan ... it's a good thing. Since when do you wear shorts? What's your secret?"

I smiled and winked. "The secret is good looking women, great white wine, and all the sex you can handle."

Billy replied, "Ah, my sentiments exactly, well, not the wine part."

* * *

The first week we were in town a new television station called MTV was also there. They were hosting their first Spring Break party. Billy and I were sharing a fourth floor room on the corner of the hotel which afforded a great view of the bands that were playing in front of the big blue ocean behind it. One afternoon we were sitting on the balcony drinking and listening to the music when there was a knock on the door.

A young male producer from MTV introduced himself and said, "You guys have the best view in the hotel. Can we use it when *A Flock of Seagulls* performs tomorrow night? We're airing it live on TV."

Billy and I said almost in unison, "What's in it for us?"

"We'll make it worth your while. You'll get all sorts of things from the sponsors like shorts, t-shirts, and their products. We'll also leave you any leftover pizza, beer, and wine from our little get together. And more importantly you'll get to party with some of the most beautiful girls on the beach."

Need I say we didn't have to think it over?

* * *

The next afternoon I went downstairs to the hotel lobby store to buy some more white wine. When I walked in, I saw the same tall brunette who had passed by me on that first day. It was then I realized she worked at the store.

I put the wine on the counter, went for my wallet to pay, and she asked, "Is that for the concert tonight? Or are you going to drink it all alone?"

Looking up I saw a hopeful face, one that reminded me of Barbie Benton, and her eyes were sparkling through her glasses, again the gleam I was always hoping for.

I confidently said, "Well it *was* all for me, unless you wanna help? I'm on the corner of the fourth floor overlooking the stage."

She jumped at the opportunity. We exchanged names, hers was Donna, and then I left. At first I was excited at the possibilities this presented to me, but then I began to wonder if she was serious, or if she flirted like that with everyone.

* * *

When the concert started I was sitting on the stairs in the hallway listening to the music with Billy's brother, Brian. I was drinking my white wine and he was giving me hell about it.

"Why do you drink that shit?" Brian said, taking a pull from the cheap can of Milwaukee's Best beer he clung to.

"I like the taste *and* the results I get from it," I replied, raising an eyebrow.

Brian just let out a long loud burp, chugged the rest of his beer, and popped open another.

The small area around us was getting crowded fast and becoming extremely loud. There were lots of intoxicated kids milling around waiting for the party in our room to start. Somehow the news had spread throughout the hotel. The guys in the next room opened their door and luckily everyone crowded in. Brian and I decided to stay in the hallway and continue our drinking. I wasn't sure he could walk anyway since he had been pounding down the beer nonstop.

I was right in the middle of a sip of wine when *she* approached us ... this six-foot brunette beauty wearing a small yellow bikini barely covered with an open white blouse.

I knew both Brian and I were staring, but I really didn't care if she caught us.

She stopped in front of us, put a hand on her hip, and said, "Phil? Do you remember me?"

To be honest I didn't recognize her at first without her glasses and her hair now hanging down loose, not to mention I was fixated by those perfect breasts.

Brian gazed at her and said in a drunken stupor, "Wow, you are the mos' bootiful gurl I ever seen. Wanna sit on my lap 'n see what comes up?"

"Seeing how drunk you are I don't think *anything* can come up." She smiled at her joke. "Besides, I'm here for him." And she pointed her lovely forefinger right at me.

Brian turned to me. "Why 'n hell would a bootiful gurl like her want yer wine-sippin' ass?"

Before I could reply, Donna chirped, "He's friendly, but not too pushy. And I like the way he dresses. I especially like the fact that he has enough confidence to have wine while all the rest of you drunkards are slurping down the cheapest beers you can find."

Brian got up and left stumbling and mumbling something about how unfair the world was to him.

As he bounced off the walls of the hallway, I was thinking about what just happened. Whatever I had done for Donna to notice me had worked, for I had just attracted a stark raving beauty that was probably way out of my league. And I was feeling a little intimidated by that.

"Thanks for the compliments," I managed to get out before motioning her over. "Come here, let's share some wine and you can tell me about yourself."

Donna sat down on the stairs so close to me her bare leg rubbed up against mine. She sipped some wine out of my glass, then said, "I'm twenty-five, divorced, and I live with my sister in her beach house. I work as a cocktail waitress over at Freedom, a bar on the strip, along with working here part-time. I'm just trying to enjoy life. How about you?"

Although in the past I've prided myself on my listening skills, I didn't really hear everything she said. I was too busy taking in her body and trying to conceal my excitement, in more ways than one.

"I'm twenty years old, but my whole life I've always felt much older than my real age. I'm new to Fort Lauderdale, staying with my dad. I always try to be upfront, so I have to tell you that I'm feeling something different around you … a kind of magnetism."

Donna nodded her understanding.

Billy came by and I introduced him to Donna. He covertly flashed me his thumbs up approval, then said to her, "I've given Phil grief ever since we got here about his drinkin' wine. I guess he is right though, the most beautiful girls really do like it. If I start drinking it, do you have a friend who looks like you that'll go out with me, too?"

"I like you, you're cute," Donna laughed. "I can think of a friend that may like you and you don't even have to drink wine. When we get into your room I'll call her for you. You just have to promise me that you can make it worth her while to come over here. Can you do that?"

Billy actually blushed as he shook his head in agreement.

* * *

Finally, the concert ended and the MTV people left. While Billy and I went through the room for what they left behind, Donna called her friend. We found two kegs of beer along with some pizza and a pleasant surprise for me—five bottles of champagne. We invited some people in to help get rid of the beer and pizza while Donna and I hid the champagne. Brian was even more blitzed than before, but that didn't stop him from walking the halls wearing a sheet like a toga looking for any girl who would want to hang with him. He filled an empty ice bucket with beer from the keg and found someone who was interested in his offer. He disappeared into her room for the rest of the night.

Donnas' friend showed up about a half hour later and as I invited her in, Billy told everyone else they had to leave. While Billy and Sarah got to know each other better, Donna grabbed a bottle of the champagne, popped it open, and the two of us went out onto the balcony.

We stood at the railing, our bodies touching, and I felt as though we were in one of those romantic made-for-TV movies. From out of the blue, soft romantic music played in the background and, as we sipped our champagne and gazed out at the ocean, I felt something come over me— my soft sensitive side was paying a visit. Instead of spouting something cocky or inappropriate I said, "You're so beautiful. I have no idea what you see in me, but I'm flattered. Would it be okay if I kissed you?"

Donna chuckled. "You're too damn polite. Do you even have to ask? I've been waiting for this since the first time I saw you pass me in the lobby."

So I was right, she did wink at me! And the movie continued.

Donna and I began to kiss and the ocean began to swirl. Strong winds kicked up and blew clouds over the full moon above us. We were plunged into a relaxing darkness as I felt her hands exploring my butt. And as *Some Romantic Evening* played in the background, Donna whispered in my ear, "It feels just like it looks, nice and tight. Now I'm ready for more ..."

I just love it when the girl starts the action!

* * *

What happened next in our romantic movie would have turned the TV censor's hair white. Donna and I rushed over to one of the rooms Billy had reserved and had sex over and over in positions that would have made the Karma Sutra couple blush.

In the morning, Donna asked, "Where'd you get to be so good in just twenty years? If you don't watch out, I could get used to this."

"They say practice makes perfect, so I've practiced a lot," I replied. But I felt something with Donna that I hadn't in a long time. I felt good about myself. Maybe I was changing.

* * *

The next few nights Donna showed Billy and me the hot spots of Daytona Beach, including Freedom, the bar where she worked. Billy wanted me to help us find more new girls, but I was only interested in Donna. Billy didn't understand, but Brian sure did. He kept trying to tell him, "Why would Phil settle for seconds when he already has the best lady in Florida?"

When Donna told me I was the sweetest guy she'd ever known, the emptiness that I normally harbored magically disappeared.

* * *

It was a warm, rainy day as I was getting ready to leave Daytona. I asked Donna, "Will I ever see you again?"

Donna swept the rain away from her cheeks. Or was it tears? "I certainly hope so. I was attracted to you physically right away, and now I'm attracted emotionally, too. You're real. There's nothing fake about you. You tell it like it is and expect the same in return. You're the best guy I've met since moving here. I would love for you to come back up here, or I can come down to you. Either way, we can't let it end like this."

And it didn't. Donna and I met every weekend. Twice a month I'd come up to see her, and the other two times she drove down to me. And over the next few months we experienced many things together—we ate at the best restaurants, drank the best wines, danced at the best clubs, and shared many nights of the best sex.

Over time, Donna showed me arrogance wasn't something I needed in order to feel good about myself. I was changing for the better, but I was also scared of what might come of this relationship. So far, love had never worked for me.

* * *

Donna was open, she was free, and she knew what she liked. She treated me as well as anyone ever had before. One afternoon she bought me a white cotton sports coat. I wore it each and every time we were together. She told me the Florida-style was to push up the sleeves. Everywhere we went, we were "the couple" people noticed. I knew they were all looking at her—but she never saw it that way. She always said we had a special connection, one that not only we, but others could feel.

There was one extraordinary experience which exemplifies this connection. It was my weekend to drive to Daytona. Normally I would make hotel reservations before I left, but this time I didn't have enough time. I figured I would find the right place when I arrived. I made my way down the long Daytona strip and passed many hotels. But when I drove by this certain one, The Palomino, I felt a strong tug in my chest, near my heart, which drew my attention to the hotel. But I ignored the feeling, and continued on right past.

I drove the entire length of the strip, turned around, and started to backtrack. This time as I passed The Palomino I felt that strange sensation again. This time I stopped and booked a room.

I put my things away in room 616 and then drove to the bar where Donna worked. But when I entered, she wasn't there. What? I thought, she always has me pick her up here.

One of the waitresses approached me and said, "Donna left earlier, but here's a phone number she asked me to give to you when you arrived."

So I drove back to The Palomino and called the number on the paper.

After six anguishing rings, Donna answered. "Hey," I said, trying to keep my cool. "Where are you?"

"I found the perfect place for us to spend the weekend. The room has two French doors which open up to a great big balcony that overlooks the ocean," she said in a lilting voice. "I have a feeling tonight's going to be special, so get your ass to The Palomino as fast as you can."

The phone dropped from my suddenly numb hand. After I picked it back up, Donna nervously asked, "What happened?"

"You're not going to believe this," I laughed. "I'm already here."

"No. Quit playing games, Phil." She seriously didn't believe me.

"Donna, I swear." I was still laughing out of my disbelief. "Room 616. Come on up and—"

I was interrupted by a faint knock on the door which connected my room to the adjoining one. I carried the phone with me as I unlocked it, and standing there looking like she was seeing a ghost, was Donna.

After hanging up our now useless phones, I gave her a long sensuous kiss to prove I was real. I then told her about the eerie feeling I'd had while driving by. It turned out Donna had been in the adjoining room both times when I passed by the hotel. There was no denying our "special connection" had pulled us together through bricks and mortar. It made us both wonder if maybe there was *something else* running our lives.

And through it all, I actually felt something I had been missing since coming to Florida. *There was a small surge of warmth in my heart.*

Could this possibly be a sign?

* * *

We had another strange connection thing happen—but this one was physical. Donna and I were sitting on the beach holding hands one afternoon when I casually looked at her right hand. I was amazed; I'd never noticed it before this. Her right pinky finger was crooked and bent to the left at the first knuckle.

"How'd that happen to your finger?" I said, trying to be gentle about it.

"It's always been that way, ever since I can remember," Donna said, covering it with her left hand. "Why?"

I lifted my right hand up to show her my pinky finger. It looked exactly the same. I said, "I was born like this."

Donna gasped and stared in amazement.

"My great-grandmother had the same characteristic. We were very close. In fact, I sometimes think I can still hear her talkin' to me," I explained.

I placed my crooked finger alongside Donnas' and we looked at each other in wonderment. A shiver went through me as I said, "I wonder if we're somehow related?"

I called my aunt back home—just to confirm that we weren't.

After I hung up the phone and gave Donna a hug she asked, "Do you believe in fate and signs from above?"

I shook my head in agreement, as a twinge of warmth radiated through my body.

* * *

On her birthday, Donna and I had an experience that made us wonder, yet another time, if our lives had been scripted for us and we were just acting out the parts.

The day before I was to drive up to Daytona, Donna and I talked on the phone. "Is there anything special you wanna do for your birthday?"

"Yes!" she gushed. "I'd love to see Billy Hughes in concert. He's in town doing a benefit for his charity. If we can get tickets, I'd love to go."

Billy Hughes was a local Florida singer who was highly popular with everyone who drank at the beach hangouts. He only did concerts in these small bars and clubs. I had heard of him before, so I agreed to go. Unfortunately, the show was sold out and Donna couldn't even find any scalper tickets.

* * *

The night before her birthday the two of us went to dinner. After sharing a nice meal, Donna and I decided to go dancing, like we normally did. We both loved to dance and were very good together. Our bodies moved in perfect rhythm, whether it was a fast or a slow song.

Now you know why our sex was so good, too.

Donna wanted to go to the best dance spot in Daytona; a dance bar on the top floor of the Platinum Building. It slowly rotated 360 degrees showing off the skyline of the city below and a fantastic view of the ocean. Most tourists didn't even know it existed, so it was populated mostly by upscale locals and visiting celebrities.

That night, instead of a band, their house DJ was playing a wide array of songs. We found a table, bought a bottle of champagne for an early start on celebrating her birthday, and began to dance the night away. As usually happened, we soon became the focal point of the room. While our bodies moved together in perfect harmony, we could feel the eyes of everyone else in the bar upon us. That always made us dance with even more intensity.

We both loved the attention.

I felt bad Donna wasn't going to get to see Billy Hughes in concert, so I asked the DJ if he had any of his music. Donna told me her favorite Hughes song was *Wonderin' My Way Back Home*. It was a slow song which most of his fans didn't know about because it was on one of his earliest albums. Obviously Donna had some type of connection to it.

To my surprise, the DJ thumbed through a stack of records and held up the album. I asked him to please dedicate the song to Donna for her birthday. He must have been a romantic himself. He added to the dedication that it was her favorite song from her favorite artist. And as Billy sang soulfully in the background, we looked each other square in the eyes and began to dance. Donna and I were the only couple on the floor so we really got into it big time. The more we danced the more we began to lose ourselves to the emotions of the song.

It was just the two of us in the world right then.

Toward the end of it, Donna rested her head on my shoulder and started to cry a little.

"Are you okay?" I asked.

"I'll be fine. This song takes me back ..." she whispered wiping away a tear. "Back to when I was married."

Donna didn't need to say anything else. I understood all too well.

The song ended and I gently kissed her lips, oblivious to everyone else in the room. Donna and I remained lip locked for a long minute until we were brought back to reality when everyone in the room started clapping for us.

We returned to our table to have some more champagne, and almost immediately a man and his wife came over. He asked if they could join us. I stared at them a few seconds as they seemed an odd couple. I guessed they were both in their mid-forties but found them totally mismatched. He was wearing blue jeans, a raggedy old shirt, had on a floppy hat with long gray hair flowing out of it and was wearing gold-rimmed sunglasses. She, on the other hand, was dressed to the max in a gold sparkling dress, white panty hose with gold heels, and was covered in gold jewelry.

I reluctantly agreed they could sit with us, and we exchanged pleasantries. The man introduced himself as William, and his wife as Jane. He first ordered another bottle of the champagne we were drinking, then turned to Donna and me, reached across the table and patted both of our hands.

He said with a thick Southern drawl, "The missus an' me, we been watchin' you guys dance—jus' like ever'body else in the joint. Yer pretty damn good tagether. There's a big ol' look-a love on yer faces an' a feelin' of belongin' you two give off. We really done enjoyed watchin' you guys dance."

He gave Donnas' hand an extra squeeze and said, "Honey, I understan' yer birthday's comin' up soon. What're you two gonna do?"

Donna was a little taken aback by his aggressiveness. "Well, I had really hoped to see the Billy Hughes concert tomorrow night, but the tickets are all sold out." She gave a little shrug of her shoulders. "No big deal, I have Phil, so I guess I don't need anything else."

William almost jumped out of his seat. "Well, hot doggie! Guess what? You two're in luck. I jus' happen ta have an extra pair-a tickets." William slapped the table with his palm. "I have me a few connections, an' Jane an' I would be very happy ta escort you guys 'morrow night, jus' cuz it made us feel so damn good watchin' you lovebirds dance to that there song."

Donna thanked him, but I could tell she didn't believe he had tickets. The four of us drank some more, laughed it up, and had a real good time together, all the same.

At one point in the conversation, William asked Donna, "Where ya guys stayin'? I'll have a car come by 'morrow evenin' an' pick ya'll up."

Donna told him, thanked him again, and we continued to down the champagne.

After a really crude joke, William glanced at his watch. "My God. Lookit the time. C'mon dear, we gotta hit the road. Bye, guys." And with that, he grabbed his wife's hand, and they were gone in a blink.

Donna and I hung around another half hour and laughed it off. What were the odds that strange dude actually had extra tickets, let alone he'd come pick us up?

"What was it with the sunglasses?" Donna chuckled. "Did he think he was Elvis or something?"

In the end we decided to be ready, but not to get too upset if the offer was all hot air.

* * *

The next night we waited in the lobby of our hotel watching the time tick away. We were beginning to feel foolish and decided to go dancing. As we walked though the revolving front door, a long, black limousine pulled into the driveway right in front of us. The driver, an older guy with silver hair, got out and approached us. "Are youse guys Donna and Phil?"

We instinctively grabbed each other's hand and nodded, somewhat stupefied.

"I'ma Guido, and I'ma here to get youse to the concert. William and his wife are very sorry that they can'ta join ya, but they were called away on abusiness. They told me to make sure youse were taken good care of. There's a bottle of champagne that youse like in the limo, and if ya need anything else just aska me."

We looked at each other, shrugged in unison, and then followed Guido to the limo.

He drove along the strip while we drank the champagne and relaxed into the moment. Once we pulled up to the concert venue and exited the limo we were treated like royalty. A young lady, in a black dress with stiletto heels, met us and escorted us to our seats, which to our complete shock just happened to be in the front row.

The concert arena was a small one, holding only about 500 people. This performance was a benefit, with all the proceeds being donated to the new charity Billy Hughes had just founded. We sat in disbelief as the lights went low. Everyone was anxious for the concert to begin, but before the music started, Billy came out on stage to thank everyone for their generosity, and for coming to see him.

He rubbed his hands together and let loose a sly smile; then said with only a slight accent, "Before I start singin' tonight, I need to share a story. Last night, the missus and I wanted to get away and relax before tonight's show. So I put on the getup I use to travel incognito. We ended up at a quiet little bar the concierge told us about, after slippin' her some cash. We were just sittin' there, listenin' to some music and having a few cocktails, when we saw this wonderful younger couple." Billy reached for the glass on a nearby stool, probably containing whiskey, or iced tea, and took a sip.

"Lemme tell ya, I've been feelin' a little down lately. I feel like no one cares about my early songs. Man, those are the ones that I really connect with the most."

A voice in the back of the room called out, "I still dig 'em, Billy!"

Billy held up his glass in tribute, took another gulp and said, "Well, last night these two kids made me feel alive again. They obviously were in love and it showed. When they danced they had an energy everyone else in the room could feel. Man, they even requested one of my favorite old songs, *Wonderin' My Way Back Home*."

By this time, Donna and I realized he was talking about us. The couple we met the night before were in fact Billy and Jane Hughes. *No wonder the Elvis sunglasses.*

"You two know who you are, so com'on up here," Billy waved to us.

Hand in hand, Donna and I walked up the steps onto the stage. Billy grabbed his guitar and began wailing away with *Wonderin' My Way Back Home*. He gestured for us to dance, and we did, but as though we were alone, not in front of five hundred people. What a connection we had! When Donna started to cry, I cried with her. And I felt a wonderful exhilaration come over me. Donna must have felt it, too. She hugged me tighter than ever and a beautiful smile told me the old melancholy feelings were gone.

Two hours later, Billy finished his third encore song. Donna and I were escorted backstage by the same lady in the black dress who greeted us, and we got to thank Billy and Jane in person. Billy, in turn, thanked Donna for being a fan of what he called his "real music."

He put his arms around both of us and said, "You guys made me feel young again. Man, I love that feelin'. Here's hopin' you guys are together forever."

Billy kissed Donna on the cheek, autographed her ticket, then grabbed Jane's hand and just like the night before, they were gone in a blink.

Donna and I just stood there with our jaws hanging open.

"So," she said self-consciously, "Do *you* think we will be together forever?"

I remembered what had always happened in the past when I let down the walls around my heart. Man, I really wanted to but I was much too scared to try. To this day, I can't remember how I answered her question.

* * *

And I certainly can't explain why, about three months of sheer ecstasy later, Donna and I finally had to admit the driving force in our relationship was our love of dancing and sex. Our love for each other never reached full-bloom.

The anticipation of seeing each other was fading fast. I was getting tired of traveling four hours just to go dancing and then get laid; and so was she. I had literally become that old joke: "I have a huge sex drive — my girlfriend lives 500 miles away."

On her last visit down to Fort Lauderdale, I knew we were through. But I wanted to end it on a high note.

Just before she got into her car to leave, I pulled Donna into my arms and hugged her with all my might. "Donna, we met at just the right time. I needed a boost in my confidence and you definitely gave me that. I hope I was able to give you something you really needed, as well."

Donna kissed me to let me know that I had.

"We were very good together, and in a different place and time things may have been different." I found myself fighting back some tears. "We both know it's over, but I have something for you. Please remember me, and all the great times we shared."

I presented Donna with a copy of Billy Hughes's album. I'd written on it: *I will always love you in my own crazy way.* I also gave her a red silk rose.

I really did try to love her, you know.

Donna started to cry.

"Please don't." I held her as tight as I could, not really knowing if I wanted her to go or not. "Remember that talk when we first met? Neither of us wanted to fall in love or get hurt again. And we both got what we said we wanted."

Donna wiped away her tears, kissed me softly, and as she drove off, forever, I was the one who was crying.

* * *

In retrospect, I have to say Donna was very good for me. She gave me the opportunity to experience being with one girl again, and I realized I could get used to that, if and when the right one came along. But I also wondered, So who's next?

CHAPTER 17
THE NEXT ONES IN LINE

I started spending many nights with Barney and Rick after Donna and I stopped seeing each other. I was missing her way more than I expected to, and the empty feeling I carried before I met her had returned, with even more vehemence. But I couldn't let them know that.

The three of us would hang out at The Liquor Store, a Fort Lauderdale bar situated right in the middle of the strip. Its perfect location made it a huge hangout for the out-of-state college girls who were visiting. There was always something good to look at as we sat and drank with each other.

Barney was originally from New York—he had that Brooklyn attitude about him which reminded me a little of Lars. He was loud, obnoxious, and truly thought he was God's gift to women. Unfortunately, no one told the women. Barney was always trying to pick up a girl, but rarely found any takers. He frequently became frustrated with me because I instantly knew which girls to ask, and he didn't have a clue how I selected them. So Barney mostly sat and got drunk.

Rick was born and raised in Lauderdale. He had blond hair and green eyes—you know the surfer boy look—and the tan to go with it. From a distance he looked good to the girls, but talking face-to-face with women wasn't his strong point. Rick also got mad at me; he couldn't connect with the ladies either. Sometimes he got by just on his looks.

One night the three of us were sitting at the bar when these three beautiful girls walked in. They were over-dressed and loud enough so every guy knew they had arrived. We had each put away several drinks by this time and were three sheets to the wind. Even though I was drunk, I knew just by looking at these ladies what their game was.

They sat at the bar directly across from us and smiled at Barney. Unfortunately he approached them first. He bought them all a drink, talked to them for a few minutes, then retreated to us with a big fat frown on his face. Both Rick and I knew he had been rejected again, three times over.

The girls then started flirting with Rick. He was just drunk enough to walk over to them, buy them another round of drinks, but returned, even faster than Barney had. The two of them resumed drinking and were finally able to laugh as they watched two more guys do the same thing.

Like I said before, I knew the game these ladies were playing. They were just getting drunk for free—compliments of the horny guys in the bar. But my gut instinct told me the girls weren't at all interested in any of the *guys.*

Barney nudged me and said, "Man, it's your turn."

I turned to him and shook my head. "No way, I'm not wastin' my hard earned money on those lesbians."

"There's no way they're lesbians." He twisted up his face. "Lesbians are all butch and ugly. Those girls just don't know a good thing when they see one."

"Really?" I smiled. "If I can prove to you that they like women, will you and Rick pick up my bar tab for the next month?"

They laughed and quickly agreed.

I snatched up my drink and moseyed over to the women in question. "Hi ladies, I've been watching you accept drinks from all the guys here, and then send them away empty-handed." I motioned over toward Barney and Rick. "My friends in particular are extremely mad."

The girls just smiled at me like they knew that would happen, and actually enjoyed making these guys suffer.

I took a sip of my drink. "I told 'em not to get so upset that a group of lesbians aren't interested in them. I know you're just here for kicks, so if you come with me and tell my friends that you aren't interested in men, I'll take you to the most exciting unisex bar off the strip, Behind the Scenes. My dad owns it, so I can get you everything for free. And I can promise there will be some very sexy bi ladies you'll be more interested in."

The three of them looked at me with astonishment. Then the prettiest of the bunch said, "How'd you know we're lesbians? No other guy can ever tell."

Over a drink *they* bought me, I explained about my mentor, Joyce, and all my lesbian friends back home. Then I pressed, "So, ya wanna go have some real fun?"

They talked amongst themselves for a minute and agreed that Behind the Scenes was worth a try.

The four of us started walking over to Barney and Rick, and I whispered to them, "Do me a favor? Will you prove to my friends that you are indeed lesbians?"

They laughed, and when we were in front of Barney and Rick not only did they kiss each other, the prettiest one flashed her full-sized breasts and said, "Sorry guys, these are only reserved for the fairer sex. Just thought I'd show you what you're missin'."

The three beautiful ladies and I walked out the door. I glanced back and saw Barney shaking his head, and Rick order them both another round of beers.

* * *

Two weeks later, Barney and Rick were still pissed at me about the lesbian incident. They were paying for all my drinks, plus those of all the girls I met. They wanted to get their money back and their chance arrived that night.

We were sitting at the bar when this dark haired lady walked in all by herself. She was smokin' hot; wearing a long red dress with slits down both sides which showed off her black fishnet stockings. Her sliver heels had to be a good six inches tall. Being that she was either Cuban or Hispanic, she immediately reminded me of Carmen and Faye.

Before I could stop him, Barney was betting me he could get her to go home with him. I had to accept the bet—even though I was sure nothing was going to happen.

After she sat down, Barney slid off his barstool and approached her. Rick and I watched him say something incomprehensible, and get no response at all. It was as though she didn't even know he was talking to her. He came back royally pissed.

The three of us watched a couple more guys try their luck and neither of them got any response either.

Rick decided he was just drunk enough to take a turn, but once again was back faster than anyone else.

My two dejected friends looked at me and then each other. Barney turned back to me and said, "We bet you *three* months of drinks that you won't get any response either." Rick shook his head in agreement.

"This is too easy," I laughed. "Sure, I'll take your money and maybe someday you'll learn."

I walked over to her and said, "Ola, que pasa, senorita?"

She smiled, then asked me—in Spanish—to sit down, and actually bought *me* a drink. We talked in her native language for a few minutes and I learned she was waiting for a group of friends. I thanked her for the drink, politely excused myself, and sauntered back over to Barney and Rick. Needless to say, they were furious. They both yelled, "What the hell?"

"Guys, she only speaks Spanish. She didn't even know what you were sayin' to her," I explained. "Ya need to be more like me, see what's really goin' on. Be more aware of the girls you meet. It just may lead to more sex for you."

That just pissed Barney off even more and he blurted out, "We need to settle this thing once and for all. Let's start another bet. Let's see who can have the most sex this summer."

Since we were all half in the bag anyway, we all agreed to this outrageous competition. But we decided to make it a fair contest, so we needed to come up with individual goals.

Barney wagered, "I can sleep with ten girls in the next three months."

"You can't even get a girl to kiss you," I said, "nonetheless sleep with ya."

We all had a good laugh, but Barney wrote down his drunken prediction on a bar napkin.

Not to be outdone, Rick said, "That's nothin'. I'll find girls whose first names start with the letters of the alphabet. That's more than ten, right?"

Again we laughed, but Rick wrote his insane prediction down next to Barney's.

The competitor in me wanted so badly to top both of them, but I didn't know how at the moment. Then I overheard the girls sitting next to us, all who had a big 'I' on their t-shirts, mention to the bartender they were from Indiana University, and were looking for a good time. It finally dawned on me.

I knew that most of the out-of-state ladies would be wearing some sort of college apparel. I turned to Barney and Rick and drunkenly exclaimed, "I've got it! I will sleep with ladies from thirty states, or at least thirty different colleges."

Barney and Rick fell off their bar stools with laughter as I confidently added my prediction to the napkin. Now that we had our numbers written down, we needed a way to prove it to each other somehow. We all knew that most guys exaggerate about their conquests.

We turned to our favorite bartender, Colleen, and explained our outrageous bet to her.

"You're all a bunch of fuckin' pigs, but I'll help just to laugh at you."

She then explained the rules. "After you sleep with someone, you have to come here and swear to it with your right hand over your heart. Only then will I add it to the scorecards I'll keep. Can you all agree to that?"

To show our sincerity, the three of us stood up, put our left hands on a drink menu Colleen had on the bar, held our right hands up high and swore we would obey all the rules.

For me, it was the perfect time for this bet. I was still getting over Donna, wasn't feeling much of anything inside, and couldn't wait to sow more of my wild oats. And I knew I'd have an edge on the other two thanks to the secret lessons I possessed.

* * *

After a week, Barney and Rick both had zero names on their scorecards behind the bar, but not for the lack of trying. They were approaching girls left and right. Problem was, they were drunk most of the time, and not very smooth, thus they were striking out regularly.

I took a totally different approach. Early one Friday evening I walked up to a pretty girl on the dance floor that had the familiar eye sparkle. After a couple dances I could sense her mood becoming even more sexual. So I took a leap of faith and honestly explained the outrageous bet we had set up. "Would you care to help me by being my first?"

She hesitated, gave it a little thought and then smiled. "I came to Florida looking for a good time, so why not?"

I drove Tonya to my house where we swam in the pool, drank a little wine, listened to some soft music in the cool Florida night air, and then had sex.

We were driving back to the bar when Tonya said, "Man that was fun. It's everything that I heard Florida was all about."

We walked in the bar together and when I approached Colleen to pledge what happened, Tonya verified, by saying she was from Georgia Tech. Not only that, she started talking to other college girls from other states. Knowing how girls like to talk about sex, I thought, This could really work to my advantage.

* * *

My biggest surprise came one Wednesday night when I was drinking at the bar alone. Colleen quietly whispered, "I don't know what's goin' on here, but these girls are all extremely giddy after they've slept with you. You should hear some of the things they've told me after you leave." Colleen hesitated for a second and then added, "I know this is probably not the smartest thing to do, but I'm originally from Alaska. When's it my turn?"

Colleen and I slept together on her night off and she changed her initial thought about me being a pig.

She said, "I think I now understood you. You just want to have fun. Just like most of us girls do. Only, unlike most Florida dudes, you're very good at it."

Colleen and I "dated" a few more times. This was the best decision I could have made. Now I had her saying good things about me to the other female customers at the bar.

So once again, just like at my hometown roller rink, I had females approaching me and blatantly hinting about sex. My nights and days off suddenly got very busy. Instead of thinking about my actions and how they may adversely affect both me and the girls involved, I foolishly went with the flow, just to prove I could hit my target number.

* * *

The three months came to an end and Colleen had the four of us meet in a separate room near the back of the bar.

With her scorecards in hand, Colleen said, "Barney, your total first. You proudly proclaimed you would sleep with ten girls, but I only have five marked down."

So much for him being God's gift to women.

"Rick," Colleen continued, "you were looking for the twenty-six letters of the alphabet. You did much better than Barney, but you missed many of them. Still, your total was fifteen."

Both Barney and I were surprised at that.

Colleen then said, "Now for the most ambitious of you all. Phil, you were lookin' for thirty states and or thirty different colleges."

Both Barney and Rick cursed out loud when Colleen grabbed my arm and raised it in the air like a champion boxer. They stalked out of the room wearing *the agony of defeat* on their faces. As for me, after Colleen's congratulatory kiss, and her departure to tend bar, I just stood there in a sort of a daze. I felt something rush through my body, but it sure wasn't *the thrill of victory*.

* * *

While I had enjoyed that summer, the emptiness I felt intensified with each of my 'conquests' and I fell deeper and deeper into denying who I had become. I wanted to understand what I was doing and why, but couldn't. I was confused and feeling more isolated all the time, even with all this attention. I recalled how Stacey L. once told me, "You're different from all the other guys in Florida who only want sex," but now I wasn't so sure. I prayed that something would happen to make me feel better, but I wasn't feeling very optimistic.

* * *

I went to see Rose, the florist, one Saturday morning to get fresh roses. It was a cloudy overcast day, but it hadn't rained in my part of town for a long time. My mind was off in never-never land as I exited the car, and I banged my head on the top of the door jamb when I tried to get out. It hurt like hell and I slumped back down into the front seat. I touched the top of my head and felt a nice bump developing, but no blood, so I continued into the flower shop.

When I walked in, and no one was there, I casually strolled around thinking Rose was in the back. While I looked at all the flowers in the store I began to smell a faint familiar scent. It was the sweet smell of fertilizer mixed with mint; the smell which always meant someone special to me was near. I turned to face the cash register and there she stood, my Nana.

"Where have you and God been?" I excitedly asked. "I've needed you and asked for you repeatedly, but you were never there for me."

"Yes we have," Nana quietly replied. "It's *you* that hasn't been here."

"What's that supposed to mean?"

"You are too caught up in your own pleasures. You took the special gift of sensitivity you were given and twisted it around for your own selfish use."

I had no idea what she was talking about. All right, maybe I did.

She continued, "You used to see all the signs that were left for you clearly, but now you're too messed up to see them."

"What damn signs?" I raised my voice.

She shook her finger at me. "How about the way certain flowers have died at your house and then mysteriously disappeared from this store? Did you ever think that might have some significance? Like when the yellow ones weren't available, it meant that you were making the wrong type of friends. Before the pink ones died, you stopped acknowledging God for what you had, and just wanted more. And when the red ones died, you stopped loving yourself, and more importantly, you stopped loving God. We left the white ones alone hoping you'd remember why you are on this journey. But that didn't seem to work either."

My anger subsided and I started listening to her.

"Those were all signs you *used* to see, but now you're too busy playing games. When we sent you Donna, she was supposed to be *the one*. God sent you clear signs which you ignored; like the feeling in your heart the day you were looking for a hotel, or the way her pinky finger matched yours and mine, and even when you were taken to the Billy Hughes concert and he sang his song for the both of you. In the past, you would have paid attention and known what they meant."

I started crying and asked for forgiveness.

Nana lightened her tone. "I know God still loves you, and always will. But you must get back to being the *real you*. Someday you'll realize that life isn't only about you. Respect the signs and you will be forgiven." And with that comment, Nana disappeared.

The next thing I remember, I was in my car coming out of a fog, and my head was still throbbing. I checked again and found there was only a bump, no blood. I got out of my car and walked to the flower shop. There sat Rose, and as I approached the counter she said excitedly, "Little Papa, we hab all you colors of roses. You wan 'em all?"

I smiled and bought two dozen assorted colored roses from her. And as I returned to my car, a warm mist hit me directly in the face.

I let out a sigh, knowing what that used to mean.

CHAPTER 18
HOOKER, HOMELESS and HARRIET

Wanting to reform is one thing; actually doing it is the hard part. Even after talking with Nana, my world in Florida went back to being one giant party. There were as many girls in my life as there were days in a month. I met these ladies everywhere, especially at work and at the bar simply by being a little different, being direct, and by being sincere, well, my version of being sincere.

In my defense, I told them point blank what I was all about, what I wanted from them, and then let them decide the next move. And after the sex, if they would tell their girlfriends about me, the vicious circle would continue.

The months flew by and before I knew it, I had been living in Florida for three years. The whole time I was feeling as though something was missing from my life, but couldn't quite put my finger on what it was.

* * *

I was transferred to another Burger Shack in a different part of town, North Lauderdale. I had done a great job opening a new store and upper management wanted to see if I could transform an underperforming unit around. They gave me a great big raise to compensate me for where they just sent me.

This section of Florida was rundown, dirty, and populated by lowlife people I had never been exposed to before. I was all at once surrounded by hookers, drug addicts, and homeless people. At first I was appalled, then I remembered what Janet taught me in grade school: *Look at what people have to offer from within, not their outward appearance or social status.*

One of the first things I did was to make friends with a group of the hookers who used the streets near the restaurant to turn their tricks. There were five — all black, and all pretty in their own way — who would come in to eat before they started their nightly rounds. They would order, go to the same table located in the back, and eat together. They were loud and crass, seemingly at ease with what they were doing for a living. All except for one of them.

I got to know Destiny better than the rest. The two of us talked sometimes in the late afternoon before the others came in. And out of these discussions I was able to see the 'real' side of her.

Destiny told me with her Cajun twang, "I be twenty-two an' come from Louisiana to Florida to fin' myself. Instead, foun' out I dint fit in. Had no frien's, nowhere to stay. So I live on the streets 'long the Strip a few months. That when I meets Nick. He promise me a place to stay, plenny—a money, lotta frien's, and the opper-tunity ta see the 'real' Florida. I done fell for his shit real fast an' now I be workin' the streets an' givin' him most-a my money, but he be right 'bout one thin', I be seein' the *real* Florida."

Destiny had been a very good looking girl when she came to town. She showed me a picture where she was smiling and happy. She was about five-foot-five and weighed about one hundred and twenty pounds, with a black afro which added more than five inches to her height. Her skin was a dark brown which matched the color of her eyes. In the picture, her eyes were big and bright.

But now—only a short two years later—Destiny looked much older than she actually was. Her skin was all blotchy and wrinkled. Her once bright eyes were now dark and empty. Every night she wore a different wig to hide the fact that her hair was falling out. And the smile she possessed back then was gone—replaced by a frown that never went away.

I felt so bad for her, but could only listen to her problems.

"My life sucks; lotta bad shit gone down. Wish I could do it over … feelin' so empty." She shook her head sadly.

"Ya know, if'n I *could* start all over, I never of come to Florida in-a firs' place. I jis wanna be happy agin."

"Why don't you just leave?" I offered.

"Cain't do dat!"

I could see the fear come over her face.

"Nick would hab nothin' ta do wit dat. He own me, an' I try to leave 'im, he hurt me real bad. Sometime I wonner if it be worth riskin' it though."

Destiny and I shared many talks like this. I learned from her that some of the choices you make can permanently change your whole life. I had never thought seriously about that before. Here I was unhappy with how I was feeling because I thought I was missing something inside, yet she had it so much worse than I did. I tried to be there for Destiny, but again all I could do was listen. Many times when she got up to leave she did try to smile at me, so I did think I was helping her in some small way.

For three days Destiny didn't show up at the restaurant. I was getting a little worried about her. That's when her friends came in and told me something bad had happened to Destiny. She'd told Nick she was leaving and, just as she had feared, he beat her up pretty bad. They said she was going to be fine, eventually, but she would never work the streets again.

Destiny finally got what she wanted, to go back home, unfortunately, she had to pay a steep price.

* * *

At about the same time Destiny stopped coming in, I met another person who also got me to thinking about life choices. May was a street person—she lived off of the beach-goers begging for food and money. She never came into the restaurant proper, but just hung around outside. I met her one night as I opened the fenced in area where we kept the garbage. I saw her behind the bin eating the remains of a sandwich. When I didn't yell at her to leave, she gave me a brown-toothed smile and said hi.

"Hi, back at ya," I waved at her. "Whatcha doin' there?"

"Eatin' my dinner," she said nonchalantly. "I know you guys got good food. So I always look ta find somethin' here."

I felt sorry for her and when I offered her something fresh to eat and drink her eyes lit up. I went inside to fix her a cheeseburger with fries and a large Coke, while she took a seat at one of our outside tables. May and I started to meet at that same table every day I worked. The more I fed her, the more she opened up to me. When I asked her to tell me her story, she said, "Well, let's see, I'm thirty-five years old."

With her wrinkled face, tanned dry skin, and raggedy old clothes, she looked like she was well over sixty to me.

May continued, "I was married once, had a beautiful young daughter and was livin' the good life in New England.

I thought I recognized her accent. But this confirmed it.

"One afternoon my husband picked up my daughter from school and on the way home they were hit by a drunk driver. Both of 'em were killed instantly."

I felt a twinge of pain in my heart.

Small tears formed in her eyes, but she quickly brushed them away. "After that I started drinkin' and doin' drugs to relieve the hurt inside. Pretty soon the bank took my house, so I hitched a ride down here cuz-a the weather, since I knew I was gonna be livin' on the streets. I got no friends, no income, and no life. I'll just go about my business till I die … sometimes I pray it'll happen soon."

Man, I felt so bad for her.

Here was another person who felt as though there was something missing inside. Although her situation was different from mine or Destiny's, we all shared that same empty feeling. I finally realized that life can be cruel—it can't always be fun and games—and that if I wanted something to change in my life, only I could make it happen.

* * *

One afternoon I was getting ready to leave work for the day when the hostess told me there was someone up front to see me. I walked up and saw my cousin, Molly, from Illinois standing there. I wasn't expecting her. In fact, I didn't know she was in town, or that she even knew I lived here. She told me she was in Florida visiting relatives, stopped by to see my dad, and found out I worked here. We decided to go out for dinner and when she asked if she could bring a friend, who was I to say no? That's how I met Harriet.

Harriet and my cousin were both in their late thirties. They'd been friends since grade school. Molly had gone through some rough times, but was finally happy with her life. She was dating a much older guy, but things were going well.

Harriet wasn't dating anyone. When we started talking about her life she confessed, "I'm not so happy these days. I came here about ten years ago to 'find myself.' But all I found was the party life, along with the constant pull of sex with a variety of different people and the resulting loneliness. I was so busy partyin' that I forgot about my relationship with God. Now I'm thirty-nine and still single. I hate the dating scene, but at the same time I can't stand feeling so lonely."

That's when Harriet shifted her attention to me. "You're lucky, you're so young. Don't forget, we all get old eventually, and we need that 'special someone' to share the good times and the bad times. All I have are memories. Please don't let that happen to you."

* * *

Destiny, May, and Harriet all taught me a valuable lesson about life choices. They also showed me there really is someone out there looking after you and that *angels* are sent to you when you need them. I hoped that I had helped them all too, somehow, even if it was only by being interested and listening to them.

After meeting these ladies, I realized why I had that empty feeling inside. The time had come — Harriet was right — I needed to find that one special person. I knew I had to stop the Florida craziness I was so wrapped up in; change my conceited ways, and focus on finding the one person who could make me feel whole again.

I thanked Nana and God for these ladies, knowing they had sent them to me. Those three ladies really came to my life just when I needed them to. Every time I hear the Beatles sing the song *All the Lonely People,* I remember them fondly. It may have been too late for them to change, but I hoped it wasn't for me.

Just as I did three years earlier, I decided it was time to take a trip. I was going back home to see what that might bring. I wondered, Is that the place that holds the key to what I need?

CHAPTER 19
BACK HOME

I really hadn't kept in contact with very many people from my past other than Billy, Lisa, and Jack, an old teammate of mine from soccer.

"Hey Jack, I'm comin' for a visit," I said, bubbling over with excitement. "I haven't been back in three years and wanna see what's goin' on. What's new in your life?"

"I finally got a girlfriend, her name is Debbie," he said, clearly happy about my decision. "Oh, and a group of us are going to The Arch Fest next week, you wanna come?"

The Arch Fest was an annual celebration with good food, great music, and down home people. "Sounds like fun. Count me in. Listen, I'll meet ya at The Roller Wheel on Sunday night. We can discuss all the details then."

* * *

I decided to take my two week vacation, due me from work. When I started on my long drive back home to Missouri, I put in a new cassette by Kenny Loggins. The song, *One Woman,* soon became my motto for the whole trip.

With Kenny singing in the background, I recalled certain events in life. My memories brought me back to when I was a little boy. Back when all I cared about was becoming a man who all women would respect.

I thought about how I had become the person I was by being different and, most times, sincere. I focused on finding the little things about the women who I met. I tried to treat them all with the respect they deserved, and most had treated me the same in return. I knew I was able to see the difference in everyone and accept them for who they were. I wanted to be friends with all of them, so instead of looking at outward appearances, I looked deeper inside and connected with ladies of all kinds. I did my best to always tell the truth, at least my version of the truth. I realized long ago girls have wants and needs, and when they are fulfilled they share their stories with other females. I tried not to let too many of the ladies I met get too close to my heart, so no one would get hurt. It didn't always end up that way, but it seemed as though I was most often the one experiencing the pain anyway. By being open to new things and practicing what I learned from a host of female "teachers" I found out it was better to give than to receive. And when it came to an end—as it always did for me—I tried to end it on a high note.

I also believed there were two parts to life—treating people with the respect they deserved, and to be accepted by others for whom we are. I wanted to work on the acceptance part, so I promised myself I would not have sex with anyone the whole time I was there.

* * *

I arrived in Missouri on a warm Saturday morning and couldn't wait to do something that night. Since no one knew I was coming home except for Jack, that's who I called. When he told me he was busy, I tried Billy and Lisa. Although they were happy I was in town, they, too, already had plans they couldn't break.

I certainly didn't want to be alone, fearing I'd fall back on my old ways, so I called Joyce. She was my lesbian friend from work who had taught me so much about how women think. She was over-the-top happy to hear from me, and when she invited me to accompany her to our old lesbian hangout, MainStreet, I accepted.

While getting dressed, I thought about how far I had come since meeting Joyce. I was an introverted high school kid, but she had sensed I was mature for my age, so she trusted me with the secret that she was a lesbian.

The two of us had experienced a lot together. She helped me through some bad times and I helped her through a painful breakup. Joyce and all of her lesbian friends accepted me for who I was, and they helped mold that shy, introverted boy into an outgoing young man. Hanging out with Joyce allowed me to experience a different side of life, one that made it easy for me to accept everyone I ever met, including my gay father. I wanted to thank her tonight for all she meant to me.

I put on my black Valente jeans and a brightly colored yellow t-shirt which Faye had helped me pick out. I smiled at the reminder of the time Joyce and her friends re-made me into Disco Phil. I slipped into my sockless Florida-style loafers and remembered when Lisa helped me buy new clothes for seventh grade, which now seemed like eons ago. When I added the white cotton sports coat that Donna had given me and pushed up the sleeves the way she liked, I cried a little.

I looked in the mirror when I was finished dressing, and saw the person staring back at me was totally put together by other people. Once again Nana had been right. *For the first time I truly realized life isn't only about me.*

And thanks to all these past friends and lovers, surprisingly I began to feel better about myself. For the first time in a very, very long time I wanted to go dancing without any ulterior motives. I had already decided no one was coming home with me, so I knew I had no one to impress.

* * *

When I got to Joyce's she really liked my new look. She said it looked comfortable on me. We hopped into her car and she said, "So tell me all about Florida. How's it going?"

I gave her the whole story, every experience I could remember that had happened to me. When I shared the stories of Destiny, May, and Harriet we both shed some tears.

"That's why I'm here," I declared. "It's about time I found the one special girl for me. I dunno, maybe I'll find her, maybe I won't, but either way I'm gonna fill the emptiness I have inside."

Joyce turned to me after she parked the car. "Listen. Don't be in such a hurry. Love seems to show up when you're not expectin' it to. I find that if you try to rush it or force it to happen, it never works out right. Just relax, take it easy, and let whatever happens happen."

I knew from past experience that whatever Joyce said somehow always came true. "Thanks for everything you've done and for all the advice you've given to me. My life wouldn't be the same without you." I gave her a hug and said, "Joyce, I love you and I hope that everything you ever want from life you get. My wish is that we can be friends forever."

"Ditto!" Joyce said, tearing up a bit.

I found myself thinking, Who would have ever guessed that a lesbian could help me feel so good about myself?

* * *

Joyce and I drank, danced, and had fun that night. It was great just to kick back with no game plan. I even got to see Carmen again.

She stared into my face and said, "Hey, straight boy, your eyes tell me that you're tired. I see you still have the moves, but you seem sexed out. You need some time to recoup all your sexual energy. It looks like you used it all up."

I couldn't argue with her. Carmen and I danced one last song together. She and I had a lot of history, too. In a strange way I felt I loved these two lesbians much more than I had loved any straight girl I'd ever known.

Just before she dropped me off for the night, I invited Joyce to come to The Arch Fest with us. She agreed to meet me along with a bunch of her friends.

* * *

The next night I went to The Roller Wheel skating rink, which had become my second home before I moved to Florida. Since I was meeting Jack and Debbie to discuss The Arch Fest plans, and I wasn't going to try and impress anyone, I guess I wasn't really thinking. Instead of my usual skating attire, I wore a pair of khaki shorts and a brightly colored t-shirt under a patterned button-down shirt that I left untucked and unbuttoned. This was what Faye called my "Florida garb." Even though I was in Missouri, it just felt right.

When I last left The Roller Wheel I was "Disco Phil" a made-up character I used to meet girls. Now that I had much more confidence, I could be just plain old me.

I walked in and ran into some of my old acquaintances. They seemed happy to see me, but weren't overzealous about it.

Steve, the owner, came over to me with his hand outstretched. "Hi Phil. Many people have heard you were coming in for a visit, so I anticipate a big crowd tonight. Let me comp you. Hey, how about doin' your old routine?"

I shook his hand and smiled. "Thanks, Steve. I miss this old place now and then. But I don't want to do the skate thing though. I'm a totally different person than before. I'd rather just blend in with the crowd and relax."

"You blend in with the crowd?" he laughed, but then turned serious. "You do seem different, much more mature; very at ease with yourself. It's nice seeing you again. Enjoy your night."

I walked over to one of the benches where I used to listen and give advice to any girl who wanted me to. I was changing into a pair of rental skates when Jack and Debbie saw me. Jack skated over, slapped me on the back, and said, "Man, you look great. I can tell you're from Florida, what with the hip clothes and the tan. You look extremely laid back."

If only these guys knew what I had been through in order to get that feeling back again.

* * *

Jack introduced me to Debbie who surprised me with a big bear hug and a kiss on the lips to welcome me home. I had never met her before, but she seemed to know all about me.

Debbie was very energetic. She was as short as he was, both of them being no taller than five-foot-two. She had long curly black hair which shaped her face well. She wasn't overweight, but she was bigger than the other girls. When she smiled at me, her great big dimples made her even cuter to look at. But most importantly, I saw what her big brown eyes had to say.

I said, "I see what Jack likes about you."

She winked at me and said, "Oh, yeah?"

"You, my dear, have the brightest sex gleam radiating from your eyes that I've ever seen," I winked back. "I bet you and Jack have spent many fantastic nights together!"

Debbie blushed, but never denied it.

* * *

Jack and I were skating next to each other when it was announced over the loud speaker a couple's skate was next.

"So, which lucky lady gets you tonight?" He reached over and attempted to pat my ass like football players do to each other after a good play.

"None of 'em," I said, blocking his hand away. "I'm here for some alone time. I don't wanna meet anyone new. I just wanna chill."

He seemed surprised, and in a way, so did I.

Next thing I knew, Debbie was between us, asking Jack if she could skate with me. When he said it was up to me, I felt I couldn't refuse.

The minute we started skating together, hyper Debbie was off and running. "Say Phil, I'm really excited about meetin' you, especially after talkin' to all the girls here that remember you. I know all about your old escapades—your trips to the parking lot and the drive-ins." Debbie again winked at me. "They told me all about how you shared your 'gift' with them all. I had no idea who you were when Jack told me you were comin' home, but he seemed real excited to see you again. And the girls, they couldn't wait for you to come back either. How's it feel? Being so in demand?"

I rolled my eyes at Debbie. "That was a different Phil back then. In fact, it wasn't me at all, it was just a character I played. That's why I came back. I found myself doin' the same things in Florida. In fact, way worse things. And I wanna stop. It's time for me to find one special person and forget about the chase. I just needed some time to reflect. And that's why I won't be having any sex on this trip at all."

Debbie flashed her knockout smile. "You're gonna make a lot of girls very unhappy with that decision."

"I'm sure they'll all get over it," I said as a joke—I think.

136

* * *

The couple's skate ended and the madness began. Steve was right; many of the girls I knew from my past had shown up. I spent the rest of the night hugging, lightly kissing, and talking to as many of them as I could. It made me feel good they still cared about me, but it also led to a question of why. *Did they like me for who I was or for what I did?*

When I would ask, "Why do you remember me?" I got the same answer over and over. The girls said I understood their needs and that I treated them with respect, unlike most of the other guys. They all said I made them feel special.

When I asked, "Would you feel the same about me if I never had sex with you?" Each and every one of them said that me being the sensitive person was the most important thing, that the sex part was just icing on the cake.

That comment meant the most to me. I now knew most of the girls I had met liked me for *who* I was and not for *what* I did.

* * *

We were leaving and Jack said, "All right, we'll pick you up at 9:00 a.m. on Wednesday at your house for The Arch Fest. After spreading the word that you were back in town, about forty people are going, so we're all gonna meet at the Jewel parking lot over on Main Street and then have a caravan to the fest."

"Forty people? That's embarrassing," I said. "I can't believe so many people wanna come with."

"Hey, everyone likes a good time, and they know that you'll make it a special time for all of us," he said, but then shook his head, "Must be nice bein' a local *celebrity*."

So much for my relaxing time alone. I sighed.

CHAPTER 20
THE ARCH FEST

Wednesday morning, Jack and Debbie picked me up at 9:00 a.m. sharp. The sun was shining, but not too hot to be outside all day. When we pulled into the parking lot, Jack was right, there were at least forty people waiting for us.

We led the caravan of cars to downtown St. Louis. Debbie turned around in the front seat. "The other night you said you wanted to start lookin' for your one special person. So, whatcha lookin' for in her? Short or tall, old or young, blonde or brunette? What kind of personality should she have?"

"I have no idea," I shrugged. "I think I need someone who can help balance my personalities. There are times I like being alone, listening to music. Other times, I really enjoy being the center of attention. I guess what I need is someone who I can be myself with when we're alone, but will also understand my need to be the 'star' when we're out with others."

I put a little more thought into it and added, "I guess I'm lookin' for someone who also believes that respect and caring are crucial. I've always said it's not what you do that counts, it's how you do it."

Debbie nodded as if she was making a mental note of what I was saying.

"I was told by a very smart friend of mine not to look for love, cuz it never shows up when you do," I said. "If it's meant to be, I'll feel it when it happens."

Debbie smiled to acknowledge she understood and said, "I'm sure you'll find exactly what you're lookin' for someday. In the meantime, have fun and just be yourself."

At least now I knew who "myself" was.

* * *

When the forty-three of us entered the gates to The Arch Fest, I saw a sign advertising that day's events. This fest was a great celebration of food and music. I smiled to myself when I saw today's band was Johnny and the Fat Girls. I knew them from both my dad's bar and Joann's prom. If they didn't know how to get people to enjoy themselves, no one did. I said to anyone who was listening, "This is gonna be a day you'll never forget!"

This gang of ours started walking through the park—tasting different foods and listening to the music playing in the background. When we turned the corner after passing the wine and beer garden, I noticed Joyce and another group of at least thirty of her friends. Right away I could tell they were all lesbians. Most of them fit the stereotype perfectly—short hair feathered back, loose fitting tops and shorts, gym shoes, and baseball caps.

I walked over to Joyce and, after giving her a gigantic hug, introduced the groups to each other saying, "Everyone, this is everyone else. Today we're one big happy family. Let's mix and mingle, let's make new friends, and most importantly, let's have some fun!"

Some bought beer and wine while others started chatting. Here we were people of mixed cultures, mixed races, and mixed sexual orientations, but at least for that day, we were all respected and accepted by all for being who we were.

That, my friends, was my mission in a nutshell.

* * *

We exchanged stories, shared some laughs, and now it was time for some dancing. The seventy of us made our way to the gigantic outdoor stage area. We stood near the back. There were twenty rows on the left side of us, a big aisle down the middle, and another twenty rows to the right side of us. Each of these benches probably held twenty people, which meant only eight hundred people could sit down while the rest of the crowd had to stand. But we couldn't have cared less about the seating, we were here to dance!

The opening band started to play and I felt as though many in our group weren't enjoying themselves enough. But that all changed once Joyce and I started dancing together in the middle aisle. Within minutes the rest of the group joined in. By the time Johnny and the Fat Girls were taking the stage, our bunch of mismatched personalities were all in the middle aisle, ready to dance the rest of the afternoon away.

* * *

Johnny opened his set with a new song I hadn't heard before. He followed with my favorite song, *Love the Feelin'*, which I loved to dance to in Florida. I immediately took control of our mixed group and made good on my promise of a day to remember.

I grabbed Joyce and put her hands on my hips. She followed suit and grabbed someone else. We started to make our way to the stage and more people grabbed on. I started to snake this dancing conga line through the bench areas. The more people we danced past, the longer our conga line became. When we finally made our way through all the benches, and I maneuvered us to the front of the stage, there must have been over 1,000 people following my lead.

Joyce and I broke from the line to do the dance I originated for this song and we saw a news camera crew filming our every move. We moved together as one while more and more people joined in. All this commotion got the attention of Johnny, and when he looked down at me and smiled, I knew he remembered me.

He put his hands up to quiet the band and said into the microphone, "I hope everyone is havin' a good time! Our little group is all about havin' fun and respectin' each other. As you can see, there is a big bunch of people dancin' right here in front of the stage. It's made up of black and white, male and female, and straight and gay. This is what we mean by everyone getting along."

A giant round of applause burst from the crowd.

Johnny continued, "I see the leader of this group is an old friend of ours from Florida. We started way back in his dad's nightclub long before this song was a hit. Phil, come on up here and show us your famous dance!"

* * *

When the song ended and I'd finished my dance, in honor of my lesbian friends, instead of a bow, I made a gawky curtsy, which cracked up the crowd.

Johnny and his band reprised their song. I jumped off the stage and started the conga line again. After getting the thumbs up approval sign from the band, I began to feed the line up onto the stage. We passed right in front of the band as they sang and then off the other side of the stage. After that I led the entire line down the center aisle and when the song finally ended — after three encores — our group was once again where we had started, back behind the benches.

My friends and acquaintances surrounded me to thank me for a great time. I was still trying to catch my breath when the camera crew appeared in front of me, along with a pretty female news reporter.

"Man, I have covered this event before, but I've never seen anyone take control of a crowd like you did. What's your secret?"

"Music is somethin' that does that rather easily. It allows everyone to feel happy and to be accepted," I said in between deep breaths. "The way I see it, life is a dance, why not choose to live it one song at a time!"

She smiled at me and said, "You are truly a unique person and I can appreciate your take on how to live."

* * *

When the camera crew moved on, Joyce rushed over and hugged me. "Man, you haven't lost anything by moving to Florida. In fact, I think you've gained a new perspective!"

"I have you to thank," I said. "The things you taught me, and the day you turned me into Disco Phil, all led me to this."

Debbie added, "I see why people like you so much. You're different, but real. I'm sure you'll find whatever it is you're looking for ... at least you'll have fun trying."

* * *

I spent most of the remainder of my visit alone in my old bedroom, reflecting, analyzing, and theorizing. I felt I had turned a corner. I now knew my true calling had something to do with bringing people together. I realized I was able to attract the right people to me by just being me, and not putting on airs. I had used my "special lessons" to bring a group of people together who otherwise would have had nothing in common. And I learned that I could make it for two weeks without even thinking about sex, at least in Missouri.

CHAPTER 21
TWANA

The trip back home was exactly what I needed—it relaxed me and helped me discover genuine confidence in myself, not the conceited kind I used to depend on. I knew I felt different, and when I arrived back in Florida my dad sensed it, too.

The two of us sat next to the pool one afternoon drinking ice-cold lemonade and actually talked about life. This became my first real father-to-son talk ever.

"I'm proud of you, and no matter what you do, or how you choose to live your life, I always will be. I'm happy that you seem to have found yourself so quickly."

Yeah, it was soooo quick.

I saw his expression change as he started to reminisce about old times. "My journey was a lot rougher. I had all these feelings locked up inside of me as I grew up a teenager, knowing I was gay, but trying to be 'normal.' I did my best to conform to the heterosexual world, but all of the time I knew that I really wanted something totally different. I've never regretted getting married and having you kids, I just wish I would've been strong enough to accept who I was earlier, so I didn't hurt so many people."

I nodded my understanding. "I know what ya mean, but I'm glad you came to accept who you are. I know my life would've been totally different if you weren't gay and if we had a normal family, but I'm happy with what I've learned as a result of the divorce. I was put into different situations when you weren't around which taught me many things, and which made me a better person. I was able to meet a lot of different people, and it taught me that we're all basically the same."

I saw my dad relax after I said that.

I continued, "People may look different, act different, and may even think they're different from each other, but inside we all want the same things … just to be accepted and to be happy."

Now my dad was smiling and agreeing wholeheartedly with me. "I see you really have learned a lot."

I shared with him my unique beliefs and how I thought I could connect with Nana and God. I told him about the signs and symbols they constantly left for me and then shared what I had been doing with my life, and mentioned some of the wonderful ladies I had met. I also let him in on some of the bad choices I'd made with women, and my intention of slowing down, and hoping to find the one special person for me.

We were locked in a man hug when something which we hadn't experienced in some time happened—it began to rain. And as my dad and I danced in it, I said, "See, God has forgiven us both."

* * *

The next day at work I shared with Barney and Rick the details of my trip back home, and my decision to stop having casual sex. They laughed, and Rick spoke for both of them when he said, "There's no way you can change. Besides, why in the hell would you wanna, anyway?"

I started to explain and was rudely reminded that most guys don't listen all that well when they just talked over me, elbowed each other, and had another good laugh on me.

I figured the only way for me to actually follow through with my "new agenda" was for me to change my routine. I started working more nights, thus eliminating the bar scene all together and the temptations that accompanied it. On the nights I didn't work, I would usually stay home, swimming and listening to my music. I rediscovered my old poetry, and began writing again. I was beginning to like the person I had now become.

I still wasn't any closer to finding that one special person yet, but I was really enjoying my own company and I didn't feel I was missing anything by avoiding the pickup bar scene.

* * *

I was called into work one Friday morning to cover for a sick coworker and was pleasantly surprised to find a new girl working. She was very intriguing—exceptionally beautiful, tall and skinny, with a fantastic smile. For some reason I felt as though she was immediately interested in me. In a "straight" kind of way she reminded me of my lesbian friend Joyce from back home. She had the same neatly trimmed afro; her eyes were dark brown and seemed to invite me in, and her chocolate-colored skin almost had a shine to it.

I found myself drawn to her, so I quickly walked up and introduced myself. Now I'd met many ladies in my life, but this time something felt different. My feelings were confirmed as I shook her outstretched hand and felt what I believed was a small jolt of electricity penetrating through it.

This beautiful black girl looked at my reaction to our touching each other and asked, "Did you feel that, too?"

"I sure did." I smiled, trying to regain my composure. "What was it, did I shock you?"

"Nah, I think it was more like fate intervening with us," she boldly said and winked at me. "I had a dream last night I was gonna meet a handsome white boy and here you show up. By the way, my name is Twana."

"That's so weird!" I said. "Listen, if this really is fate, we would never forgive ourselves if we let this moment pass us by without seein' what is meant to be. How about goin' with me later on for a drink and a 'get to know each other' chat?"

Twana smiled her acceptance of my offer.

Later that afternoon, after we both got off of work, Twana and I set off for Casey Maxfields. When we walked in I sensed a mixed reaction from the regulars who I knew so well. I didn't understand why. I usually received a great big welcome from them all—you know, like Norm on *Cheers*—but today I was greeted with just a few quick glances my way.

The two of us were making our way through the crowded bar toward an empty table in the back of the room when I overheard a faint voice say, "Yeah, go to the back, that's where she belongs."

I looked around trying to locate the owner of the voice, but was unsuccessful. Thankfully, Twana didn't hear the comment, so I let it drop.

We sat down and Brenda, the waitress who was a previous *acquaintance* of mine, hurried over to serve us. She was nice enough when she said to me, "Hey there, stud! I see you have a new friend." But then she then turned her gaze toward Twana and said, "We don't get too many of your kind here, hope there won't be any trouble."

Twana was taken aback. I looked Brenda in the eye and said, "What's that supposed to mean?"

"I don't mean any disrespect," she shrugged, "but a black woman with a white man, that don't sit too well with most us Southerners."

I became agitated—I never cared what color a person's skin was, and I didn't realize that some people in the bar I called a second home did. I grabbed Twana by the hand, stormed past Brenda and all the other of my so-called friends, and out of that place for the last time ever.

We got to my car and I said, "I'm so sorry for that. I hope you don't judge me by my friends."

"Don't let it bother you," Twana blew the whole thing off. "I get it from time to time. There are just some people who'll always hate to see blacks and whites mixing. I know—my dad is the same way. In fact, he'd be really pissed with me if he knew I was with you right now."

"Why's that?"

"He's old school. He believes a black woman's place is in the home takin' care of the cookin', raisin' the kids; he calls it 'barefoot and pregnant,'" Twana said, rolling her eyes. "He blames all of his life's troubles on the white people. And he thinks all of us young black girls are lookin' for a better life, and think that only a white guy can give it to us. He's just a bitter old man who will never change."

"Wow, I never knew."

Twana kissed me gently and said, "Can we go back to your place and talk?"

We went back to work first where Twana picked up her car and followed me to my house. On the way I began letting off some steam. I thought the human race was past all that trivial garbage, and it sucked that Twana and I had to be rudely shown the opposite.

I had cooled off by the time we arrived at my house. I gave Twana a quick tour, then grabbed a bottle of wine and two glasses, and led her out to the pool to sit and talk.

"Here you'll always feel accepted," I said, turning on the cassette player. With Rod Stewart singing quietly in the background, I prompted her, "So, tell me more about you."

Twana slowly drank her wine, and in between sips said, "I was born and raised right here, and they say no one is from Florida. I just graduated from high school and have no idea what's in store for me. I'd like to go to college, but I know my family can't afford it. So I'm hopin' to meet someone special, get married, and have some kids, hopefully in that order."

I laughed, but knew what she meant.

Twana took another sip of wine, and then confessed, "Phil, I need to tell you something. I like you so far—so I wanna be honest. I learned all about you when you were away on vacation, the girls at work do talk, you know."

Yes, I knew that all too well.

"I need to let you know right from the start," she continued, "I'm a virgin, and I have no intention of losin' that right now. I've heard that sex is very important to you, so if you're gonna try and pressure me about it, let's not even start anything. I don't wanna get hurt."

I stared directly into her eyes. "Twana, you have absolutely nothin' to worry about. My trip home helped me realize that I needed to change my behavior. The person you heard about was the *old* Phil. And let me tell you in all honesty—I have never, and will never, pressure any girl into having sex. In fact, I always let the girl make the final decision."

I sensed Twana relax after that.

"What I want now is to find that special person and develop a serious relationship. I know we just met, but I have a strange feelin' that if you want it, you could be the one I'm lookin' for."

Twana leaned over and again kissed me. "So is that you askin' me out on a date?"

By kissing her back, I didn't even have to answer her question.

After a few minutes of simple playful kissing, I pulled back. "I do have a small favor to ask. I'd like you to be the one in charge of what we do together—it's been a long time since I was out on a 'regular' date. I used to just drink, dance, and have sex. So I'll be your puppet on a string, if ya let me. I'll do whatever you ask, and the two of us can experience anything you want to. Is it a deal?"

Twana laughed. "That's no problem at all. I love being in control!"

* * *

For the next two months Twana and I had regular dates just like everyone else in the world, well almost. Since we were a mixed couple we did get some rude stares and some crude comments, but we didn't let that bother us. This was "their problem", not ours. We went to the movies, to the museums, and even to the beach. We attended all the local festivals, went to many of the finer dining establishments along the coast of south Florida, and we danced our way into each other's heart. And we began being regulars at the new horse track, Pompano Raceway.

Even without having sex, I was having the time of my life. Although, there was still the emptiness I had gotten used to lingering in the background.

During this time, the people at work, even Barney and Rick, all noticed a change come over me. I became nicer than I had ever been before, I had more patience with those around me, and I was able to return to listening and giving advice to those who wanted it. The lessons I learned so long ago had reemerged, and I was actually using them the right way this time. With Twana by my side I didn't need the spotlight shining on me as much; my quieter side became my dominant one. I was happy and I actually felt—for the first time in I can't tell you how long— that God was on my side.

* * *

About three months into our relationship we were eating at a fancy restaurant that overlooked the ocean when Twana shocked me with, "Tell me all about sex. I wanna know how it feels, how to enjoy it, and how to accept it. Tell me about your first time—how'd it make you feel? Did anyone else notice? And how did it change you?"

"Listen," I put the forkful of salmon back on my plate, "here isn't the place to discuss this. If you really want to talk about sex, we should go somewhere we can be alone."

Without missing a beat, she said, "Then let's blow this joint and head to that pool in your backyard!"

* * *

When we passed through my kitchen, I stopped to grab a bottle of wine—if I am going to lead her first "sex talk" I may need some more confidence.

I opened the bottle; Twana took off her shoes and sat on the edge of the pool with her feet dangling in. "So, are you surprised by my frank questions about the subject you thought I wasn't interested in?"

"I was at first," I said, "but the best way to learn is to have others share their experiences with you. I'm actually flattered you trust me enough to talk about it. Most people never talk, or listen, enough. They just go ahead with the physical act, and then many later regret their decision."

Twana shook her head as if she knew the feeling I just described.

I sat down beside her, and lowered my feet into the pool next to hers. "I'll tell you my story, if that's what you want."

She grabbed my left hand, looked very innocently into my eyes, and shook her head yes.

"I was just like you at one point of my life—not wantin' to have sex till I got married. I was told by a priest long ago that if I did give in and 'do the deed' I would go straight to hell, and that God would forever hate me. So I stood by that decision for a long time and actually lost girlfriends because of it. One fateful night I gave in to the pressure of a girl I thought was special, but she left me shortly after getting what she wanted."

I took a sip of wine to wet my mouth. "You asked me how it made me feel. Well, right afterward I was confused, mostly because I felt as though I let someone else decide something so personal for me. Then I wondered if what I did was right or wrong. I thought everyone knew what I had done, but much to my surprise no one said anything, not even my mom. Soon I found myself takin' care of the needs of many more of 'em, although I wasn't sure if I was getting what I needed in return. What I eventually came to realize was, even though I thought I was helpin' these girls discover their sexuality, I, myself, was losin' more and more self-respect."

Another pause for a sip of wine helped me collect my thoughts. "Now I'm not sayin' this'll happen to you, but you can only lose your virginity once, make sure you really know that the person you share it with is someone special."

Twana slid as close as she could to me, kissed me, and gave me the biggest hug I had ever gotten from her. "I really think I'm in love with you, Phil. I've never felt this way about anyone else before. I have to be honest, I'm a little confused as to what these feelings are tryin' to tell me. But I'm seriously considering havin' sex with you tonight. I want to feel loved back."

"Stop right there," I put my finger to her lips. "That's not gonna happen … not tonight anyway. Tonight is way too early for you to clearly decide about sex."

Twana hugged me again. "You're so special, but I can wait, if you think that's best."

I had truly surprised myself. This self anointed lover-of-all-women had objectively turned down sex. I was hoping I had really turned the corner this time.

* * *

Twana and I continued to date and the subject of sex didn't come up as often. It was still lingering in the air, but was not pressing for action on it.

We dated for another six months—the longest I had gone without sex since I was a virgin many years earlier.

It was our ten month anniversary and Twana had planned a great night for us. She'd put aside some money for the occasion and wanted to take us out for a great dinner—she said it was the least she could do for me. We then went to a club to dance. I forget the name of the place, but I could feel Twana was very comfortable there. We actually felt as though we belonged. We finished a slow dance, then polished off the last of a bottle of champagne, when Twana kissed me and whispered in my ear, "Let's get outta here. I wanna be alone with you. Let's go for a midnight swim, you-know-where."

Who was I to argue?

And as I held open the car door for her to get in, I swear, for the first time, I saw the sex gleam radiate from Twana's eyes.

* * *

As soon as the car stopped, and I had opened the front door of the house, Twana ran to the pool flipping off clothing as she went. When I got to the backyard, I saw the most beautiful glistening brown skin shimmering in the moonlight. Twana said, "Whatcha waiting for? Get those clothes off and join me in here."

She was in complete control, so I followed her orders to a tee.

The two of us met in the middle of the pool and Twana started kissing me—totally different than ever in the past. There was much more passion and feeling this time. She stopped for a second and then whispered in my ear, "Okay, I'm ready."

"For what?" I said, as if I didn't know.

"For you to make mad passionate love to me!"

I started to object, but Twana put her finger on my lips as if to silence my qualms. "I'm ready and tonight you can't talk me out of it."

We moved to my bedroom. I opened the French doors to let a small breeze flow through, lowered the lights, put on an Air Supply tape, and then turned to give Twana what she wanted. I began the erotic moves that had always come so naturally to me. However, that night I found myself to be clumsy and awkward because I was so out of practice. But slowly, as we both began to relax and enjoy what was happening, the movements I had perfected long ago came back to me.

I focused my attention on Twana and I know I made her feel things she never had before. She did the same for me. I felt wanted and needed and loved all at once. And the emptiness I was accustomed to started to fade away.

We were cuddling afterward when I saw small tears form in the corners of her eyes. "Are those tears of joy or sadness?"

"They are definitely tears of happiness," Twana said. "You've made me feel so special tonight. I feel complete … I feel whole … and I feel like shoutin' out to everyone just how much I love you."

My own eyes started to get misty now. "I feel exactly the same way."

And much to my own surprise, I meant each and every word!

* * *

Twana and I grew more and more in love. Although we felt this way, and she spent more and more time at my house, I never got to meet her parents or visit where she lived. I did get to know her sister, Sherry, and she called Twana on my house phone many times. I never even got a home phone number, Twana always called me. She told me she was embarrassed by her neighborhood, and her parents would never understand, so she made me promise never to bring up the subject.

Again, I just listened and followed her requests.

* * *

Three more months passed since the first time Twana and I made love and we were practically inseparable. One night we decided to go to Pompano Raceway with a group of her friends. I had to work late so we agreed to meet at the track bar at around 8:00 p.m.

I walked into the bar. The front end faced the track, and the rear was far away from the commotion of the people who were there only to bet. I found Twana and her friends sitting right next to the back windows looking out to the parking lot. Luckily there was place to bet right in the bar, so we didn't have to leave it at all. I gave Twana a kiss, sat down next to her and ordered a bottle of white wine. We were all having a great time, actually winning some money, and laughing way too much—and way too loud—for our own good.

That's when it happened.

I noticed a large silhouette approaching our little group. This shadow I saw looked to be an older gentleman and he was staggering. He probably had too much to drink.

Even before he reached our table, the shouting started. "What da hell 're y'all kids doin'? Black and white folk together? Dat so wrong."

That's when the silhouette turned into an actual person.

"Oh, my fuckin' God," he exclaimed.

I looked at Twana and saw fear on her face.

"What's wrong?" I asked her rather loudly.

"Twana-Jo, what da hell're ya doin' wit' *him*?" the man demanded.

Twana whispered to me, "That's my dad."

"Get off-a yer ass, youn' lady. Y'all comin' home wit' me. Now!"

I started to say something, but Twana beat me to the punch.

"No, I'm not," she yelled back. "This is my boyfriend, and you just gotta accept that. We're in love an' you can't change nuthin'."

"Maybe I cain't change yo' feelin', but I sure 'n hell can make sure y'all don' see 'im no mo'," the old man spat out. "Now git off-a dat black ass-a yourn an' let's go. I'm takin' y'all home. Long as y'all live in my house, y'all follow MY rules."

"He's a little drunk," Twana quickly turned and explained to me, "I'll go home with 'im, and when he passes out, I'll come over to your house. Don't worry. I know how to handle 'im."

I wanted to object, but saw her eyes meant business. I gave her hand a squeeze and watched as her father grabbed her by the arm and marched out of the bar with her in tow over to a fire engine red Cadillac. We all watched as he yanked open the passenger door and all but shoved Twana into the seat. He then stumbled around to the driver's side, started the Caddie, raced the engine; then peeled out of the parking lot like a teenager just showing off.

I shook my head and thought, Grow up, old man.

* * *

I arrived home at about ten o'clock. My dad was home early and had the television on. I thought this odd. Dad was never home at night; he owned the bar and this was their busiest time.

"Hey, what's up, why ya home?" I said, tentatively.

"Dewey isn't feelin' too well, so we had to call it a night. Lars said he'd close up for us. How about you?"

"I finally met Twana's father tonight. Didn't go over too big. She's gonna deal with him and then come over."

While we were talking, in the background, a TV reporter said that highway I-95 was closed near Pompano. We both turned our attention to the TV screen. A car had veered out of control in front of a police car that was attempting to pull it over and crashed head-on into the center cement divider.

The station switched to their helicopter flying above the accident, and the picture on the screen showed a spotlight focused on a *fire engine red Cadillac* ... crushed like an accordion.

I lost it right there. My dad had no idea what was happening and I was unable to tell him. I couldn't breathe, tears were flowing fast and furious from my eyes, and I had an extremely large empty feeling in what used to be my heart.

The broadcast then returned to the regular scheduled program, and for the next two hours I was inconsolable. I just knew Twana was in that horribly mangled car, and I could only imagine the condition the occupants were in. But I didn't know where Twana lived, or even a phone number to confirm it was her, and find out if by some miracle she had survived. I had no idea what to do.

That's when the phone rang. It was Twana's sister, Sherry. I could tell she'd been crying. And her voice had that heart-wrenching hesitancy that always precedes bad news.

I was devastated. Another person I let into my heart had been taken away from me. I didn't feel like going on. Without Twana I felt my life was over. After all we had been through, why did God let this happen? What had I ever done to offend the Lord? Well, I guess I had done some bad things in my past, but bad enough to have this happen?

* * *

I quit my job a week later, said good-bye to my father, and moved away from Florida. I left late one night and soon found myself on a deserted part of the highway. As I drove alone with my thoughts, I heard a voice — I couldn't tell if it was female or male — only that it was calming, and I really needed that feeling right then. This voice left a profound and mystifying message for me. One I couldn't really comprehend, but knew I needed to put it away for another day.

In this life phase there has to be balance — you must take the bad with the good. Eventually this will allow you the ultimate luxury of becoming a whole person. Without this balance in your life, you could not learn and grow. Becoming whole is the key, and the only true way of coming back home.

I had no idea what that meant. Or why I got this message when I did. Or who was speaking. The more I drove along in silence, the more I prayed to God — for help and direction. When I didn't get an immediate response, I just kept driving ... and praying ... and wondering, Now what?

CHAPTER 22
THE WEDDING

I crossed the Missouri border depressed, and exhausted, late on a rainy Saturday night. I found a hotel room in a small town I knew nothing about, and tried to get some shut-eye. But with the constant lighting and thunder, and the memories of Twana running through my head, sleep was impossible. After tossing and turning until about 1:00 in the morning, I decided to go down to the bar located in the lobby of the hotel. I ordered a glass of white wine and waited for the answers to all my problems to be solved.

I didn't have to wait too long—a short, red-headed lady with an "I'm lonely" look radiating from her eyes sat herself down next to me. She was way too perky for her own good.

The ready and willing babe said, "You look like you need to talk, what's up?"

I really wasn't in the mood to conduct a long and drawn out conversation about my troubles, so I shaved the truth a little bit. "I just drove up from Florida, and I'm feelin' a little road-weary is all."

"Is there anything I can do to help?" she winked at me.

Without another word, she grabbed my hand and led me to the elevator. Neither of us talked on the ride up to my room and we never even learned each other's name. When I woke up it was almost noon and her side of the bed was empty.

And just like that I was back to my old unfeeling self, like it or not.

* * *

In the next month I found a job, at another Burger Shack, and a small one bedroom apartment about a mile away. I made sure I was close enough to my family, but far enough away to be on my own. It was the first time in my life I was actually alone; no parents, no so-called girlfriends, not even Nana or God seemed to want to be around me.

I decided to start buying roses—only the red and white ones—to spread throughout my apartment. In the past, the red ones meant I should love myself and God, while the white ones meant remembrance.

I had no one else to fall back on and I found myself doing what I had always done in my past—engaging in casual sex with the ladies I would meet at work and at the bars I hung out at.

For the first six months back in Missouri I was feeling pretty much numb—just going through the motions. The old emptiness was back again, but this time much deeper and much more apparent. I was depressed, I was lonely, and I couldn't stop wondering, *what the hell has become of my life?*

The only thing that seemed to help me temporarily forget my problems was to drown myself in these meaningless sexual relationships, like some people drown themselves in alcohol. Being the consummate overachiever, I was doing both.

* * *

A few weeks later, I got a phone call from Jack and Debbie, my old soccer teammate and his girlfriend. They announced they were getting married and asked me to stand up for them.

"Great," I said sarcastically. I realized how I must have sounded, and tried to cover for it. "Really, I'm happy for you guys, you deserve each other. I'd be honored to stand up for you."

Debbie sensed my depression. "Phil, how are you *really* doing?"

When I didn't answer quick enough, she said as if she knew something I didn't, "I bet your life is gonna take a turn for the better very soon."

The night before the dress rehearsal I was way down in the dumps. I sat on my bed, reviewing my life, trying to decide what it all meant. I couldn't make heads or tails out of what I had become. Right now this so-called life of mine made absolutely no sense to me. I was confused, tired, and often cried myself to sleep. All I wanted was to be part of something that felt real, but my prayers were never answered. Although I couldn't sleep, I closed my eyes in order to rest in the quietness of my room. Soon after, I felt a presence sitting next to me on my bed and I knew it was Nana.

I felt a quick calm come over me as she gently started to rub my head. "Well, here we are again, Phil. This time I have very good news. I know you have had a very rough time lately. There've been many times when you've felt alone. Times you were frustrated. Times you gave in to the dark side, but you've always found a way back. God is very happy with you."

"Then why was Twana taken from me?" was all I could come up with.

"That I don't know, but everything has a reason whether we can see it or not," Nana said.

I just shook my head.

"Promise me you will begin using your gift of sensitivity again. There will be more signs and symbols coming your way, and I know you'll be able to see them clearly. Your journey is not complete, stay on the straight and narrow and always know we are both there for you. Now get on with your life, sweet boy."

Her visit didn't give me any concrete solutions, but I still slept the best I had in a long time. My dreams were all in vivid color and were about happy things like being back in Wisconsin, and the smells—fresh cut green grass, hamburgers cooking on an outdoor grill, and mint—that I used to adore as a kid. I took this as one of the signs Nana talked about.

When I awoke the next morning, there were two more symbols I recognized right away. The first was the rain. It told me that God had forgiven me, and I wanted to return the favor. I vowed to change and become the person the Lord wanted me to be.

The second meant even more. The white and red roses on my dresser caught the sun in such a way that they had a glow around them; this made me take notice and really remember what they meant. I took this as a sign God was apologizing for taking Twana away from me, and needed her soul for a higher purpose than I could understand.

* * *

The next night was the dress rehearsal. I had bought a pair of black pin-striped slacks which I paired with a light blue metallic shirt and a thin black tie. Instead of my slip-on Florida loafers, I wore a new pair of black cowboy boots. I added the white cotton sports coat Donna bought me, pushed up the sleeves the way she liked me to, and I stared into the mirror. What I saw looking back at me made me smile. The depression that had been locked in my body had somehow abated—replaced by a renewed sense of calmness, order, and a confidence I hadn't felt in some time.

* * *

I walked into the church, the first one I had visited in over ten years, and was more than surprised by two initial things. First, I saw red roses everywhere. And I felt a warm sensation cascade through my body.

Secondly, I realized I was the only one dressed up; everyone else had jeans and t-shirts on. This made me feel a little different—something I always wanted to be—and I knew everyone else was staring at me.

Finally, I was back in the spotlight again.

Jack and Debbie, who were walking around hand in hand and smiling profusely, saw me. They came over to introduce me to the others

155

in the church. I felt a moment of shyness again, just like I always had back in school, realizing I didn't know anyone except Jack's parents.

Luckily, Jack's mom came up just then and made me feel comfortable with a big hug. "Wow Phil, you've certainly grown up since the last time I saw you. I've always liked your unique style. Even tonight, look around, you're the only one here all dressed up—that shows confidence. Whatever you did in Florida, it sure looks good on you."

I blushed, but was able to say, "Thanks!"

Jack, Debbie, and I started our walk to the front of the massive church, and I could feel a pair of eyes on me. I searched for the owner and a feeling of anxiety came over me and I didn't know why.

I scanned the room and found the culprit; she was sitting across the room, but was definitely locked on to me. The second I laid eyes on her I felt something I'd never felt before, even with Twana. My emptiness seemed to disappear and I could feel the high security walls around my heart loosening up. I actually became a little scared, remembering Joyce's admonition, *Don't rush love.*

This girl's looks would probably be described by most as "ordinary", about five-foot-eight, with short brown hair, and brown eyes. I guessed her age to be about twenty, and her weight, maybe 140 tops; but she was very athletic and in good shape.

Her fantastic smile, and the resulting dimples, put me instantly at ease—even more so when I noticed a yellow rose strategically placed in her hair. This was always a sign of friendship to me.

"Who's the girl across the way?" I whispered to Debbie, "the one so obviously staring at me?"

"That's my friend, Rosalin," Debbie smiled. "She's the one you're standin' up with. You wanna meet her?"

"No time like the present." I was anxious, but wanted to be cautious all the same. "But please don't tell her anything more about me. I need to stay a mystery right now."

Debbie looked confused. "What's that supposed to mean?"

I took a deep breath. "Look, I know this is gonna sound silly, especially comin' from me, but I have this strange feeling in my gut that she's the girl I'm supposed to marry, and rarely does my gut play tricks on me. I've never felt this way before."

When I said that, Twana came to my mind and I realized that even she never made me feel the way I was feeling right now.

"This one scares me. Although a part of me desperately wants to meet my soul mate, I know if she comes into my life too early I'll just mess it up somehow. So, I'll stand up with her, but it has to end there—until we're both ready for more."

"I just knew the two of you were right for each other," Debbie smiled again. "I don't understand your logic, but you always seem to know yourself pretty well, so I'll listen to you."

Debbie introduced Rosalin to me, and when I shook I her hand for the first time, just like with Twana, it was like an electric pulse rushing from my hand to my heart, only this time much more intense.

I was polite to Rosalin, but was also very short with her. But when I told her I liked the tiny pendant on her necklace, she was impressed that I even noticed it.

* * *

A short time later, Jack's mom came up to me. "You seem to have an admirer over there." She moved her eyes in the direction of Rosalin. "She's asking lots of questions about you. She told me she likes the way you dress, the way you handle yourself, and the air of confidence you brought in with you as you walked into the room. Who knows, this may be the one you've been looking for your whole life."

I was scared she just may have been right!

* * *

The next day, a beautiful sunny one, I actually made it through the wedding with Rosalin standing beside me the whole time. Once again, I was polite, and although I was, I tried not to act too interested in her.

We were dancing together at the reception when she asked, "So, how do know Jack and Deb?"

Maybe ten words had passed between us up to that point. I started to sweat and stammered as I tried to answer her. "J-J-Jack and I played soccer together i-i-in high school."

Rosalin smiled at me and I saw what I always wanted to see emanating from female eyes—the trust sparkle. Only instead of relaxing me, this time it just made me even antsier.

She noticed this. "Rumor has it you like to be the center of attention, so how is it I make you so nervous?"

I blushed, but answered her honestly. "You make me feel things I don't wanna feel right now. I think I may like you even though I don't even know you. And I'm not ready for what may come of it."

"You're really different than other 'boys' I know, almost a man, but I like different." She winked and then got serious. "You seem to have experienced more than the average guy. Your eyes tell me you've been through a lot in life—some good and some bad. I can also tell that you're honest, probably sometimes painfully so, but that's okay with me." She stopped to consider her next words very carefully. "I'm not sure what I feel for you either, but don't worry, I promise I won't get in your way. If anything is supposed to happen between us, it will. If it doesn't, it wasn't meant to."

With that, Rosalin took the same yellow rose she wore yesterday from her hair, handed it to me, and said mysteriously, "I know you know what this means. I'll be waiting."

CHAPTER 23
THE 'DATE'

In the weeks following the wedding, I continued to meet more ladies. I wasn't completely over the Twana tragedy and needed much more time before I could fully commit to anyone, especially Rosalin. I was worried that my heart just wasn't in it, and I wanted to give this girl a fair shot at helping me achieve true love. So until I was ready for an exclusive relationship, it was back to good ol' meaningless sex. But the whole entire time Rosalin lingered in the back of my mind. In fact, I even put her yellow rose in a plastic bag to preserve it, and to remind me of the true friendship I really wanted.

The lady I hooked up with the most was Ranja. She was four years younger than me. Here I was a mere twenty-two, yet feeling I was closer to forty-four thanks to my experiences. Ranja, eighteen, looked more like she was twelve. She was less than five feet tall, with short black hair and dark eyes to match, and had no girly shape to speak of. She did have a winning personality and a healthy sexual appetite, so naturally I found myself attracted to her.

I was roller skating by myself one lonely night when she decided to approach me and the rest was history. We had absolutely nothing in common, except a burning desire for sex. But that didn't stop us from dating for three months.

On our first night together Ranja said, "Obviously, you can see I'm from India, but I'm adopted. My life has been hard, it seems like I'm always getting hurt by the people I trust. I like sex cuz it allows me to lose myself for a short while, and forget all my bad memories."

I can totally relate to that!

* * *

Speaking strictly for myself, our routine quickly became dull. We would either go skating or dancing, or hang out at either the racetrack or the bowling alley whenever we weren't having unemotional sex with each other. Most Monday nights, Ranja would come watch me bowl in a league I was in with my new friend, Jim. After bowling, the three of would go to the local bar, start drinking, and Ranja would either find a girl in the bar, or call a friend for Jim. Then the four of us would go back to my place and retreat to separate bedrooms. This became our Monday night tradition. It was taking me nowhere fast, but it had become my life, and I accepted it.

* * *

One spring Monday night, Jack and Deb surprised me at the bowling alley. They had brought Rosalin with them. Luckily, Ranja didn't show up that week.

Deb took me aside and said, "I've decided that since you haven't called Rosalin yet, I would help out. She keeps askin' more and more questions about you, so I thought you'd like to answer 'em yourself."

With the three of them watching me, I became real nervous. Although I was a pretty good bowler, I was more preoccupied with the fact I couldn't talk directly to Rosalin; I couldn't even look in her sweet brown eyes without starting to sweat and stammering about. Here I was, a man who'd been with more than his share of ladies, and I couldn't even carry on a simple conversation, not to mention roll a stupid strike. So, I did what any man in my position would do—I drank.

Bowling ended unceremoniously and Deb suggested the four of us go back to their place. I was rather drunk and had nothing better to do, so I agreed. I was going to follow the three of them in my car, but as I unlocked the door Deb pushed Rosalin over to the passenger side. So we rode together on the longest car ride ever.

When she tried to talk to me, although I prided myself on being a good listener, I found myself totally unable to focus on anything she had to say. All I could remember out of the whole conversation was for me to call her Rose, for short. By the time we reached Deb's place, I was sure Rosalin, Rose, hated me.

The four of us went in, had one drink and I listened to Rose and Deb chatting back and forth. I tried to be nice, but it was apparent I wasn't paying attention to what they were saying. I took advantage of a point in the deep conversation when they both came up for air to politely excuse myself and leave, not even getting Rose's phone number.

About an hour later when I walked into my dark apartment, the red light on my answering machine was blinking. It was a message from Deb in a serious tome. "Phil, you just left here, but I need you to call me as soon as you get home."

I thought something bad had happened. I rapidly dialed the number and blurted out, "What's the emergency?"

Deb casually said, "Nothin'. You just forgot to get Rose's phone number, and she wanted me to give it to you so you can call her tonight."

"It's twelve-thirty-eight," I quoted the time on my answering machine readout. "I'm sure whatever she wants can wait until tomorrow."

But Deb insisted, so I called Rose.

Rose answered the phone sometime after the fifth ring and seemed a bit miffed. "What're you doin' calling me at this late hour?"

I was confused and there went that damn stammer again: "D-D-Deb told me you needed to talk to me right away. I'm just followin' your directions, so don't get mad at me."

"I didn't say anything of the sort," Rose huffed. "I got the message loud and clear tonight that you don't ever want to call me. You sure don't seem to be interested in me like you said you were at the wedding. And that's fine. At first I thought you were different than the others. But so far I've not seen anything to confirm that. Either you're very short with me, or you can't even talk to me. And I'm certainly not gonna beg for your attention."

"I'm sorry," I said as humbly as possible. "You're right. I did have special—no, extra special feelings for you at the wedding. But I wasn't ready to deal with them yet. And tonight, well, I wasn't exactly expectin' to see you guys show up. You need to understand, my life is really mixed up right now. I'm basically just going through the motions, and tryin' to get back on track. You haven't seen the real me at all yet."

I stopped, pondering my next move. My mind went into overdrive. I know *I'll use Nana's advice and be different.*

"How about you and me doin' something unusual this weekend?"

Rose didn't say anything, but I knew I had her attention.

"Look, I have plans to attend a professional wrestling event. I know the owner of the company. I can get three extra tickets—yeah, this isn't your typical first date—but how about you, me, Jack, and Deb all goin' together? This time I promise to show you the real me."

There was a pause that lasted a lifetime and then Rose let out a laugh. "Okay, you're right. That's not your typical first date, but I'm game." Rose laughed again. "This *is* different and so far I like what I hear."

* * *

That Friday night the four of us went to the wrestling match. I decided to keep it a secret that once a week I got paid to harass the wrestlers, and to incite the crowds. The manager was a friend of mine from Sidewinders, a bar I frequented. He'd seen my alter ego, Disco Phil, in action at the roller rink in my "younger days" and knew I was perfect for the gig.

I went over-the-top crazy that night. Yelling and screaming when the "bad" guys "cheated", whipping the crowd into a near riot frenzy. I waited until after the matches, when I picked up my check, to break the news to Rose that I was a professional rabble-rouser. She got a real kick out of that, having no idea such a job existed.

On the way back to the car I asked Rose, "Is it okay if I hold your hand?"

Rose looked at me and blinked her amazement. "No one has ever *asked* me if holding my hand was *okay* before. It's kinda nice."

Rose reached over for my outstretched hand and once again there was that little surge of electricity.

We sat in the backseat of the car as Jack drove us home, and I said, "Rose, how about just you and me goin' on a real date next week? We can go out for dinner, take a drive, and talk. I'll let ya see yet another side of me."

She smiled, and gave me a small peck on the cheek in acceptance of my offer.

* * *

I was happy with myself, well, at least until I got home. That's when I saw the red blinking message light on my answering machine. It was Ranja. For several days now, I had forgotten all about her. I knew I needed to talk to her, but didn't know what I was going to say.

I took a deep breath, called her, and just let it all out, "This is hard for me to say, but I've met someone new. I know I told ya that I'd never hurt you, and I hope that I don't. But I just think we have so little in common, our life has become stale, and I know you have much more to offer to someone who really cares deeply about you."

Ranja started sobbing. "I get it. I just knew this would happen. Everyone I let into my heart turns around and hurts me."

As I hung up the phone, I was crying myself.

* * *

For a guy whose mission in life was to be liked and respected by all women, I sure felt like a gigantic failure. I grabbed a can of lemonade out of the refrigerator, and lay down on my bed. I popped in a Rod Stewart cassette, closed my eyes and almost immediately the life lessons I learned so long ago came to mind.

During this reminiscing, I thought about how I've always believed that when someone needs an emotional rescue, God sends an angel their way. I realized there were times in my life when I *needed* that angel and there were times when I *was* that angel. And I didn't feel as big of a failure as I originally thought.

I sat up on my bed and took a sip of lemonade. The cassette played on and I came to the conclusion I was a better man than the boy who started that journey, although the detours I took made it a longer than expected one. All the while Rod belted out in the background, *I Wouldn't Change a Thing*, a song which meant the world to me.

* * *

Just as I was drifting off to sleep a loud noise from outside made me snap to. Then the sweet aroma of fertilizer entered my apartment and I instinctively knew by now Nana was here for another one of her magical visits. I wiped the sleep from my eyes, and there she sat right next to me.

"I can see you are at another crossroads in your life."

I just shrugged my shoulders, not sure whether or not I agreed.

"Keep this thought in the back of your mind for later: *There are no endings, only new beginnings.* There will come a day when you'll fully understand what this means."

Nana touched the top of my head gracefully, and as tears made me blink uncontrollably, she was gone just as fast as she'd appeared.

CHAPTER 24
ROSE

Rose and I went out every night the next week and got along as though we had known each other forever. Soon we became an item—dating seriously for a few months, and then we started hanging out with many of her married friends. Along with them, the two of us joined a bowling league and a volleyball league.

Whenever we would go out to a club as a group, Rose and I always were the center of attention—and more so when they saw the two of us dancing as one. We were constantly asked, *When are you two getting married?* Rose and I just laughed it off. After all, we hadn't even taken the first step toward that yet—we hadn't consummated our relationship.

There was a time when I wanted to wait to share the sexual experience with only one special person. But that idea was blown out the window long ago. Rose had this same wish. She was much more outwardly religious than I, and was always worried about how she would be judged at the end of this life. She needed to be sure she could justify her actions when the time came.

Sex wasn't a topic of discussion between us, and that was just fine by me. I truly believed this was the girl I had waited my entire life for, so I knew there would be a day the sex part would happen. We went at her pace so neither of us would get hurt. We used dancing as our special way of showing each other how we felt. And we used it a lot! Dancing was far more acceptable than sex in Rose's world.

* * *

Before I knew it, Rose and I had been going out for two years. We still hadn't had sex and now I *was* becoming a little antsy about it. This was a long time for a man who craved sex to go without, but the signs continued to point to us "doing it" someday, so I hung on. I had lost lovers in the past because of sex. It was too important or not important enough and either way I wasn't going to allow that to happen again.

Instead of pushing myself on her, I used dancing with Rose as a pacifier.

* * *

I picked up Rose one early May morning. We were going to see my great-grandfather—I called him Gramps—up at his house in Wisconsin. This was the very same cottage where my Nana and I would spend long summer nights, when I was a kid, talking and drinking lemonade as she helped me understand life.

Every time I revisited this sacred place of my past, I became uncontrollably emotional. This time was no different. When we pulled into the long gravel driveway next to the grassy hillside where I used to lay and look aimlessly into the blue sky for answers, I saw the two rocking chairs on the screened-in porch where Nana and I would do our talking. I totally lost control of my emotions. It was the first time in the two years of dating Rose had seen me cry.

When I was able to control myself, I said, "Sorry, but this place brings back so many great memories of my Nana that I just can't help myself. This is one of the few places on this earth where I feel so connected."

Rose seemed to understand; she gently placed her hand into my left one. When she kissed me I felt a different kind of warmth come over me.

It was also the first time I saw the sex gleam in her eyes.

The day was magnificent with a cloudless blue sky above us, the lush green grass on the hillside next to us, and the lingering aromas from my younger days penetrated the crisp air ... fresh cut green grass, hamburgers cooking on an open campfire from the campground down the road, and that unique odor of seaweed lying on the beaches along the lake. Rose was able to smell them, too, and understood why I liked them so much.

We walked hand in hand into the cottage. When Rose met Gramps they immediately clicked as though they had known each other for years. The three of us made our way to the screened-in front porch. Rose and I sat next to each other rocking on the hammock, and Gramps surprised us with a box he'd brought out. It was an old, beat-up cigar box held together by two green rubber bands. When his old, but nimble, fingers undid the rubber bands and he slowly opened the box, I was able to smell one more distinct odor from my past—sweet fertilizer. That unique smell was the scent of my Nana, it was neither too feminine nor too masculine and it was her through and through. Nana once told me that this distinctive smell of hers came from many years of living on a farm, and countless summers of planting flowers here around the cottage.

Gramps sifted through this box of memories and that's when he began to cry. I could tell his whole life was wrapped up in that box. He took out some items which made no sense to Rose or I, but obviously meant the world to him. He then pulled out an old worn down pencil which he told us was the very pencil Nana used to solve crossword puzzles every summer. He found a small yellowed handkerchief which was also Nana's, and she carried it on the day they got married so long ago.

Next he retrieved a small thimble, and as he started to tell us the story about what it was and what it meant to him, he stopped to dry his eyes. We never did get to know about it.

Finally, he was able to find what he was looking for; it was a faded black and white photograph. Gramps handed it to me and said, "Look closely and tell me what you see. There's something special in the picture."

I gently took it from him and looked for any clues as to what he wanted me to see. The picture captured Nana with a little boy sitting on her lap. Obviously it was me. Next to her was a table with lemonade glasses and baked desserts on it. I showed Rose the picture and she somehow knew exactly what Gramps was talking about, although I still didn't.

I asked what I was looking for and got this response from him, "You were always her favorite, you know. She knew you had a rough time with the divorce of your parents, and she absolutely loved the times the two of you spent talkin' here on the porch. She was always so concerned you would get hurt even more and wanted to be able to protect you. Remember when you moved to Florida and I gave you the special gift?"

That's when I saw it. In the picture, Nana was wearing the old Saint Christopher medal she had found while digging a garden for her flowers here at the cottage. I was now wearing that same medal around my neck.

Gramps said, "I gave it to you to keep you safe and sound, and it apparently worked because you're home no worse for the wear. I was hopin' I can have it back, as I plan on takin' a trip soon and would like to carry it with me. It looks as though you don't need any special help anymore, now that you have Rose. It feels to me like you guys are really meant for each other. You know, I seem to remember that somebody important once said, 'Everyone will find that special someone sometime, you only must wait your turn.' Well, it looks like this is yours."

I reverently took the medal off my neck and handed it to Gramps. When I did, my right hand touched his and I felt a small icy sensation. It was an extremely hot day for early May, so I knew his hand shouldn't be that cold. When I asked him about it, he only said, "You'll understand some day."

We drove home the next day. Rose had been in deep thought for some time before speaking up, "He's such a nice old guy, and to keep all those small treasures for his entire life shows he really cared about your Nana. You did the right thing giving him the medal back, it made his day. You've been lucky to have two such loving people in your life. I'd be extremely happy to have someone just like him to share my life with," and then she winked at me.

* * *

Two weeks after our visit to Wisconsin, Gramps went on his *trip*. While Rose and I sat listening to a priest we didn't know tell us how good a man he was, we both started to cry. When they slowly lowered him into the ground, we each threw a red rose on top of his casket to show our love, and wish him well on his journey.

I sensed a different feeling come over Rose after the funeral. She appeared to be much closer to me than she had ever been before. And the longer we stayed together, the more I believed she was falling in as much love with me as I was with her.

* * *

It was time to make my move—June 10, Rose's twenty-first birthday. I wanted to do something extra special. I organized a dinner and dance party and invited all of her family and friends to join us at the St. Andrews Country Club for a special bash. In order to make this a truly unforgettable event, I decided to buy her a significant present.

We all shared a great dinner of steak and lobster, her favorite, and many bottles of champagne. And now it was time for my present. I had a gift wrapped box the size of a washer wheeled in on a cart and placed right in front of her. This was the biggest box Rose had ever gotten for her birthday. Everyone gathered around as she anxiously ripped away the paper, opened the box, and was totally surprised to find a smaller gift wrapped one inside. Rose tore into that one, and the same thing happened, and so on and so on. Five boxes later, she was holding in her trembling hands a very small package, wrapped in white paper adorned with red roses. She gently pulled away the wrapping of this final box and now held in her hand a small black velvet box. I slowly held out my hand and she passed it to me.

In front of everyone she loved, I got down on one knee and said, "Rose, I love you and hope that you love me, too. I want to have the kind of life my Nana and Gramps did, and I can't think of anyone else but you that I'd want to share it with. Will you make me the happiest man on Earth by marrying me?"

Rose was crying, her mom was crying, and there were many "oohs" and "aahs" emanating from the people gathered around us when I opened the box to reveal a half carat diamond engagement ring. She held out her left hand and I slipped it on.

I was on top of the world. Here I was, only twenty-four and I had finally arrived. I thought, Look what finally happened to Phil, the king of all women chasers?

Many congratulations and slaps on the back later, Rose and I were able to slip out of the party. After two and half years, that night we finally were able to consummate our relationship. I gave my heart and soul to Rose that night. We immediately became as one, and I dedicated my life to making her, above all others, feel special.

CHAPTER 25
THE PSYCHIC

Rose's family wanted to throw a party for the Fourth of July, and combine it into an engagement party so I could meet some of her relatives from out of town. Also invited were some neighbors—Mr. and Mrs. Margolis. Mr. M. was a fantastic singer who loved crooning old Frank Sinatra songs and Mrs. M. was a homemaker who'd raised their six kids almost single-handedly.

The neighbors from the other side of Rose's house, an older couple named Bobbie and Rich were also there, along with their three grandkids. There were two girls—Allie, fourteen, and Janet, eleven, and a little boy, Billy, eight.

We all hula-hooped together to the loud disco music blaring in the background, and when Allie said I did a good job for being such an old man, Rose laughed, saying she'd never forget how I looked when Allie said that.

At one point, Allie came up to Rose, bursting to ask a question. "So, are you guys gonna have kids?"

"Maybe. Why?"

Allie never even hesitated. "Cuz I got mine all planned out already. My girl will be named Penelope and I like Trent for a guy."

That's just like a girl to have everything planned out so far in the future.

We were making the rounds showing off her ring to those who hadn't seen it before, and I was able to sense a connection with her grandmother on her dad's side, and also with Mrs. M. I pulled over a chair and started talking to these two wonderful ladies. We had a very long and enjoyable chat about families, the past, religion, and finally, the afterlife. I happily found out both of them shared my fascination with the occult and with the belief God leaves us signs in order to become a better person. Mrs. M. even let me know her youngest daughter, Margaret, was a psychic and had the ability to tell me about the future if I so desired.

I was intrigued and wanted to know more.

Margaret was summoned over by her mom and the three of us went inside to be alone. We sat down at the kitchen table. Margaret looked directly into my eyes and said, "I will only tell you about what you want to know. I can talk about the past, the present, and the future. Sometimes I speak only in symbols, that's why my mom will take notes and we will discuss things afterward. Please don't say anything until the reading is over. The one thing I can't tell you is when you will pass from this life form. Do you want to know everything, or just something specific?"

"Let me know it all. God only gives me what I can handle."

Margaret clasped my right hand between both of hers and then closed her eyes. "You are a messenger of God. You use your ears more than your mouth and physical touching as a way to help others. You have helped many, many people already. Your gut and your right hand have special abilities—always trust them. I see a picture of a family and it's ripped in two. I feel isolation and reflection. There is someone over your left shoulder—it looks like a spiritual advisor—she's a girl who says she was once deeply hurt by a man, and she is watching over you to help you be the total opposite of him. She says her name is Olivia. Over your right shoulder I see an older lady, a farm, and a green leafy herb—but I can't tell what it is. I see blackness in the head area and sickness. I feel religious faith, but no actual church presence. I sense a lack of trust in men. I'm experiencing the death of a friend and a deep guilt on your part, but it's not your fault. I see a green hill and a lake. I feel calmness, and see the same older lady that's over your right shoulder. There is a trip taken laden with a broken path, desperation, and loneliness. I feel three human formed angels were sent to you, then sunshine. There is a row of three black hearts, two small pink hearts, and then a great big red heart. I see two spirits, one black and one blue. I see a long golden bridge and then again that blackness in the head area. I see no more."

Margaret opened her eyes and took a drink of cold water. She was entirely drenched in sweat. Margaret then asked her mom to start reading back the notes. She wanted to review the symbols she saw, and to find out if anything made sense to me. When Mrs. M. finished recapping the readings, Margaret asked me if anything sounded familiar.

I nodded. "Most of it. I listen closely to most people and try to help them solve their problems. I've always been told I've been blessed with the God-given gift of sensitivity. I trust my gut feeling and first instinct, but I don't know what you mean about my right hand. My mom and dad were divorced when I was little, and I spent lots of time in my room alone, so I assume that's the ripped picture of a family. I don't know of any Olivia, but I totally understand her message. I know the other lady is my Nana and the green leaf you saw is mint. She used to put it in her lemonade as we talked for hours about life. Nana still visits me now and then to give advice. I have no idea what the blackness in the head area means, but I do get the lack of trust between me and other men. I understand the remark about feeling responsible for the death of a friend, and it comforts me to know that I wasn't really to blame. Both the green hill and lake are at my happiest place, it's a cottage up in Wisconsin where Nana lived, and it's the area where I'm most comfortable at. I moved to Florida to 'find myself' and eventually was able to, but not till after some rough times, so that's probably the trip you saw. The so-called angels were real people who helped me choose to return here. The rest— all the hearts, the two spirits, the bridge, and the blackness in the head again, I don't understand at all."

Margaret seemed satisfied I'd correctly accounted for most of what she saw or felt, then asked, "Have you ever been sick for any length of time?"

I thought about it and remembered back in sixth grade when I had a kidney infection and extremely bad headaches. I suggested those headaches were the blackness in the head she was talking about.

Margaret nodded in agreement. "The many hearts mean different things. The first three black ones are loves lost. The next two smaller pink hearts that follow are women who will teach you more, and eventually help lead you to the large red heart—your true love. The two spirits are probably children this true love and you bring into this life. The black means the entity never made it to human form and the blue means a boy. The long golden bridge represents that you will live a full life, but be careful of those headaches, they may return. Do you understand this?"

I was stunned. I always was intrigued by the occult, but this was scary. It was as though Margaret had seen a movie of my life in her head. "I get most of it, and it's uncanny how you well you read my life. I do have a few questions though—one about the children part. You say that they are descendants from my true love and me. Did you see another one that came way before the black hearts?"

Margaret shook her head no, and I was now positive Loretta, my old girlfriend back in Florida, had never gotten pregnant, at least not by me.

"What I don't get is the last part, the part about bein' led to my true love but not until *two* more ladies enter my life?" I looked at her puzzled. "You do know I'm engaged to Rose and we plan on getting married this October? Are you *sure* that everything you see is always right?"

Margaret put up her hands. "No, not everything I sense happens exactly the way I see it. Use it as a caution though. Maybe she isn't the one for you after all?"

"Margaret!" her mom jumped in. "Don't scare the man."

Mrs. M turned to me, put her hand on mine, and said, "Some of what she says can be just mumbo jumbo, so don't let it bother you. Go ahead, live your life, and don't let anyone's 'predictions' dissuade you. Follow the signs God gives to you, and trust in the way of the Lord, even though you may not always totally understand everything. I believe that our God works in miraculous ways, so let that be your guide."

I relaxed a bit when she said that. But when I went to shake Mrs. M's hand I felt the same icy sensation I experienced when I touched Gramps just before he passed on.

I looked into her old and tired eyes and she understood I knew what was to follow and whispered, "Don't say a word to anyone, I have come to grips with my upcoming journey home, and don't want to worry anyone else. Let's keep this a secret between you and me, understand?"

I nodded yes while small tears appeared in my eyes. I now realized what Margaret meant when she said that my right hand had special abilities.

* * *

Rose and I spent the rest of July getting ready for our upcoming wedding. We talked to the young priest who was to marry us and a church date was reserved—October 25th. Then we, actually I, started to put deposits down on the necessary items: a reception hall, limo, band, cake, invitations, and finally Rose's special wedding dress. This cost me all of my savings, but I knew it was money well spent. I was happier than I could ever remember.

Rose and I also were spending most nights at our favorite bar, The Cave, drinking and dancing. Right before my eyes, she was morphing into a different person. Her drinking had accelerated and it was like she'd lose herself to the excitement of the bar. She clearly loved the devil-may-care feeling. I figured these changes were for the good. After all, the drinking was bringing out her latent sensuality. Rose especially loved "dirty dancing" and I wasn't going to complain. The way we moved together reminded me of what Carmen said years before; that dancing is the foreplay to what follows, and it also helps you see how compatible you are with your partner. I was feeling very excited about both.

* * *

The last week of July I received a terribly saddening phone call. Rose informed me that Mrs. M. had passed away.

The night we arrived at the funeral home I hugged Margaret. "Sorry about your mom, she was a lovely lady. I'll miss her, but she's in a better place now."

"You knew this was going to happen that day I met you, didn't you?" Margaret quietly responded. "I saw the look on both your faces when you touched her hand. I told you your right hand could be trusted."

She changed subjects before I could say anything, "You're right, though, she is in a better place and she has moved on to the next phase of her life." Then Margaret abruptly asked, "How's it going with Rose?"

I shrugged my shoulders. "I think she's changin'. She's not exactly the same person I fell in love with, but the feelings are the same. Everything is a go for October, so it can't be all bad."

"How about bringing her over here so I can do a quick reading?" Margaret offered.

I called Rose over, explained what was going to happen, and Margaret looked deeply into her eyes. "I see a short vacation of sorts coming your way soon. It will lead to the realization of what you really want for your future. Be open to seeing what is being shown to you or your life may not turn out the way you want it to. Make your choices carefully, or else you may hurt someone you care for, and yourself, in the long run."

Rose laughed it off, and walked away saying, "Get real, Margaret."

Margaret hugged me good-bye and whispered in my ear, "Watch her closely. I see someone else in her near future. She cares for you, but she's not truly in love with you. If she doesn't come clean soon, she'll hurt you badly. You'll make it, though. Your life will be a fine one."

Margaret left, and I never saw her again. I took her words with a grain of salt. I really loved Rose, and there was no way I would give her up that easily, no matter what a psychic believed to be true.

CHAPTER 26
THE TRIP TO FLORIDA

Another few weeks went by—Rose and I continued organizing our big wedding during the day and dancing away the nights. One Saturday afternoon a box arrived in the mail. It was addressed to the both of us and it was the first time Rose saw my last name appended to her first. We opened the box and saw it contained our wedding invitations.

Rose started to cry. "You make me feel like the only girl in the world. I love how you're always there for me. I can't wait till we're married."

I felt the same way, all of it. Well, except for being the only girl in the world!

And as she continued to look through the invitations, I took one of them and put it away for another day.

* * *

That Saturday became a turning point for us. Rose and I started drinking only white wine while we were together. I told her that my grandmother believed a glass of wine brought you closer to God. Rose began to think the same, and got real close to God with almost a bottle per night.

I had my own reason for drinking wine, though—it made me horny. As soon as the sweet taste hit my mouth, the feelings of love trapped inside of me began to escape. Not only did they intensify, but so did the time I was able to perform.

We would drink, dance, and then go back to my place and make passionate love the rest of the night. The more we did this, the deeper I let Rose into my heart—the walls surrounding it had been broken down long ago—and I knew we really belonged together, no matter what Margaret had said. I hadn't felt the old emptiness I was once so accustomed to in a very long time.

The closer we became, the more I felt God was back on my side, and that I had read the signs correctly. I hadn't seen Nana lately and wondered why, but I was so busy loving Rose it didn't matter.

* * *

The third week of August my father called and invited us to fly to Florida so he could meet Rose before the wedding. He also said he had something important he wanted to talk me about.

Rose asked if her sister, Ann, could come along. Dad picked up the tab for all three of us, and we arrived in sunny Florida a week later. When my father and Lars met us at the airport Dewey, my dad's life partner, wasn't with them. I found that odd as these three gay guys were practically inseparable. I assumed he was resting at home after a long night at the club.

Dad drove us the four miles to my old house following the initial introductions of everyone. I shared my knowledge of South Florida with Rose and Ann, and noticed both Lars and my dad were abnormally quiet on the way.

The girls were chit-chatting the whole ride and when I pointed out The Liquor Store, my old stomping grounds, I saw a look of excitement in Rose's eyes. I heard her whisper to Ann, "That's where we wanna go one of these nights."

* * *

The two girls wanted to go swimming after arriving at the house and getting a quick tour. I took that opportunity to ask my dad about Dewey.

He turned dead serious. "That's what we need to talk about."

Lars, my dad, and I sat around the big glass table in the outside Florida room.

"There's a new disease spreading like wild fire, not only here in the gay areas of Florida, but everywhere," my dad explained. "It's a deadly virus called AIDS. It attacks a person's insides and literally eats them away. It's only spread by sexual contact, not shakin' hands or drinkin' out of the same cups or things like that, so don't be afraid of catchin' anything. Dewey caught it from a friend of ours, and he died a month ago."

He stopped for a minute as tears welled up in his eyes. It was the first time I had ever seen him cry, and I felt very bad for him. Even though he made my life a little rougher than it needed to be, I still loved him, and knew this hurt him very much.

"Even though Dewey and I were together for so long, I'm still symptom free—but probably not for long. All of our friends, with few exceptions are now gone."

I saw the tears again. My dad took a deep breath and added, "It looks like this AIDS thing will wipe out gays all over the whole land. Some people believe that it was sent by God to rid the planet of us. I just wanted you to know what was happening ... that I love you and always will."

I had a lot of questions, but he held up his hand. "Look, you know about this now, but let's stop talkin' about it. You're here for some fun, so let's not have this stop us. Don't tell Rose, I don't know if she will accept me and my lifestyle, and we don't want her or her sister worryin' about catchin' somethin' while they're here. Let's just drop it."

Later that night, we all went to Behind the Scenes, the club my dad owned. This was both Rose's and Ann's first exposure to the gay lifestyle, but I was very impressed how they both accepted what they saw, and that they treated the gays the same as they treated everyone else. In fact, I felt they enjoyed the exciting energy in the club. The drinking, the poppers, and the loud atmosphere intensified the feelings of freedom they were experiencing. Rose danced around, with both men and women, looking more alive than I had ever seen before.

I went upstairs to relax and try to be alone for a few minutes, but Lars followed. We sat down at a table overlooking the dance floor and we watched Rose do her thing.

Lars said, "Watch out for her, she seems to like the bar scene a little too much. That gets a lot of people in trouble if they can't handle it. I can tell she loves the attention she's getting. I know you love her, but does she love you back?"

I shrugged my shoulders. "I hope so, but I'm starting to feel the same thing you do. She's changed a lot since seein' all the variety the world has to offer. I do know that she's only slept with me, so I think I can handle sharing the spotlight, as long as she comes home with me every night."

And right on cue, just after I said that, we watched Rose sniff a popper with a young Cuban lesbian, then kiss her square on the lips. I knew I should have been mad, instead I was strangely excited by the thought of where this could lead. The more she danced and touched this girl, the more the anticipation grew within me. If Rose really enjoyed sharing time with me *and* other girls, the sky was the limit.

* * *

The next night Rose and her sister were going to The Liquor Store without me. I was staying home under the pretense of being too tired — but it was really to talk more with my father about this deadly new disease called AIDS. I walked them out to Dad's car, handed over the keys, and told them to be safe, be careful, and that after a nap I'd be waiting up for them at the pool when they got home.

I joked, "Watch out for these Florida guys — they lie, steal, and make you do things ya don't wanna. Just because they look good doesn't mean they're good for you. Ann, keep your eyes on your sister for me please, I'm really looking forward to getting married you know."

* * *

It was about 2:00 in the morning. I was sitting in the pool under the dark Florida sky when I heard a car pull up and only one door slam shut. I waited to see who it was, but no one came out to the pool. About thirty minutes later, another car pulled up and another door slammed shut. This time I heard a faint conversation, and knew it was Rose and Ann talking. I heard the front door of the house open and close, and finally saw the two of them walking toward the pool through the open Florida room.

They slowly approached me. Rose tried to talk low, but I heard what she said. "Ann, please don't say anything to Phil, he'll just get mad and I don't need that right now. Let's just forget about tonight."

Ann whispered back, also too loud, "Trust is what's important right now. You should tell him what happened and I'm sure he'll forgive you."

Rose shook her head. "I know *he* will, but I don't know if I can."

* * *

The two ladies entered the pool area and Rose took off her clothes to join me in skinny dipping. Ann kept her clothes on and sat down on a chair near the pool.

I was chomping at the bit. "So how was your night? And what will I forgive you about?"

Rose blushed. "We'll talk about it later, right now I just want to relax."

The three of us lounged around the pool for the next half hour, soaking up the moonlight and looking at the stars in the Florida sky, exchanging very little conversation. Ann excused herself and went to bed, leaving Rose and me alone to discuss what happened.

She let out a deep sigh and said, "Okay, I was dancing with Ann when this good lookin' guy, Bert, comes up and starts dancin' with us. Pretty soon he asks if he can buy us a drink, but Ann wasn't interested and went back to our place at the bar. I said he could buy me *one* drink, but after more dancin' and talkin' I actually had more than one. I think he may have put some type of drug into one of my drinks because I became very aroused. The more we danced, the more I felt like I do when we're together."

Uh-oh, where is this going?

177

"I got closer and closer to him and we started to dirty dance. Before I knew it, Bert was kissin' me and I found myself kissin' him back. What kept runnin' through my mind was 'I wonder how good he is in bed?' I wondered if he'd be different than you and if I should follow through on this thought."

Not exactly what I wanted to hear.

"It was like Bert read my mind cuz he asked if I wanted to leave with him. I told him I couldn't—that I had a fiancé waiting for me at home."

Good girl. I knew I could trust you.

"To which he replied, 'What he don't know won't hurt him.'"

Double Uh-oh!

Rose stopped to kiss me. "Ann came to get me to say she was tired and wanted to leave. I gave her the keys to the car and told her we'd follow behind her so that Bert and I could spend some more time together. Well, we left at the same time, but somehow Ann got stuck in traffic, so I showed Bert how to get here. When we pulled in the driveway, first he turned off the car, had me slide over next to him and he started kissin' me again. I didn't want to. I started to struggle a bit, but he forcibly took my hand and had me touch him through his pants. Then he unzipped his pants, took his dick out and told me to stroke it. I was scared—and still a bit woozy from all the drinks and whatever else he gave me—so I did."

Please stop this.

"In a matter of seconds he had my shorts off and was just about to enter me when I realized what was actually happenin' and tried desperately to get away. Bert locked the doors and his personality changed quickly. He said, in a strange and eerie voice, that he knew I wanted him from the minute we first started dancing. He said my eyes told him that I needed a real man and that *he* was my dream come true."

So, I guess I'm not the only man in the world who knows about the sex gleam.

"There we both were, naked from the waist down. He began tryin' to have sex with me again, but by now I was sober. He tried to climb on top of me but I grabbed at his thing and dug my fingernails into it as hard as I could. He screamed out in pain and I was able to unlock the doors. I got out of the car as fast as I could, and ran around to the side of the house and hid. About a half an hour later, Ann finally showed up. We talked about what happened as we were walkin' back here."

Rose let go another deep sigh. "Phil, I'm ashamed I got drunk. But I'm more ashamed I let a creep like Bert sweet talk me into almost havin' sex with him. I hope you can forgive me."

Of course I will. You were as honest as honest could be.

I exhaled a deep breath for emphasis. "Rose, you need to be more careful."

I grabbed a hold of her shaking body. "Maybe you need to stop drinkin' so much so you can stay in control of yourself when you're out at bars. I don't want you getting hurt, and I sure don't want ya to get raped. You know I forgive you, but I'd never forgive myself if somethin' bad happened to ya."

Rose kissed me and told me she loved me. We went to sleep with me satisfied she'd learned her lesson.

* * *

The next morning when I woke up, Rose was still asleep. I decided on a quick swim and then I'd have some coffee next to the pool. After a few minutes of rigorous exercise in the water I sat down at the table and let the sun warm my naked back. I read the local paper, *The Fort Lauderdale Journal*, and then said a quick prayer of thanks to God that my father was still healthy, and that Rose didn't get hurt the night before.

I was reading the results from yesterday's horse races at Hialeah Park when Ann joined me at the table. She poured herself some coffee. "So did she tell you about last night?"

I shook my head yes continuing to study the form for today's races.

"Aren't you mad at her for what she did?" Ann said, wide-eyed.

I looked up. "It wasn't her fault—the guy was a jerk. I'm just glad she didn't get hurt."

Ann just stared at me like I was nuts, or maybe a fool? "For the record, what'd she tell you happened?"

I started to retell the story I'd heard last night but Ann immediately shook her head no and stopped me. "That ain't at all what happened. I'll tell you the truth, but you gotta promise to give her a second chance. I know she's my sister and all—I really like you, and want you to be part of our family."

Ann opened the flood gates.

I didn't want to hear what she was saying and really only comprehended the last things she said.

"...I'm waitin' outside on your porch when Rosalin and Bert show up. Rosalin gets outta the car and I see her kiss Bert on the lips. I hear her say 'Thanks for a great time.' She sees me, and I could tell right away they had sex. She quickly makes up the story she told you and begs me to go along with it." Ann made a sad face. "I'm sorry to be the one to tell you this."

I could feel the blood drain from my face.

Ann reached for my hand and said, "I'm sorry I didn't try to stop her, I feel like shit."

I tried to regain my composure. "Ann, this isn't your fault. She's a big girl and can make her own decisions. Thanks for lettin' me know the truth, though."

"So, what happens next?" Ann's face was white. "Are you gonna talk to her? Or ask for your ring back?"

I thought it over for a minute. "I think it's better we keep this to ourselves. I'll work through it on my own, and hopefully it's just a onetime thing. If she wants me to know, she needs to come clean on her own. Nothing's gained by getting mad, it's all over now."

Ann shook her head in disbelief. "You're a better man than most. She's lucky to have found you. I just hope you're right and she doesn't blow it."

You're not the only one.

CHAPTER 27
PANDEMONIUM

All through September, Rose and I continued planning our future together. We found an apartment where we wanted to live, decided on what kind of cars we wanted to drive, and also discussed the possibility of having children. She wasn't too keen on kids, but I was. I had it all planned out. I wanted two, one of each, and even had names picked out. I liked Trent Michael for a boy and Nicolette Lynn for a girl.

Rose teased me and said that I was acting all girlie—just like Allie.

During this time she was also spending more and more nights with her girlfriends. She said she wanted to "sow her wild oats." Before the trip to Florida I never even knew she had any oats—let alone wild—but I trusted her, and her friends, to keep it sane.

Many of those times they would end up at Pandemonium, a dance club we all frequented. That was where Rose really let loose. According to her friends, she would drink, dance, and flirt all night long. They all told me I taught her well—she knew how to have a good time, and made sure everyone around her did, too.

I was okay that she was getting the wild life out of her system. After all, I had already done my share. And I'd rather she do it now than *after* we were married. I felt that as long as she came back home to me that same night, I was fine. There were many a time when we would go dancing as a group and she would take off on her separate way, only to return to me near the end of the night. I trusted her not to do anything really stupid that would jeopardize our relationship, and kept the negative thoughts at bay.

* * *

One night near the end of September we went out together with a group of our friends and Rose did her own thing. I was drinking with the other guys and didn't realize she had strayed from the group. Most of the time Pandemonium played fast dance music, but occasionally they slipped in a slow song. About an hour before closing time the DJ put on an old Air Supply song I really liked. I got the urge to dance, but couldn't find Rose.

I had a friend of hers look in the ladies room while I scanned the bar area for her. My search ended when I saw her on the dance floor with another guy. They danced the whole song so close they were practically inside each other's shirts. And when it ended, all of us watched Rose tongue kiss this guy while he grabbed her ass.

I sat at the bar and proceeded to get drunk. No white wine this time. Stoli vodka for me, thank you!

An R-rated version of the Florida episode was happening, only in front of all of her friends and me.

Karen, one of the girls in our group, was sitting next to me. She shook her head sadly. "I know that musta been hard to see. You need to know this, Phil—it happens all the time. Take my word, I'm here a lot with her and this ain't the first time she's behaved like that. I don't know what happened to Rose, but she's not the innocent little girl you fell in love with."

I downed a Stoli shot in one gulp. "Yeah, I know you're right. I love her so much, but how much can a man take? I wish I knew whether this is just a phase or if it's who she really is."

"I hope it all works out for you two." Karen tossed her head in Rose's direction. "Except for *that*, you guys really are perfect for each other."

Karen walked away and I said a silent prayer asking Nana for help.

* * *

It was twenty-one days until our wedding. I was anxious and Rose seemed nervous. I took that as a good sign. I never told her I saw her with that other guy, and she hadn't brought it up, so I thought it was over.

That night I went out with some friends from work to the local OTB to bet some horses and just relax. We watched these graceful animals run around in circles all night while I continued to drink one Stoli per race. By the end of the night I had lost all my money, was stinking drunk, and was feeling pretty down about myself.

When I walked into the apartment Rose and I shared, she was sitting on our couch all wrapped up in a down blanket watching an old black and white movie in the dark. I sat down next to her and noticed she had tears in her eyes.

"What's wrong?" I huffed. "I should be the one cryin'. I lost a ton of money tonight."

Rose looked up. "I'm lost and confused, and I don't know what to do."

"About what?"

"We need to talk," Rose barely mumbled.

That was the first time I'd ever heard that infamous cue, if I'd heard it before, I would have been ready for what was coming next.

Rose told me she didn't know herself anymore; that she also wasn't feeling good about herself and she had no idea what she wanted. Rose held my hand tightly in hers and started to tell me about the night in Florida, but I stopped her and said I already forgave her for that.

She began telling me stories about Andrew and Betty, friends of ours who were going through a tough divorce. Everyone thought they were the perfect couple, but they were never on the same page at the same time.

"I don't wanna be like them," she sighed. "I really want a relationship that will last forever, not end up where people just fight all the time."

"I promise we'll never let that happen," I stated firmly. "We both love each other too much for that."

"I know that I love you, and that you truly love me." Rose let the tears flow unobstructed. "But I find myself feelin' different than before. Ever since you have shown me how to enjoy life—ya know, the dancin' and drinkin' and partyin'—I just want more and more. I know I'm being selfish, but I think I'm too young to settle down. I know that's what you desperately want. I don't want to hurt you, but I think we should postpone the wedding. I'm just not ready. Can you ever forgive me?"

I was flabbergasted and deeply hurt, but being drunk I swallowed my pride. "I guess I understand. Listen, Rose, you're the only one for me, but I heard a saying once, somethin' like: 'If you love something, let it go free. And if it ever returns it's yours forever. If it doesn't, it never was in the first place.' Tonight, Rose, I set you free."

Rose hugged me tightly, and said in between sobs, "You're the best. I hope someday I come to my senses. Can we still be a couple, though? I really want you in my life. I just don't want to be married right now. I just want to feel good about myself again."

I half-smiled when my old saying popped into my mind. I said somewhat sarcastically, "Yes pretty lady, I can help you feel good."

CHAPTER 28
GRAM

Rose gave me my ring back, and I put it in a safe place, hopefully for a later day. It became my job to tell everyone the wedding was off. All our friends couldn't believe it, nor could they believe I was still going to be involved with Rose. I got sympathy, I got empathy, and I got respect from all these people and from the companies I gave deposits to.

What I didn't get was any of my money back.

When I talked to the priest who was to marry us, he said it was a shame—we looked so good together. He would have sworn we were in love, but that God must not have wanted it to happen. He reminded me the Lord only gives us what we can handle.

All this kept me busy. It was a good thing, too. I knew I was going to lose my mind if I wasn't staying in motion. I prayed for God to help get me through these times and to keep me strong. I wanted to maintain my composure around other people. I needed them to think I was strong enough to handle this, even though I was sure I wasn't.

* * *

One of the last people I called was Rose's grandmother. We had become pretty close since the engagement party. She lived in Wisconsin and we could only talk on the phone, but had weekly conversations regarding many a different subject. I loved her almost as much as I loved my Nana, and I trusted her insights just the same. She was very angry with Rose about her decision, but I calmed her down.

"Look, I understand Rose. She's young and wants to live. I can't fault her for that. I sure have done my share," I said. "At least she still wants me around."

"That's very adult of you. You're so much more mature than she is."

"Yeah, I try."

"Since you guys are gonna try and stay together, how about a little visit up to see me. Let's do it on the weekend that the wedding would have been held. At least it will give you a break from people feelin' sorry for you—for a little while, anyway. And if it's not too cold we can sit on the pier by the lake, talk about life and drink until we're all so drunk we can't stand up anymore."

"Sounds like a plan to me," I said, smiling and looking forward to seeing her again. "I'll run it by Rose."

* * *

On October 24, the day before we were supposed to get married, Rose and I drove up to Wisconsin to spend the weekend with her grandparents.

Luckily, the weather was clement for that time of year, and the ride went quickly. But the whole way up Rose was quiet. I was hoping she was thinking about us and what this day, and especially tomorrow, should have been all about.

When we drove past Delavan, the town where my Nana and Gramps had their cottage, I began to cry a little. Rose understood what I was feeling and cried with me.

Even though we weren't getting married, at least I felt like we still shared a connection with each other.

We reached our destination, Whitewater, and surprisingly I felt an eerie calm come over me. We pulled into the long narrow driveway of her grandparent's house and I was actually in complete control again.

Rose's grandmother was waiting for us on the porch and rushed up to me first as we exited the car. She gave me a big, loving hug and whispered, "I'm so glad you came. I love you like a grandson. I want you to call me Gram from now on. Don't you worry, we'll survive this together."

She then went over to Rose and repeated the action while I shook hands with her grandfather. Kevin was a quiet man who rarely spoke. I had met him twice before and never heard him speak. Even though he didn't say a word to me, his handshake made me feel welcome, and also let me know he understood what I was going through.

Rose and I unpacked the car and I asked where to put our things. Gram replied with a twinkle in her eyes, "Put 'em in the second bedroom on your left. That'll give you enough room for both of you, and I won't be able to hear whatever sounds emerge from behind the closed door tonight."

Rose blushed as she walked past her. I winked at Gram, knowing she was going to do everything possible to give Rose a hard time the whole weekend.

* * *

We had a quick dinner, as it was late, and then both Rose and Kevin decided to call it a night. Gram and I walked to the back porch, sat down in a couple of old rocking chairs, and started chatting. Right away it reminded me of the talks Nana and I had years earlier and I smiled.

"That's a great smile you have," Gram said. "It's nice to see you can still use it even after what my granddaughter has done to you."

"Well, I believe that God only gives us what we can handle and this is definitely a test of that," I returned. "Besides, life is all about learning and that's what we're both doin'. I just think we're learnin' different lessons."

"Interesting," Gram nodded. "So what have learned from her?"

"That's easy," I said. "Rose has shown me how to be me, and actually believe in myself again. Before I met her, I was self-destructive one moment and self-centered the next. She has taught me patience and humility. Without her I'm sure I wouldn't feel as whole as I do right now."

Gram smiled. "Even the bad sometimes bring us good."

* * *

When we got back from Wisconsin, Rose moved out of our apartment. She said she needed to have her own place. We still saw each other, and continued to meet her married friends for dinner and things, but we were really two separate people. The only time we were connected was when we were making love—and it was still making love to me—not just having sex.

I was sure she was having more than her fair share of that with whoever she brought home at night, as her likes in bed had changed since she moved out. Once again I tried to be the bigger person and never said anything. Inside, though, I was dying. I knew it was just a matter of time before she moved on forever. And that empty feeling was inching its way back.

* * *

December 18th came and I realized I hadn't seen Rose for about two weeks. I figured she was having her fun and didn't want me getting in the way. I had been feeling rather low anyway; it was better she wasn't around. So I was taken by surprised when she appeared at my doorstep that night without any warning. I could see she was upset.

"What's wrong?"

She walked right past me and sat down.

"I have some bad news," she said. "Gram just died … thought you'd like to know. You guys seemed so close."

"I'm so sorry." I went over and hugged her. "Is there something I can do to help?"

"Just hold me for a while, and then let's make love," Rose said quietly.

* * *

I went to Gram's wake by myself. Since the night Rose told me about her death, she hadn't called or dropped by at all. I slowly made my way around the funeral home and ran into people who didn't expect me to be there. I felt as though it was my wake, not Gram's.

Rose was very short with me and everyone in the room could feel the tension. It was the first time I felt out of place around her since Jack and Deb's wedding, almost three years earlier. There was nothing but cold air between us.

I took the hint and moved on. Ann and her new boyfriend were there, along with some of the married friends Rose and I used to hang around with. They were all very polite to me, saying it was nice of me to be there for Rose.

They didn't realize I was there for Gram, not her.

I sat down in the back row and a few minutes later I felt someone touch my left shoulder from behind me. A feeble voice said, "Finally, someone I wanna see. You look like how I feel. Can I sit next to you for a while?"

I turned around and was shocked to see Kevin. This was the first time Rose's grandfather had ever spoken to me. We sat together in silence and he looked lost. He was quieter than ever, if that was even possible, and was extremely white in color. His eyes were set back into his face with dark circles around them. All he did for the next twenty minutes was twiddle his thumbs without moving any other part of his body.

He surprised me again when he said, "I'm just half a man now. She meant everythin' to me, and now I feel nothin' inside. I died along with her, ya know. This is why the man should always go first. We're nothin' without a woman by our side."

I reached over with my right hand to try and control his trembling body, and felt the same icy sensation that was present just before Gramps and Mrs. M. passed away.

I didn't say anything out loud, but thought to myself, You'll be with her soon enough.

Kevin left and I remained at the back of the room. That's where I overheard Betsy, Rose's aunt who was in charge of the funeral, ask Ann's boyfriend if he would like to be a pallbearer the next day. I assumed she would ask me next, as I knew her mom much better than he did. But she never did. I was deeply hurt and wondered why I wasn't asked.

I made my way between mourners and over to Rose. "Why wasn't I asked to be a pallbearer, Rose?"

"My aunt doesn't know who you are, she's never met you." She brushed me off. "She doesn't know you had any kind of relationship with Gram."

"Well, can you tell her?" I pleaded. "I really want to do this, and I bet Gram would rather have me there by her side than Ann's new boyfriend, who she never met."

"Just get over it, will ya?" Rose whispered angrily. "This isn't about you anymore, it's about family and you're not part of it."

That was the final straw. I said good-bye to Kevin, for what would be the last time. I went up to pay my respects to Gram and placed a red rose in the casket next to her. I started to cry and that's when Betsy came up to me and asked, "Who are you? And how'd you know my mom?"

I looked her directly in the eyes. "I'm Rosalin's ex-fiancé, and I loved your mom almost as much as I did my own great-grandmother. I realize you don't know this, but we had a special bond, go ask your dad. I'm really gonna miss her, and will never forget her."

When I left the funeral home, like Kevin, I, too, felt as though a part of me had died. I cried most of the way home, all the while cursing out Rose about ever having met her.

I told myself I wouldn't be able to forgive her this time.

* * *

Two days after the funeral, Rose came by with a hand-written message from her aunt.

Phil, I'm so sorry I didn't know you when I saw you and that I didn't know your feelings for my mom. I realize now that I should have asked you to be a pallbearer, as you really did share a bond. I hope you can forgive me. Kevin says that she wanted you to have something special, so please accept this, and my apologies about everything.
Sorry, Betsy

Rose handed me a small figurine. It looked like an angel, but I wasn't sure. She explained, "This was Gram's favorite. She always believed God was a woman, so this figure was what Gram prayed to. She called Her Azna and said that She helps deflect all the negative powers in the world. Gram also told us that Azna is like a guide. She helps you get over all the small, and some of the large problems you encounter in your life. She's always there, watchin' over you when you need someone to believe in. I don't get it, but Kevin told me to tell you that Gram knew you'd totally understand all this."

I took the figurine from Rose and stashed it away.

I knew exactly what Gram meant.

* * *

Over the next three months I was trying to get Rose back into my life full-time, but she was only interested in going to bed part-time. Rose only called when she wanted sex and I always gave in. I hoped the lovemaking would bring us closer again. But the more I expressed my love for her, the further she drifted away.

One night in March, Rose called and asked if we could get together. Like always, I said yes. This time when she arrived, she prefaced our love-making by saying, "Phil, I owe you so much. You have made me who I am today and you've always been there for me. I know this is going to hurt, but tonight is the last time I'll call on you for help."

Rose stopped to give me a kiss. "You've always been honest with me, so this time I will be, too."

Then she started to cry. "I've met someone and I've decided to move in with him. But I don't want to leave without something to remember you by."

I had tears in my eyes too, but I knew what she wanted.

Rose and I spent this last night together and I gave it my all. When it was over I was trying desperately to hold onto the moment forever. I gave into my emotions and burst into a nonstop flood of tears. No matter what I tried I couldn't stop. My heart was breaking in two. Rose was crying, too, and finally couldn't take it anymore so she just got up and left without even saying good-bye.

I lay on my bed for hours crying inconsolably. I begged for help from God or Azna or from my Nana, but got no response from any of them.

I gave up and was able to cry myself to sleep. During this restless slumber, it happened. A "vision" of Nana appeared to me. It wasn't for very long, but it was memorable.

Nana wiped away the tears from my eyes. "Remember, I told you to be very careful with this one. I know it may be hard, but you must try to forget the heartache, but don't forget what she taught you. You're a better man for the time you spent with her, and this will help you move on. God and I love you very much and are always there for you, even when it seems like we aren't."

CHAPTER 29
CHRIS

Just as fast as the last two months had flown by, the next four dragged on and on just as slowly. I was depressed, lonely, and angry at how Rose had treated me. I had always been there for her when she needed help, and I'd put my life on hold for three years while she "decided what was best for her."

My days consisted of attempting to wake up and go to work. But I was constantly coming in late and leaving early. Each night when I returned home I would drink heavily. I changed my favorite drink from white wine to Stolichnaya vodka. The wine just made me horny, while the vodka simply got me drunk—fast—and that's exactly what I needed right now.

Most nights after getting inebriated, I would assume the fetal position on my couch in the living room or hide under the covers of my bed searching for answers. When none came, my old reliable standbys of Air Supply, Bread, and Rod Stewart once again became my best friends.

At least I knew I could always count on them to be there for me.

* * *

There were no positive emotions in my body and I saw no future for me. It was like Rose had taken the best of me and left me with just a shell. I felt like Kevin did at Gram's funeral. The impenetrable wall which once surrounded my heart, was once again rebuilding itself, brick by brick. And another old friend of mine—emptiness—came over for an extended visit.

* * *

Every night after work, the first thing I would do was check for messages on my answering machine. I'd walk into my dark apartment alone and immediately look for the red blinking light telling me that someone, anyone had called. Rarely did the light ever blink back at me, and so I'd spend the night with my other close friend, Stoli.

One Friday night, I came home and again no messages. I headed right for the liquor, then pulled up short. I was so bored of being bored I forced myself to get out of my apartment. There was a time, back in Florida, I enjoyed the horse races and I thought I'd give that a try, instead of the usual mind-numbing TV.

I arrived at Washington Park, near the Missouri-Ilinois border— bought a program and proceeded directly to the bar. Yes, I was still alone, but at least other people surrounded me. I sat down, placed a hundred dollar bill on the bar, and said to the blonde bartender as I read her nametag, "Hey, Chris, start bringin' me Stoli tonics with three olives until the money is gone. Don't wait for me to ask, when ya see an empty glass just fill 'er up. I promise to leave ya a nice tip if you help me forget why I'm here."

"I know how you feel. I'm on a bad streak myself. Do you need ta talk?" Chris said, placing the first of many drinks in front of me. "I'm right here, and it's a slow night."

"Not now. First I'd like to get drunk, and hopefully not lose all of my money," I politely said. "I'll let ya know if I need you."

I scanned the race program and found a horse named Anza running in the second race. That name was close enough to the mother God figurine Gram had bequeathed to me, and I decided to bet it. I was standing in line to place my bet when the feeling in my gut told me there was no way this horse was going to lose. I glanced at the odds, saw she was 50-1, so I placed a C-note on her nose.

I went back to the bar, and as Chris poured me another drink, I confidently said, "When I win this race, I'll give you a $100 tip."

"Are you sure?" Chris piped up. "What do I need to do?"

"Just keep the booze flowin', pretend to be my friend, and hope and pray number 7 wins."

The race went off as Chris and I watched together. Anza took the lead and never looked back. The adrenaline rush I felt was unbelievable. After the last few months of total numbness, this was excitement at its best. But it was nothing compared to how I felt when I gave $100 to Chris after cashing in for $5000, and said, "Maybe this will end your losing streak."

"It looks like a good start," she smiled, plucking the bill from the bar and tucking it in her bra.

I downed the next vodka tonic she placed in front of me and looked over the next race. I was blown away when I saw a young female horse named My Golden Gram. I flashed a smile at Chris. "Here's another one I can't lose. The same deal goes as last race."

I plunked down another $100 at the window, this time on number 6. Her odds were 10-1. Chris and I yelled and high-fived as "Gram" crossed the finish line first. I was $1000 richer, and she had another $100 tip.

I raised my arms into the air like the winning prize fighter, and said, "Told-ja your bad streak was over."

I was feeling very alive for the first time since Rose left me. I had made a complete 180 degree turnaround after only 45 minutes at the track.

There were no horses in the next few races I liked, so Chris and I just talked. "It's so cool to see someone win and actually smile once in a while," she said, while wiping down some beer mugs. "Many of the guys here don't have lives, or anyone for them to go home to. It's normally a pretty lonely place. So, just why are you here?"

"Cuz I have no life," I laughed. "I guess I fit in just fine."

I gave Chris the short version of my failed engagement.

"I'm sorry to hear about your ex-fiancé and all," she said. "But if you dole out money like this all the time, I'll gladly go out with you."

I smiled, and I felt like I was back in control.

I was scanning through the program again when I came upon race nine. I saw horse number 3 was Rosie Is Right. I instinctively wanted to bet it. But then a strange feeling rumbled through my gut, and even though *he* had won the last nine races in a row, and was the "Best Bet" of the night according to those "in the know" I knew he was going to lose. I smiled at Chris and said, "I'm gonna give you another $100 when he gets beaten tonight."

"There's no way that happens," she laughed. "He's the best horse on the grounds. He never loses."

"Trust me," I winked. "He will tonight."

Some of the other guys at the bar heard me say this and took Chris's side. I was so sure "Rosie" would lose I bet five of them a drink. All of them accepted my wager and then eagerly awaited their free alcohol.

The race was exciting as Rosie went to the lead, only to lose it to another horse around the first turn. They were head to head for the first half of the race and I felt my heart start to pound faster. My palms started to sweat and my voice got louder as I rooted *against* the horse everyone else had bet on.

Man, I was feeling alive again.

At the end of the race, there was a very close photo finish between horse number 1 and Rosie. All the guys sitting at the bar argued over who won. When the official numbers on the placing board stopped blinking everyone saw number 1 had won the race and Rosie Is Right was indeed second.

I happily gave Chris her $100 and even told the others not to worry about the drinks they owed me. I said, "Hey guys, I had an unfair advantage in that race. There was no way that horse was gonna win. Rose is the name of my ex-fiancé."

They all laughed as if they totally understood what I meant.

I was so elated that I could joke once again I actually bought *them* all a drink and toasted, "Like Billy Joel sings, here's to sharin' a drink called loneliness."

Chris thanked me for the money I was giving her. "This will really help me and my three kids. I'm divorced and work full-time during the day, and then three nights a week here just to stay afloat. Every little bit helps and this is more than I make in tips in a week."

I felt sad for her, realizing she was just one of us.

* * *

The last race of the night was upon us, and as Chris and I looked over the horses we both turned and stared at each other when we saw number 8 was Dontworryitsover.

"I know this horse," Chris said. "Not only hasn't she won in a year, she always finishes last."

"Tonight will be a first then. Look at her name, isn't that what we've been sayin' all night long?" I said, getting up to place my bet. "It's time for you to start believing your unlucky streak is over, and for me to get that my life with Rose is done."

"There is no way in hell," Chris laughed, "that horse won't win, place or even show up-'cept dead last."

I put down a conservative $100 on number 8 at 99-1 odds to win, and as an afterthought placed another small wager.

Before the horses lined up behind the starting gate, I glanced upward and said a silent prayer to Azna, the mother God. Gram believed She could help with both the small and big problems, so I pleaded, "I don't need the money, but Chris does. Don't let her down. Please handle this for us."

The race started and poor number 8 had trouble getting out of the gate.

"You should've listened to me," Chris shook her head.

But after the first turn my horse started a small comeback. By the halfway point, she had gotten into fifth place and was still moving up steadily.

And when, around the turn for home, ol' Dontworryitsover had moved into second place, Chris was yelling, I was screaming, and all the guys at the bar joined in.

Down the stretch they came, neck and neck, nose to nose. I was sweating cannon balls—but more than anything I felt electrified. I closed my eyes to thank God for reviving me, whether or not my horse won.

I knew I was back to my old self.

The horses crossed the finish line and once again the photo finish sign went up. Chris and the gang eagerly awaited the outcome while I quietly sat and sipped on my last vodka tonic. I tipped the glass trying to get the last drop of alcohol out of it and swear I saw a vision of what looked like an angel in one of the ice cubes. At the same time, I felt a warm sensation in my heart again.

I knew this time it was Azna and that we had won the race.

Before I went up to collect my winnings I said to Chris, "I have a surprise. I made a little bet for you and your kids."

I handed her a ticket listing a $50 win amount. We turned our heads to the tote board and saw our horse had paid $225.80 to win. That made her little paper ticket worth over $5000 and mine worth more than $10,000.

Chris started to cry and threw her arms around my neck, hugging me tight. "This is the best day of my life. I'm so glad you came here tonight. You're like an angel sent from above."

CHAPTER 30
LIFE GOES ON

By the time I got home, both the alcohol and the high of winning big had worn off. It was well past midnight when I walked through the parking lot of my apartment building. I approached my door knowing that inside it would be as lonely as it was before I left.

I put the key into my front door, pushed it open, and I saw it. At first I was excited, but then I was concerned. Through the deep darkness of my apartment, the red light on my answering machine was pulsating. Someone had finally called me, but who was it, and what did they want?

I flipped on the light and made my way to the dining room where the phone sat on the counter separating it and the kitchen. I hit the # button and a computerized voice announced I had two messages. I was feeling anxious as I pushed the "play" button, but the first message was only a hang-up.

I wasn't ready for another disappointment. I walked around the counter and opened the upper cabinet where I kept my drink glasses. There were no clean ones available so I grabbed a dirty one from the mess in my sink. I washed it, tossed in a couple ice cubes, and filled it to the top with ice cold vodka from my freezer.

Although I drank tonic with my vodka when I was out, I had become accustomed to drinking it straight up at home—that way I caught a buzz much faster.

I downed the drink rather quickly and then refilled the glass. I returned to the answering machine and sat down at the dining room table, where I contemplated whether or not I should hit the button again.

I took a big mouthful of vodka, and pushed the dreaded button. I almost choked on the cold liquid when I heard: "Hi, Phil. It's me, Rose."

I hit the "pause" button, not sure I wanted to hear the rest, fearing her next words would be, "I'm getting married." Another swallow of Stoli gave me the courage to hit "play". It wasn't what I expected when her voice continued.

"I know we haven't talked in a while, but I need to see you again. I'm not sure if you wanna talk to me, but I'm at Deb's and I'll be here all night. Call me at whatever time you get this message. I'll be waiting."

I sat back in my chair, poured the rest of my drink down my throat, and contemplated my next move. Here, after four months of loneliness and depression and on the very night I had finally been able to feel like I could move on, Rose was asking for my help.

I got up and refilled my glass again with some more liquid courage.

* * *

I spent the next fifteen minutes creating a mental list of the pros and cons of returning Rose's call. A part of me desperately wanted her back in my life, yet I couldn't just forget how she'd treated me. In the end, my curiosity as to why she was calling won out.

I punched the numbers on the phone that would connect me to Deb, and ultimately to Rose. The phone rang one time, and when the eager voice on the other side said, "I was hopin' you'd call," I knew I was caught up in Rose's web again.

Rose wanted to know if she could come over. I was drunk, I was missing her, and I wanted to see her again, so against my better judgment, I agreed.

Rose arrived only minutes later and before she rang the doorbell, I had the opportunity to down one more Stoli. I buzzed her in, and then listened to her footsteps the whole way from the entrance door to my first floor apartment. I was looking through the peephole as she quietly knocked on my door.

She had on a purple sweater covered by her spring jacket, tight blue jeans, and black boots. Her hair was longer than the last time I saw her and also was dyed blonde instead of her natural brown. Even at this late hour, her makeup was still perfectly applied and her hair was as neat as ever. She was a sight for lonely eyes and I prayed she was coming over to tell me she had made a big mistake and wanted to marry *me*.

I opened the door and Rose entered without me asking her to. The first thing she said was, "Wow, you look plastered."

I couldn't deny it. All the alcohol I'd imbibed had finally hit me.

"*You* look fantastic," I spat out. "But why are you are here?"

"If you get me a drink, I'll explain," she shrugged. "White wine, please."

"Sorry, don't have that anymore," I said curtly. "I only keep vodka in the house. Helps get me through the night better."

"What's that mean?" she raised an eyebrow and then quickly changed the subject. "I'll try it, but don't know if I'll like it."

Rose followed me to the kitchen.

"Man, you're a pig." She indicated the mess I'd become accustomed to. In the past, my house was always immaculate.

"I just don't have the energy, or the drive, to clean when I know no one's comin' over."

I picked up another dirty glass, washed it out, and filled both it and mine with more ice and vodka.

"Here's your drink, I'd sip it if I was you," I suggested. "So what's goin' on?"

Rose took a small sip and I saw her eyes squint as the liquor hit her throat. "Tom left me. I guess we weren't as compatible as I thought. I constantly compared what he did to what you used to do, and he quickly got sick of it."

"So, I wasn't all that bad after all," I said sarcastically.

"You treated me fantastically—that wasn't the problem," Rose said, pausing for another small sip of her vodka. "*I* was the problem."

I nodded my head in agreement.

"Look, I think I made a royal mistake when I left you," Rose said. "I'd like to try again. Can you ever forgive me?"

I was considering her question when she asked another, "Why don't you have any wine? This stuff tastes like shit!"

"Wine gets me horny," I said, as if she'd understand. "And since there's been no one to share those feelings with I started drinkin' vodka. It helped ease the pain of you leavin' me, and helps me forget I'm a failure."

Rose ignored the failure comment. "You haven't been with anyone else the whole six months? What have you been doing?"

Just trying my damn best to survive.

* * *

I slurped down another drink while Rose rambled on about her life, her decisions, and finally got to the real reason she called me.

"After leaving you, there was one thing I could never get out of my mind," she said. "I can't forget how I felt when we made love. Oh, I tried hard to suppress it, but I wasn't able to. Tom made love like we were on some kind of schedule. And he isn't as gentle as you. It felt like it was all about him getting off—never mind me." She gave me a sad, puppy-dog look and said as she led me to my bedroom, "Whaddaya say my stud in shining armor? How about sharin' some of your magic with me tonight?"

I was numb, not from what she had just told me, but from all the alcohol I had ingested that night. "Yes, pretty lady I can help you."

And that was as far as I got before I passed out next to her.

* * *

The next morning, as I tried to wake up, I wondered if last night was all a dream. I couldn't remember exactly what had happened. Some of it came back when I saw all the money I'd won falling out of the pocket of my jeans, laying on the floor next to my bed.

I stumbled out of bed with nothing on and was making my way to take a shower when I heard the water running. I opened the bathroom door and the room was filled with steam and the smell of my shampoo and body wash. I called out, but no one answered. I walked in and slowly slid the shower curtain to one side. There Rose stood, naked before me, and she looked like she was expecting me to drop in.

"Good morning, sleepy head. Are you comin' in so I can help you return from the dead?" She glanced down at my wilted member.

I shook the sleep from my eyes. "So last night did happen after all."

Rose laughed, "Everything except for what *I* really wanted, anyway."

I climbed into the shower with Rose and it reminded me of the good ol' days when the two of us were living together. We'd shower together at least once a week just for the fun of it. This time I mostly wanted to clear the cobwebs from my head.

While she was lathering me up, Rose said, "I really miss this. How about me movin' back in and we pick up where we left off?"

"How about I get my head on straight and then we'll talk?" I mumbled.

Rose hopped out of the shower and I stayed in trying to recoup my wits. I propped myself up in the corner and closed my eyes, trying to concentrate. The water fell onto my pounding head and a vision of Nana suddenly appeared. She didn't talk—only stared at me with a stern face like I was a little boy who had just made a mistake. And I swear, as I saw her pointer finger start to go back and forth five times, I heard her say, "Tsk, tsk, tsk, tsk, tsk."

I shook it off, got out of the shower, dried myself, and started to brush my teeth. My head was still groggy as I looked at myself in the steamy mirror and wondered what that brief visit by Nana meant.

I got dressed and was going to meet Rose in the dining room. I passed the kitchen and saw she had already cleaned up all the dirty dishes and was busy cleaning the rest of the apartment.

"Now, doesn't this look and feel better than the God awful pigsty you were living in?" She gestured to her handiwork.

"I guess so," I shrugged. "Now, let's talk about why you're here."

"Like I said last night, Tom didn't treat me the way you do. Yeah, he had some good qualities, but mostly he was selfish."

I could tell it was hard for her to admit she was wrong, but she forged ahead.

"Look, Phil, I'd like us to be a couple again … even move in together … start all over. Whaddaya think?"

My gut told me not to trust her, but after a minute of agonizing silence, I found myself saying, "I'm willin' to try, but you can't move in here."

"That's good enough for me," Rose smiled. "I promise I'll never to hurt you again."

* * *

An apartment in the same complex as mine, only on the other side of the parking lot, had just been vacated. She couldn't afford all the rent by herself and convinced her sister, Ann, to move in with her. The two of them became frequent visitors to my place, which was adjacent to the pool we often used.

Rose and I picked up right where we left off. We signed on for another bowling league and a volleyball team with some of her married friends. This time, Jack and Deb also joined us. We were having tons of fun together again, and in no time I was feeling extremely positive about my decision to let her back into my life.

One night, after bowling, Deb put her arm around my shoulder and said, "So, are you happy again?"

"Right now," I said. "But you know me, I always think the worst, so I'm sure somethin' will happen to change that."

"Just relax, she's not goin' anywhere this time." Deb gave my arm a confident squeeze. "She told me she wants her ring back, but she doesn't know how to ask you for it."

"*That*, I'll need to think about."

CHAPTER 31
OKAY, NOW WHAT

We had been together for another four months when September arrived. The summer had been very good to us. Rose and I spent lots of time at the zoo, the festivals of St. Louis, and took short trips to Chicago.

The two of us also had our own separate lives going on. I would go to Washington Park race track every so often to see Chris. We agreed to keep it platonic, and we both thoroughly enjoyed each other's company. I didn't give her any more lumps of money, just normal tips. Sometimes I won and sometimes I lost, basically I broke even on the horses, but was way ahead on the friendship side of things.

Since Rose didn't like horse racing, she went to the bars with her sister. This time I got good reviews. According to Ann, Rose was behaving.

We were getting along very well, and I was seriously considering that I might give her the engagement ring back after all.

* * *

Mid September, I received a phone call from Florida.

"Your dad isn't doin' too well." Lars breathed a heavy sigh into the receiver. "He has the AIDS virus and is in the hospital. The doctors think you should come down."

I quickly called Rose to let her know what was happening, and flew down to Florida that very afternoon.

When I walked into my dad's small private hospital room, I became confused. It was painted a stark blue and the sunlight that beamed through the window made it even brighter. Lars was sitting in a chair next to the bed. My dad was sitting up in bed, and they both were having a good laugh.

I became incensed. "I rushed here thinkin' you were on your deathbed, only to see you guys are laughin' and jokin'."

My dad reached out for me. "This thing comes and goes. Today is a good day."

We hugged and I noticed my dad was much thinner than I remembered.

Dad felt my unease. "You don't want to see a bad day when I'm in so much pain I just want to die. The doctors are doing all they can, but I've already lost over thirty pounds and I'm not done shedding weight."

As he told me more about the disease and how long he'd actually had it, I realized that this was only the second time in my life he felt like a father to me—the first being when we shared that father-son talk on the side of his pool.

I smiled as I went to hold his hand, and felt a warm sensation knowing that I had done the right thing in rushing to be with him. Unfortunately, I got a cool icy feeling when my right hand touched his.

* * *

Dr. Peters ducked his head into the room and asked to see me in the hallway. I joined him and he looked at me with a dour face.

"Your dad is very sick. We can keep him going by giving him a cocktail of pills, but he has a living will which will not allow us to keep him alive by means of mechanical devices. You are the final decision maker, though. If and when he goes on life support, you must let us know if we should continue or not."

That was a heavy load for me. How was I supposed to play God? And I found myself thinking, Why me?

When I returned to the room, my dad was asleep. Lars and I went for a cup of coffee in the hospital cafeteria.

Lars seemed relaxed when he said, "Your dad's ready to die. He has his will all made up, has the funeral arrangements made and paid for. He told me he wants to donate some money to the AIDS charity. I'm the executor of his will, but I'll need your help. He wants to be buried in Missouri next to his mom and dad. Can you help me with that?"

I started crying when I realized what we were talking about.

"Don't," Lars said, again in complete control of his emotions. "This is what he truly wants, and he told me that he feels very comfortable with his fate. He has accepted it and is actually lookin' forward to whatever's next. That's why he signed the living will. He said that he needed everything to be in place for those he leaves behind. He believes that this is not an end, but rather a new beginning. Let's be strong and support him."

I agreed without saying anything else.

* * *

That night I called Rose from my dad's house. She wasn't home, but I talked to Ann. I explained the situation and said I would be making trips in between Missouri and Florida in order to get everything arranged. I told her to let Rose know what was happening. In case Rose wanted to talk to me, I gave Ann my phone number. We hung up and I felt as though Ann was hiding something from me, but I was too emotionally drained to worry about it.

Over the next three weeks, I made weekly trips back and forth finalizing all the arrangements, looking in on my dad, and trying to keep my life as sane as I could.

This whole time, I wasn't able to see or talk to Rose, but I was too busy to realize it.

* * *

The cool, but sunny, morning of October 18 found me in Florida, and the day started out normal, in fact, way too normal.

Lars and I ate breakfast and discussed more estate things. We decided not go to the hospital until later that afternoon. Dad was doing well the last few days and Lars and I needed some time to just veg out.

We went to dad's bar, Behind the Scenes, to see what was happening with the impending sale. Neither Lars nor I had the time or the desire to continue on with it, and a local businessman had made a nice offer. He was a friend of my dad's, so I knew he would do right by it.

We walked through the empty dance club and many, many memories came rushing back to me—thoughts of Loretta, Stacey, and Joann. As we did, the faint recollections of all the music, the dancing, and the mild drug known as poppers came to my mind. Even the thought of what happened behind the black door with Lars made me smile.

For a moment, I wished I could keep this place, but I knew that running a bar wasn't my destiny, especially a gay one.

We left for the hospital and when Lars and I entered the empty lobby a different feeling came over me. We got on the elevator and my gut told me something was very wrong. A very anxious Dr. Peters was waiting when we exited the elevator and started walking us down the hallway to my dad's room.

"Your dad has taken a turn for the worse. The pills will no longer work, so we had to put him on a machine to keep his heart beating last night, because he lapsed into a coma," Dr. Peters explained. "He goes in and out of the coma. Right now he is fine, but this is considered life support in the state of Florida. I'm sorry to say this, but you have a decision to make."

I swallowed hard. "I'll be right back."

I walked slowly into the room not knowing what to expect. Once again, the sun was shining brightly through the window, the place looked brilliantly alive, and my dad seemed just fine, although he did have many more tubes hooked up to his arms.

"Good afternoon," he said calmly. "I think it's almost my time."

I started to cry, but he stopped me. "Don't. I've had a good life, made some very good friends who are all gone now. I even got to be very proud of all my kids. There's nothin' left for me to do. Please make sure I am buried next to Mom and Dad, even in bad times they always supported me. I want to be close to them once again."

I gave my dad a kiss and hug and promised him all of his wishes were already taken care of. I told him l loved him for who he was. And then I made that dreadful walk back to the doctor in the hallway to sign my dad's life away.

* * *

Shortly after, Lars and I entered the room again and watched Dr. Peters remove the IVs out of my dad's arm and turn off the machine he was attached to. My dad told him he was a great doctor, and a better friend. For the longest time after the tubes were taken out, nothing appeared any different. The three of us talked, we smiled, and we all reminisced about my dad's life. He looked very happy and content.

Since Dad was stable, I went down to the cafeteria to get some coffee. I was gone only ten minutes. But when I returned the difference was amazing. The room itself, which moments ago was bright, warm and sunlit, was now gray in color. I felt a coolness in the air and the bright sun was nowhere to be seen.

I sat down next to my dad and looked at him closely. His skin, which used to be soft and tanned golden brown, due to years in the Florida sun, had become gray and rough. His red lips were now purple and chapped. The marks that were left by the IV's in his upper arms were bruised and black and blue. The strong and confident voice that resonated from his mouth just minutes before, was now gone. His throat was so dry he couldn't talk. I looked in his eyes and saw nothing but darkness staring back. Minutes earlier they had been very alive and taking in each precious moment. Now they looked like deep pools of mud emitting no feelings at all.

I was scared for both him and me, but as I grabbed his arm, his eyes softened and I actually saw a minuscule smile form on his dry mouth.

A minute later, he was gone.

I sat next to his body—numb—as the doctor came in and pronounced him dead. His eyes were still open and as I stared blankly at them, strangely I felt that warm sensation in my heart again.

I continued to gaze at his body and something miraculous happened. I swear I saw a white spirit emerge from his chest area and hover above his head for a brief moment. Then just as quickly, it disappeared upward.

As it left, the room again became bright with color, warm to the feel, and the sun shined brightly through the window.

I still couldn't let go of my dad's arm go. Slowly, as if by magic, the skin which was gray just before he died turned golden brown again. The marks on his arms were all gone. Before my very own eyes, I saw the purple chapped lips around his mouth turn red again, and finally I saw his dull brown eyes change back to a tiny sparkle.

The fear I was experiencing, and all my negative thoughts of death suddenly evaporated into thin air. God just taught me another life lesson—I truly realized our body is simply a cocoon which we use in this life phase. Just like a caterpillar uses theirs to transform into a beautiful butterfly, our souls inhabit the human body form before we morph into the next existence.

Not only was I now happy for my dad, but as I carefully shut his eyes for the last time, I was actually looking forward to the day I could experience the same euphoric feelings myself.

* * *

Yes, I was happy for my dad to be released from his pain, but I was still deeply affected by his passing. And I was lost as what to do next.

Lars drove me back to my dad's old house, which had now become mine. I walked through it alone, silently, and many of the memories I'd been holding back surfaced. I remembered both the good and the bad times. Each room meant something different to me. The Florida room and the pool area brought back memories of all the girls, of all the wine consumed, and of all the fabulous times I spent in them. Visions of Loretta, Stacey, and Joann ran through my mind as I wondered what they were up to now, and if their lives turned out the way they wanted them to.

Although it pained me, I knew I'd have to put this place of my past up for sale. I needed to get on with my life in Missouri.

I was sad, I was tired, and I needed someone to share my feelings with. I called Rose. Each time I tried to contact her over the last month I was unable to reach her. She never seemed to be there when I needed her, although I was always waiting to console her when she needed me. This time was no different. I didn't even get a recorded message, only a continuous string of unanswered rings. This left me more frustrated and confused.

I angrily hung up the phone and quickly dialed Deb's number. Maybe she would listen to me for a while?

Deb answered the phone on the second ring and when she realized it was me, she spoke apologetically. "I'm so sorry, I knew you'd call."

"How'd you know I was going to call?" I was taken aback. "And what are you sorry for?"

"Who else would you call?" she sighed. "I was the one who got you guys together, and I told you that I'd take the blame if anything went wrong."

I was confused. "Okay, let's start all over. I'm calling from Florida to see if you can help me ... my dad just died, and I really need someone to talk to, and I can't reach Rose. What are *you* talking about?"

"Uh-oh," Deb got quiet. "Sorry about your dad." There was an interminable pause. "So, you don't know anything about what's been happenin' here, do you?"

"All I know is that I can't get in touch with Rose and I really need her right now," I replied, my anger rising.

Deb asked me if I was sitting down. "There's no easy way for me to say this, so here it goes. I know you and Rose were getting along again, and that the summer was a good time for you guys, but on the days you weren't together she was hangin' out at the bars again."

"I know that already," I interrupted. "But Ann told me she was behavin' herself."

"Well, not really," Deb hesitated again and the silence was absolute torture. Finally she let it all out. "She was meetin' guys all the time. Ann was coverin' for her cuz she thought if you knew the truth, you'd just die."

A distinct numbness came over me. "So, what you're telling me is I've lost my dad, and Rose too?"

I could sense the impending answer Deb had for me. I didn't even wait for her to say the dreaded words. I began to let all the pent up emotions of the last few months rise to the surface. I was crying uncontrollably when I heard her say, "Yes. And this time it's for good. She got married yesterday in Las Vegas."

* * *

I hung up with Deb and did what used to come very naturally to me in this situation—I started drinking ice cold Stoli—only this time, right out of the bottle. I couldn't be bothered with refilling a glass.

Once again in this topsy-turvy life of mine, I was on a downward cycle.

The death of my father combined with Rose's sudden marriage, drained the very life from me, and I immediately succumbed to the isolation that once plagued me as a youngster. I sat alone in the calm pool under the abnormally cool Florida night and slowly drained the bottle.

It occurred to me that every time I began to feel good about myself something would immediately happen to change that. I was helping others get through their issues, but there never seemed to be anyone around to help me when I needed it. I prayed that someone or something could come to *my* rescue once in a while.

Half a bottle later, I came to the realization I was meant to be the "helper" in this life phase, not the recipient. I needed to try and find comfort in the knowledge that by being there for others, I should be happy, too.

I also began to believe I would never be totally satisfied with my life.

* * *

At about three-quarters of the bottle empty, I gazed into the night sky and saw a falling star. I made a quick wish. I was sure it wouldn't come true, as many of my prayers and wishes had been ignored lately, but I hoped for the best anyway.

I got out of the pool and laid down on a chaise lounge. I closed my eyes hoping to rest my weary mind for a while. Right away, a blurry vision appeared to me. It started out as two small white lights which were approaching slowly and deliberately toward me. The first to materialize fully was Nana. I hadn't seen her in some time and was happy to finally get some advice from her. The second one remained fuzzy, hovering in the background.

"It's nice to see you, my sweet child," Nana said in her grandmotherly voice.

I was happy to see her, but I was also angry. "Where have you been?" I snapped. "I keep asking for help and neither you nor God ever answers. Don't you care about me anymore?"

"We always care about you, but there are some things you need to learn on your own," she said, smiling beautifully.

"I don't get it. What am I supposed to learn from my dad dyin'? And from Rose gettin' married?" I demanded. "Those are lessons I can do without."

Nana reached for my hand. "This life is not always about having fun and getting everything you want. The number one priority is to grow. You must learn from the past and apply it to the future in order for that to happen. If you don't see the hidden messages you are doomed to repeat your past mistakes and that will slow you down on your journey. Now, think back and tell me what you have learned from these two unfortunate events."

I thought long and hard. "Okay, I guess from Dad dying I finally got to see that death is not the end, rather another beginning. It's somethin' to look forward to and not to be afraid of."

Nana smiled and nodded yes.

"Rose taught me how to be myself, how to be patient, and most importantly, to value the time we spend with each other, no matter how long or short it is."

"That's very good." Nana gave me a kiss on the forehead. "Don't forget about Karma, though. It's written in the Bible: *As ye sow, so shall ye reap.*"

I had no idea what Karma was, and the "sow" message just made me think of Rose sowing her wild oats. I must have had a strange look on my face because Nana said, "Just remember—what goes around, comes around."

That I understood. I wished right then that Rose would someday come back around and realize what she had thrown away for good.

Nana continued, "There will be some more hardship to come, but remember, it is all for the betterment of your being. I will be there watching, as will God, and one more person you know and love."

Nana started to fade away, and the blurry vision behind her now came to life right before my eyes. I thanked God for making my wish on that falling star come true—I got to see my dad happy and content one last time.

But I also found myself wondering, when is it my turn to be happy?

CHAPTER 32
HELLO DARKNESS, MY OLD FRIEND

The next few days were crazy busy as Lars and I packed up all my dad's belongings, donating most of them to the local AIDS charity. I headed back to Missouri with a small truckload of memories. The next couple of weeks remained very emotional for me. We had a memorial and a funeral for my dad. He would have been very happy to know I was able to bury him in between his mother and father, just as he requested.

It was three weeks before my life returned to "normal" and that's when it hit me again—the hurt, the loneliness, and the anger at Rose for leaving me without even saying good-bye. I fell into another deep depression just like Nana had warned me. The headaches I used to get in sixth grade returned, although they weren't as bad as back then; I didn't have the cold sweats usually associated with them.

I knew I was making one person very happy with all the vodka I was buying from him, the corner liquor store owner. Once again, through one of my personal tragedies, I was still able to help someone else.

* * *

I never knew how to openly accept help from others. I always tried to show everyone I could tough it through anything God threw at me. Even in my lowest of times, I faked my way through so others didn't know how much the situation at hand was taking its toll on me. This time was no different.

I tried going to work and doing my best, but I was sure that my coworkers knew something was up. I was constantly late and even when I wasn't, I couldn't be the reliable guy I used to be. When they tried to be nice and asked what was wrong, I made something up to cover.

Every night when I returned to my apartment, the answering machine never had a message for me, the doorbell never rang, and I didn't even get any interesting mail. I was desperate and hoping for a miracle. I prayed every night to God to bring Rose back to me, but never got a response. I wasn't sure why I wanted her in my life so bad, she had hurt me so many times in the past. But I wanted to be with someone who knew me and understood me, rather than reverting to one night stands that just left me feeling more empty than I was now, if such a thing were possible.

One night when I was extremely drunk the doorbell rang. I was in no mood or shape to see anyone, but I dragged my sorry ass off the couch and over to the buzzer. It was Deb.

"Hey," she said. "Lemme in. I wanna see how things are goin'."

"No," I slurred into the intercom. "I'm fine and even if I wasn't, no one cares anyway. Jus' go back home an' live your own life. I don't need anyone worryin' about me. Leave me alone."

"I'm not leavin' till I see you," she demanded. "So you better let me in."

It took two tries to hit the button, and then I heard her coming down the hallway. Since the apartment had a safety door, I rarely locked my front door. I slumped back to the living room and flopped down onto the couch, but not before I was able to snag the bottle of Stoli.

Deb knocked, and I quietly said, "Come on in, if ya really wanna."

When she entered, Deb wasn't ready for how I, or how my apartment, looked. I had always been a neat freak, but not anymore. Garbage was strewn all over the place, dirty clothes tossed haphazardly around, and several empty vodka bottles littered the floor. But that was nothing compared to my appearance. I had completely let myself go. The clothes I wore were the same ones I had on since two days ago, my hair was disheveled and dirty, and anyone could tell I had been crying and was quite obviously drunk.

"What the hell?" Deb exclaimed. "What's with you?"

"My life is over and I'm done tryin' to ignore the reality of it," I sniveled. "No one cares about me, I have nothin' to live for, and I feel like I just wanna die."

"No you don't!" she scolded me. "There are many people who care for you and you have lots to live for."

"Whatever," was my sarcastic reply. I took another pull on the vodka.

"Look," Deb sighed heavily, "I got you into this, so I'll help you out of it. I'm gonna call you every night, and if you don't answer I'm comin' over. You need to talk this out and get on with your life."

Again, I just mumbled, "Whatever."

* * *

The next night, true to her word, Deb came over; this time to clean my apartment, and dole out some advice. "You wouldn't be feeling so bad if your place didn't make you feel that way."

For the next month, every night exactly at nine o'clock, the phone would ring. Deb was on the line to let me cry my heart out, assure me everything would be fine, and she wouldn't hang up the phone until she knew I was back in control of my emotions. I really looked forward to those calls. Without them, I was sure I would've killed myself.

* * *

Before all this confusion and depression had overtaken my life, I was on a Monday night bowling team. I missed about two months because of my dad's death and how low I was feeling now. When I finally showed up, I was surprised to be greeted with empathy and sympathy. All through my life it seemed that most of the men in it had been loud, obnoxious, and undependable. It was a unique twist of fate that *these* men all understood what I had gone through, and actually felt bad for me.

Dwayne was the oldest and the most concerned. We were sitting side-by-side when he put his hand on my shoulder and said, "How's it all goin'?"

"To be honest … very bad," I said. "I feel like I can't stop grieving over losin' them both. No matter what I try or what I do, they're the only things on my mind."

He looked me square in the eyes. "Are you sure that's the real problem?"

"Whaddaya mean?" I said, surprised by the question.

"When my wife passed away I felt the same as you do now. The doctors, my friends, and even my priest all told me it would get better with time. But none of the external symptoms disappeared until I realized I missed her companionship. Yes, I missed *her*, the person, but what I truly missed were the feelings of being a whole person she gave me. I've gotten better, but still have bad days." He gave my shoulder a gentle squeeze as he got up for his turn to bowl. "Phil, you need to go deep inside yourself and find the real cause of your pain."

I thanked Dwayne, but I didn't think his little talk had helped me that much. I was still very unhappy, depressed, and believed no one really, truly cared for me.

I was still sitting down, waiting my turn, when a young lady came over. She was short, with dirty brown hair, and wore a serious expression, accented by understanding eyes.

"Hi, I'm Sherrie. Sorry to hear about your losses."

I was sure I'd never met this woman before, but she proceeded to sit with me the whole night, and even made me smile a few times.

When I was getting ready to leave, Sherrie gave me her phone number and asked for mine in return. "I know what you're goin' through. When my husband died, I felt lost and alone. Luckily, I had a good friend to help walk me through those tough times. Lean on me when you need support. I'm just a phone call away."

All the way home I tried to remember where I knew Sherrie from, but nothing clicked. I wasn't sure if I was going to take her up on her offer, but at least it was an option.

I didn't have to wait long to see how this would play out. I entered my apartment and there were two messages on my machine. The first was my nightly call from Deb making sure I wasn't dead. And the second was from Sherrie, offering to come over. I called Deb to assure her I was still alive and to let her know I actually went out that night.

Then I called Sherrie.

Seeing it was so late at night, instead of her driving over, we talked on the phone—for hours. We discussed how I was feeling, our religious views, and life in general. I shared with her my visions of Nana and the lessons she taught me. I was excited to learn Sherrie believed God left signs for her to follow. She also believed in guardian angels and spirit guides. When I said, at times I thought I was a human angel, she didn't laugh, letting me know she agreed with me.

I finally got around to the question that had been bugging me all night. "How'd ya know all about me, and what I'm goin' through right now? We've never met before, have we?"

"Nope, I saw that some guy needed help, in a dream of mine, and I knew instantly when I saw you, I was the one picked to help," she said. "I just followed the feeling in my heart."

"I get it, you're *my* human angel," I said, feeling a little more comfortable.

* * *

Over the next few months, with the help of both Deb and Sherrie, I began to get revitalized. I was slowly accepting the fact that Rose did not want me, and just let the lessons she left behind sink in. Each and every day the pain became easier to bear.

I finally realized the sun would come up, and the world would continue on either with or without me. And the empty feeling inside of me shifted to a mere annoyance.

Deb still called every night and Sherrie either called or came over. With their help I cut way back on my drinking.

Thanks to these ladies, I was able to maintain a somewhat decent life. Day by day, I got stronger and eventually the pain receded. I could finally talk about my dad's death and losing Rose without breaking down and crying. What once were intense negative feelings became sweet positive remembrances of their best qualities.

* * *

One Tuesday night, Sherrie came over and we discussed my progress. "You seem in control of your life again."

"I'd still be a hapless soul if it weren't for you and Debbie."

"It just goes to show you, if you let people into your life, and accept their help, without any strings attached, this thing we call life all seems to come together."

When she left, Sherrie gave me a big hug, then handed me a little black book containing quotes from the Bible. She explained, "Whenever you feel the need for help, these verses will be there for you."

I thanked her with a hug. When she left I put the book where I knew it was safe. That was the last time I saw or heard from Sherrie. When I tried calling her the next night, her number was mysteriously disconnected.

I guess God decided I didn't need her any more.

* * *

I learned many things from Sherrie and Deb during this short period. I truly believed they were my human angels sent directly from God. They helped me get back on the straight and narrow, and taught me how to live again, just like the three ladies in Florida, Destiny, May and Harriet, made me realize what I was missing years ago.

This experience reconfirmed that God does indeed help those who need it.

And I finally got the BIG lesson: Even though I thought I was grieving the whole time, I was experiencing those nightly panic attacks, the sudden chills and the breathless moments, it wasn't really grief after all. It was more of a *fear*. I was able to look deep inside myself, like Dwayne suggested, and found what was really at the bottom of what I was feeling.

Even though throughout most of life I was introverted, and consequently on my own, I finally understood the irony that I was deathly afraid of being alone.

CHAPTER 33
NOW WHAT?

I could vaguely remember a time not so long ago when I was confident, in demand, and even the life of the party.

It had been only four months since Rose left and my dad passed, but it felt like two lifetimes to me. I wanted to belong again, I wanted to live again, and I wanted to be myself again.

It was the middle of a cold February and I was feeling rather depressed when Valentine's Day came around. Once again I was celebrating a holiday all alone—well, not really alone. I was with all the other lonely guys at Washington Park that Thursday night who were drinking, cursing, and rapidly losing their money. Even Chris had been able to find someone new, and didn't work at the bar anymore.

It was one of the worst nights I ever had at a track.

Jim, my friend from the Monday night bowling team, was looking for someone to bowl with him on his Friday league. I accepted the offer. At the very least this would be another night of the week I could be too busy to remember I was all alone and lonely.

The next Friday I took off work and went for a long drive. Just after passing The Roller Wheel, my old stomping ground, I drove by the place where I spent many a Friday night, which now seemed like eons ago, helping young girls find themselves—the old private parking lot. Both of these places were where I'd felt the most welcome and comfortable. They brought back some nice memories, but I was sure it could never be the same again.

After driving around dredging up memories all day, I arrived at the bowling alley early that night, both a little depressed and feeling rather neglected. So I sat at the bar alone to wallow away my sorrows. Lucky for me, the more I drank the sadness began to dissipate.

When the bowling started I felt a transformation taking place. Our team was bowling on the lanes adjacent to an earlier league. While our teams were compromised of all men, this other was a mixed league with both men and women on the same team. We were very competitive and serious, but I could tell they were there just to have fun.

After three frames of our first game I was "clean," meaning I had thrown nothing but three beautiful strikes. The alcohol I'd consumed earlier had me relaxed, and by not concentrating as hard, I found myself in a zone.

I stepped up to the lane for the fourth frame and from the corner of my left eye I saw the lady next to me start her approach. She was clearly much drunker than I was. She couldn't even walk straight, and was way more interested in talking to her friends than bowling. She staggered toward the line and let the ball unfurl from her right hand. Suddenly, she tripped, let out a scream, and landed almost halfway to the pins. At first I was upset at her obnoxious behavior; but when she didn't get right up, I set my ball down on the ball return and went over to help her up. I walked gingerly on the oil laden alley, held out my hand to help steady her, and finally was able to get her off the lane.

"Thanks for the help, man," she said, embarrassed. I noted a Spanish accent.

"Think nothin' of it," I said to ease her mind. "Glad to be of service. But maybe you shouldn't drink so much when you bowl; you could get hurt."

I went back to my lane and casually registered another strike—my fourth in a row. When I approached the lane looking for a fifth straight strike, I noticed the same girl lining up again. This time she cradled the lightweight ball in her hands, staggered forward, and as she made her backswing, the ball flew out of her hand and almost hit me in the foot.

"I am sho sorry," she said, slurring her words. "I almost killed you thish time."

I shot a disgruntled smile her way. "Let me reiterate what I said before—with a minor change—stop drinking, you could hurt *someone else* when you bowl."

She continued to apologize, then suddenly stopped and blurted, "Hey, I knows you."

"I doubt it, unless you lived in Florida, or maybe visited there in the last four years," I said, clearly annoyed.

"No, thaz not it. But I knows I knows you." Her eyes got larger and I swear I saw steam flowing from her brain. "It'll come to me soon a-nuff."

The rest of the night this mysterious lady kept staring a hole through me. It affected my game and I ended up with no more strikes and only three spares. I found myself preoccupied with trying to figure out if I knew her, too, but nothing came to me. I was sure I would have remembered if I did indeed know her.

She was Hispanic, about five feet tall, weighed around one hundred pounds soaking wet, and had the blackest black hair I had seen since Faye back in Florida. Best of all she had the biggest and prettiest gray eyes. She'd surrounded them with glittery blue eye makeup and had bright red rouge on her cheeks. She was wearing tight grey sweatpants, pink leggings, and a red shirt which was just as tight as the pants. She had pulled the upper part of her blouse down off her shoulders to show them off. Her shirt was so tight; her big chest was prominently displayed for the whole world to enjoy. I always liked my girlfriends a little on the trashy side, so I knew she would have made an immediate impact on me if I had met her before.

I even checked the scorecard hanging above her to see what her name was. But only the initials JJ were used and those didn't ring any bells.

* * *

Before JJ left that night, a girlfriend of hers, Ronnie, came over to me. She slipped me a piece of paper with a phone number on it. "I've watched you and JJ starin' at each other all night long. Obviously there's some mutual interest. She's a little shy, not to mention drunk right now, but she wanted me to give this to you. She'll be waitin' for your call. By the way, what's your name, so she knows it is you when ya do?"

"I'll take the number," I put it in my pocket, "but can't promise I'll call."

"Why do all you guys say that? Do you think you're too good for her?" Ronnie pinched her face. "Or is it cuz she's Mexican?"

I swore I had heard that saying before, but couldn't come up with when or where.

"No, nothing like that," I assured her. "I'm just not lookin' for anything serious."

"Believe me, I know she isn't either." Ronnie said, with a hint of sarcasm. "She's just lookin' for a friend."

"Well, we all could use more of them," I said. "My name's Phil. I'll try callin' her later this week."

* * *

But I didn't call JJ that week; in fact, I lost the piece of paper. It wouldn't have mattered anyway. Soon as I walked into the bowling alley the following Friday night, there she was waiting for me.

She hopped to her feet and gleefully exclaimed, "I knew I knew you. You're older, taller, and got less hair, but you're still you. You're Disco Phil."

I hadn't heard that name for years, and honestly it took me by surprise. She must have noticed my reaction.

"I'm Juanita … from skating," she explained. "I finally put two and two together—your comment about Florida and your name, and voila, I remembered you. I shoulda known it right away, but I'd had a few too many drinks. Your eyes haven't changed at all, they're still dreamy."

My mind went into overdrive. Juanita was the girl who had a crush on me the whole time I skated, but even though I talked to everyone else, I considered her too young to associate with. The last time I saw her she was like fourteen, and I was almost eighteen. Now at thirty, those four years, which seemed like such a big obstacle back then, weren't so daunting.

"And you're still as pretty as you were back then," I smiled. "I should've known it was you."

Juanita and I had no interest in bowling that night. We headed for the bowling alley bar to reminisce.

"So what's new?" I asked, slowly sipping my Stoli tonic.

"Where do I start?" she replied, nursing her Miller Lite. "After you moved away, the skating rink went downhill. I guess I grew up over the next few years. I met a guy, dated him for a while, and one day woke up married. After about six months, we divorced. It just didn't feel right."

She stopped to finish off her beer. I ordered her another one, and she continued, "I started hangin' round the bars when I hit twenty-one and met a white guy—well, really he was just a boy. This time, after about five years of dating, I got pregnant, so we decided to do the 'honorable' thing and got married, but it only lasted about a month. So here I am twenty-six, with a three-month-old girl named Carrie Jo and on my own again. Can you top that?"

"You've been married twice already?" I downed the remainder of my drink and signaled the bartender for another one. "No, I can't say that I can."

She laughed. "Tell me all about the great 'Disco Phil' and how he's used that special 'gift' of his these last ten years or so."

"It's a long story that I'm sure you don't really want to hear," I said dejectedly.

"I've got nothin' but time," she said. "I really wanna hear about your adventures. Besides, my mom has the kid until later."

Juanita and I sat alone in the dark bar listening to a selection of 1970 and 1980 music the DJ played for us and I told her my story.

I started with Florida—the good and bad times, the emptiness I felt that led me back to Missouri, my failed engagement to Rose, the death of my dad, and anything else she wanted to know. The more I talked, the bigger the sparkle of trust emanated in her eyes.

"Do you remember what I told you that night we were together at that famous parking lot of yours?" She reached over and squeezed my forearm.

I had never forgotten that night, or what Juanita had told me. I closed my eyes to pretend I was thinking, but immediately answered, "I think it had somethin' to do with hoping to find someone like me one day and getting married."

Juanita was impressed I actually remembered. And the sparkle of trust turned into the sex gleam.

"I'd really like to spend some more time with you," Juanita said. "You never know what may happen."

Even as depressed as I was about being alone, I certainly wasn't ready to start another relationship. "Look, there are many other things I didn't tell you about. My life is in a shambles, I am totally confused, and I'm not the person I want to be. I'm not ready for a serious relationship, especially one with a mom and a kid. I suppose we can spend some time together, but don't fall in love with me, I'm no good for you."

"Come on." Juanita seemed surprised, even offended. "After two failed marriages, do you really think I'm lookin' for a third? I'm sure you're not as bad as you make yourself out to be. I really just need a friend right now anyway."

Well that I could always be.

The two of us proposed a toast to friendship. Just then her mom walked in carrying a small bundle of multi colored blankets; wrapped inside was Carrie Jo. The minute Juanita uncovered her tiny pink face, I was hooked. And for some reason the empty feeling I normally carried with me left my body.

For the first thirty years of my life everything I had done ultimately was with only one person in mind—me. Sure I *was* there to help others, but there was always the underlying reality of how *I* would benefit from my kindness in the long run.

Looking at this little child, who had no idea about life and where it could lead you, I found my reason for living change right then and there. Memories of Jane and her son Bobby from Florida came flooding back to me. At that moment I knew I needed to be there not only for *Juan*, but more importantly for Carrie Jo.

CHAPTER 34
SOMETHING DIFFERENT

Juan and I started "dating." It was more of a get-together on Saturdays where we would take Carrie to the zoo, to the lake to see the ducks, or just for a walk.

Our first month hanging out together consisted of me driving the forty-five minutes to Juan's house, picking up these two lovelies, and going wherever they wanted to go. There were no thoughts running through either of our minds about what *we* wanted; it was all about the kid.

I began looking forward to each opportunity to spend time with these two and, surprisingly, found myself falling in love with little Carrie. Every week I would bring some new toy or clothes for her as I knew her mom couldn't afford very much. For the first time in my life I never asked for anything in return—from either Carrie or Juan.

One Saturday, Juan came to my apartment with Carrie and we ended up spending the day at a small petting zoo, laughing with each other. As she was leaving, Juan said, "This has been the best day Carrie and I've had in a long time. Nothing can change how we feel right now."

Famous last words.

About an hour later I received a call from Juan. She was very upset and frightened. After I got her to calm down, she told me, "When we walked in the door, I could see we were robbed. All my jewelry and most of my small electronics are gone. I don't care about the stuff, but I'm really scared. I tried calling Ronnie, but she's not home."

"Would it help if I came over and spent the night to watch over you guys?" I suggested.

"You're wonderful," she said with a sigh of relief.

When I arrived, Juan was sitting on the porch in a rocking chair holding Carrie. "I was too afraid to go back inside. I'm really glad you came."

She gave me a little kiss on the cheek and the three of us walked into the house together. We put Carrie to bed, then Juan and I sat on the couch and I held her—just held her.

"It's so nice to have someone care for me again," she said trembling.

"You look tired, why don't ya go to bed and I'll stay here and keep guard in case someone comes back?"

She started for her bedroom and then stopped. She turned around and walked right into my arms. Juan gave me the biggest hug and the sweetest kiss I ever had. It was a soft innocent kiss which said thanks, and the hug seemed to say she liked the strength I showed her. Either way, both of these actions combined made me realize we had just become more than friends.

I spent the whole night wide awake watching the front door to keep the two new ladies in my life safe and sound.

* * *

It was late April and spring was coming. Juan and I finally had a real date. We went to a Jimmy Buffet concert at an outside theater called Popular Creek. I had seen him before and became a fan. Juan liked him because he sang about fun, sun, and good times. She told me, "He's also one of Ronnie's favorites."

The best part of the venue was the big green hill we sat on to watch the show. It reminded me of the one I used to love next to Nana's cottage up in Wisconsin.

It was a beautiful afternoon, the sun beat down on us, but it was still cool enough to enjoy — we sang and we laughed together. We danced to the music as though we were made for each other; our bodies moved as one. Not only did that surprise me, but I think we surprised each other with how well we got along without Carrie. It was the first time in our relationship we were able to temporarily forget she was part of this, too.

On our way home, Juan leaned over close to me in the front seat and kissed me gently on the cheek. She started to softly cry. "You've been a savior for me and Carrie. I love the way you treat her like she's your own. I can tell that you love her and she adores you, too. For most guys a kid would probably get in the way of a relationship. Even though neither of us wanted a serious one, I believe that's what we have. Thanks for being there."

I was feeling rather pleased with myself. I never thought I'd be good for kids. I figured all I could do was teach someone how to drink, gamble, and have sex. But this was proving to me I was ready for a family, and I actually liked the idea of a ready-made one.

"I'll always be there for both of you, but please remember our agreement, neither of us should fall in *love*," I emphasized.

We had Ronnie, Juan's best friend, babysitting that day, and as we slowly pulled into the driveway at Juan's small but adequate house, I noticed it was only nine o'clock. Since it was too early for us to officially end our date, we backed out and went for a drive. We took the back roads that weaved along the banks of the Mississippi River. Juan pointed out the place gangster Al Capone had used as a hideout; his old house had been turned into a pretty cool bar and restaurant. Only the locals of the small town knew about it, so we stopped in to have a quiet drink.

We found a table, sat down, ordered our drinks and talked about what Juan envisioned for her future. For the first time, I got to see inside this person. She was a scared little girl looking for someone to help her get on the right track. Even though she put up a front that always portrayed she was in control, I realized she really wasn't.

"Whaddaya want from life?" I asked.

She didn't hesitate. "I want to be happy, treated well, and I want to go back to school so I can get a degree. I wanna be able to afford all the things my little girl deserves. I want her life to be much better than mine."

"Is it okay if I help?"

I saw her hesitate a little, but then she said, "If you want to."

We finished our drinks, and I asked her for directions back to civilization. I was very surprised when we ended up at the very same private lot where Juan and I had parked before I left for Florida years ago.

It came as no surprise that after twelve years there was no locked gate anymore, or that no one else was parked there. Juanita and I got out of the car, grabbed the blanket we had used earlier at the concert, and walked closer to the banks of the Mississippi.

We sat down on the grass and watched as the river passed us by. I reminisced about the many nights I had used this very spot in my past. A smile spread across my lips as I said, "Ah, the memories."

Juan shot me a devious smile, and said, "I've never forgotten that night we were here, you know? You treated me with utmost respect. Whaddaya say, this time we do it for real?"

The last time we visited this place was the night Juan begged me to bring her here and have sex, but I helped her to see she really wasn't ready.

I laughed, and tossed out my old saying, "Yes pretty lady, I can help you feel good."

Juan and I gave ourselves to each other that night along the banks of the Mississippi and I found myself doing the one thing I thought sure I wasn't ready for—*falling in love again.*

CHAPTER 35
FAMILY LIFE

With May upon us and the two of us getting along better than ever, I wanted to help Juan spruce up her hundred-year-old home. It was a small place—you walked into the front door and right into a living room, two tiny bedrooms were attached to it off to the right, and a cramped kitchen situated just beyond it. And finally, connected to the kitchen, was the extremely cozy bathroom. It was a nice size for two people, but sure could use some updating. In fact, her dad had built a new garage next to the house which was bigger than the house itself.

Juan did have some nice land, though. Her place was situated on about two acres of green grass, tall weeds, and dead trees. With some help it could really become a home, not just a house on a lot gone to seed.

"Hey, do you mind if I help renovate the place?" I offered.

"I don't want you spendin' all your money on me, but," she couldn't resist, "whaddaya got in mind?"

"Just a little cleanup around the yard," I shrugged, "possibly a new roof so it stops leakin' over your bed, and screening in the front porch so we can sit outside at night, even if it rains."

Juan's eyes lit up, "That would be wonderful. Can you do all that by yourself?"

I wasn't at all a handyman kind of guy when it came to outside yard work. While most young boys who needed extra cash growing up in the summertime mowed lawns, I was busy babysitting. While their fathers taught them about pruning hedges, laying concrete, and fixing roofs, my mom taught me what she knew best—how to call a professional.

"Hell no, I can't even cut grass," I laughed. "But I'll find someone to help."

I called Jim, my friend from bowling, who happened to be a groundskeeper at a local golf course. Between the two of us, we spent all of May cutting down dead trees, chopping away the tall weeds, and putting down new sod where needed. He even showed me how to build a fire pit in order to burn all the wood so we didn't have to haul it away.

With bowling over for the summer, sitting next to the fire pit, with a cooler full of beers, became our new Friday night hangout. I was never a beer drinker, my palate was soothed by a nice cold vodka, but Juan never touched the hard stuff. Even though I found most beer to have an awful aftertaste, I finally tried Amstel Light. It was easier to go down since it tasted pretty much like water, and thus had no lingering bite. Plus, it was cheaper than Stoli. So this became my summer beverage.

When the yard cleaning was all finished, Jim called his brother, a contractor, who gave me a bid on the roof and the porch. Juan, Carrie, and I watched them fix her roof in one afternoon and we had an enclosed screened porch the next day.

The little house was becoming more like a home every day.

* * *

July came quickly, which meant my brother Tim would soon be holding his annual Fourth of July party. Ever since he got married and had kids of his own, this had become a family tradition. It was his way of showing off. I hadn't been able to attend any of them as I was either in Florida or busy with Rose and her family. Even if I'd been able to attend, I probably wouldn't have. Since returning from Florida I had become a somewhat distant person to my family. No one understood why I left in the first place, and I think they resented that I got to know my father better than they did.

Deep down I believed they also thought I had become just like him — gay.

After Rose left me, I felt like a fool, as if I had failed at being a man, and these little family get-togethers just emphasized that fact to me.

This time, when Toni, my brother's wife, fulfilled their obligation to call I was happy to say that Juan and I would love to attend, along with *her* daughter.

Obviously, Toni didn't hear me correctly, and had told everyone something totally different. When we walked into the house that day everyone let out a visible sigh of relief to see Juan was actually a girl. Clearly, they all thought *she* was going to be a *he*.

I guess I now had confirmation of what my family really thought of me.

As I shook hands with one of my uncles, he said, "That was close, we thought you went over to the other side."

* * *

Juan and I continued to grow closer over the next few months, and I began to spend some of my nights at her place in the country. Even though we didn't have sex regularly, because Juan said she was afraid of getting pregnant again, it was so nice to feel wanted, and I got very comfortable being in her world. But this led to some minor discomfort for me. Her tiny bathroom had an old four-legged tub I couldn't even fit in.

My brother, a plumber by trade, kindly added a shower so both of us could get clean in comfort.

One Saturday night near the end of August, Juan and I were sitting around the fire pit as usual when I up and asked, "How'd ya like to go back to college and take some of those courses you were telling me about?"

Juan smiled. "I'd love to, but can't afford it right now."

"I meant that I'd pay for it," I said. "There are night courses on Tuesdays and Thursdays starting next month. I'll even watch Carrie on one of those nights for you."

She gave me a big hug as a thank you and then asked, "Can I call Ronnie and tell her the good news?"

"Sure," I said, not really knowing why it would be so important to Ronnie.

I was finally excited about where my life had taken me. I thought I had seen the signs God left me and followed them correctly. Nana always told me that if I did it right, they'd bring me to places I couldn't imagine and let me experience feelings I never had before. Once again I believed she was correct.

* * *

Juan started her business classes and I watched Carrie every Thursday night. Ronnie volunteered to watch Carrie on Tuesdays and I began to notice she was always hanging around. I wished she would get her own life, but remembered how she once told me that Juan needed friends who were there for her, so I didn't make a big issue out of it.

* * *

Christmas came and we had the biggest celebration ever. I spent way too much money on Carrie, but really enjoyed watching this one-year-old girl playing around with her toys and even the empty boxes. I finally realized Christmas was indeed for children.

The three of us were getting ready to go to her mom's house for dinner when I said, "Juan, I've got a big surprise for you. But first, I need to know if you really and truly like where we are right now. I'm very happy with our situation, but there's one more thing that will help all of us come together more as a family."

I saw a look of fright come to her face as she contemplated what I said.

"Don't worry—I'm not going to ask you to marry me. We're not anywhere near that," I said. But added under my breath, "Yet ..."

That made her smile. "Anything else would be just fine."

At her grandparents, we watched Carrie open even more presents, with her grandma's help. I gave Juan a package. She took off the wrapping paper, and as her mom and dad watched, I saw her eyes begin to tear up.

It was a hand-drawn picture of a house, the dream house Juan always wanted. We had talked about this while sitting under the stars all summer long and wished that it could happen.

"In order for you and Carrie to have the life you want, I think we should build this on the land you own. Jim told me his brother would be happy to oversee the construction, and that he could do it for only $150,000. If you say yes, he will start as soon as spring breaks. We could have a new home by June."

That was the first time Juan told me that she loved me.

* * *

The rest of winter went by fast; Juan was taking her classes and the two of us began working on what we wanted our new house to look like on the inside. Luckily, I had been promoted and was overseeing the operations of five Burger Shack restaurants, so money was no issue.

The plans all came together rather quickly—we both had the same taste. Besides, all I really wanted was a set of French doors that opened up to a balcony overlooking the river from our second story bedroom.

More and more, I could feel Carrie giving me back the love I was feeling for her. When I came over, she was either waiting for me at the door, or swinging outside and would run up and give me a great big hug. The three of us were in our own little world surrounded by love. I felt more and more drawn to this family thing, even enough to reconcile with my own family and to resurrect the closeness we once had, as well.

* * *

The weather finally broke and the construction started taking shape. Another idea popped into my mind. I always put a lot of importance into the kind of car I drove. In the past, it was mine and only for me. I was driving a convertible Chevy Corvette most of the time and there was no back seat, so no room for Carrie. I had already bought a used Chevy Nova to drive when the three of us had to go somewhere together, but I decided to take another gigantic step by trading in both of my cars for a real family vehicle. Juan was surprised, but also impressed, when I drove up one night in an Oldsmobile Bravada SUV.

"What's this?" she laughed. "Has the confirmed bachelor man suddenly changed into Mr. Family Man?"

All I could say was, "A man has to do what a man has to do."

She was right, though, I had changed. I had given up all the selfish things I was accustomed to: drinking heavily, gambling, and my toys just to see that Juan and her little girl were happy. In turn, that made me even happier.

Again, Juan told me that she loved me.

* * *

By June the house was complete and I was ready to make another big move. My lease was up in August and I informed my landlord of seven years I was moving out. When I told her about my ready-made family, she congratulated me on my decision.

I finally thought I knew what happiness was all about. It had absolutely nothing to do with drinking, gambling, or lots of sex. The truth of the matter was, in order to be truly happy I simply needed others who cared around me. I needed Juan and Carrie in my life.

* * *

August arrived and with it my move to Juan's new home. Jim and my brother helped me move all my stuff to "our" place and while most of it ended up on the street corner for the garbage collector, my prized possession was able to stay.

When I was a kid, the hallway in our house had a picture of a copper horse amidst a black background. My name, and that of my father, meant "horse-lover" so I grew attached to that piece of art. I later learned it was a gift given to my mom and dad on their wedding day by a friend, and that my mom hated it. When they divorced, Mom put the thing in the garage and forgot all about it. When I moved into my first apartment, I asked if I could have it. It's been with me ever since. Juan knew the significance of it and the personal meaning it held for me. She consented to let me hang it in the hallway as you entered our new house.

Later that month we decided to have a house warming party and everyone was invited, including Ronnie. When I showed my mom through the house I had built from the ground up, she started crying. "I guess my little boy has truly grown up. It took you longer than I expected, but with all you've been through, I'm glad you're finally happy. Family life looks great on you."

I felt the exact same way.

In fact, Juanita's mom said the same. "We're so glad that Juanita met you, you're just what she needs. Responsibility and anything adult have never been her strong suit. You guys complement each other so well."

I saw Ronnie and Juan talking in the corner of the front porch, and they were smiling and really laughing it up. It was so cool to see my girl enjoying herself so immensely.

At the end of the party, when everyone was gone and as we were cleaning up, Juan and I exchanged a look of pure contentment and happiness.

* * *

We had spent one year together living as a family and things were going very well. Juan continued to take her college classes on Tuesday and Thursday nights. Carrie continued to grow taller, and I remained a happy family man.

I had everything I thought I wanted, except that Juan and I still weren't married. I knew we both started this arrangement with "no commitments", but everything pointed to the fact we had outgrown those guarded feelings long ago.

On a Saturday night late in September Carrie was spending the night at her grandmother's house. Juan and I went out for a romantic dinner and along with it, some serious adult conversation.

"Are you happy with your life now?" I opened.

She replied, "I couldn't be happier."

"I know how I feel—but how do you really feel? I remember we began this relationship without any expectations and not wanting to fall in love with each other, but much to my surprise I have," I confessed. "You've changed me for the better and I don't wanna lose that feeling."

"I feel the same," she said as she put a forkful of linguini into her mouth.

"So how about us getting married and makin' it last this time?"

"Wow," Juan said, clearly not expecting that. "Well, okay, I think I'm ready."

Even though she wasn't as deliriously happy as I'd hoped she'd be, I felt she was with me on this.

The next day I went to the jewelry store and bought Juan a one-carat diamond engagement ring. I knew her size, so the jeweler made it especially for her while I waited. That night, in front of her parents, Carrie, and Ronnie, I slipped this ring on her finger and while Juan looked happy, she still seemed slightly reserved in her excitement. I chalked it up to nerves and then noticed that Ronnie didn't look all that excited, either. This I wrote off as jealousy. Ronnie never was able to keep a boyfriend longer than a few weeks. I thought it had something to do with her being sexually uptight, but never said anything.

* * *

Two days later, Juan called me at work. "Hey, my grandmother, my mom, Ronnie, and I have to go to Tennessee for a funeral. A distant aunt of mine passed away. Can I use the SUV so we can all go together?"

"Do you want me to come with?" I asked.

"No, it's a girl thing," she explained. "Besides, you've never met her."

"No problem. What about Carrie?"

"She's gonna stay with Rick. Her dad hasn't seen her since we got together and he needs to fulfill his fatherly duties."

I was taken aback. His name had never surfaced before and I didn't even know he was still around. He never sent any child support or Christmas presents, and he never seemed to give a damn.

"Is that safe?" I asked. "Wouldn't it be better if she stayed with me or your dad?"

"Just let it go, everything will be fine," Juan said, talking to me like I was overreacting.

I trusted her, so I did as I was told.

* * *

I first kissed Carrie good-bye, and then watched Juanita drive off that night. I felt really alone again for the first time in a long while.

I went back into the house—the big, empty, lonely house—and after opening a cold Amstel Light, I retreated to our master suite on the second floor. I opened the French doors, which immediately allowed a cool breeze to flow through, and turned on the record player. I put on an old dusty album, Billy Joel's *The Piano Man*, and as he started to sing about sharing a drink called loneliness, I dozed off.

She came to me in an instant. I hadn't seen her in quite a while and welcomed her visit.

"Look at you," Nana said. "What a difference since I last saw you."

"I'm truly happy for the first time since you died," I confessed.

"I'm glad, but don't forget what life is all about—learning from your mistakes."

"What's that supposed to mean?" I raised my voice. "I am learning new things every day. Are you tellin' me somethin' bad is about to happen?"

"I'm just saying it's nice to see you again, and to always remember my saying: There are no endings ... only new beginnings."

With that Nana left me without any other explanation.

I wanted to forget she'd visited me, but her unlikely appearance stirred up other lost memories. I recalled my meeting with the psychic who told me there would be *two* other ladies in my life before I met my 'one and only.' I was sure, after thinking about it for a few moments that Rose was one, and either Deb or Sherrie was probably the second.

I drifted into sleep happy, believing Juanita was indeed my true love.

* * *

Three days later Juan, her friend Ronnie, and the rest of the family returned from the funeral, and I immediately sensed a difference in her. She was quieter, and seemed to always be off in a faraway place, and she wouldn't directly answer any of my questions about it. Other than that our life went on as normal.

I was on my way home from work on a Friday October afternoon when my car phone rang.

"Hi, do you have time to talk?" Juan opened.

"Of course," I answered.

"I've been doin' a lot of thinkin' and I feel it would be better for us to stop seein' each other," she said with no emotion whatsoever.

I was sure I had heard wrong. "Come again? I think we have a real bad connection."

"No, it's just fine. I said we need to stop seeing each other."

I was confused and also a little distracted; trying to drive in heavy traffic, I couldn't give her my total attention. I said, "Let's talk about this when I get home."

"No, I can't bear to see you again," Juan said. "Don't come here tonight. Find somewhere else to stay. I'll have your belongings out on the curb on Sunday so you can pick them up. Oh, yeah, I do really love you, you know?" *CLICK!*

When Juanita hung up, I hit the redial button over and over until I finally realized she wouldn't answer the phone anymore.

I was stunned, but found a hotel room, bought the biggest bottle of Stoli I could find, and then proceeded to get stone cold drunk.

I was once again alone and lost, and I didn't even have a clue why. Did I do something wrong?

* * *

October was fast becoming the single worst month for me. I was supposed to be married to Rose in October; I lost my dad in another

October, which was also when Rose married someone else. And now I lost Juanita, my home, and my happy life this October.

I emptied the vodka bottle as fast as I could, and quickly found my way to the restroom, as I knew what was to follow. I threw up everything I just ingested, and passed out right there on the bathroom floor.

Nana picked that moment to pay another visit.

"Why? What did I ever do to deserve this?" I cried out in anguish.

"It's not you, you did just about everything right," Nana said gently. "Just like you threw away loves in your past because you weren't ready, she is doing the same. She's confused, and literally, not thinking straight. But there is nothing you can do about it. It's just another lesson."

"That's bullshit," I screamed. "I put all of my heart into her and her daughter's life, not to mention all of my money. What lesson is this supposed to teach me this time?"

"Calm down and you tell me what you learned."

I felt myself relax a bit and gave her question a few minutes of thought. At first I came away empty; but as I continued to dig deeper I was able to say, "I truly understand that my life really isn't only about me. Carrie made me feel things I never had before. I learned how to take care of, and to help others with no ulterior motives. I was able to feel good about what I did. And finally I was able to experience true responsibility, and actually did rather well at it."

Nana gently wiped the tears from my eyes and said the same thing Gram had told me before, "See, once again from the bad in life, some good comes."

Before I could comment she disappeared. I actually slept very well there on the bathroom floor, and when I awoke hours later, instead of vomit, I smelled the welcome scent of mint.

* * *

I didn't even bother to try to call Juan after that. I knew she was stubborn and I wouldn't win, even if I was right. I went to *our* house that Sunday with Jim to pick up my things. The finality of the relationship was apparent when I saw the mailbox on the side of the road, just days earlier it listed both our last names, but now had only hers.

All my stuff, except for my horse picture, was boxed up and sitting near the garage. I knocked on the front door, but no one answered. I tried my key in the lock and it had already been changed.

Just as fast as I had entered her life two years earlier, I was now thrown out of it.

* * *

I moved in with Jim and tried to go on with my life. I never did get any response from Juan; no reasons for her decision, not even a letter. I missed her, but I missed Carrie even more. Even though I spent a fortune on them and never got to enjoy most of it, I was still able to feel a warmth deep down knowing I had helped them out and made a difference in their lives.

Three months later, I received a letter, and my horse picture, from Juanita's mom. I didn't know how she knew where I was. The letter read:

Phil, I'm so sorry that my daughter treated you the way she did. I told you acting adult and being responsible weren't her thing. She's moved to Arizona with Ronnie to "find herself" because now she thinks she may be gay. I'm sorry to say, she's pawned your ring ... she told me she tried so hard to be "normal", but finally had to give in to her "real" feelings. I sold the house you built for her, so I've enclosed a check with all your money back, plus some. I hope you can forgive her. Love, Mom

CHAPTER 36
ALEX

There was no mourning this time around, although I did start drinking Stoli vodka, gambling on the horses, and having meaningless sex again. At least it didn't take as long to get over Juan as it did for me to get over Rose. However, I felt the old emptiness of my past return. It was a gigantic void, but this time I tried to focus more on the lessons I'd learned from Juanita and Carrie. Instead of moping around like a zombie as I did before, I eagerly anticipated the last and final love that was supposed to come to me according to Margaret, the psychic.

* * *

I needed a fresh start, so I took the money Juanita's mom sent me and quit my job. I spent a few weeks just hanging out at the race track, meeting many new and unusual people who were all clearly worse off than I was.

I drove to Wisconsin to see the old cottage Nana and Gramps had called home for so many years and found it all changed. The new owners had painted it a different color, put on an attached garage, and finally the thing that hurt the most; they enclosed the screened-in porch with glass. All the charm and character the old place once had was now lost. It was the last time I ever visited it.

I also spent many a day at the cemetery where I was able to sit alone and think next to the plots of Nana and Gramps, my father and his family, and all those others who had passed through this life phase. Over time, it was here where I would eventually understand the meaning of life.

* * *

Jim and I moved to a bigger townhouse on the other side of town and I set out to find a new career. One day, coming home from the track, I noticed a restaurant, Poppa's #3, with a "Help Wanted" sign and applied for their open manager position. I was hired on the spot, along with Sandy, an older lady who was going to be my assistant. We started training together at the Poppa's #1 location and the two of us spent the next four weeks learning the ropes and all about each other.

Sandy was about fifty years old and had led a rough life, ending up living in a rundown mobile home park. She had drifted from job to job, from marriage to marriage, and from drink to drink.

The two of us sat at the busy bar in the restaurant each night after work. I watched her drink many a guy under the table and fondly recalled Juanita and her penchant for doing the same thing. Sandy reminded me of a long ago friend of mine, Sally, from my youth bowling league. She had the same color blonde hair, was a little overweight, and had the same "Woody Woodpecker" laugh. This made it very easy to talk to her—well, that and being drunk most of the time.

Four weeks later, we were sent back to Poppa's #3, the busiest of the three restaurants this owner had. The main dishes were barbeque ribs and fried chicken. The dining room was gigantic and held about 500 people, but the small see-through open kitchen where all the action took place in front of the customers was long and narrow.

We walked in and were rudely greeted by the manager and his assistant. They weren't exactly happy to see us. Although they were eventually going to open a new location, they really liked this one. The main guy was about my age, tall, and was very quiet. He stood placidly in the dark corner just observing while he let the assistant, a young white lady in her early twenties, do all the directing and the yelling. The minute I saw her I swore I had seen her before; but seeing she was so young I decided that wasn't possible.

This girl was short and petite, about five-foot-three, weighing only a handful, with brownish hair that was held up off her face in a ponytail. Despite her size, she seemed to enjoy wielding control of things.

Her caustic demeanor came across very clearly to Sandy, me, and all the staff. But nothing seemed to faze her, as she ramped up the control freak attitude. She sent Sandy to the back kitchen to help prepare the chicken, while I was ordered to stay up front in the open, next to her, overseeing the rib pit.

I extended my hand. "Hi, the name's Phil. I'm looking forward to learning from your expertise."

"Alexandra, call me Alex," she ignored my proffered hand. "Now, let's get to work."

The rest of the night I sweated, I cursed, and I bit the bullet listening to this young girl tell me what to do, even though I was probably ten years her elder and obviously had much more restaurant experience.

When the night was over, instead of telling me I did a good job, she just said, "You need more work." Although she did it with a half smile, I missed that point.

I was pissed and Sandy could tell it. While the two of us sat at Summers, a bar down the street, drinking Stoli after Stoli, she also told me something I couldn't believe.

"D'wanna know somethin' 'bout that young girl who was pushin' all your buttons tonight?"

"I couldn't care less about her. She's a pain in my ass and I hope she's history when we take over."

"She may be, but she won't be forgotten."

"What's that mean?"

"She's got the hots for ya. I can see it in her eyes. Watch out, Phil my dear boy or you'll end up hitched to this one."

I almost did a spit-take with a mouthful of Stoli. "I highly doubt it."

I shot Sandy a look of reproof—like she'd had one too many. I hadn't seen anything in Alex's eyes, no sparkle of trust or the sex gleam. I didn't know what Sandy saw that I couldn't.

We drank the rest of the night away in silence. Melody, the tall good-looking bartender, continued to refresh my glass over and over, and constantly winked at me time after time. I continued to wonder about what Sandy had said. Even though that lingered on my mind the rest of the night, when I was done drinking I still took Melody home with me.

Regardless of what Sandy's take on Alex was, I knew I wasn't looking for love, I didn't want love, and I was sure I couldn't handle love. But was it there at my doorstep again?

I made it my mission not to let that happen. From then on, I deliberately treated Alex badly. I ignored her, I berated her in front of the others, and I even yelled back at her. But the worse I treated her, the nicer she was to me.

* * *

One busy Friday night about a month later, the first one Sandy and I had worked, Alex and I once again were up front and I was getting frustrated, not at her but at the customers. One older couple in particular got my anger flaring. The crotchety old lady came back up to our counter and said her ribs were overcooked.

Alex whispered to me, "I'll handle it—this lady's a pain. There's always something wrong with her food so we have to comp it every week. It's getting a little annoying."

"This food is shit!" the lady bellowed, taking both Sandy and me by surprise.

Alex calmly replied, "What's wrong *this* time?"

"I don't like your attitude, young lady. Who's in charge?"

"You know very well that I am," Alex again said very calmly. "We go through this every week. What can I do to make it right, Mrs. Simms?"

"You can apologize to me for being so rude, and then comp my food."

I watched how this young girl handled this overly aggressive customer for a few minutes. Even after getting her way, the overbearing lady never stopped complaining and berating poor Alex. It was apparent Alex was now getting quite perturbed and may even have been ready to cry, her face turning a fiery shade of red. When Alex started to breathe heavier I thought for sure she was going to blow.

I stepped in to ease the situation. I used all my fifteen years of restaurant management experience, but I soon realized I couldn't calm the lady down either.

She started in on me. I was able to maneuver her away from the crowd and over to the side of the counter, a small area where we announced customer's pick up orders were ready over a loud speaker. She continued to swear directly at me and indirectly toward Alex, who had already disappeared into the safety of the kitchen.

I made a quick decision.

"Be quiet and listen to me. You've been getting free food from this place for months now, complaining nothin's ever right. So why do you keep coming back?"

She was shocked that I stood up to her. "Well, I never—"

"I think you have, and probably all over town. Its one thing to criticize food, but it's another thing all together to dehumanize a person. You come in here and abuse Alex, week after week, just to get your jollies. I think you and your husband better leave this place and never come back. We don't need your type of customer, nor do I want any of your money." I thrust my forefinger toward the door.

She started to speak, thought better of it, then huffed and made her way out of the restaurant, husband in tow. That's when I realized the microphone we used to call out numbers when the customer's order was ready was activated and the whole dining area had heard our entire conversation. I was expecting to be fired until many of the customers who minutes ago were eating, now stood up and were clapping.

At first I was surprised, but then another regular Friday night customer came up to me and said, "That's tellin' the bitch. Maybe now we can eat in peace again without her constant whining."

I went in the back to see how Alex was doing. She gave me a peck on the cheek and said, "Thanks for havin' my back."

I saw the sparkle of trust in her eyes and her hard exterior shell had melted away.

"Yeah, that's what I'm here for."

* * *

The rest of the night flew by and after work Sandy, Alex, and I went over to Summers to relax. When the three of us walked in, Melody, who had by now become much more than a casual friend, asked if I wanted my usual.

I smiled, gave her the thumbs up, and pointed Alex to a stool between Sandy and me at the bar.

"Whaddaya drink?"

"I'll have a Miller Lite."

"A beer? Where's that coming from?" I grinned.

"From too many years of college parties," she said.

Melody rounded up our drinks—Stoli straight up for me, Sandy's vodka and cranberry, and Alex's beer.

"So, are the customers always so hard to deal with?" I asked.

Alex said, "Nah, just Fridays. That's when they let the lunatics out."

Alex took a sip of her beer and I found her to be totally different outside of work. Sandy and I learned a lot about her that night—like the tough cop act was just that, an act. She did it to get respect from the staff and the customers. She said she didn't care what they thought of her. The more we drank, the less the act appeared.

Two rounds later, I was three sheets to the wind and said, "Alex, you're still so uptight. Look at Sandy and me, she's undone her bow and I've taken my shirt out of my pants, unbuttoned some buttons, and took my tie off. You're still all put together. Why don't ya let your hair down and relax?"

She removed the two purple scrunchees that were holding her hair in that tight ponytail, and shook her head from side to side. Almost immediately I saw a new and improved Alex emerge. When her long brown hair settled down along her face, she looked much younger and much prettier. I guess I was unconsciously gawking because Sandy said, "Now I see the same look in your eyes as she had the first time. You two will be a perfect couple."

"What's that mean?" Alex said all innocent-like.

"Sweetie, you know exactly what I mean. I can tell you're infatuated with him. A lady's eyes never lie, you know."

* * *

Alex and I started hanging out after that night. I had to get rid of Melody, but that was easy. She understood we were just two ships passing in the night.

When Sandy was fired for showing up drunk one too many times, Alex became my temporary assistant for a while. We weren't exactly dating, but we did see a lot of each other—and many times without our clothes on. In fact, Alex started spending most nights at my place. It was much closer to the restaurant than her apartment. I didn't realize just how much time she was there until Jim brought it up one night while we were drinking together.

He took a sip of his third beer, and said, "I like Alex and everything, but when is she gonna start payin' rent?"

"What?" I was shocked at his comment.

"You know she's moved in don't ya?"

"Nah, she just stays here some nights."

"Really?" he said sarcastically. "Let's take a walk and see."

Jim led me into the kitchen and pointed to a handwritten note on the second shelf of the refrigerator: *This is my shelf and everything on it is mine—Do not touch!—Alex.*

"That doesn't mean anything," I said.

Jim opened the sliding doors which hid the washer and dryer and handed me a detergent bottle and dryer sheet box that wasn't either one of ours. When we passed through the living room, he pointed out many magazines and books which obviously we, as men, would never be interested in—*Cosmopolitan* and romance novels.

I followed him to the hall closet. Hanging inside was a long lady's winter jacket and another couple of hangers covered in plastic. There were four or five boxes on the floor and I knew they weren't mine.

"So she's brought some things in. She still isn't living here," I said, trying to convince myself.

"Let's check your bedroom next," Jim laughed.

I opened my closet and was surprised to see it was mostly filled with Alex's clothes. I never knew just how much stuff she had brought over. There were dozens of pairs of shoes littered on the floor I had never noticed before. When we looked through the drawers in my dresser, I realized I was regulated to only one of the four existing areas.

"When did all this stuff get here?" I asked dumbfounded.

"She comes over when you're at work, does her laundry, and brings in a load of stuff each week," Jim said. "We talk all the time."

I just shook my head still not believing she'd actually moved in. "How'd she get in?"

Jim said, "She has a key. I thought you gave it to her."

I shook my head again, wondering out loud, "There has to be some mistake, she would have asked me if she really wanted to live together, wouldn't she?"

"There's one surefire way to prove to you that she's truly moved in, and when you finally give in can we start dividin' things by three?" Jim said, dead serious.

"Sure, I'll pay more, if you can really prove it."

Jim walked into my bathroom and returned seconds later with a large box of tampons.

I started paying for two.

* * *

Alex may have been able to sneak her way into my life and into my house, but there was one place she could never get into—my heart. I had been hurt way too many times before and never wanted to experience that again. I essentially turned my heart off to everyone and everything after Juanita.

One night about four months after she "officially" moved in, as we were sitting around the dining room table eating Chinese takeout, Alex said, "You're really a nice guy. Is there a reason why you're so hardened and distant?"

I fidgeted with the long wooden chop sticks in my hands before saying, "This way I won't get hurt."

"What's that supposed to mean?" she asked, slurping a long noodle into her mouth.

So I opened up to Alex. I shared all my previous experiences, my loves, and my devastations. I helped her understand my life before her. And even though when I was done talking and I knew she truly understood all I had been through, I still couldn't let her into my heart— the walls were still way too high.

"I get it now," she said. "Don't worry about it. I really like you, but I won't push anything. We can go at your speed. I'm here for you."

That made me smile. It brought back memories of how I used that same phrase back when I was "helping" young girls find themselves.

* * *

Alex was right; she never pushed me too far. We had sex once or twice a week, but *that* wasn't the glue that held us together. Maybe I was sexed out, or maybe I was finally growing up. We both enjoyed each other's company much more.

She took what I had to offer and after five years of living together, she still hadn't asked for anything except for being in my life. But the longer we stayed together, the more I discovered the real me.

On the outside I was still distant and aloof, but on the inside change was coming over me. I never let on totally, but I began to depend on Alex like I never depended on anyone ever before. She became my saving grace, and my reason for living.

CHAPTER 37
ONE BECOMES TWO

Five uneventful Octobers passed and I was becoming encouraged. I hadn't seen nor heard from Nana since Juanita left me. I didn't need to ask for any help from Azna or from God, and I actually found myself sleeping very comfortably throughout the nights. The anxiety and fear of getting hurt seemed to have disappeared, and I actually thought that maybe Margaret, the psychic, could have been right. She'd told me that a big red heart would follow two smaller pink ones and that would be my true love.

* * *

Christmas was always a big time for my family. We would all get together on the night before to open gifts, have some food and wine, and share the positive things that had happened to each of us throughout the year. Ever since my move from Florida, and especially after my failed Rose and Juanita relationships, I never shared any of mine—I never had any.

I did, however, listen to what the others had to say to me.

Toni, my brother's wife, cornered me in the basement. "I really like Alex, and she's been comin' around for about five years now. So what are ya waitin' for?"

"What?" I pretended ignorance.

"I've seen a big difference in you since she's been around. Come on admit it, I know the 'old you' better than anyone else in this family. She's got you feeling again and in a good way. So, whatcha waiting for?"

Toni and I had always shared a special bond, maybe it was all the drinking, dancing, and sex *we* shared together before she met and married my brother. She always said I was good at making a girl feel better, but that wasn't always what a girl wanted. I never pushed her for an explanation. Still, I found she was always right about me.

"I'm scared and not ready yet," I confessed.

"I guess I need to be the one to say this to you." She grabbed me by the shoulders, pushed me down on the couch, and started her lecture. "First of all, she's great. You know it and I know it. Second, none of the others will ever come back to you. Rose is married now and besides, she screwed you so bad. Juanita, and her *girlfriend,* is nowhere to be found. Don't let this one get away."

I blushed and said, "We'll see."

It seemed to me that over the course of my life I let others make decisions for me because I wasn't strong enough to stand my own ground. So I listened to what Toni had to say, but still wasn't sure of my next move.

* * *

The next day was Christmas and Alex and I went to her parent's house. I was always very quiet around her family. I already felt as though I was pushing the envelope pretty far by living with Alex; *in sin,* as her sister always reminded me sarcastically. This time was no different.

I sat in a rocking chair on the closed in back porch which overlooked about an acre of woodlands behind their house. I rocked back and forth, drinking one Stoli after another, surveying the white winter wonderland in front of me. Someone sat down in the rocker next to me. I turned to see Alex's eighty-year-old grandmother, Cora.

"Hi," she said. "So you like to be alone, eh?"

"Sometimes, and in some places," I answered. "It's just easier this way."

"I know what you mean. They are givin' you a hard time about you and Alex livin' together, right?"

"Just like normal." I smiled at her.

The more we chatted, it reminded me of the times long ago when Nana and I would sit on the front porch of her cottage up in Wisconsin looking out at the darkness and talk about life. I felt the same calmness now I always did back then.

"Don't let 'em change you, my dear."

"That's easier said than done."

"You love her?"

"Don't know. I do know there's somethin' filling the void I carry inside—can't be sure it's love though."

"Want an old lady's advice?"

"Sure, shoot!"

"Love is funny. You don't need a little slip of paper to show that you care. As long as you're both happy with what you're doing, why worry about them?" She tossed her thumb back toward the house.

I smiled and winked, letting her know I understood, and couldn't help thinking older women sure have a way about them.

"Either way, have a baby ... quick. I'd like to see a great-grandkid before I die and you're the best shot I got," Cora said, getting up.

Two people, two very different people, telling me the same thing— Alex was the one for me. Those thoughts resonated in my head for two months before I knew what to do. Alex and I never talked about marriage, our true feelings, or our future together. We were just two people sharing the same life, silently knowing that neither one could make it without the other.

* * *

February 14th, the sacred day of Valentines, a day most single people hate, and probably many married ones, too. If you didn't give flowers or a card to those you were with, you were considered cold and unfeeling. If you didn't get flowers or a card, you were usually alone.

Since I always had roses in my house, a throwback to my upbringing and a tribute to my grandmother, I didn't have to buy Alex any, although I did get her a card and small present. I already knew she wasn't getting me anything. I never wanted anything materialistic from her. She knew I sort of hated most holidays, except for Christmas. I normally dismissed them as concoctions for the retail world to make a fast buck.

That afternoon, sitting on the coffee table in the living room was my little package for Alex, along with the card. The writing on the envelope said: *Open this first, then call me.*

It was three o'clock. I was still at work when my phone rang.

"Hi, it's me!" she said. "I love you, too."

I knew she had opened the card; this was the first time I acknowledged to her that I loved her. I never said it out loud, and based on my actions, she probably never thought I would.

"That's good to know," I replied.

"Can I open the present now?"

"That's what I bought it for."

I heard the paper come ripping apart. Then I heard nothing. For about two minutes, there was complete silence on the other end. I was imagining what was happening and how she was feeling when Alex cried out, "Okay! I mean YES!"

I could tell the tears were flowing and that made me smile. Without saying another word, Alex hung up.

I then made a call myself—to Toni.

"Happy Valentine's Day," I said calmly.

"Same to you, what's new?"

"Nothing, unless you consider getting engaged something."

"It's about fuckin' time!" Toni blurted out.

* * *

I don't know if it was because Alex worried I'd change my mind or because she had this all planned out well in advance, but we were married in June. During the reception, we showed a video montage of our families and there were some pictures of people who had passed on—my dad, his parents, and Nana and Gramps. There was a picture of Alex's maternal mom and dad, and for a moment I thought I recognized them from somewhere, but just as quickly forgot about it.

It was a festive event with a lot of laughter, way too much drinking—and lots of dancing; my favorite way of letting people know I was happy. That night I danced with everyone: my sister, Pat, and my brother Tim, and his wife, Toni. I even got to see Alex's younger sister, Jan, and her brother, Bill, dance with their dates. I really enjoyed this time. This was family to me.

I was taking a break, trying to find some space to be alone and catch my breath when I ended up in the men's bathroom. I continued to sip from my never-ending glass of Stoli and was surprised by the priest who had married Alex and me.

"I can tell you're very happy about this," he said.

"Contrary to what I thought, I am!"

"You guys will be together a long time, I can sense it. Many couples these days are so much younger and in such a rush. It really seemed like you took your time to find the right one. Can I give you a little suggestion to help make it last?"

"My ears are always open."

"Some people will tell you to always treat her well, others will say to bring her presents every day, while even others will say to never go to bed angry—but all you need to know are three little words from now on."

"I love you?" I said, thinking I had beaten him to the punch.

"Nope—*I am sorry*," he laughed at his own joke. "Say those words to her first thing every morning when you wake up and then again just before you go to sleep every night, and they will cover everything you can possibly do wrong in between."

* * *

I took a few more minutes of much needed rest, then returned to the reception to dance some more. The combination of alcohol and music sometimes makes you do things you never did before. I was about to do two of them.

First, I actually danced with my mom. She had been my hero as a little boy when she helped make my life as normal as she could after her and dad got divorced. We shared everything back then, but as I grew older I changed. I wanted to live my own life and thought she just got in the way sometimes. When she remarried, I felt as though I had been replaced by her new man, Bob. And when I chose to move to Florida, I think that hurt her even more.

"It looks like you finally made it," she said.

I put my cup of Stoli down on a nearby table, and then we slow danced to an Air Supply song I can't remember.

"Maybe."

"Are you happy?"

"As happy as a thirty-seven-year-old getting married for the first time can be." I smiled as I thought about that comment.

"You know, I'm proud of you. You've always been your own man. I may not have liked what you were doing or understood why you did it, but by the smile on your face I have to say it all worked out. She's a good kid, treat her right. Remember the lessons!"

"You know about my lessons?" I was astonished. After all these years, I never knew.

"Of course!" she said. "Your teachers told me how you learned from the other kids in school. They always said you were very aware about those types of things. And believe it or not, after your father died he actually visited me in a dream to tell me how well you turned out and about your little talk with him by the pool that night in Florida. I still miss him, you know."

"You do?" I was surprised. "How can you miss him after the things he did to you and to us kids?"

"He, too, was his own man. I loved him for *who* he was, not *what* he was, just as I love you for who you now are, not what you've done in the past."

"What about Bob?"

"The feelings Bob and I share are special, but your dad was the true love of my life and always will be."

Like I said before, alcohol and dancing make you do things you never did before. "I love you, Mom," I said to her for the first time in my life.

* * *

Right after that song ended I refilled my glass, sat down to relax some more, and this time was joined by my maternal grandmother, Jean. She had just won a long battle with cancer, and was drinking as much red wine as I was vodka. She'd always tell me, "Drinking wine brings you closer to God."

"Finally, I can stop worrying," she said.

"About what?"

"You and I have been through a lot together, honey, and I never slept too well thinkin' about how your early years affected you. You were a quiet one, but then you also surprised me sometimes—like when you showed me that picture of you dressed as some weirdo in fishnet stockings."

That brought back memories of high school when I routinely attended the weekly showing of *The Rocky Horror Picture Show* and dressed up as Dr. Frank-N-Furter, the transvestite star of the movie.

"Yeah, I sure have two sides, don't I?" I smiled.

"I'm so happy for you and Alex. She's what you need right now."

"I guess so."

"Are you thinking about kids?"

"Yeah, and I think we'll start tonight," I laughed.

"Just remember this old Bohemian saying: *When one life ends, another starts.*"

"What's that supposed to mean?" I wrinkled my brow.

"Just don't rush what will eventually happen," she said, kissing me on my cheek.

* * *

Too much dancing, too much alcohol, and way too much psychology made me take a walk outside for a breather. I followed a narrow path around a small lake until I was alone in the dark, ever-present Stoli in my hand. I sat down on a lawn chair which overlooked this man-made water hole and I smelled it. At first I thought I was imagining it, but the scent continued to get stronger and stronger. I looked around for what I knew was about to happen, and that's when I saw her.

From behind a bush my Nana emerged, along with the smell of sweet fertilizer mixed with the over-powering scent of mint, Nana's signature aromas.

"Hey, sweet child," she gracefully said. "You look well."

"You're a sight for sore eyes," I responded. "Where ya been?"

"Just watching."

"Am I doing okay?"

"You tell me, how'd you get to this moment?"

I knew what she meant. Nana told me long ago our time on earth was all about learning and growing, so the real question she was asking was, 'What did I learn from the people in my life to lead me here.'

I traced the near past. "Well, I learned how to be myself again from Rose. I learned how to accept help from others when I needed it whether I liked it or not from Sherrie and Debbie. Juanita taught me how to accept kids, and to be more responsible. And finally, Alex showed me how to love and enjoy life again."

Nana smiled.

"It's just like you told me years ago. Follow the signs, put them together piece by piece, and they will lead me to important things I've never experienced before. Thanks!"

"That's a good student, but we're not done yet. There's still more to learn."

"Please, not tonight?" I laughed, half serious.

"You never know where God will lead you. Just remember you never get more than you can handle. Now go back and enjoy yourself, but maybe change the drink you have to lemonade. It will help you think better."

I liked seeing Nana again, but I knew there was no way in hell I was changing to lemonade.

CHAPTER 38
TWO BECOMES THREE?

The party was over for most of the guests, but for Alex and me the night was just starting. We retreated to our honeymoon suite located high above the hotel, in order to "officially" become husband and wife. I had been told many times before in my life not to rush things, like love, because these things wouldn't work out correctly if I did. I tried to listen to that advice, but tonight I couldn't. I wanted to make love to my new wife and I wanted to give Cora the great-grandchild she so desperately wanted. Although we always had used condoms before, tonight we decided not to. And after a few hours of intense love-making, both Alex and I passed out together on the bed.

* * *

Three weeks later, Alex was feeling a little under the weather and had her mom take her to the doctor. She thought she was catching the flu—her stomach was always queasy and she constantly felt hot. A few tests later she was extremely surprised, as was her mom, when the doctor told her it wasn't the flu—she had the mommy virus.

Both of them were ecstatic and couldn't wait to spread the news. Alex called me at work, and while I should have been happy too, I felt a twinge in my gut. That distinct feeling usually told me that something bad was going to happen, but this time I ignored it.

However, I did say, "Let's not tell too many people about this yet. I wanna be sure."

So Alex, her mom, and I were the only ones who knew what was going on. While I really wanted to tell my family, especially my mom, I also thought it best to wait.

About a week later, my grandmother called. When she asked, "What's new?" I gave in and said, "Please don't tell anyone else, but we just learned that Alex and I are pregnant."

"That's nice, but I'm not ready to go yet," she replied.

I was confused. "What's that mean?"

"Nothin'—you'll understand one day. So, do you wanna girl or a boy?"

"Either, as long as it's healthy."

We hung up after she promised not to tell the rest of the gang.

* * *

Alex set up a doctor appointment for her ten week checkup. Even though Alex and I still hadn't told anyone, the rumors were swirling. I finally let the cat out of the bag when my mom called and asked me about it. I found out Alex's mom couldn't resist and called her to congratulate her on becoming a grandma.

"Why didn't you tell me?" she said, clearly agitated.

"We were just waitin' for the right time," I said. "I don't have a good feeling and just want to be sure."

"That's just the first time jitters."

"We'll see. We have a doctor's appointment tomorrow where we'll get the ultrasound picture of the baby. Once I see that, I'll probably calm down."

Alex and I walked into the doctor's office together. We were both nervous, but for different reasons. She was excited and hoped she'd be a good mom, while I was still feeling that strange twinge in my gut. I couldn't wait to see the picture and get this thing over with.

We were ushered into a room that was dark and cool, in order to keep the mom-to-be comfortable. But for me it brought back memories of the hospital room my dad was in just before he passed away.

Brenda, the young nurse preparing Alex for the ultrasound, looked over at me, and seeing I was much older than Alex, said, "So, how many does this make?"

"One," was my short answer.

"Really? I'm sorry. It's just that with your age—and you're so cool and collected—I just assumed you've been through this before."

"Inside I'm not that composed. I just want to get this over with so I can see for my own eyes that I'm going to be a dad."

Brenda continued to rub jelly on Alex's stomach, explaining the procedure and how it never hurts the baby inside. She went about her business as she would hundreds of times a day. She turned on the machine and a small hum filled the room; surprisingly the noise calmed me down. When Brenda started to run an apparatus over my wife's belly, I actually began to get excited. I was anxious to see the little person I helped create.

Brenda continued to move the equipment over and over Alex's belly without saying anything. With this our first time, neither of us understood what was happening. I was watching the ultrasound television but didn't see anything resembling a baby. Brenda put a stethoscope on Alex's exposed belly and listened for a heartbeat. I wasn't sure how she would hear one with the loud humming in the background.

Brenda went back to using the apparatus and also turned her attention to the screen.

"I seem to be havin' some trouble with this equipment. I'll be right back."

A few minutes later she returned, this time with Alex's physician, Dr. Marks. He used the ultrasound equipment himself explaining that Brenda was having a hard time finding the baby.

"This sometimes happens when the baby moves," he said casually.

He spent a few minutes moving the probe around and looking at the screen, then listening for a heartbeat himself. A few times I saw his eyebrows move upward unexpectedly, but thought nothing of it. The whole time he was searching, he didn't say a word.

"I'm going to move you to a new room. I have more sensitive equipment closer to my office. Brenda, help get Alex cleaned up and then bring them back. I'll see you in a few minutes," Dr. Marks said to us as he left the room.

"What's happening?" Alex gasped.

Brenda forced a smile. "We're just having a difficult time finding the baby and hearing the heartbeat. The equipment he has is much more sophisticated. Don't worry. I'm sure everything is fine."

Instead of taking us to a new examination room, Brenda led us to Dr. Marks's office, asked us to take a seat, and then quickly disappeared. As we waited for him, Alex and I tightly held hands.

Dr. Marks entered rather solemnly and sat down. "We couldn't find a heartbeat and that's not normal. At ten weeks, all vital signs should be available to us. They were there on your last visit. This is your first pregnancy, right?"

"Yes," Alex said nervously.

"Well, I have some bad news for you. Something has happened, as sometimes will the first time, and the fetus has died."

Alex started to cry. And much to my surprise so did I.

"It's nothing you did. Many times when this kind of thing happens it means there was something physically wrong with the fetus. This is God's way of making up for the mistake," he said softly.

We sat there in a stupor while Dr. Marks explained what was going to happen next, not that we actually heard any of it. Then he took Alex away.

I remained in his office. My mind flashed back to the summer before I was to marry Rose, remembering what Margaret told me. She had seen this happening years ago. Instead of getting angry, I felt a strange sense of calm come over me as I also remembered her saying that my true love and I would have a little boy.

* * *

A couple hours later, Dr. Marks returned with Alex. He started to explain the operation to me that he had just finished. Alex was still out of it, so I wasn't all that concerned with what he was saying, I just wanted to make sure she was okay.

"So, it's over then?" I said, holding my breath.

"The physical part," he said. "I'm sure there will be some mental mourning to come, but she's strong—she'll get through it."

"Can we still have kids?" Alex asked out of the blue.

"In most cases, your insides will be back to normal in three months. You can try again then."

I shook Dr. Marks's hand and he said in a low voice only meant for me, "Help her through this and I know I'll see you again in five months. I can tell you guys will be parents some day."

We eventually told everyone what happened and were greeted with not only sympathy, but also with knowledge. Alex and I learned that many of our aunts on both sides had the same experience their first pregnancy. That information was enough for Alex to regain her vigor and she eagerly awaited the three month time period to try again.

* * *

Thanksgiving finally came around and Alex and I did try again. This time when we went to the ten week observation in February, Dr. Marks heard the heartbeat and we got a picture of our baby from the ultrasound, not that I could make heads nor tails of the black and white piece of paper I was looking at.

"Do you want to know what it is?" he asked.

"It's a baby, I hope," I joked.

He laughed. "He's a boy and every indication is he's very healthy."

This time I had a different feeling, one which made me believe everything was going to be just fine, and that Alex and I would make wonderful parents.

We couldn't wait to tell everyone, and started planning visits to our families that very night to share the news and the so-called picture with them. Everywhere we went the mood was one of joy and celebration, especially with her grandmother.

"I knew I could count on you," Cora said, hugging me joyfully.

I had just made another lady feel good, but this time in a completely different way than I was accustomed to.

* * *

That weekend we went to my side of the family. Everyone was happy for us, but there was one disturbing thing that happened.

I noticed my mom and grandmother talking in the corner. I couldn't hear everything, but was able to overhear the end of their conversation.

My mom said, "It's nice that he'll finally have a family of his own, that's what he needs to really grow up."

"I'm happy for him, too," my grandmother said. "And although I'll never see my grandson, I'll always be there watching over them."

* * *

In mid March my grandmother suffered a massive stroke and wasn't expected to live. I went to see her in the hospital alone one day.

How's the pregnancy? She wrote on a piece of paper, unable to talk anymore.

"Everything seems fine. How about you?" I asked.

She wrote: *Ready to join Nana and Gramps, so this one will live.*

I was confused and started to get emotional, but she stopped me with a hand motion.

Don't cry, she jotted down. *Remember the saying: One life ends, another replaces it?*

I nodded my head yes.

This is how the world revolves. God knew I wasn't ready last time. He has a plan for us all. Love you very much and promise I'll always be around just like Nana.

I had no idea she knew Nana visited me.

* * *

One month after my visit, Grandma Sutter died.

The baby growing inside of Alex had always been a quiet one; by that I mean he never kicked. During the song *Amazing Grace* at Grandma's funeral, Alex felt him rear back and kick her extremely hard. We took it as a good sign from above that Grandma had made it "home" safely.

* * *

Things were going well for Alex the next few months. She was gaining weight in the right places, had a glow about her, and she was very excited about being a mom. We bought all the necessities—a crib, baby clothes and breast pumps. All the check-ups with Dr. Marks went well also. We were all eagerly awaiting the anticipated August delivery, and it couldn't come fast enough to suit me.

* * *

It was June 26, our one-year wedding anniversary. I had planned a big romantic dinner and evening for the two of us. That very morning Alex had a doctor's appointment at the hospital, and I went with her. I took a seat in the waiting room and actually was able to relax. This was the first time in a long time I was by myself and I enjoyed it. It was quiet and serene as I visited the happy place in my mind once again.

Brenda, the same young nurse as before, came out and said, "Dr. Marks wants to see you inside for a minute."

So much for quiet and serene, my mind started to race. The last time he wanted to see me, Alex miscarried. What was going to happen this time?

"I want to keep Alex here." His face held concern.

"What?" I gasped. "Today's our wedding anniversary and I have special plans for tonight."

"Those plans have just changed. We're going in to get the baby."

"But we're not expecting till August."

"This one is special, and he can't wait to come out. Go home and pack a bag for her—toothbrush and pajamas. I'll call you when we're ready for you."

* * *

I did as Dr. Marks ordered and on the way home I called both of our parents. I told them what was happening and to meet me at the hospital later.

I suddenly realized no one cared it was our anniversary.

I wasn't home five minutes when I got the call. Brenda told me to rush, that it was time and the baby wouldn't wait any longer. While I drove a hundred miles an hour, I called everyone again and told them I'd meet them as soon as they could get there. I never knew my car could go that fast and thought God was again on my side when I didn't get a ticket or lose control of the wheel during the frantic drive to the hospital.

I was told to come directly to the delivery room and I ran up the three flights of stairs instead of waiting for the elevator.

Brenda was waiting for me and helped me get into a pair of green scrubs. She said Alex was already in the operating room, to wait in this room, and as soon as they could let me in they would. "It should be five minutes at the most," she concluded, then left.

I waited anxiously for her to return, but she never did. Five minutes became ten, and then twenty. I heard nothing coming from behind the big closed doors and no one entered or left. Then *BOOM!* The doors crashed open and I saw a nurse run past me with a small blue baby in her arms, rushing for the incubators. I was tempted to follow, but I wasn't sure if it was my son or not. I saw two more nurses run past me, neither stopping to tell me what was happening. Two minutes later, I heard the sounds of a baby crying from down the hall.

I can't tell you how relieved I was when Dr. Marks came out and congratulated me on having a baby boy. He explained the situation, how my boy was only four pounds in weight, but otherwise healthy. As we were talking, Brenda rushed in and interrupted us. She and the doctor huddled up a few feet away from me. They left together and I wondered what the rush was. The first thing that crossed my mind was the baby — what is wrong?

But then I realized they went the other way. *Maybe this involves another patient?*

Minutes later, Dr. Marks came out and said Alex was having trouble and he needed my help. He said that many times a familiar voice helps a person come back from anesthesia. While I followed him through those big doors, I quickly said a prayer to everyone—God, Azna, and all the angels from my past—I needed all of their help.

I finally got Alex to talk to me. Dr. Marks thanked me and then had Brenda introduce me to my new son. He was so small he could almost fit in the palm of my hand. I turned to Brenda. "How can he be all right being so little?"

Brenda smiled. "Oh, he has some growing to do. But we'll feed him through his nose until we know he can drink breast milk on his own, and then he'll develop as normal as he can. He may be small but he's a fighter, he's been through a lot already. You can see it in his eyes, he's something special."

I was able to bring in all the grandparents and was proud to show off the newest addition to our family. There was joy and happiness in the room. But as we were talking, Dr. Marks, ominously, came into the small isolation room we were in.

"I'm sure you don't want to hear this, but I want to keep Alex for observation," he frowned. "She's having a harder time than the baby. I'm sure she'll be fine, but just want to make sure."

The air went out of the room rather quickly. This should have been one of the happiest days of our lives, but Alex and I couldn't even share it together, and on our anniversary no less.

But at least we were given the best gift anyone could hope for.

* * *

For the next two months, Alex was in ICU on the fourth floor of St. Luke's Hospital, and our son was in infant ICU on the third. We hadn't even named him yet. I spent those months working a few hours a day, then running from floor to floor in the hospital to make sure all was well with the two most important people in my life. I was getting exhausted, I was getting antsy, and I was once again riding an emotional roller coaster.

I was finally able to take Alex home, and together we made the daily pilgrimage to see our son. One day as Alex was pumping breast milk and holding him at the same time, Brenda asked us his name. I hadn't thought about names since Rose and I were supposedly getting married. I was flabbergasted when Alex suggested Trent. That was the name I had in mind way before I knew her.

* * *

Two months later, little Trent, Alex, and I at last made our way to our new home. When we were leaving Brenda reminded us, "Remember, I was the first one to tell you that he's going to be something special."

CHAPTER 39
FAMILY LIFE PART 2

The three of us grew into a nice little family. Alex and I decided not to have any more children—we didn't want to risk her life, nor the one that we shared. Instead, we went about spoiling this little boy of ours, as did everyone else in the family. Cora was especially nice. She showered him with clothes, toys, and even set up a college fund for him.

She adored him, and I was very angry when God took her away from us when Trent was only two years old.

* * *

While Trent was growing up, I began to fully understand what being a parent really meant. The realization that your child comes first became apparent immediately, and I once again gave up many of the things I thought I needed—like gambling, drinking, and new clothes—to make sure he could have a better life than I did. That fact was not lost on my mom at Trent's third birthday party.

"Now you know how I felt, don't you?"

"What's that supposed to mean?" I asked, not really getting the question.

"Your life gets put on hold when a son comes around, doesn't it? As a parent, you begin to live through him, and you want only the best for him. That's how I have always felt about you, even in the tough times. I always knew that you'd make it through and make me proud. The look in your eyes today tells me just how much you care and understand."

"I'm glad! It's all because you did such a wonderful job raising me, you know?"

My mom gave me a great big hug. "Cherish the moments, life goes by fast," she warned.

* * *

She was right, the years went flying by. I changed jobs, Alex became a stay-at-home mom, and Trent continued to grow. Although not as fast physically as the other kids, mentally he was a real brain child. He had many friends in the neighborhood and they all admired his abilities, especially in the area of math. He understood mathematical problems way over his age, and could even explain them to anyone who asked.

A few months before Trent turned five, I retired from my upper management job at a local restaurant chain that went national, and was able to cash out all the stocks I had earned. For almost my whole entire life I had resided in Missouri—cold and snowy Missouri. I hated it when every winter came around. Now I had the chance to get back to some warm weather. Alex and I debated on the location and we finally agreed upon Nevada—our small three person family was moving to fabulous Las Vegas.

Look out sin city, here we come!

* * *

None of us knew anyone in Nevada, and on our drive I decided to teach Trent the ten life lessons I had learned so long ago. In addition to them helping him, I thought they'd come in handy for Alex and me, too.

We drove through the grassy prairies of Kentucky, the barrenness of Kansas, the mountains of Colorado, and finally the desert of Nevada while I let my little secrets out. Alex and Trent heard about Nana and how she taught me to be different, sincere, and to make the females feel special. Trent laughed when he heard about Jenna, her green balloons, and how she helped me understand that girls remember and cherish the small things you do for them.

Alex listened as I explained about how Nancie taught me that girls hold onto the good you do for them, and sometimes reciprocate back at a later date. When I talked about Julie D. and her book on trusting your inner feelings and how to see the difference in everyone, Trent clapped his approval.

Lisa and Sally were my first real friendships, and as I reiterated how important that was in life, both Trent and Alex nodded their heads in agreement. We talked about Janet, bobbing for apples and how to see past appearances and concentrate on what a person has to offer from the inside. During a lunch stop we talked about emotions and how it was okay for a boy to cry in order to show he is sensitive and caring.

Both Alex and I shed a few tears as I told Faith's story. She taught me age doesn't matter when you connect with someone, or when they need your help, and then how Faith died a few weeks after I learned that important lesson from her.

And finally, after I explained that listening is very important to girls, and they show trust by a certain sparkle in their eyes, I watched Trent drift off to asleep. Then I noticed the same sparkle I'd just talked about becoming stronger in Alex's eyes.

* * *

When we pulled into the driveway leading us to our new house and our new life, I was feeling very good about where my life had taken me. I had paid attention to all the signs and symbols God and Nana laid before me, and figured I'd come out ahead of the game.

I felt like my dad did on the day he passed away—happy and content.

We started unpacking and as Trent went across the street to meet the little girl who would soon become his new best friend, I unloaded the items that would be placed into "my room." All of the moving boxes were labeled with words like "Bathroom," "Living Room," "Master Bedroom," and the one most important to me: "Dad's Memories." After putting together my room, many different emotions went through me—I was happy, I was sad, I was excited, and I was nostalgic. All I truly knew was that I was feeling good.

Once all the other rooms were set up to Alex's approval, I sat behind the big old desk under my picture of the golden horse in my room and just relaxed. I opened a bottle of white wine and closed my eyes to reminisce. I had brought my old record player and some older albums with me, and no sooner had Rod Stewart started to sing directly to me, Trent walked in and hopped on my lap.

"Love ya, Daddy," he said.

"Right back at ya."

He looked around the room. "What's in der?"

Trent was pointing to my box of memories—actually it was a big oversized jewelry box my dad gave me before he died. Luckily it was big enough to hold all my important papers and my journal. It also was the place I kept all my most prized possessions.

"Just my life," I said. "That's for me and no one else. Don't let me catch ya goin' in there. It's not for little boys, only grown-up daddies."

* * *

Shortly after we settled into a daily routine, I realized I wasn't cut out for retirement. I was bored, creatively stymied, and felt that if I didn't get back to work I'd grow old fast and die young. I was hired by a small warehouse chain that needed someone to oversee the operations of their local stores. It was easy work, it was fun, and it allowed me meet many new and interesting people.

Fortunately, or unfortunately, I was promoted within the first year and became the operation head for the whole Southwest region. Now I was constantly flying into Southern California, Utah, Arizona, and New Mexico. This had me being away from home more than I was being there while Trent was growing up. When this job first started, he seemed to miss me and didn't understand why I had to leave so often. But as he grew older, and some of his friends' dads did the same, he began to get it.

Alex was okay with me being gone as she was always so busy anyway. She became a PTA president for the elementary school Trent attended, and then a substitute teacher. She really enjoyed the interaction with children and decided to get her Master's degree online in order to become a full-time teacher.

My being away brought the two of them much closer, and I felt somewhat like I did back when I was younger—that no one really knew or cared about me. I was *only* the guy who showed up for all the important baseball games, the school plays, the science fairs, and later, the math meets. When they were over, I'd go back on the road to face the same loneliness I used to be accustomed to. However, during the times I was home, Trent and I would talk about the lessons I learned growing up. I was thrilled that those lessons, which were taught to me by my Nana and other females in my life, were still effective today, nearly forty years later.

Although I never truly felt like he understood everything, the more often we talked, the more I knew we had connected. I told my son how much I loved him and that no matter what he did in his life, I would be proud.

I always made sure my schedule was clean for *all* holidays. I never once missed a Valentine's Day, a Mother's Day, either Alex's or Trent's birthday, or most importantly, a Christmas.

I also made sure my family continued the tradition of having roses in every room of the house to remind us of the love we shared.

* * *

It was Trent's senior year of high school. By this time, Alex had become the principal of *the* private middle school in Nevada, and a very big player in Clark County education. Trent was eagerly awaiting college offers, checking the mailbox with regularity. Every other day a new college had accepted him, but he wasn't satisfied yet. There was one special place he wanted to go to. He had aced all his college prep classes, his tests and whatever else he needed to attend the best of the best. He and his mother had visited universities across the country trying to find the correct fit.

Trent was still a brain at math and at logistics. It was a bit mystifying to Alex that not only did he understand the beginnings of numbers, and how to apply them to anything, but that he also believed in Numerology. It really bothered his mother when he used numbers to run his life and help with major decisions. I had always been interested in the occult, ESP, and astrology, so he must have gotten this from me. For whatever reason, after he did all the figuring, his lucky number became 4.

* * *

In late March, Trent was accepted to Northwestern University in Illinois. They offered him a "free ride" and I hoped he was leaning toward attending there.

"Congrats," I said. "That's a pretty good college. Not just everyone can get in."

"Yeah I know, but I really want to go to MIT."

"But you can't look a gift horse in the mouth. These guys want to pay for everything," I urged.

Trent just shot me a strange look. "But I did all the calculations and the numbers say MIT is the best college for me. Why haven't I heard from them yet?"

"Some things you can't rush. Look at your mom and me. If it's meant to be, it will."

* * *

Early April came and there was still no envelope from MIT. I was getting ready to leave on another long business trip and really hoped I could be around if and when he got the answer from them. I was packing and Alex was helping me that spring night when Trent walked in later than usual.

"Any mail for me?" he bellowed out.

Alex replied, "Haven't gotten it yet. Go out see for yourself."

We heard him swear as he walked out the same door he had just entered. A scant few seconds later the door blew open and we heard Trent screaming and yelling, but couldn't make out a word of what he was saying. We rushed downstairs and he was waving the acceptance letter and doing a little dance.

"I knew I would make it," he exclaimed.

I read through the letter and sure enough Trent had been accepted to MIT, his number one choice. And they also offered him a free ride. Mom and son were hugging, and Trent blurted out, "I told you the numbers never lie. I was destined to go there because the number four is so prevalent in my life and I just proved it."

She just shook her head and let out a patronizing chuckle, but as she did I held the letter under her nose and said, "Look at when this letter was written."

The three of us quickly shifted our attention to the date line. Alex's eyes registered sheer disbelief as she read what Trent and I already knew — the date was 4-4.

* * *

Senior year ended and Trent was the school valedictorian, which meant he had to make a speech. I cleared my calendar and was able to be a proud parent. I met all of Trent's friends and some of Alex's, and although many of Alex's friends didn't even know I existed, and teasingly called me Mrs. Alex, I was still elated my son had made one of his dreams come true.

While I was happy on the outside, the feelings I harbored inside were different. Even though I had given my all to help raise Trent, I often wondered if my being gone so much had affected him in any negative way. I felt he and his mother had a better relationship than he and I did. She was always there for him when I couldn't be, always there to comfort the blows, and to revel in the celebrations.

I wondered if I was a second class person in his life.

* * *

Alex and I sat proudly in the first row as Trent approached the stage to give his speech. He was roundly welcomed when his name was announced by the principal — it looked to me that he had many, many friends.

His speech started out the same as all speeches did — some jokes, some references the parents didn't understand, some motivational sayings, and finally some thank-you's.

"I want to thank two people in particular today," Trent said into the microphone. "You all know my mom, Alex ..."

When she was introduced, the whole crowd rose as one and applauded for her. Everyone knew of her, and her contributions, to the education system and this was their way of letting her know that she was greatly appreciated.

"... she was there right by my side the whole way. She has taught me many things I will continue to use as I grow up. But there is another person that many of you don't know ... my dad. He was away a lot on business, but he was also there for many of the most memorable times in my life. I learned some very important things from him, too — things he probably doesn't even know I remember. My dad's life hasn't been easy, as many of our parents' weren't. His mom and dad got divorced when he was eight and he made a pact with himself to be a different type of man than he'd seen others be. He learned ten lessons from the ladies in his life and has used them ever since."

Trent went on to tell the crowd about the "secret insights" I taught him when he was just a boy. I found myself crying as I listened.

"My dad told me about special visits from his deceased great-grandmother, and how he believed that she and God have left him signs to help him grow and learn, as that is the primary purpose of our time here on earth …"

As he continued, I hoped the assembly didn't think I was crazy.

"He emphasized that roses have hidden meanings and are meant for much more than just looking at. They can show others what you're feeling at any precise moment in time. Mom and Dad please come up here. I have something I want to give you."

Alex and I got up uncomfortably and made our way up to the stage, hand in hand. We heard the sound of applause start out slowly, as though no one knew what was going to happen next.

"Mom and Dad, here is a bouquet of roses from me. I'm sure everyone knows the red ones stand for my love for you, but the white ones are so you'll remember what you mean to me."

The applause started to get louder, but Trent raised his hands to silence the crowd.

"I know some will think less of me because I'm getting all emotional up here, but the biggest thing my dad ever taught me is that we are all here for only a short time and we all have a mission. That mission is different for each of us, but there are few things we all want from this life—that is to be accepted for who we are and to be as happy as we can be. Today I am the happiest young man graduating, not only for what I may accomplish in my life, but because of the lessons my dad shared with me as I grew up. Dad, you're my hero and I hope I can be half the man you have become."

My eyes welled up with tears, and the whole crowd stood up and clapped for me. That felt pretty good, but it was nothing compared to the joy in realizing my boy had indeed understood all the talks, all the mysteries, and all the beliefs I had shared with him.

CHAPTER 40
ANOTHER LESSON

It was mid-August, Trent was leaving for college and he asked his mother to accompany him. They decided to drive out together so he could have a car, get situated in his new apartment, and then Alex would fly home a week later. But before he left, Trent wanted to talk to me alone.

"Dad, I truly appreciate all you've done for me—the lessons should come in handy in a new place—especially the second ones," he said with a smile.

"How do you know about the second ones? I never shared *them* with you," I raised a suspicious eyebrow.

"I must confess," a look of guilt momentarily crossed his face, "after you started leaving on business trips, I used to go into your room and look around. At first I just sat on the floor looking at all your old baseball cards—and missing you, a lot. Then I found your special box of memories and went through it a few times. Most of the things meant nothing to me, but I did find your old journal and started reading about *all* the lessons. Hope you're not mad."

"Nah, use them well," I said, after all, my son was old enough for sex. "Just be careful."

"I need to tell you something else, but you can't tell Mom." He got real serious. "She hasn't said anything to you, but she gets these terrible migraine headaches at times. They really knock her out, sometimes for days on end. When she does, she spends most of the time in bed, in the dark with the covers over her head. Just watch out for her."

It was the first time I heard about this, but I promised Trent I'd do my best. We exchanged a manly hug, and then I kissed my only son good-bye so he could start living his own life.

* * *

That first night alone in my own house was one of mixed emotions. I was happy my son could realize his dream of attending MIT. I was anxious for him to do well, and I was extremely happy I had decided to retire *again*, this time to spend more time with my wife of almost twenty years so we could re-discover each other. But I was a little scared about what Trent had told me about Alex.

To get my mind in order for what was next for Alex and me, I needed to relax. I made a tall glass of lemonade, went into my room, put on an old worn record Rod Stewart recorded about forty years earlier. I sat behind my desk in the big leather chair Alex had surprised me with on one of my many returns from a business trip. In front of me was a big square mirror and underneath it was a small table where I always kept a full vase of colorful roses: pink, yellow and white ones this week.

I sat back in this chair and took a deep breath, closed my eyes—which were red from crying—and expected to look back at what my life had become. I must have fallen asleep instead.

The record started skipping, as an old album that was played much too often would naturally do. This woke me up and as I turned in the direction of the mirror I saw her. Staring back at me through the mirror was my beloved Nana. It had been many years since I had a visit from her, and even though I had aged, she looked exactly the same as I remembered.

"Well, well, my child," Nana said. "It's been too long. I see that your life is going along nicely."

"Thanks to you and God, I'm very comfortable with where I am right now."

"Yes, you've learned very well, even after the inauspicious start you had. And I see you still appreciate the colors of the rose."

I nodded in agreement.

"You're still not done learning though, I've come to remind you of a saying you once heard," Nana said. "Do you recall, *In this life phase there has to be a balance—you must take the bad with the good. It allows you the ultimate luxury of becoming whole. Without the necessary balance, not only would life be dull, you could not learn or grow. Becoming whole is the key and the only true way of coming back home?*"

I thought back and did remember hearing something like that, although I couldn't exactly recall who had said it to me.

"Just keep that in mind as you continue on your journey. The plans are already in place and eventually they will lead you back home," Nana said, smiling.

The image in the mirror was now just a reflection of me.

* * *

Alex made it safely back home after escorting Trent to college and we started on our new life without him. We made some plans to travel, basically going to Missouri to see some of our family who still lived there, and to give me some time to visit the cemetery where everyone else in my family was buried.

It was early October when I went out for some groceries. I was only gone a few minutes and when I returned I found Alex in our bedroom. She was buried under the covers and had the drapes drawn so that the room was very dark.

"Hey, what's wrong?" I asked, anxiously.

"My head hurts, real bad," she quietly explained. "I've had headaches before, but this one takes the cake."

I told her I would leave her alone and to yell if she needed me. I went into my room and was sifting through some of my memories when I heard Alex scream my name at the top of her lungs.

I rushed to our bedroom as fast as I could.

"What?" I asked out of breath.

"Just sit with me. I'm not feeling too good. Maybe some quiet talk will ease the pain and help me feel better."

I smiled to myself when I replied, "Yes, pretty lady, I can always help you feel good."

"You're the best thing to ever happen to me, you know?" Alex said out of the blue. "I love you with all my heart. Remember how we met?"

The two of us reminisced about our time together and I reached over to hold her hand. I was totally appalled when I touched her with my right hand and I felt the icy sensation that I had felt only a few other times in my life—always when someone was about to pass on.

Tears came to my eyes, and I ran out of the room and into the bathroom.

Why, why now? I demanded of God, or whoever else was listening.

When I returned, a few minutes later, to my utter shock and disbelief, Alex was already gone. I quickly called 911 and they assured me the ambulance was on its way. When they arrived, I was told that Alex most likely died of a brain aneurysm. Even though the two paramedics reassured me there was nothing I could have done, I still couldn't help feeling that in her time of greatest need I wasn't there for her.

And the emptiness so prominent in my early years returned to become my constant companion.

Once again Margaret, the psychic, was correct. She'd predicted this blackness in the head, this time it just wasn't mine. Alex and I had shared a lifetime together, brought one child into this world and had helped many others between the two of us. All that good was gone right now. I asked for help from God and from Nana, but got no answer.

I remembered the last visit from Nana and now I knew why she had come by. She was trying to warn me and that's what her message really meant. Balance needed to be achieved, and once again I was the one who got hurt, and again in October. What was it about this month?

CHAPTER 41
THE PAST REVISITS

I made it through Alex's memorial in Nevada and her funeral back in Missouri, but really didn't know how. I now felt just like Kevin did when Gram died. I listened to all the good things people had to say about Alex, but didn't really hear them. I could only focus on the fact that once again I felt lost and all alone.

Trent wanted to quit school and move back home to make sure I'd be okay, but I was able to talk him out of it. We decided he would come home for Christmas and we'd try to have a good time then.

I returned to Nevada and tried to live normally, but soon found myself absorbed in my memories and regulated myself to my room. My life had finally come full circle. Each day I sat in this room surrounded by articles from my past which took me back to another place and time. I played the old albums I had once relied so heavily on, changed my drink from lemonade back to vodka, and talked to pictures of Alex, even though I knew she wasn't there.

I truly had become less of a man and I blamed God once again for letting me down.

* * *

It was mid November when Trent came home from college for the holidays. He seemed to be in good spirits considering it was less than a month since his mother passed away. I on the other hand, was a mess. Trent knew I was having a hard time. Whenever we talked on the phone I was always very short with him and let no feelings come through.

Trent brought with him a bouquet of red roses and filled my empty vase with them. Immediately the house had a different feeling to it. He had also brought another surprise with him—a girlfriend. Now I knew why he was feeling so good, he had a girl by his side.

"I'm sorry about your wife," Shannon said to me when Trent introduced us. "My dad just passed away a few months ago, too. Trent and I are helping each other get through the pain."

"Togetherness always helps to ease the loss," I said without much feeling.

When I looked at Shannon closer, I thought I saw something in her eyes, making me think I knew her, but I realized that was just silly.

Trent said, "Shannon is here to see her mom, too. She lives about twenty minutes away. She moved to Las Vegas to live with her sister after her husband died."

"See, I told you togetherness helps," I shrugged.

I had forgotten my manners, even though neither of them fully expected me to have them anyway, but I quickly rebounded, "I'm sorry. I haven't been the same since my wife died. I feel like only half a man, which is why the man should always die first. I tend to forget things, like would you two care for something to drink?"

"That's funny. My mom told the priest at my dad's funeral that she was glad he went first, so he wouldn't feel that exact way," Shannon said. "Do you have any white wine?"

"No, I'm sorry. I have vodka and lemonade."

"That's a shame," Shannon said. "There's something about wine, I find it brings you closer to God."

That was my grandmother's old saying and it seemed odd to me Shannon would know anything about it, but I didn't press the subject.

"Lemonade is fine, then," she smiled.

The three of us were sitting around the living room drinking lemonade and chatting when the subject of my youth came up.

"So, where did you grow up?" Shannon said.

"Born and raised in a small town in Missouri, near St. Louis. I lived a while in Ft. Lauderdale, then moved back and finally settled here in Las Vegas for the weather."

"Really? My mom is from Missouri and I was born and raised in Florida, up in Jacksonville. Dad liked the weather there, just enough hot and cold to please anyone."

Trent could see I was losing interest, and so he turned the subject to the one thing he knew I liked—my room and the memories locked away in it.

"Dad, I shared with Shannon the lessons from your journal. Do you think you can show us some more of what's inside your secret vault?"

"I'm sure she doesn't want to know about ancient history."

"No," she chimed in. "It would be a pleasure."

I shot him a look of annoyance, but I got up all the same and went to fetch the box of memories. When I entered my room, I noticed there was a slight aroma of mint. I felt as though Nana had visited, but couldn't find any actual "physical" presence of her.

But as soon as I picked up my box, I felt a distinct calmness come over me, one that I hadn't felt since Alex was alive.

* * *

"This is my box of memories. I've had it since I was small," I announced, returning to the living room, "Whenever something significant happens in my life I add it in."

I reverently opened it up and started to sift through it. I reached to take the pile of old papers out of the box and one of them dropped onto the table. Shannon looked down, scanned it quickly, and then said, "Before you share all this with us, do you think I can call my mom? I was thinkin' maybe she can come over. I'm sure that you guys both being from Missouri may stir up some good ol' memories."

"Sure, I'm all about making others feel good," I said sarcastically.

Shannon called her mother and then left with Trent to pick her up. The idea of company my own age had me feeling a little better. I quickly straightened up the house, put on some clean clothes, and even went to a nearby liquor store to pick up some white wine for Shannon.

I was pulling into my driveway when I heard the voice again. It was the one that was neither male nor female, yet it was very calming. It repeated the same message as the last time I heard it, about balance and taking the bad with the good.

I also swore I heard Alex say, "I love you and I am waiting for you, but you're not ready yet. Live each day to its fullest."

I was confused, but at the same time calm and feeling in control for the first time since Alex died. I wasn't feeling terribly sad or lonely anymore.

* * *

I was in the kitchen when Trent, Shannon, and her mom pulled into the driveway. I had opened the bottle of wine; my stereo was playing smooth jazz and my nose picked up the fresh scent of the red roses Trent had brought with him. The feel of the house was totally different from just a half hour ago.

I walked into the living room, put the tray of drinks down on the table next to my box of memories, nodded to Trent, and was expecting to meet Shannon's mom, but she hadn't made it in the door yet.

Shannon entered the room next, followed by a tall lanky lady with short gray hair which was expertly styled. She was wearing a long blue dress, white panty hose, and black flat shoes. Although overdressed for our little get together, she looked perfect. She, too, was holding a bouquet of roses, pink, in front of her, so I still hadn't seen her face. But as soon as Shannon moved over to be closer to Trent and this lady lowered the bouquet of flowers, I saw her eyes. They were the beautiful brown eyes I had seen before—and also had a hint of recognition when I first met

266

Shannon. This lady, Shannon's mom, was none other than my ex—Rosalin.

"Oh, my God," I stepped back in disbelief. "It's you."

"Yes, it is. I'm just as surprised seeing you again, too."

"You look great, age looks good on you," I said.

Here I was in my late fifties with a bald head, a pot belly, and as many age spots on my arms as could fit. But Rose looked practically the same as when I first met her—just a little older.

Rose and I gave each other a quick hug. Then I glared at my son. "Trent, did you know about this?"

Shannon cut in, "Neither of us did. But when I saw the piece of paper that fell off the pile earlier, I noticed it was a wedding announcement that had my Uncle Jack and Aunt Debbie's name on it. They're not really related to us," she explained, "they're just very good friends of my mom, that's why I had to call her. I hope you don't mind."

"I was surprised as hell," Rose said. "I had no idea you lived here in Nevada, none-the-less so close. I was extremely nervous about seeing you again, but I figured that reliving some memories may do both of us some good."

I nodded, hoping for the same thing.

"We stopped on the way to buy these flowers, so I could thank you for everything."

I was surprised she remembered what pink roses meant.

"There were so many things you taught me. Many times over the years I've told my girlfriends about your unique perspective on life. They were all very impressed. Even though time marches on, I never forgot you."

That made me smile. I wondered how many other people have been somehow influenced by me and if I'd ever find out.

Balancing out your life—now I thought I understood the strange message. Through all the good and bad you experience in life, people are what matter the most, and how you treat them can change their behavior, their thoughts, and their actions—even if you never get to see it happen.

* * *

The four of us sat in my living room and I was in a daze. There were times in my life when I hated Rose, times when I loved her, and times when I cursed her—now I was just glad to see her again.

She talked about her life and her husband, and I related stories about mine and Alex. Time had cured us both of any feelings of romantic love we once had for each other, but as we continued to reconnect I think some of the feelings started to come back.

Trent opened another bottle of wine and as he started to pour all of us a glass, Shannon said, "So, can we see what's in the box now?"

This time I was happy to share.

I opened the box again. There were things in there no one would understand, like the small red metallic Ford Mustang I got from my mom when I wanted a convertible for my 14th birthday. The orange ping-pong ball I had gotten from some young girl who said when she gave it to me she wished she could give me the moon, but that *it* would have to do instead. The gold tiger pendant my dad had given me so long ago was still shiny, although the chain was all tangled in knots. The Gemini charm Nancy bought me was still there right next to the letter "H," for healer earring she also had me wear. I also found my old Playboy Bunny earring Joyce bought me to let everyone know what I thought I wanted to be.

The more of my past I brought out, the better I began to feel. I saw smiles on the faces of the other three people in the room as I once again felt a twinkle come to my eye.

I started to go through the pile of papers and first came across a playbill for the junior high play I was in; then a poster a cheerleader had put up on my locker back in high school, and the school newspaper that had my pictures of an old magnolia tree that was to be cut down a long time ago. Then I found the little black book with Bible quotes Sherrie had given me.

I had the anniversary card I forgot to give to Alex on our first year together. I had a birth announcement from the local Missouri paper telling the world Trent had been born. I had obituary cards for all those who had passed, and I noticed a tear in Rose's eyes when she saw the ones for Mrs. M. and Gram. The tears became more intense when I pulled out the little statue of Azna which she gave me after Gram died.

But those tears were nothing compared to what was to follow, because the next few items were all about Rose. First, I found the program for the wrestling meet we went to on our first date. Then I found ticket stubs to old Cardinal baseball games and from our trips to the zoo, and even some old scorecards from our bowling league.

When I pulled out a small black box which contained the engagement ring I had given to her so many years ago she gasped. But when I pulled out the invitation to *our* wedding, it was Niagara Falls. To my surprise, she just grabbed another Kleenex from her purse and encouraged me to continue.

The last item I removed was a small plastic bag. It was old, it was dirty, and it was fragile. But as I opened it gingerly, everyone could see it contained a dried up yellow rose. The very one Rose had given me when we first met at Jack and Debbie's wedding. I had kept it all these years and explained to everyone that to me it was a sign of true friendship.

"You still have that?" Rose looked at me in amazement.

"Do you remember what you said when you gave it to me?"

"No, I'm sorry, I don't."

"You told me you'd never rush me into anything, that you understood I wasn't ready to meet you yet, and that you'd be waiting."

"Now I remember what I liked the best about you—you were different, sincere, and you always treated me special. It's nice to know that some things never change."

* * *

The four of us, along with Rose's sister, Ann, spent some time together over the rest of the holidays. We told stories, exchanged memories, and we all helped each other get over the devastating losses we had all endured.

Trent and Shannon went back to college and I went back to my life. I wasn't as isolated as I had been before seeing Rose again. In fact, the two of us spent many wonderful evenings in the months to follow going to restaurants and dancing just like the good old days. It was like we had turned back the hands of time.

Although we hadn't been together in many years, and both of us were older, we still could dance just as gracefully as before. Instead of the dirty dancing we used to love, Rose and I became very good slow dancers. Once again our bodies moved as one and when we were on the dance floor, the other couples would stare in awe.

"You know, we were good for each other," Rose said one night. "I think we met at precisely the right time when we were younger."

"I don't know. You put me through some real hell. There were a few nights I thought I'd never make it through."

"Yeah, I did treat you pretty bad, but when Al came along I knew right away he was the one."

"How was he different than me?" I was dying to know the answer. "What made you love him and not me?"

"But Phil, I did love you, well, I loved the feeling you gave me when we were together," Rose said, not mincing any words.

Since I had her attention, and she was answering questions so honestly, I decided to play all of my cards. "So, why do you think I lost at love so many times?"

"That's an easy one," she said without hesitation. "You kept confusing great sex with love and acceptance, and the girls just played you most of the times. You're real good at understanding what women want and need in bed—and always gave them what *they* wanted, but you didn't strike a balance. It begins to feel off when it's always about the other person for you. I have to say, I was as guilty as the rest."

It was hard to hear this, but I knew she was right. I had even thought this about myself when I was younger. "Is that all?"

"Now that you ask," she grabbed my hand in hers, "No, there was another reason. There was almost a feeling of desperation around you. You wanted to feel wanted so much. You always sought perfection in your life, but that's not what girls really want. Girls like to tinker with, to fix their guys shortcomings—you know, train them by themselves. But you were already 'fixed' in a way. You were like the male version of 'the girl you don't bring home to mom', if you know what I mean."

This was so hard to hear, but wow, I knew she had nailed it. However, there was at least one exception, and the gold band on my left hand had proved it.

"So, what about Alex?" I tossed out since Rose was being so candid with me, "What made her different?"

"Well, I didn't know her, but I bet because you were older, sex didn't play such a major role for the two of you. She probably got to see the 'real' you and just fell in love. You needed to grow and learn how to just be yourself, flaws and all, before anyone could love you back the way you wanted them to."

I changed the subject before it reached a point where I couldn't handle any more truth. "It all worked out just like Margaret said it would. You remember her, don't ya? She was Mrs. M.'s daughter."

"Wasn't she a physic or something?" Rose rolled her eyes, still the skeptic. "I never believed in all that, you know."

"I know, but I did and I still do."

I told Rose that most the things Margaret had predicted years earlier did come true. That she'd said the second lady I met after Rose would be my true love. And that turned out to be Alex. And that Alex had suffered a miscarriage just like Margaret had envisioned. She also saw that we would have a son.

"Did she see us getting back together?" Rose interjected with a sly smile.

"Are we?" I blinked, surprised by the question.

"If you wanna be," she shrugged pleasantly. "I never stopped loving you."

"Well, I like these times we're spendin' together, but you must know Alex was my true love and always will be. I'll never forget her. We can continue to see each other, but it will never be like what Alex and I had."

"The same goes for me and Al," Rose said. "So, I'm okay with that."

* * *

For the next ten years Rose and I remained dear friends. We never got married and we never had sex, out of respect for both of our true loves. What a difference in perspective I finally achieved. Like Rose pointed out, for most of my life sex was the driving factor. It helped me spend my time, it helped me choose who to date, and it screwed me up more than a few times. But with age comes wisdom—and I finally had acquired some. There's so much more than the so-called pleasures in life. Sacrifice and self-understanding are necessary to achieve balance.

Although we did many things together, we also had our separate lives. Rose often went to bingo with her sister, while I spent a lot of time in my room, listening to dusty old albums and reading. I became interested in books about religion and death, and how the two went together. I took a special interest in Sylvia Brown, a renowned psychic who wrote many books about the afterlife, and John Edward, another psychic who claimed to be able to talk to the dead. I was intrigued by these two and actually tried all their techniques to get Alex to "talk" to me, but to no avail. I hoped she wasn't mad at me.

* * *

The late summer in August of my sixty-seventh year, Rose and I decided to take a trip back to Missouri. She wanted to see her other daughter, Debbie, who was about six or seven months pregnant. Additionally, we both wanted to visit the cemetery where all of our other family members were buried. The areas where Rose and I grew up, even though we had lived in different towns, were very close to each other and they shared a common cemetery.

When we drove into Queen of Heaven Cemetery, there were some smells present I remembered from my youth—the scent of fresh cut green grass, a faint aroma of hamburgers cooking by the lake situated in the center of the cemetery, and fresh wild flowers—reminding me of Nana's cottage in Wisconsin.

We went to see Rose's family first. I parked the car on the side of the road and we walked through the lush grass about a hundred yards when she saw the first gravestone. The plots were set up just like a family tree—to the left were her grandma and grandpa on her mom's side, and then on the right were Gram and Kevin. Seeing her name again brought a few tears to my eyes as I remembered what a special lady she was. Below them were Rose's parents and finally Al, Rose's husband.

I was very surprised at how close her family plots were to those of mine. We spent some time with them and then walked another fifty yards away where my family sites came into view.

First I introduced Rose to my dad's mom and dad, and when she saw my father's headstone in between them she cried heavily.

"Why the tears?" I said, taken aback.

"Just seeing your dad's name in the stone reminds me that someday you'll be gone, too. *You know, the name is the same,*" she explained.

I told Rose how I felt, and how *he* felt, the day he died. Death was not something for us to fear. It is the day everyone will be together again. Although it didn't stop her crying, she seemed to understand.

We walked a few paces more, to the center of the cemetery, and came upon the graves of Nana and Gramps. Next to them were my grandma and grandpa on my mom's side and all of Nana's other children. Below Grandma were my mom and Bob, along with all of my aunts, uncles, and cousins who had already passed through.

Off to the left a few more steps were Alex's family—her grandmother and grandfather, her mom and dad, and finally my dear Alex.

I kneeled down next to her stone and Rose stood over my left shoulder looking down. First she read Alex's full name, then looked at the other headstones behind it.

"I don't believe it," she exclaimed.

"What?"

"I knew her, and so did you."

"Obviously," I said, rolling my eyes. "I was married to her for almost twenty years."

"No, that's not what I mean," she pointed more forcefully at the headstones. "Alex's grandparents lived next to me. They were the Smileys, Bobbie and Rich.

I looked at their stones and indeed the names Roberta and Richard Smiley were etched there for eternity.

"Do you remember our engagement party?" Rose looked at me intently.

"Of course I do."

"Remember playing hula-hoop with three kids?"

"Yes."

"The oldest one was Allie, or now Alex."

I was stunned as my mind reeled back in time to when I met Alex for the first time at Poppa's, and had sensed that I knew her from somewhere. This answered the question of why we agreed on the name Trent so easily.

My reverie didn't last long. Rose had changed her attention to the stone next to Alex's. It was mine—for when it was my turn. It already had my name, date of birth, an etched white rose, and below that the epitaph: *It's not the end, just a new beginning.*

"What a nice sentiment," Rose said sweetly.

Rose and I walked back to the car. We agreed the world we lived in was indeed a small one in which we truly are all connected. And as we drove away, we also hoped the other side was a far better place than where we were now, one with no pain.

A sobering thought passed through my mind—and I let it stay there—as I turned to look back at my past just before I exited the cemetery for the last time. I know far more people who have passed through this life than I know who are still alive.

And for the very first time I wondered when it would be my time to move on.

* * *

Rose and I returned to Nevada and went about our separate lives. I found myself more at peace and calm than I had in the near past. Most of these feelings probably resulted from the visions I was getting at night again. This time my visitors never spoke to me, and there were many more people showing up, some I knew and some I didn't. They all had one thing in common though; they were all holding red roses.

CHAPTER 42
BALANCE

Another October had arrived, although you'd never know it by the hot Nevada weather outside. Fall was the one thing I did miss about the Midwest. Back home at this time the leaves on the trees were so many different colors and constantly falling from their branches, while the piquant aroma of them being burned filled the air day and night. Most things alive were busy getting ready for the long winter ahead, like the animals gathering food, the farmers fertilizing their barren fields, and the kids were getting ready for their second most favorite holiday, Halloween.

In Nevada it was just another time of the year.

Middle of the month, Rose came over and said, "I'm taking another trip to Missouri. My Debbie is ready to have her baby and being it's her first, she wants me there. Do you wanna come with?"

"Thanks, but I'm goin' to hang out here for the holiday."

"Suit yourself. I'll call you as soon as she has the baby to let you know the good news."

"You take care of yourself," I said. "I'd never be able to forgive myself if something happened to you."

"Come on, you've always been there for me, even when I hurt you."

"Yeah, they say what goes around comes around," I joked. "I just had to wait a little longer."

"Love ya," Rose said as she gave me a gigantic hug, one like she was trying to take back all the bad she had ever done to me.

"I've always loved you, too." And I'm sure it was good for my soul that I was finally able to forgive her.

* * *

On October 24, a week since Rose left, I was feeling especially nostalgic. I spent most of the day in my room just reading my journal, looking at old photographs, and drinking lemonade. Before I knew it, night had fallen and I felt myself becoming very tired. I went to my bedroom, looked out at the clear Nevada sky, put on some old albums by Rod Stewart, and fell asleep.

Just before I nodded off for the night I heard the phone ring in the background. I decided to let the machine pick up, but faintly listened to what was said.

"Hi, it's me Rose," it began. "Debbie just had her baby, it's a boy. I'll see you in a few days. Love ya."

Her voice trailed off and I drifted into sleep, or what I thought was sleep. The minute I closed my eyes I had a vision that started with a big white flash of light; it sort of looked like a gigantic candle flame flickering in the night. Instead of just one red rose like my other visitors, this one had a bouquet of them floating in front of it.

Then I was embedded in the best sleep I had ever felt. In a dream state I saw a smaller white flickering flame that began talking to me.

"Phil, it's me Olivia," the sweet calm voice said.

I struggled to put a face to the name. Then I remembered Margaret telling me about my spirit guide and that her name was Olivia.

"I'm your spirit guide," she confirmed, as if reading my mind, "and it's time for you to come home. Just get ready to follow my light and soon you'll be experiencing things that before you could only imagine."

I felt myself lift away from my sleeping body and hover above it for a few a seconds. There was an eerie calm which came over me and I felt as though I was twenty again. I had no aches and no pains, no worries and no fears, just a fantastic feeling of calmness surrounding me.

I saw Olivia's light up ahead of me when I thought I entered either a long black tunnel or an elevator. Just before I started to follow her I heard it, the music of my life—Jim Croce, Bread, Air Supply, and of course, Rod Stewart. It was faint, but I heard every word as they sang my favorite songs to me.

I floated through this darkness and saw images of my life on the two walls around me. There was Nana—with me sitting on her knee as a young boy. Jenna was there and we were watching her green balloons fly through the sky. I saw Nancie and her smile, just as she looked in second grade. Julie D. and her books flashed by me. Lisa and Sally, my first true friends, waved as I passed them by. Janet from sixth grade was there, holding an apple, while Barbara and Claire smiled their approval. Faith, the senior who helped me relate to others in high school, was smiling beautifully as I passed her. Terri, the head cheerleader, was smiling at me and had the sparkle of trust she taught me about emitting from her eyes. And I got to see Twana once again. I was so happy to see her. I tried to ask her if she was happy, and if she missed me as much as I missed her, but all I got in return was a smile a mile wide.

I also got to see some of the other loves of my life. I wasn't sure if they knew what they meant to me, but when Mary, my first girlfriend, and Kim, my first real love, passed me by I realized that they both made a big difference in my life, especially Mary. She was the first girl I trusted my heart to and although our time together only lasted a few months, I had so much to thank her for. She taught me the basics when it came to being around girls. She taught me how to take my time when dealing with ladies. And most importantly, she taught that first loves never go away. They may not stay in touch physically, but their memory is always lingering in the backgrounds of your mind. I really wished I could have experienced what could have been.

There were many, many others; some I knew and some I didn't. I wasn't sure what was happening, but it sure made me feel good. In fact, I felt as though I was glowing and each time one of these images passed me I felt the glow intensify.

I finally caught up with Olivia and was standing in front of a fantastic solid gold gate. Behind it were the most beautiful colors I had ever seen, although the details of what lay ahead were fuzzy and out of focus to me. She said, "There is someone I want you to meet."

I looked up and saw before me a huge ball of white light, the same image that had come to me earlier holding the bouquet of roses. Whatever this was it floated right in front of me. There was no outline to it, but as I continued to stare I did see two eyes emerge.

"Welcome, my dear child." The voice was neither male nor female, just extremely calming. I immediately recognized it as the one who had talked to me before in my dreams. "Today, you have made it home."

"What, am I dead?" I gasped, in a state of disbelief.

"You have passed through your earthly life, so in a way yes. Although no one really dies, balance and wholeness have been achieved with the birth of a new spirit to take your place. And poetic justice allowed it to occur in October. All of the seemingly *bad* things that have happened to you in October were just the precursor to this, the greatest day you'll ever experience."

"So my life was planned in advance?"

"Before you were born into that phase, *we* wrote the book of your life together and you merely played the part perfectly."

"Can I ask who *you* are?"

The voice chuckled, "I am the only God you ever chose."

"What with all I've been through I thought you'd be a man, but what exactly are you?"

"I am everything. I am more of a feeling than a concrete image. I can be male or female, any color of race, even a smell that you experience. I am what you want me to be. I came to you in different forms, like the gut feeling you always trusted, the warmth in your heart, and even the scents that you enjoyed so often—the smell of fresh cut green grass, the aroma of grilled hamburgers cooking on an open flame and the smell of sweet fertilizer and mint. You have learned your lessons well and followed the signs I left for you perfectly. You now arrive at the place most people long for and to see if you can stay."

"May I ask a question?" I asked.

"Yes, of course."

"What is the meaning of life?"

"You already know that answer. But more so, life is about both compromise and taking risks, about putting yourself out there for others to see, and ultimately realizing that who you are, and what you become, is good enough."

I listened to the words carefully; then remembered the earlier statement. "Wait a minute, those lessons you talked about were given to me by my Nana and *she* helped me through."

"I have a little secret to tell you. Those visits by Nana were actually me. I had to find a way to appear to you so you'd relax and trust me. *Her* image helped me help you through all the hard times."

"So that's why all the messages were the same and came to me just when I needed them. Did you send all the human angels, too?"

"Not only to you, but I also sent *you* to help many people. You did a wonderful job spreading the word of love. You were respected, accepted, and liked by the majority of those you met. You should feel very happy about yourself."

And I was.

"As you know, the main priority of your time on earth, which you have mastered, was learning and sharing, and you did both. They will come in handy in the next phase you will enter. Remember there is no such thing as endings, just new beginnings. But before all that begins, there are some people who want to see you again."

I looked past the God I had chosen and began to see thousands of other lights, although I couldn't be sure how many, approaching the gate. Although none had solid human forms, I knew many of them just by looking into their eyes. Standing right in front of the group were Nana and Alex, both of whom were the brightest lights.

"Welcome home, my dear child," the voice said. "Before I let you in I do have one more question for you. Are you ready to enter and learn what true happiness is all about? I know there are some people just waiting for you so that they can feel better?"

The gates slowly opened and I floated into what I figured was heaven. I turned around and looked back into the bright eyes of my chosen God, and they were reflecting back the sparkle of trust I always longed to see in a *female*, and I said for what would be my last time, "Yes pretty lady, I can help everyone feel good."

* * *

P.S. For those of you wondering, "If you died, how are you writing this book?"

This is how I see my passing. It is based upon information that was given to me by those 'powers' that have guided, prodded and provided me with lessons to live a better life.

I was always told that when you die you have to defend your life and the decisions that you made and that only God would make the final judgment. But I learned that when you pass through the gates of heaven after meeting your maker you must go through a series of observations to make sure you can stay.

One of those is the ability to tell your life story to a group of "life judges" who will listen to how you saw your life and compare them to the real-life movie of what really happened. Using your own words, these judges then turn the most interesting stories into the books we read.

Thanks to these judges allowing me to share, you now got to know my side of the story. I hope you learned from it because life really is all about learning, sharing and growing.

About the Author

Philip Nork was born in Chicago, Illinois and is the oldest of three children. His early years were devastating as he endured the divorce of his parents, the death of his beloved great-grandmother, and the resulting feelings of isolation and loneliness. While these events took their toll, they also shaped the man he grew up to be.

Phil had a different perspective than his friends and his experiences were totally unique. As his young male friends were busy playing baseball, defending their turf, and hitting on girls, his time was spent reading, listening to music, writing his feelings down in his journal and trying to understand the differences in people and to figure out how "we can all get along."

After graduating early from high school, he entered the work force as

a way to help support his mother and his siblings. To get away from the reality of his life, Phil spent much of his off time with his friend Joyce, a lesbian. She was able to help him experience women at his own pace and taught him many of the lessons he was to put in place. As more and more straight ladies entered his life, these experiences allowed him to learn more about human nature and he was able to turn these special times into the stories in his book.

Phil lives in Nevada with his wife and their son. He mixes work with his love of writing. He spent the first 25 years of his working life in the restaurant industry. He took all the knowledge from his early days at McDonalds and parlayed that into a successful stint with Panera Bread. He rose from the day to day operations of a general manager to become an Area Manager and then a Training Manager for that organization. Teaching and speaking in front of hundreds of trainees day in and day out helped him perfect his easy going style. He is now an Area Manager for CDS, a marketing and sales firm which specializes in working with the vendors of Costco Wholesale Warehouses.

In addition to writing, Phil is a baseball card collector, an avid reader, and enjoys listening to the music of his youth, especially Rod Stewart and Air Supply.

www.ingramcontent.com/pod-product-compliance
Lightning Source LLC
Chambersburg PA
CBHW051535260626
47170CB00003B/939